THE McALLISTER FI

PATRICIA H. RUSHFORD

HARRISON JAMES

SECRETS LIES & ALIBIS

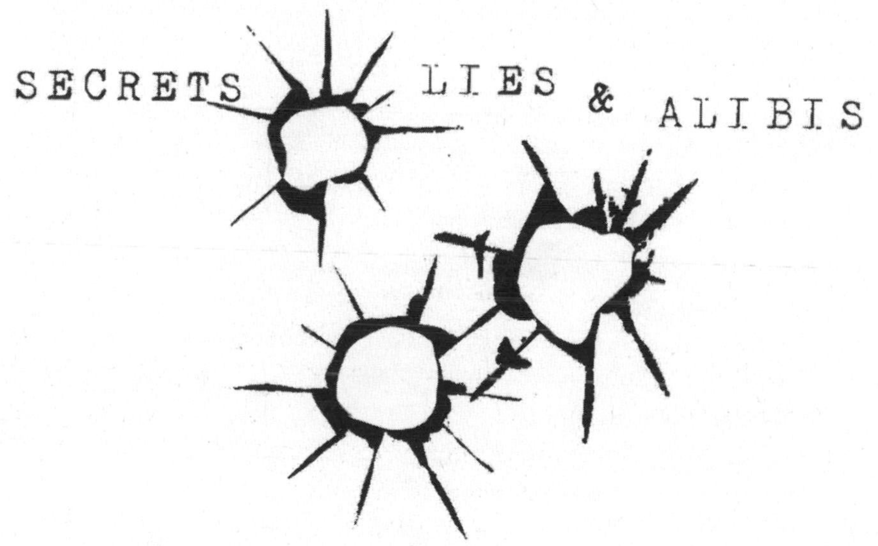

INTEGRITY
PUBLISHERS
Nashville

SECRETS, LIES & ALIBIS

Published by Integrity Publishers, a division of Integrity Media, Inc.,
5250 Virginia Way, Suite 110, Brentwood, TN 37027.

HELPING PEOPLE WORLDWIDE EXPERIENCE *the* MANIFEST PRESENCE *of* GOD.

Published in association with the literary agency of Alive Communications, Inc., 7680 Goddard Street, Suite 200, Colorado Springs, CO 80920.

Cover Design: The Office of Bill Chiaravalle | www.officeofbc.com
Interior: Inside Out Design & Typesetting

Library of Congress Cataloging-in-Publication Data

Rushford, Patricia H.
Secrets, lies, and alibis / by Patricia H. Rushford and Harrison James.
p. cm.

ISBN 1-59145-081-0 (tradepaper)

1. Police—Oregon—Fiction. 2. Man–woman relationships—Fiction.
3. Oregon—Fiction. I. James, Harrison. II. Title.
PS3568.U7274S77 2003
813'.54—dc21 2003010477

Printed in the United States of America
03 04 05 06 07 BP 9 8 7 6 5 4 3 2

The authors would like to dedicate *Secrets, Lies & Alibis* to our country's fallen law enforcement officers and their families, who have given the ultimate sacrifice to their communities.

To my wife and daughters. I love you so much.

—Harrison James

Acknowledgments

Thank you to our families for their patience and understanding during our long hours of writing and editing. To our agent, Chip MacGregor, and the people at Integrity Publishers who believe in us and in our project. A special thank you to the Oregon State Police. And thanks to the folks at Brewed Awakenings for providing great lattes and a perfect place to work out snags.

Chapter One

The wind lifted Megan's hair as she floated skyward on her backyard swing. Her father's hands lightly brushed her shoulders as she returned to earth for another push. The sun warmed her face. She peered through squinted eyes at the wispy clouds. Megan could almost touch them as the swing lifted her higher and higher.

Her saltwater sandals pointed toward the sky as she leaned back in the familiar rubber seat, supported at the end of two rusty chains. The chains creaked and groaned with each push. Megan found comfort in the sounds. The rusty chains joined with the distant hum of a neighbor's lawn mower. Rustling leaves complemented the backyard symphony.

The sounds reminded her of home and safety.

But Megan was not home. And she was not safe.

MEGAN SLIPPED BACK INTO CONSCIOUSNESS, back into the nightmare. Her neck was bent backward over the edge of the bed. The swing of her youth had been a dream, an oasis in the desert of her desperation. She tried to inhale. Her nostrils found no air, only the black plastic bag that had been wrapped around her head.

Can't breathe. She stiffened and tried to move as panic set her heart racing once more. *Oh, God, will it be over soon? Please make it be over.*

She cried out when her attacker straddled her on the creaking bed, swearing and punching at her face and chest.

Megan swallowed harder, trying to choke down the salty blood that filled her throat. Duct tape covered her lips and cheeks, and a rag stuffed in her mouth degraded her screams to guttural moans.

Please God, let me die. Take me home. Would He hear her pleas after all these years? *God, how could You let this happen?*

No. How could I do this to myself? I came here on my own. I didn't know . . . Hot tears cascaded from her eyes into her hair.

In the distance, a child laughed, oblivious to the horrific crime occurring in the dark, dirty bedroom of the low-rent apartment building. Megan prayed for her dream to return. She longed to be a child again, floating on her swing in the endless summer days of her youth. To feel her father's hands upon her shoulders. To know his love. She was the oldest daughter of an Episcopal priest, and a devoted Christian until . . . When had she stopped? *When he died.*

Daddy, I'm sorry.

Her tormentor tore the ornate silver cross from her neck, breaking the chain.

No! Please. She had little time to think about the cross and its significance. It had been a gift from her father on her confirmation.

Thick, hard hands closed around her throat, crushing her fragile windpipe. The bones in her neck cracked and Megan's desperate prayer was answered.

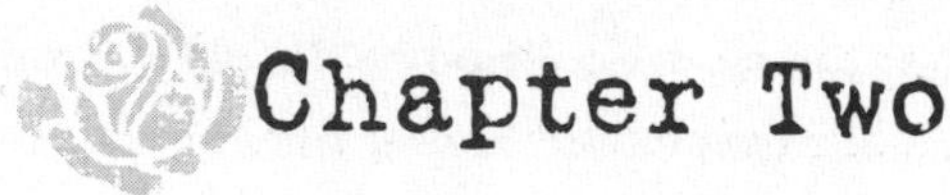

Chapter Two

Friday, August 23
3:12 P.M.

Preston Collins drove along the frontage road of his riverside property. He lifted his faded straw hat and mopped his brow with the sleeve of his stained denim shirt. In addition to the local news, the radio in his 1971 Chevy pickup filled the cab with static. Still, he could make out the five-day weather forecast for the Portland-Metro area: "Mid-nineties with no rain in sight."

"Great. Just great," Preston grumbled. Hobo, his black-and-white Border collie, sat in the passenger seat panting heavily. Hobo gave his master a shared look of contempt for the weather before hanging his head out the window of the battered pickup.

"If we don't find that calf pretty soon, old boy, the coyotes will." Preston veered off the main road and headed toward the river. A new calf had escaped through the downed fence and stood little chance of survival—especially in this heat.

As Preston eyed the wooded area along the river for signs of his missing livestock, he noticed several magpies floating down into the brush. "Looks like those birds have found a carcass of some sort." He spat out the window. "Hope it's not our calf."

Hobo's ears perked up as he sniffed the stale summer air from the open window. Preston turned his truck into the dusty wayside to inspect the magpies' target.

The bent yellow license plate that was wired to the old pickup dangled in the dust as Preston eased closer. He set the emergency brake and worked the door latch from the outside. The pickup door's inner assembly had been broken for years.

"You better wait here, Hobo. I don't want you smelling like a gut pile."

As he made his way to the river, Preston noticed trash and broken glass scattered alongside the road. "Darn kids," he grumbled. "They've turned this place into a garbage dump with their booze and drug parties." He kicked over a shiny object on the dry summer earth, his curiosity rewarded with a bottle cap. While he owned a prime piece of property, he had the misfortune of bordering Bonneville State Park.

Preston pulled a cigarette pack from his left front shirt pocket and tapped the pack on the palm of his hand as he walked down the grassy slope to the area where the birds had landed. While he watched a magpie hop along a fallen maple, Preston paused to light up. The magpie didn't much like Preston being there, but it didn't seem all that interested in leaving either. The wind shifted a bit and the putrid smell of rotting flesh sank into his nostrils. His stomach rolled and he backed away.

Preston looked at the afternoon sun. *Must be going soft.* He'd experienced tropical heat in a combat zone for Pete's sake. *Not soft,* he decided, *just old.* He tucked the lighter back into the pocket of his khaki work pants. Whatever was giving off that stink could wait awhile. It was way too late for a rescue.

He took a long drag from the cigarette, then another, ignoring the growing ash column. When he'd smoked the cigarette down to the filter, he was ready to face whatever morbid carcass had attracted the birds. Preston ground the butt into the ground, making certain there were no stray ashes. The last thing they needed was a forest fire.

Preston descended the dry overflow ditch that ran adjacent to the road. At the far side of the ditch he spotted a mass of long blonde hair. Preston waited for his eyes to adjust to the shady, tree-protected slope. The hair on his arms and neck rose, sending a chill through him.

"Dear God! What in tarnation is that?" He took in a gulp of air, realizing he had not taken a breath for the last twenty seconds.

The hair was attached to a human skull. The skull lay several yards away from the remains of a nude female torso. It was partially obstructed by ferns and ground foliage, but he could see it well enough—too well.

He turned and scrambled back up the incline, his heart and lungs heaving with the exertion. When he reached the top of the ditch, Preston looked back. Had he really seen what he thought he'd seen?

Preston climbed back in the truck with Hobo. Still trying to catch his breath, he stared out through the dusty windshield. Although he had not seen a dead body since the war, he had not forgotten the look and smell of decaying human flesh. He caught a glimpse of himself in the rearview mirror, noting the horror reflected in his eyes—the pallor in his deeply lined face.

Hobo turned around in the seat twice, whimpering and licking his master's hand as though offering his condolences. Preston blew out a long breath, then pulled another cigarette out of the package. With the cigarette lit and dangling from his lips, his composure slipped back into place.

Preston scratched Hobo between the ears. "C'mon, boy. Ranger station's closer than the house. Let's head on over there. I gotta make a phone call."

Chapter Three

"Eleven-twenty-five." The dispatcher's voice sounded scratchy over the car radio.

"This is eleven-twenty-five." Dana Bennett responded quickly, her heart fluttering. She'd only been on her own as a state trooper for two days and was still learning the ropes.

"What is your location?" Dispatch sounded annoyed.

Dana flushed with embarrassment, hoping she didn't sound too much like the novice she was. "Oh, sorry. I-84 near the Troutdale exit." She'd just written a ticket to a guy going eighty in a fifty-five mile per hour zone and was still parked on the shoulder of the freeway.

"Proceed to the entrance of Bonneville State Park; contact reporting party, Preston Collins, on report of a twelve-forty-nine."

Dana checked her laminated twelve-code cheat sheet on the visor of her patrol car. The code was new to her. She thumbed down the sheet. "Let's see, twelve-forty-nine—here we go, twelve-forty-nine is a . . . Oh my gosh. A homicide investigation." She twisted the key in the ignition and eased onto the freeway.

Dana flipped the visor back up and gripped the steering wheel with both hands. "Homicide." She gulped and thought back to her one-hour class on crime scene preservation that she'd had during her basic training two years ago. She hoped she could remember everything.

"Eleven-twenty-five, did you copy?"

Dana jumped. Would she ever get this right? "Yes—I mean, copy." She took a deep breath and let it out slowly. *You can handle this. You know you can.* It wasn't as though she didn't have experience in police work. After graduation from police academy, she had worked in the Portland Police Bureau, with a goal of eventually becoming a homicide detective.

Then her sister, Laina, had developed breast cancer. Dana quit the bureau and moved to Iowa to care for Laina and her four children while she went through chemo. With Laina newly divorced and the cancer recurring, the brief stay turned into two years. Her sister had died six months ago. Laina's ex-husband took the kids, and Dana eventually moved back to Portland, where she applied for a job with the Oregon State Police and went through their training program.

For two days she'd been driving solo, and both days had brought new experiences.

She could and would do fine, she reminded herself, and eventually she'd achieve her ultimate goal to make detective.

The dispatch came in again. "Eleven-twenty-five, Detective Sergeant Evans will be notified and the medical examiner will be en route."

"Eleven-twenty-five, copy." She tried to sound intelligent even though she hadn't quite digested all the information. "I'll advise status upon arrival," she added, feeling the need to say something over the police airwaves so her peers had the impression she had control of the situation.

"It's not that big a deal," she mumbled to herself. "All I have to do is secure the scene until the homicide detectives get there. Make sure none of the evidence is disturbed." Her nervousness diminished as she determined her responsibilities and decided she could handle them just fine.

As she approached the ranger station where she'd been told the reporting party would be waiting, she spotted an old broken-down pickup. An older man, who didn't seem to be in much better shape than his vehicle, paced back and forth, smoking a cigarette and looking extremely nervous.

Dana's stomach tightened. He was probably a very nice man, but she hoped she wouldn't have to spend too much time alone with him. "Just don't turn your back on him," she muttered to herself as she opened the door of her patrol car and walked toward the man.

DETECTIVE SGT. FRANK EVANS sat at his cluttered desk in a cubicle at the detectives' office in Portland. He supervised the area's violent offender section of the Oregon State Police. Frank had the misfortune of reviewing every crime report generated by his team of detectives, including violent person crimes ranging from sex abuse to prison crimes to homicide.

Frank scanned the stack of police reports heaped on the in-box that demanded his review and signature before being routed to the district attorney's office. He picked up the report on top of the pile and looked over the summary. It detailed a prisoner at the Oregon State Penitentiary who had been assaulted by another inmate. Both suspect and victim refused to talk to police. Other inmates reported they had not witnessed the assault.

"Humph. Dirt bag versus dirt bag; no human involved." Frank put his initials on the report and threw it in the out pile. "Prosecution declined."

Frank scanned the rest of the reports, then he leaned back in his chair, loosened his tie, and glanced over at the picture of his family that had been taken at the beach a few years back. He wished he could be lazing on the beach now instead of sitting here in his stuffy office. Heck, he wished he could be anywhere but here. Well, he soon would be. He stacked the reports in a neat pile and slid them into his briefcase. They could wait until he got back from vacation.

As Frank grabbed his sports jacket from the back of his chair, the pager vibrated on his left hip. "Shoot." He tossed the jacket back on the chair. "Should have left ten minutes ago." Before checking the readout he knew it would be one of those Friday afternoon calls. He'd had far too many of them in his thirty years on the job. The investigations invariably kept him away from his home and family. Family outings had always been a rarity, but these days with all of the budget cuts, they were practically nonexistent. He glanced at his pager and groaned. *12-49, Bonneville State Park, advise ETA.*

Frank hit the speed-dial button on his phone to the state police dispatch center, which dispatched emergency calls to troopers in the majority of the state.

"State police dispatch."

"Yeah, this is Sergeant Evans. The supervisor just paged me."

"One moment, sir," the woman responded.

While Frank waited, he transferred the call to speakerphone. With his hands free, he removed his .40 caliber Glock from the top desk drawer and placed it securely in his black leather hip holster. He also clipped his badge to his belt and slipped a pair of stainless-steel handcuffs around his belt at the small of his back. He remembered a time when his gear hadn't given him a sore back at the end of the day. Seemed like a long time ago.

"Thanks for holding," the dispatch supervisor answered. "This is Sue."

"Yeah, Frank here. Got your page on a body call."

"Hey, Sarge. Looks like the real deal on this one, not just another animal bones call. We have a trooper at the scene."

Frank hoped the reporting party was mistaken. "Make sure the troop doesn't disturb anything until we get there. I'm en route from the Portland office."

"You got it, Sarge. The medical examiner has been notified. You should get there about the same time. I'll let Trooper Bennett know. She's standing by with the reporting party."

"How many victims?" Frank wouldn't ask too many detailed questions. The answers were usually unreliable by the time word sifted down through the ranks. Still, he wanted some idea of what he would find.

"Only one reported, further details unknown."

"I'm on my way." He hung up and groaned. "Another weekend shot to . . ." He caught himself midsentence. He'd talked to several of his people about cleaning up their language and he should be setting an example.

Frank slipped on his jacket then strode to the cubicle next to his. "Hey, O'Rourke. You're up."

"Up for what, Boss Hog?" Eric grinned as he dropped his feet to the floor.

Frank ignored the nickname. He didn't mind as long as Eric and the other guys didn't use it in public. The tall gangly redhead reminded Frank of a teenager who hadn't yet filled out. Unfortunately, Eric was about as well rounded as he was going to get. He was a vegetarian and looked the part. Though Eric didn't appear to have much in the way of muscle, Frank sure wouldn't want to get on his hit list.

"Homicide at Bonneville Park. You're the lead on this one, pal."

"No way." Eric's grin widened.

"I'm leaving with Connie and the kids to go to the Islands for a week, remember? We got nonrefundable tickets." Frank frowned and muttered, "At least I hope I'll be going."

"Sorry, I'd forgotten. But don't worry, Sarge." Eric stood and gave Frank a friendly slap on the back. "You know I'll take the wheel while you and Mama are gone."

Frank nodded. "I know." Eric knew how badly Frank needed a vacation. Heck, so did the entire department—mostly because they were all in the same boat. Frank and Eric had worked together for years. The guy loved his job. More importantly, Frank trusted him. "Just remember, as acting sergeant, you have to lead the investigation and not get tied up with evidence or interviews. Leave that to the rest of the crew."

"Breaks my heart." Eric faked a despairing sigh. "No reports, no court appearances with defense attorneys." He chuckled. "I'll take the lead anytime."

"You're sure?"

"Yeah. You go have yourself a great time." Eric swung his narrow hips from side to side. "Do a little hula, go to a luau. Work on your tan."

Frank grinned. "Thanks. I'll drive out to the site and see what we're dealing with, then you're on your own."

Eric gathered extra cassette tapes and latex gloves from the stash in his desk.

"What's up?" Detective Kevin Bledsoe walked in and tossed his jacket on the chair in the cubicle next to Eric's. Kevin was a big man, around six-two, who carried what looked like two hundred pounds of pure muscle. Though Kevin and Frank were close in age, Frank envied the man's ability to stay in shape while, even with regular exercise, his own muscles seemed to droop and sag, especially around his belly.

"Hey, Kev," Frank hailed him. "Saddle up, my friend. We've got a homicide at Bonneville Park."

"Whose lead?" Kevin asked.

"Mine," Eric answered with a grin barely visible through his thick red mustache.

"Figures. I do all the work and you take the credit." Kevin feigned a pout.

"Looks like another unsolved case for the taxpayers," Eric shot back.

Frank shook his head, wondering how those two ever got

anything done. They'd been partners for years, but just recently, Kevin had been shifted to the new guy—a trainee from the child abuse unit by the name of Mac McAllister.

"Are you two ladies going to exchange recipes all day?" Frank ducked back into his cubicle and snatched his briefcase. "We've got work to do."

"Mellow out, Boss Hog. They don't get any deader," Eric replied.

"Is *deader* a word?" Kevin pushed his arm through his blue nylon jacket with State Police imprinted on the back in yellow letters.

"It is now," Eric replied. "Let's go, partner."

Eric opened the door that led from the detectives' offices to the hallway. "Age before beauty," he teased, letting the two senior officers walk ahead of him.

Frank admired and respected both men. Kevin, at age fifty-four, was the senior detective in his work group. He had been involved in hundreds of death investigations statewide during his twenty-six years of service with the Oregon State Police. He had trained all the other detectives in his unit, including Eric. Eric was ten years younger than Kevin, but there was no generation gap between them—at least none that Frank could see. They understood each other all too well. They'd been through a lot together, both on and off the job. They had worked well together—maybe because they went to the same church and shared the same faith.

"Hey, Kev, how's the new partner working out?" Eric asked.

"You mean Mac? He's been in orientation, so I haven't done more than say hello when he toured the place. Looking through his files, though, I think he'll make a fine addition to our team. Maybe I'll even be able to teach him a thing or two." Kevin paused. "Why don't I give him a call and have him meet us out there? He could use the experience."

"Sounds good," Frank agreed. The men separated at the door and Frank headed for his Chevrolet Caprice. "I'll be on the radio and my cell phone is on," he shouted to the two men as they walked toward Eric's car. "See you there."

Frank pulled out of the lot in the car everyone referred to as the "hammer wagon." He wasn't certain why the old beater got that particular nickname—probably because it looked like it had been beat up with a jackhammer. Or maybe it was because of the knocking noise its engine made, regardless of the work he'd had done on it. It was one of the old squareback Caprices with peeling paint and a leaky trunk.

Frank could have gotten a new car anytime but always gave the new cars to his detectives. He couldn't really say why. Maybe he was resistant to change or just preferred the companionship of his old car. The moaning siren and the clunking knock of the hammer wagon accompanied Frank as he headed east up the gorge toward Bonneville State Park.

Chapter Four

"What are we doing tonight?" Linda asked.

Mac's gaze roamed over his fiancée's face. Linda Stewart had the classic beauty of a model—dark shoulder-length hair and deep chocolate brown eyes. She was Italian. So was he, but she didn't know that. His gaze settled on Linda's full mouth as he pulled her into his arms. "How about this?" Mac kissed her.

After a few breathless moments, she pushed him away then ran her forefinger across his lower lip. "Maybe later. I was thinking about a movie. There's one with Meg Ryan I'd like to see."

"Why don't we rent a movie?" Mac grinned. "That way we can both have what we want."

"You're impossible." She straightened the collar on his cotton golf shirt.

Mac shrugged. "But lovable, right?"

She rolled her eyes. "After the movie we can—"

"Make out?"

"Honestly, Mac, don't you ever think of anything else?"

"Sure. Lots of things—like food and . . ."

"Work." She frowned. "Which reminds me . . . You don't have to work this weekend, do you? I was thinking maybe tomorrow we could go out on the boat with my parents."

"Sure, unless I get called in."

She wrinkled her nose. Linda didn't much care for his line of work. She was especially upset when he'd told her about his recent move into the homicide division. "We'll have to pray that doesn't happen."

Mac almost wished he would get a call. Linda was starting to annoy him with all her talk about prayer and God's will.

"About tonight." She hooked an arm through his. "I'd really like us to talk."

Mac groaned. *Talk* meant she was getting more serious. She probably wanted to talk about commitment.

"Honey, please," she prodded gently. "We've been going out for six months and I don't know anything about your family. I'd like to meet your parents."

Mac folded his arms. He did not want to talk about his family—or lack of one. He felt like walking out the door and slamming it behind him. "Why?" His voice was strained, and the veins in his neck tightened.

"Because I love you. Mac . . . and that's another thing. I don't even know your real name."

"Tony." His tone was so sharp she backed away as though he'd hit her. Well, she'd asked. "Antonio James McAllister. There, are you satisfied? You know it. Let's go."

Linda took another step back. "I'm not sure I want to go anywhere with you now. I mean, what's so bad about your past that you can't tell me?"

"Leave it, okay? Maybe someday I'll tell you, but for right now, leave it alone."

"Fine." Linda strode to her bedroom and returned with her purse.

Mac watched her walk back to him, feeling like a jerk. "I'm sorry. I didn't mean to snap at you."

She turned around and hugged him. "You're forgiven. But if you expect me to marry you, I want to know what I'm in for."

"Right."

He'd fallen in love with Linda Stewart the minute he'd met

her. Mac had gone to the hospital to check on a woman who'd been badly beaten by her husband. Linda was the nurse assigned to her. She was the best thing that had ever happened to him. He wanted to tell her everything, but how could he? He'd be opening old wounds, and who knew what it would cost him? If Linda knew too much about his past, she might change her mind.

He'd just opened the door when his cell phone rang. "Hey, partner. This is Detective Kevin Bledsoe. Ready to tackle your first case?"

"Sure," Mac responded without hesitation. He glanced over at Linda. She would not be happy.

"Good. We got a farmer out by Bonneville State Park who says he found a body out on his property."

"Okay." Mac tried to suppress his excitement but couldn't. This was what he'd been waiting for since he met Detective Bledsoe during his orientation. Still, he didn't want to seem too eager. "Where do you want me to meet you?"

Kevin gave him the information. "Oh, and Detective McAllister, welcome aboard."

"Thanks. I'll see you in about twenty minutes." Mac turned off the phone and slipped it into his pants pocket. He turned to Linda. "I have to go."

"I know. You don't have to look so happy about it."

Mac didn't know what to say. "I'll be back. Maybe even tonight."

"No, you won't." She gave him a wistful smile and kissed his cheek. "Take care of yourself."

Mac had a feeling he was losing her—that he'd moved too fast in asking her to marry him. But now was not the time to think about Linda or what they meant to each other. He had a death to investigate with the best detective in the state of Oregon.

Chapter Five

A short time later, Sgt. Frank Evans eased his old Chevy onto the shoulder of the frontage road on the southeast end of Bonneville State Park. He made note of the time on his dash-mounted clock and on his yellow legal pad wrote, *Arrived on scene, 1723 hrs.*

A black-and-white patrol car was parked on the right shoulder of the roadway, with its rear amber emergency lights flashing. The red and blue overhead lights were on as well, though not as piercing to the eye as the amber strobes. The red light on the left side of the light bar wasn't rotating.

Frank popped the trunk of thc Caprice with the dash-mounted button then activated his own four-way emergency flashers. He climbed out of his car and watched the trooper as she walked toward him. Nodding at the light on her vehicle, he said, "Needs a new rotor housing."

"Yes, sir," Dana answered. "I'll take care of it." She reached out her hand. "Trooper Dana Bennett." Her blue patrol uniform was neatly pressed and her leather shoes polished to a high shine.

Frank glanced at his black leather dress shoes. They looked like he'd polished them with a chocolate bar. Taking her proffered hand, he introduced himself. "Sergeant Frank Evans." He raised an eyebrow in recognition. "I remember you from my crime scene class at the academy. You sat in the front row, didn't you?"

She smiled, revealing a pair of dimples. "Good memory. I guess that's why you're a detective."

Frank smiled back, not mentioning the fact that she would be a hard woman to forget. Not that he had any ideas along those lines. He was a happily married man, but he wasn't dead. She struck him as competent as well as attractive. Trooper Bennett met him eye to eye, making her about five-eight. She wore her long blonde hair back in a thick braid, twisted into a bun at the back of her head to comply with regulations. The bulletproof vest gave her a boxy torso, but he remembered from class that she had a nice figure—not superthin, but nice just the same. The most attractive part of her was her smile.

Frank opened his trunk and began to assemble his gear, forcing his attention back to why he was there. "Is that the reporting party?" The passenger door was open on the trooper's vehicle, and Frank saw a scruffy-looking man sitting in the right front seat with his hands folded. The man glanced back at Frank and Dana, then he faced forward again. He seemed nervous and scared, but who could blame him?

"Yes." Dana adjusted her straw campaign hat. "His name is Preston Collins." She opened her police notebook and flipped to the most recent page. "Um . . . dispatch gave me a twelve-forty-nine call when I was out near Troutdale. They had me meet Mr. Collins at the ranger station at the main entrance of the park. He said he found the body while looking for a lost calf. He thinks the victim is a woman. Or was."

"He looks pretty shaken up." Frank eyed the man.

"Yeah, seems like a good old guy. I have to admit I was a little nervous being with him at first, but he seems harmless. He had a hard time explaining where he found the victim, so I drove him down here. His dog and his rig are back at the park ranger's office. He said the body is about fifty yards off the road, near that gully off to the right." She pointed out the location. "I haven't been down there. I didn't want to disturb anything you guys might need to examine."

"Good. Why don't you back up your car and I'll drive ahead to the other side of the pullout? We'll string the tape between our cars."

"Yes, sir."

"What time does your shift end?"

She smiled again. "About two hours ago, Sergeant Evans. I don't mind extending, though . . . for the experience."

"And the time-and-a-half pay?" Frank offered a lopsided grin.

"Yeah, that too."

As Frank positioned his car in the roadway to string the crime scene tape, Kevin and Eric pulled behind the marked patrol car. Frank reached in the trunk of his car and pulled a fresh roll of plastic yellow Crime Scene Do Not Cross tape. He fastened the tape to the left side mirror of his car, walking the line back to the left side mirror of the black and white. He tied off the end, stretching the rubbery tape until it was taut.

Frank glanced toward the two detectives approaching them. "Like I said back at the office, I don't want to get too involved in this one. You guys know what to do. The scene is yours. Start with the outer crime scene. The troop said the body is just over the rise, down in the ditch. We can't remove the body until the medical examiner gets here." He glanced toward the main road. "Someone from their office should be here anytime."

Kevin and Eric walked up to the black and white, introduced themselves to the trooper, and looked in on Preston, who nodded a tentative greeting.

Detectives Phil Johnson, a.k.a. Philly, and Russ Meyers drove up in a maroon Ford Thunderbird, blocking in Kevin and Eric.

"Good afternoon, ladies," Philly rolled down his window. "I thought you'd be packing your Bermuda shorts by now, Sarge."

"All in good time, Philly, all in good time. My plane doesn't leave for four hours yet."

"Cutting it close, aren't you? Don't forget about all that added security since September 11."

"I'll bring my badge. I want to find out what's going down here. I need you two to talk with the reporting party—Mr. Collins in the black and white. Take him back to the station and get a statement. Trooper Bennett has interviewed him, but I want you two to do it as well. He found the victim and apparently lives nearby. I want details. The scene belongs to Eric and Kevin—and the new guy, McAllister, when he gets here."

"You got it, boss. Who's the lead while you're working on your sunburn?"

"O'Rourke. And I'm out of here once we identify the victim." Frank said it more for his benefit than for theirs.

Philly nodded and opened the car door. "Come on, Russ. I know when we're not wanted. Let's grab Mr. Collins and get out of here."

It took two tries for Philly to get his nearly three-hundred-pound body out of the car. A shower of breadcrumbs fell from his tight-fitting black polyester pants when he finally got to his feet. His silver tie tack, a small pair of miniature handcuffs, smacked his horseshoe-shaped pinky ring as he brushed the crumbs from his lap and protruding belly.

He glanced at Frank as if to apologize. "I had to stop for a bite on the way, Sarge. I was fadin' away."

"That'll be the day." Frank didn't much feel like getting into a lecture on health and fitness. Philly knew the drill. "I'll get with you two knuckleheads later."

Russ rolled his eyes and ducked into the backseat of their vehicle. He pushed briefcases and notes behind the driver's seat to clear a hole for their unexpected third passenger. Russ Meyers was a three-year detective out of L.A.—competent and cocky. He had an average build, leaning toward stocky, with brown hair and hazel eyes. He was usually quiet, unless you gave him the opportunity to talk about himself. That didn't happen often, as Philly tended to dominate the conversations. Russ and Philly were a little unorthodox in their investigative methods, but if the end results were all that mattered, they made a good team.

Philly walked around to Preston, who now stood outside the patrol car smoking a cigarette. "Mr. Collins." Philly displayed his badge and photo identification. "I'm Detective Johnson, state police. Would you mind coming with us? We need you to make a formal statement and answer some questions."

"Do I have a choice? It's feeding time at my place. The Mrs. will be wondering where I disappeared to."

"I'm sorry, but we really need your cooperation on this." Philly laid a beefy hand on the farmer's shoulder and led him to the Thunderbird. "We'll give your wife a call from my car."

Preston flipped his cigarette butt to the ground, stepped on it with a slight twist, and then climbed into the backseat.

As the Thunderbird drove away, Frank felt sorry for the guy. Do a good deed by reporting a crime and get hauled downtown in the back of a police car. Frank headed back toward Dana and his two top detectives. "Trooper Bennett, I wonder if you'd do me a favor. I need to let Connie—my wife—know I'll be late, but I intend to make the plane one way or another. Tell her I may have to meet her at the airport."

"You could leave now, you know," Eric told him.

"Right—I could, but I won't." Frank wasn't certain why he had such a hard time letting go and leaving someone else in charge. Maybe it was curiosity. He had to know what they were up against and what or who was out there.

"You saying you don't trust us?" Eric said.

Frank shook his head. "It isn't that and you know it. I want to see what's going down. Habit. That's all."

"Dana." Kevin turned back to the trooper. "While you're at it, you may as well have dispatch call for all three of us."

"Sure, what's the code for that request? I . . . um, don't remember."

"Twelve-fifty-nine," the three detectives chorused.

"Sounds like you've used it once or twice," Trooper Bennett teased as she picked up her radio microphone.

"Or twice." Frank walked toward his car and glanced at his watch. "Wonder what's keeping the M.E.?"

A green Pontiac Grand Prix pulled up.

"There's Mac," Kevin said. "Is it me or are they making detectives younger these days? The guy looks like he's fresh out of diapers."

"It's you, old man," Eric teased. "Mac has to be at least twenty-eight."

"Sorry I took so long," Mac apologized as he unfolded his six-four frame from the car. "A traffic accident on the Glen Jackson Bridge slowed me down."

"No problem," Frank said. "Our victim isn't going anywhere, but I am." He reminded himself of his mission to make the plane. When the familiar county-owned white Dodge van joined the other vehicles, Frank breathed a little easier. Kristen Thorpe, the Oregon State Police medical examiner, eased the van to a stop, parking parallel to the crime scene tape. Frank waved her over so he could fill her and the new guy in.

MAC FELT LIKE HE'D BEEN DROPPED onto a movie set. He recognized Dana Bennett. He'd dated her several years ago. "Hey, Dana." He gave her a wide grin. "When did you sign on with OSP?"

She beamed at him. "A few weeks ago."

She looked good and Mac wondered how she'd feel about going out with him again. He brought his thoughts up short. An engaged man should not be thinking about dating another woman. He cleared his throat and glanced at a muscular, gray-haired guy who looked to be in his late forties. The man, Detective Bledsoe, glanced briefly at Dana then looked back at Mac, obviously curious about the interchange.

"Kevin Bledsoe." The detective offered his hand and a smile. "Glad you could make it, Mac."

"Yes, sir. I met you during my orientation." Mac wasn't about to go into a lengthy explanation about his relationship with Dana, so he changed the subject. "Where's the body?"

Kevin raised an eyebrow. "We're just getting ready to check it out."

"I'm surprised you haven't been down there yet." He was curious and eager to get started. The others still didn't seem to be in all that much of a hurry.

"Had to wait for the M.E.," Kevin answered.

"Oh, right." Mac hadn't wanted to seem too eager but was managing to do just that.

"Why do you have to wait?" Dana asked.

Drawing from his classes on the matter rather than from experience, Mac answered, "In Oregon, a corpse can't be disturbed until the medical examiner or one of the deputies makes a general ruling on the cause of death. The deaths are preliminarily determined to be of natural causes or by unnatural means. That includes criminal homicide. The deputy medical examiner then has the authority to forward the body to the state police medical examiner's office in Portland for an autopsy to determine the cause of death." Mac cleared his throat. His explanation had sounded like he'd read it out of a textbook.

Dana didn't seem to notice. "Sounds like a cheery occupation."

"Beats stopping cars in the rain." Dr. Thorpe's grin took the edge off her sarcasm.

Dana rocked backward on the heels of her boots, apparently startled by the comment and by the woman herself.

Mac wasn't sure what to think. Being new to homicide, he'd never met Dr. Thorpe, and now catching his first real look at her, he held back a yelp. Her hair was short and spiked, blonde, and highlighted with bright orange dye. She wore no makeup—didn't really need to as far as he was concerned. She was a natural beauty, with thick eyelashes and porcelain skin. The doctor reached for Mac's hand. "Kristen Thorpe. And you are?"

He was surprised by the strength in her grip. "Mac, um . . . McAllister. Detective."

Dr. Thorpe reached into her bag and pulled out a pair of latex gloves. "Don't let the hair fool you, Mac. Regardless of what some people think, it doesn't interfere with my intelligence."

Mac hadn't been thinking that at all but didn't bother to correct her. *So much for getting off on the right foot.*

Frank finished loading his 35mm camera. "Do you all know each other?" Without waiting for a response, he finished making the introductions.

Mac didn't need to be introduced to Eric. His cousin raised a hand in mock salute to him. He wondered if Eric had told the others anything about their relationship, or more importantly, about the family. He hoped not. There were family secrets he'd just as soon not divulge to anyone, let alone his coworkers.

Eric gave him a sly grin and turned to the M.E., a glint of approval in his eyes. "Glad you could join us, Doc."

"You think we could get started now?" Frank asked. "We're burning daylight."

"At your service. What brings us out on this fine occasion?" Dr. Thorpe asked.

Frank explained the circumstances of the find to Dr. Thorpe. "We haven't been down to the body yet. We're still working our way in," he told her.

"Here, Dana." Frank removed a single white sheet of paper from his binder. "I'd like you to keep the crime scene log for us."

"The log? Sure. What do I do?"

"Just note on the form when people arrive. Fill in the box for the person's name, time of arrival, and purpose for entering the scene. Make sure you write down the checkout time too."

She nodded. "Okay."

"And one more thing. Nobody, I mean nobody, gets past this crime scene tape without my say-so. Is that clear?"

"Crystal."

"Now if you all will excuse me, I have some photos to take." Frank walked away from them and began shooting pictures.

Kevin and Eric had both outfitted themselves in their crime scene attire—blue nylon jackets with yellow State Police insignias on the back. Mac dug his out of his trunk and slipped it on. He hoped his deodorant was still working. The heat from the late afternoon sun and the high humidity made the place feel like a sauna.

The detectives placed white paper booties over their dress shoes so as not to leave footprints at the scene. More importantly, the disposable footwear protected their shoes from any unpleasant substances they might step in during the scene processing. Mac was beginning to feel more at ease. He knew the procedure—it was the actual experience he lacked, and now he was getting that as well.

Eric stretched a pair of standard issue powdered latex gloves onto his hands. He handed a pair to Kevin and another to Mac.

"I hate these things," Eric complained. "White powder gets all over everything and my clothes look like I've been eating powdered doughnuts all day."

"I wouldn't worry, Eric," Kevin teased. "Everyone knows you stick to carrots."

Mac grinned at the two men who'd been partners for many years. He felt like an intruder having been assigned to Kevin and hoped Eric wouldn't hold a grudge. Detective Kevin Bledsoe was the best, and Mac wondered why Frank hadn't made Kevin the lead. Not that it mattered. Maybe Frank thought it would be better if Kevin was out in the field. The man sure knew his stuff.

"Hey, Kev."

"Yeah, Frank?"

"I shot three rolls of film of the roadway and outer crime scene. Why don't you and the doc move inside the tape while I sketch the area and take a quick video? I'm going to stay out of the ring on this baby so I can avoid any grand jury testimony while I'm on vacation."

"Sounds good, Sarge." Kevin motioned to the trooper. "Log us in at 1725 please, Dana."

"Um—that's 5:25 P.M., right?"

"Right."

Mac couldn't stop staring at the medical examiner. Kristen Thorpe broke the mold. She couldn't have been too much older than he was, maybe in her mid-thirties. She checked the documents on her stainless-steel clipboard and raised her gaze to his.

He glanced away, then back again.

"I know that look." She raised an eyebrow. "You're either flirting with me or you want to know what I'm doing."

Mac shifted his gaze to his shoes as heat rose up his neck.

She chuckled. "If it's flirting, talk to me later. If it's the latter, I'm just noting the weather conditions."

He couldn't do much but smile back at her as she checked the thermometer and noted the day's temperature—92 degrees.

Dr. Thorpe attached her pen to the clipboard and picked up a large red plastic case. A white sticker had been glued to one side. The large bold letters read, "My day begins when your day ends."

Seemed as though it was like that for all of them. For a brief moment he wondered what it would be like to have a girlfriend who really understood what being a police officer was all about. Linda kept saying she'd get used to it. Maybe she would in time.

Kevin grabbed his own camera equipment, and they ducked under the tape just as Frank rejoined them.

"Okay, guys, you know the drill." Kevin handed his camera equipment to Mac, who put the bag's strap over his shoulder without comment. "Follow me single file; don't disturb a pebble on the way in. Let's confirm we have the real McCoy before we go all the way with the scene process."

"I've got the video rolling with the audio on, guys," Frank reminded them. "So watch your language."

"Yeah, like we need the warning." Kevin moved forward, stepping over the tire tracks in the dusty earth. Eric, Mac, and Dr. Thorpe followed. They walked along the paved roadside to the overflow ditch, attempting to take the path least likely used by the suspect or suspects.

As they approached the edge of the sloping earth, Dr. Thorpe caught her breath and whistled. "Looks like you guys are working the weekend. I can see the torso and pelvic girdle. Human remains. No doubt about it."

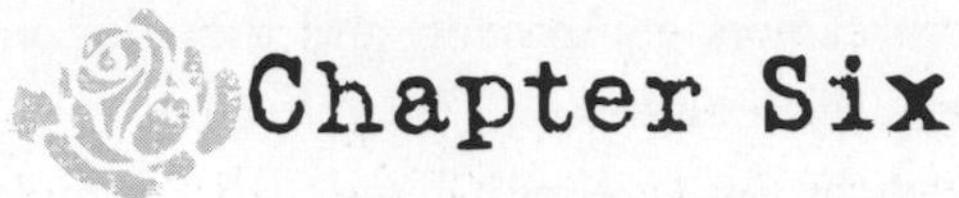

Chapter Six

Mac again tried to suppress his excitement. Adrenaline buzzed through him.

"Let's photograph our way in," Kevin said. "Mac, you take the digital photos with your setup and I'll get the video camera from Frank to document the rest of the path."

"Will do." Apparently Kevin didn't believe in just letting the new recruits stand by and watch. Mac appreciated having an assignment—an important one at that.

Kevin jogged the short distance back to Frank, who stood at the edge of the crime scene tape. "We'll be able to recover the body tonight, but we'll need to hold the scene overnight to process all this garbage. We'll need a crew out here tomorrow."

Frank nodded. "I'll call in and have dispatch send a shift car to relieve Trooper Bennett. We'll lock up the scene until we're done." Glancing over Kevin's shoulder, he added, "How does it look?"

"Nude female. My guess is she was dumped there. Hard to tell, though."

Mac glanced around the litter-strewn area where high school and college kids tended to party. It was a popular spot, with an abundance of shade trees and secluded areas. Patches of grass and a sandy beach bordered a wide spot in the river where people could swim and fish. Working patrol, he'd stopped more than one carload of kids coming from here. Kids too young and too drunk to drive and still trying.

"Could be that one of the parties got too rough." Kevin echoed Mac's thoughts. "I'll take the video from here, Sarge."

"Right." Frank handed over the camera. "I hate to leave you guys with this."

"We'll handle it," Kevin assured him.

"I'd like to get her name before I leave town."

Kevin grunted. "Like that's going to happen."

Frank checked his watch. "While I'm waiting for you yahoos to get back, I'll have dispatch scare up all the recent missing person teletypes from the last month."

"Good. See you in a few."

Kevin reached Mac's side and turned to watch his boss settle into the front seat of his car to make the calls. "Poor guy. Just can't leave it alone."

"Do you think he'll go on his trip?"

"He'd better or we'll have another homicide on our hands. His wife will kill him." Kevin smiled.

Mac and the veteran detective joined the others and moved forward to where they could see the remains.

"Whoa!" The medical examiner squinted to take a photograph with her own digital camera. "That's no boating accident."

"What?" Mac scrutinized the dumpsite.

"You know, that shark movie. When they found the shark attack victim on the beach and took her to the morgue, remember? The examiner said, 'That's no boating accident.' Remember that one?"

"Oh yeah, right." Mac sighed and rolled his eyes. Dr. Kristen Thorpe was one strange woman.

"I loved that movie." Kristen placed the camera back into her plastic tote box.

"Doesn't anything bother her?" Mac muttered to Kevin when Dr. Thorpe's back was turned to them.

"I guess that's how she copes, making light of the situation. Probably keeps her sane. We all have our ways of doing that. You'll see."

"To each his own, I guess." Mac stood above the scene, catching a whiff of the corpse even though the wind was blowing most of the smell away from them.

Eric pulled out a menthol nasal inhaler and used it. "You have one of these?"

Mac shook his head. "Are you serious?"

"It helps. I don't have an extra one. Just breathe through your mouth as much as you can."

"Okay, people." Kevin lowered the camera. "I'm finished with the scene for now."

That meant only one thing. They were ready to recover the body. Mac's stomach lurched as the team moved forward and the smell grew stronger. He swallowed back the bile rising in his throat and closed his eyes for a second. *You are not going to throw up,* he told himself in no uncertain terms. Mac closed off his nose and pulled slivers of air through pursed lips.

Solemn as mourners at a funeral, the team stood silently for a moment as if to pay their respects. Mac wanted to turn around and run. The lush Oregon climate and shaded earth had been a fertile setting for the ferns and soft ground foliage where the body rested. The victim's torso lay parallel to the trunk of a fallen maple tree, her left shoulder and hip partially hidden under the tree's girth.

The legs were bent at the knee, with the feet folded behind her buttocks. With the right side of the torso exposed, Mac could easily make out the victim's right breast and pubic area. Her arms were stretched above her shoulders, also parallel to the trunk of the fallen tree. The left hand was tucked under a mass of ferns and not visible from their vantage point. The right hand was clearly visible, clinched in a loose grip as if she were holding someone's hand. Mac swallowed back the tennis ball–sized lump in his throat.

Stay objective. Don't think about it as a person. Mac tried to take photos, but his vision blurred. His nostrils rebelled. His stomach lurched. Mac ducked his head and took a step back, colliding with a tree. He twisted around and plunged forward, depositing his lunch on the riverbank.

He felt a movement at his side. "Keep your head down for a minute." Kevin pressed his hand to the back of Mac's neck.

"I-I'm sorry." Mac gripped his stomach and heaved again.

"Don't worry about it." Kevin pulled a handkerchief out of his pocket and dipped it into the river, then handed it to Mac. "Wash your face. Take a minute to pull yourself together, then get back up there. I'm counting on you to get those photos."

"Yes, sir." Mac gasped for air. The smell was worse, but somehow his stomach began to settle down. He drew the wet cloth down his face, catching his tears as he went. He'd messed up. First time out and he'd blown it. He'd probably get demoted and go back to being a trooper. Maybe standing out in the rain handing out tickets wasn't such a bad thing.

Mac straightened up and with new resolve made his way back to the scene. He started taking photos again, trying to see without seeing. *Be objective,* he reminded himself again. *You have a job to do.*

The victim's head was over three feet away from the torso, with most of the flesh removed from the skull and jaw. Only the large muscles of the lower mandible remained on the yellowish skull, along with a mass of matted blonde hair. Green fungus accented by bird droppings now covered the dark skin along her torso and legs.

"I wonder why her skull is detached and nearly bleached white, while the rest of her is still intact," Eric said.

"Could have been cut off by her killer," Kristen answered. "Or not. If the head was attached to the body when she was dumped, the critters start at the easiest opening to the body. That's usually the mouth and eyes, then they work their way in. Once they got around the neck, the buzzards could have severed the head from the body and continued to pick on it."

Shut up, will you? Mac wanted to shout. He couldn't, though. It was bad enough that his stomach was starting to roll on him again. Whatever had made him think he wanted to investigate crime scenes? As a trooper, he'd seen corpses, but nothing like this.

"How far back do you put the death?" Kevin asked the M.E.

"I'd say a week, maybe two. It's hard to tell in this heat. Once we get her up to my place I can do an autopsy and run some tests, so I'll be able to tell you more."

"All right." Kevin straightened. "Follow me down to her; try to step in my tracks. I'll video while you and Eric process her."

Kevin removed some paper masks from his jacket pocket, handing one to Eric and another to Mac. He held a fourth out to Kristen.

"No thanks. I sweat too much in those things."

The older detective produced a small jar of cologne, giving one spray of the fine mist into the mask. "Want me to do yours?" he asked Mac.

Mac nodded. He'd do anything, even use cheap cologne, to keep the smell down. He placed the smelly mask over his nose and mouth and secured the elastic string around his head. "Ugh. This is disgusting. Where did you get this stuff?"

"Father's Day, 1978." Detective Bledsoe lifted the mask over his face. "Comes in handy from time to time."

The medical examiner pulled a rubber-coated body bag from her plastic tote box and stretched the bag alongside the victim. She then pulled down the large zipper to open the bag. Inside the pale blue bag was a clean white sheet used to cover the body and a smaller plastic bag for personal effects.

Kevin videotaped the scene and Mac shot another role of 35mm film while Eric and the medical examiner looked over the body for any obvious signs of injury. Aside from the detached head, there were no detectable marks of injury due to the advanced stages of decomposition. Kristen placed a single paper bag over the exposed right hand, tying the bag around the wrist with cotton string.

She glanced up at Mac as she pulled the woman's left hand out from under the log. "This will protect any trace evidence for the forensic lab."

As the left hand was exposed, Dr. Thorpe let out a long whistle. "Someone or something beat us to this one." The majority of the left hand was missing, with obvious signs of animal scavenging. All four fingers were missing, with only part of the thumb and palm remaining.

"Go ahead and bag what's left," Kevin said. "Let's roll her over and get a look at the rest of her."

"We need to be careful when we pull her out from this log—looks like the skin is sloughing," the medical examiner warned.

"Sloughing?" Mac asked.

"Her skin is falling off the muscle and bone. Good thing we got to her when we did. There wouldn't be much left to examine in a few days."

"There isn't much now." Mac found that the cologne was actually helping. Bad as it was, the scent was strong enough to overshadow that of the corpse. He helped Eric and the doctor roll the body from her temporary grave. Mac looked away in disgust. Cripes, he was going to vomit again.

The left side of the victim's body was writhing with maggots. He wasn't the only one to be affected. Eric had covered his face with his sleeve. Kevin squeezed his eyes shut and shook his head.

"It never gets any easier, does it?" Kristen grimaced. "Let's get her into the bag."

They worked as a team, rolling the body into the bag while Eric put in the skull and hair as well. Dr. Thorpe placed the white sheet over the victim's body and worked the heavy zipper closed on the bag. With the body out of sight, Mac could almost breathe again.

They searched the immediate area for trace evidence, but the ferns and nearby garbage dump made the search futile.

"We'll have to keep the scene overnight," Kevin said. "We'll conduct a methodical grid search of the area tomorrow. Let's work on her identification, Eric, and see what we can find before Frank leaves."

The four of them emerged from the body dumpsite, carrying the victim in her temporary rubber-coated bag.

"Don't look now," Eric muttered. "Looks like the vultures are here. And I don't mean birds."

Chapter Seven

Mac glowered at the dozens of news vans and reporters waiting outside the crime scene tape, microphones in hand and cameras aimed at the approaching investigators. Dana was still at her post, and the media were apparently keeping her busy.

A hush came over the reporters and rubberneckers when they saw the body bag. The bright lights of the cameras and the red lights on the microphones seemed to come on simultaneously.

"Doesn't take them long to find the story, does it?" Eric muttered.

"Not long enough, partner." Kevin sighed. "Not nearly long enough."

"SERGEANT EVANS, CAN YOU GIVE US A STATEMENT?" The television news reporter thrust a microphone into Frank's face.

"All I can tell you is that we have recovered the remains of an unidentified person and the death will be under investigation. I have no additional information at this time." Frank ran a hand through his thinning gray hair.

"Can you comment on the state of the body? Do you have the

identity? Do you know the cause of death? Is it Megan Tyson?" The questions came at him like bullets, and Frank wished he could fire back with the real thing.

One of the reporters pressed against the crime scene tape that Frank had ducked under when he saw his team come over the rise.

"That's far enough." Trooper Bennett stepped in front of the reporter.

"You folks are so helpful." The reporter glared at her.

"Glad to be of assistance." The trooper glared back.

Frank grinned at the exchange. He'd have to remember to put in a good word for Dana.

Turning his back on the reporters, Frank headed out to meet the medical examiner and his crew. They didn't have much to report. Not that Frank expected a lot. They told him about the find and the condition of the body. One week, maybe two. Probably because one of the reporters had mentioned it, Frank thought about a missing person case that had recently made headlines. Megan Tyson, a lovely young woman about to be married, had suddenly disappeared. When they came back to the vehicles, he helped the trooper keep the reporters at a safe distance while Kristen and his detectives took care of the body.

MAC STOOD TO THE SIDE as Kristen pulled the shiny metal gurney from the back of her van, setting it down on the pavement next to the body bag. With a quick lift, Kevin and Eric settled the body onto the metal stretcher. Dr. Thorpe extended the legs with a quick shake downward, then she effortlessly lifted the weight of the body and platform and locked the device into place with her foot.

One of the reporters who'd had little luck with Frank yelled at the medical examiner, "Can you give us a statement?" Kristen ignored them, muttering something under her breath that sounded anything but complimentary. She buckled the gurney's two nylon straps around the body bag, pulling them snug with a jerk. With a quick push, she pushed the collapsible contraption into the back of the county-owned van and slammed the double doors shut.

"I'll transport the body up to my office." Kristen pulled off her gloves and stuffed them in a plastic bag behind the driver's seat. Glancing at Eric, she added, "I suppose you want this autopsy done yesterday."

"Yeah, as soon as possible," Eric replied.

"I'll have to juggle things around a bit, but we should have a preliminary report by noon."

The M.E. saluted as she climbed into the driver's seat and started the engine. "Gentlemen, it's been a pleasure."

Before taking off she scratched a few notes on her clipboard and put on a headset. Mac could make out the strains of rock music as she adjusted the volume on her portable compact disc player and began to move her head and shoulders with the music's beat. The medical examiner eased the van onto the roadway and headed west toward Portland.

"There goes one weird chick," Mac murmured. "I think she enjoys her job a little too much."

"She's coping," Kevin told him. "You'll get used to her."

Frank Evans stood with his hands on his hips, looking back at the scene. The summer sun was just beginning to set and a light breeze began to blow. Kevin and Eric removed their latex gloves and pulled down their masks, letting them rest around their necks.

Frank came back over to them. "I talked with Philly and Russ just before you got here. They wrapped up their interview with Mr. Collins." Giving them a frustrated look, he added, "I've assigned them to locating all the recent missing person reports. There's so much to do on this. There's no way I can leave on vacation now."

"You are not missing that vacation, Sarge." Eric shook his head. "You're going to be on that plane tonight if I have to hogtie you and drag you there myself. I've got this one, buddy, so why don't you clear out now? We'll have the scene secured overnight and we can take up the search for trace evidence at first light. Kevin and Mac can attend the postmortem in the morning."

"I don't know." Frank brushed some dust off his jacket.

Settling a hand on Frank's shoulder, Eric said, "We've got this one covered. Now get out of our hair."

"Maybe. But if I do go, I'm calling in every day and I expect to be briefed on what's going on every step of the way. Once I reach the motel, I'll leave my room number on your voice mail. If you have any problems, call me and I'll be on the next plane."

"There won't be any problems." Kevin chuckled. "Besides, it'll be kind of nice not having the brass in the way for once."

"All right, all right. You knuckleheads win." Frank folded himself into the driver's seat of the hammer wagon. "Don't forget to keep the lieutenant in the loop—give him enough information to keep him happy. And hold down the overtime; don't use it unless you have to."

Eric and Kevin folded their arms. "Go," they said in unison.

"You two are such jerks." Frank smiled as he turned the key. The old car grumbled in protest and on the third try roared to life in a cloud of gray exhaust. "Thanks, guys," Frank yelled as he pulled away from the scene. His cell phone was pressed to his ear before his automatic transmission shifted gears.

"Okay, Kev," Eric said, "let's get down to business. I'll take care of scene security and tomorrow's processing. You and Mac attend the autopsy while Russ and Philly work on gathering the missing person info."

Mac released a shallow breath. Eric had assigned him to watch an autopsy? His stomach rebelled at the thought of it. They were definitely including him in the process—and that was good, wasn't it?

"Man, and I thought Frank was bossy." Kevin grinned.

"You ain't seen nothin' yet, partner. Um, do you need me to write all this down for you? I know your memory starts to go when you start aging."

"Punk. I should have washed you out years ago when I had the chance. It was bad enough working *with* you; now I have to work *for* you." Kevin stepped over the crime scene tape.

Watching their banter, Mac felt like an outsider, but that was to be expected. These guys had worked together for a long time and it showed. He hoped Kevin and Eric didn't hold it against him for coming on the scene and causing their separation.

Eric followed behind Mac and Kevin, stepping over the glossy yellow tape that momentarily caught on his camera case. "Trooper Bennett, log us out of the scene at . . . 2045 hours."

"Eight-forty-five it is," she replied, writing the times on the crime scene log.

"I'll hang out here until the relief trooper arrives," Eric said to Kevin. "You can take my car back to the office; I'll get a ride back with Trooper Bennett. I want to be here at first light, so let me know what you find out at the autopsy."

"You got it. Want me to bring you a cup of joe?"

"Nah, I'm okay. Thanks, though. Have a good night, Kev. You, too, Mac," Eric said as an afterthought.

"Hey, Eric," Mac said. "You don't look too thrilled about staying behind. If you want to get back to your family, I'll be happy to stay."

"I'm sure you would." His tone had a teasing quality, indicating his suspicion that Mac and Dana might have a thing going.

"But I need to stay and make sure the place stays secure." Eric pursed his lips and added, "Um . . . Mac, we haven't seen much of you lately. We'll have to get together sometime."

"Thanks. I'll think about it." Mac wasn't sure what to make of the invitation. The cousins hadn't spoken socially since his grandmother McAllister's funeral last year.

"See you two later." Kevin eased Eric's car back onto the

frontage road, stopping momentarily to push the seat backward and adjust the rearview mirror.

Mac said his good-byes as well, to Eric, then to Dana, whose eyes offered an invitation to call her. Though Mac didn't say anything that might encourage her, he felt certain his admiring gaze and smile had left an open door.

Driving over the I-205 bridge into Vancouver, where he had an apartment in the Fisher's Landing area, Mac felt a blend of trepidation and excitement. His first case, though gruesome, promised to be intriguing. Things were definitely looking up—a new job, a new partner who was one of the best in the business, an apartment in an upscale neighborhood. Life was good, he thought as he watched the beginnings of a glorious sunset. From his vantage point on the bridge he had a spectacular view. The Columbia River flowed beneath him, wide, deep, and swift. The sun had disappeared behind the Coastal Mountain range to the west. But to the east, the peak of Mount Hood still sported a luminous pink-and-lavender shawl—compliments of the setting sun. The almost twelve-thousand-foot, snow-covered peak provided a landmark to residents and travelers in Oregon's Willamette Valley, not to mention a wide variety of winter and summer sports.

Mac thought about going straight to Linda's apartment just off Mill Plain. But he didn't. She'd want to *talk,* and he wasn't in the mood to delve into the subject she'd want to talk about—marriage. Not after what he'd just seen. He needed time to think and to process the find. A woman had been murdered and dumped in a place no one was likely to find her. Even though the woman meant nothing to Mac, it seemed sacrilegious somehow to do anything but grieve over her passing.

AS DETECTIVE KEVIN BLEDSOE left the crime scene, he thought about the grisly murder. The clear day and Mount Hood's glorious cloak almost dimmed the horror of finding the Jane Doe. The girl had a name—she was someone's daughter or mother or sister. He prayed they'd be able to make a positive identification soon. Though he tried to take his thoughts in another direction, he couldn't. Instead, he found himself praying for her family and wondering what had happened to her. How had she ended up as fodder for scavengers and maggots?

In a way, Kevin wished he, too, was on his way to the Islands or to some exotic place with his wife. Jean would love it. Maybe he'd surprise her and set up a cruise for their next vacation. Kevin was glad to be going home, thankful that unlike Frank and Connie, he and Jean had maintained a fairly healthy relationship during all these years. He couldn't count the number of times he'd been late for dinner or the nights he hadn't come home at all.

Jean always seemed to understand. Over the years, she'd learned not to count on him. She'd learned that if she was going to survive and keep the marriage together she had to be flexible. She had her church activities, quilting, knitting, and the kids—and now grandkids.

He was one of the lucky ones. Kevin thought of all the failed marriages within the department. He thanked God for his stable home life, knowing full well the bond he shared with his wife could still not be taken for granted. *I just wish I didn't have to spend so much time away from home.*

Stop feeling sorry for yourself. You're in this job because you love it and can't see yourself doing anything else. A passage from the Book of Isaiah came to mind. "*Then I heard the voice of the Lord saying, 'Whom shall I send? And who will go for us?' And I said, 'Here am I. Send me!'*"

Kevin, being what many of his peers called religious, knew it wasn't just his love for the job that kept him going. This was where he felt God wanted him—where he needed to be.

The reminder set things in perspective. In a few minutes he'd be home. He'd eat the dinner Jean had saved for him, watch a little television, and then go to bed. He'd curl up beside his wife, and, hopefully, there he'd stay until morning—until the autopsy.

He wondered briefly about the wisdom of having his new partner there then dismissed it. *He'll have to learn sometime, and this is as good a time as any.*

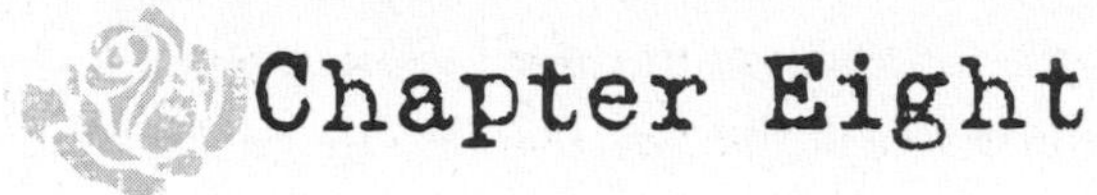

Chapter Eight

Saturday, August 24
7:50 A.M.

You want whipped cream on that?" the attendant at the drive-through window at Brewed Awakenings asked.

"Sure, sounds great." Mac reached out the car window to accept the hot raspberry mocha latte. "Thank you." He popped the chocolate-covered coffee bean that she'd placed on the lid into his mouth.

"Have a great day." She adjusted her headset and gave him a wire-laden smile as he drove off.

Mac pulled his unmarked patrol car out onto 164th Street and headed south toward the freeway, trying to get comfortable in the driver's seat of the Pontiac Grand Prix. The form-fitting bucket seat fit well under normal circumstances, but with the added girth of a .40 caliber Glock handgun and a set of handcuffs, he needed an additional two inches on either side.

He turned his car radio to the AM dial, tuning in to his favorite news radio station for the eight o'clock headlines. Mac parroted the opening remarks of the news program in the deepest voice he could muster. "Watch it tonight at five, read about it tomorrow, or hear about it now. It's time for the news." He laughed out loud, then looked to see if anyone had seen him clowning around. His integrity appeared intact for now, and he took a sip of his latte.

Not surprisingly, the top story on the news was that of the body recovered by Oregon State Police at Bonneville State Park. "Assigned to the case is Master Detective Mac McAllister," Mac added in his reporter-like voice.

The news reporter continued on despite Mac's aside. "Confidential sources close to this reporter are saying the body recovered could be that of Megan Tyson, the thirty-four-year-old Troutdale woman who was reported missing ten days ago. Oregon State Police have yet to officially identify the remains. In other news . . ."

Mac frowned, wishing reporters wouldn't make speculations like that. What if it wasn't Megan? The family's hopes would be lifted and then dashed again.

He knew all about the Tyson case, and though the state police hadn't been directly involved, he'd followed it with interest. He'd seen Megan's picture in the newspaper and on television. She'd worked at a place called Fitness First in Troutdale, where coworkers described her as petite, athletic, and attractive. Mac also remembered she was engaged to be married, turning up missing a few weeks before the wedding. He wondered if the young woman had gotten cold feet. If so, he couldn't much blame her.

Then he wondered if she was now awaiting his arrival at the medical examiner's office. For some reason the thought turned his stomach, and he wished he hadn't ordered the rich coffee drink.

AT THE OREGON STATE Medical Examiner's Office in Portland, Dr. Kristen Thorpe took hot water out of the microwave and dunked the chamomile tea bag in and out a few times before discarding it in the wastebasket beside the small sink. She sipped at the herbal tea as she made her way to her cluttered desk. Setting down the cup, Kristen scanned through the intake records from the previous day, reading over the list of bodies transported to her office for autopsy.

She was the lead medical examiner for the state of Oregon, supervising five medical doctors at her office and fifty-four deputy medical examiners statewide. With all of her people busy or unavailable, she'd been the one to go out to Troutdale yesterday to bring in the decapitated corpse, which in her view was a victim of a criminal homicide. Rather than assign the Jane Doe to one of the other doctors, she planned to do the postmortem exam herself. She didn't usually take a personal interest in the cases that came into her office, but something about this particular victim haunted her. Kristen suspected the woman had been brutally murdered, and she wanted to be the one to discover the secrets her body held. She wanted to have a hand in seeing the murderer brought to justice.

She'd have company this morning. Kristen smiled as she noted Detective Mac McAllister's name along with Detective Kevin Bledsoe's on the note her secretary had placed on her desk that morning. Apparently Detective Eric O'Rourke had called after she'd left the scene last night. While Bledsoe knew the ropes, Mac was the new kid on the block. She'd enjoy taking him through the hoops. She wondered if he'd ever been in on an autopsy before. "Better have some smelling salts handy." She grabbed a couple out of her bottom desk drawer and slid them into the pocket of her scrubs.

"Let's see." She settled a pair of half-glasses on her nose and began reading down the list. "Overdose. Overdose. Accidental drowning." Nothing that couldn't wait a few hours.

"Okay, where did you guys put her?" She found the Jane Doe label and followed the line across. "Cooler number three." Kristen took the last sip of tea, jotted the ID number on a neon pink Post-it, and escaped the office and the paperwork. Closing the door behind her, she headed across the hall to Henry's office.

Henry Thiele had been her aid since she started working here five years ago. She turned the knob and poked her head in. "Hey, Henry, how goes it?"

"Morning, Doc."

"Ready to go to work?"

He sighed. "Can one ever be ready?" His black hair and ebony eyes twinkled despite his hangdog tone.

Henry took off his denim jacket and placed it over the back of a black stool, already wearing his faded blue scrubs underneath. "What are we working on this morning, Doc?"

"A Jane Doe. I brought her in last night. She should be in cooler number three unless someone switched her." Dr. Thorpe handed Henry the note. "Here's her ID."

When Kristen had arrived with the van the previous night, two swing-shift guys had helped her unload. She left the victim in their capable hands and went home. She had almost stayed and gone right to work on the woman, but common sense got the better of her. Her little boy needed her far more than a corpse.

"I'll go get ready while you put Jane in the autopsy room," she told Henry. "We have a couple of detectives observing. They should be here any minute."

MAC PULLED INTO THE PARKING LOT of the old red brick building that housed the state medical examiner's offices. As he was getting out of his car, a gold Ford Taurus pulled into the lot and parked beside him.

"Morning, sir," Mac said over the roof of his Grand Prix.

"Morning." Kevin closed the driver's door behind him and leveled a hard gaze on Mac. "One thing to remember if you plan on getting along with me, Mac."

Startled, Mac took a step back. "What would that be, sir?"

"Drop the 'sir' bit; I work for a living. Have you been to these things before?" Detective Bledsoe opened his trunk and leaned in.

"Oh yeah, once or twice." Mac had no idea why he'd just lied to the man. Wanted to make a good impression, he supposed. Truth was, Mac had managed to avoid autopsies until now.

"Good. I'll photograph and gather the evidence. You package the items I give you and log them on Form 65."

"Form what?" Mac cleared his throat.

"Form 65—you know, the department's evidence sheet."

Embarrassed, Mac nodded. "Oh sure. Um . . . I don't have one with me."

"You sure you've been in on an autopsy before?"

Mac looked toward the building and licked his lips.

Kevin grinned and slapped him on the back. "I thought so. Look, son, let's get something straight. You don't have to pretend to know more than you do. You're here to learn. I'm here to make sure you learn right. So don't try to impress me. And for heaven's sake, don't lie to me. If you're going to be my partner, I need to know I can trust you."

Mac bit into his lower lip and ducked his head. "Yes, sir—Kevin. Sorry."

The senior detective pulled out the hard plastic case of his 35mm camera. Then he reached in again, this time withdrawing a second black plastic case marked Evidence on the outside in white stenciled letters. This he handed to Mac. "Let's go, partner." He closed the trunk and hurried toward the building with Mac trailing by a few feet. Kevin stretched out his wrist and glanced at his watch. "Right on time." He grinned back at Mac. "Punctuality is a good measure of a man."

Mac felt as though he'd committed a major sin and been redeemed. He was beginning to understand why his new partner had such a good reputation.

They entered through the north door of the building and

walked into the room on their immediate left. "This is where they'll be performing the autopsy. The administrative offices are down a hall and the walk-in coolers are to the right."

In the center of the autopsy room stood two stainless-steel tables, each with a grated top to allow liquid waste to pass. There was a sink at the foot of the tables, with an extended water hose at the top. Above the tables hung a scale, the type you'd find in a grocery store to weigh produce.

Cabinets filled with various medical supplies and containers lined the walls. Below the cabinets, a number of wooden pegs held single large rubber gloves and heavy black rubber aprons. The six heavy industrial aprons looked alike, except for the one on the end. The apron under the name Thorpe had pink lace across the chest area and along the neck strap. As Mac entered, Kristen caught his eye and winked. "I'll be right with you. Say, would one of you mind giving Henry a hand with the body? He's in the cooler."

"I need to get set up," Kevin said and turned to Mac. "Why don't you give him a hand?"

Mac nodded and headed into the cooler, which was separated from the autopsy room by a hallway. The cooler was like an enormous walk-in refrigerator with a freezer section. Bodies lay in plastic bags on gurneys, most likely on hold for the morticians or awaiting autopsy.

Inside, Henry stood over a steel cart containing a body bag and reading the label affixed to the zipper. His once-black hair had streaks of gray that made his hair look frosted.

"You must be Henry. I'm Detective McAllister. Dr. Thorpe sent me to help you with the body." Mac could see why she'd asked. Henry looked far too thin and frail to be lugging around corpses.

"Appreciate that," he said, looking far from pleased. "This is the one." He then pointed to another body. "Pull that other stiff outta the way so I can get her through."

"Sure thing." Mac examined the frosty handle on the steel cadaver cart before grabbing hold.

"Go ahead, son; he won't bite," Henry said impatiently, waiting to push the other cart out.

Mac pulled the cart out of Henry's way and noticed something that looked like milk crates in the back of the freezer. He asked about them.

"Spare parts," he said. "Why, you missing something? Lookin' to upgrade maybe?"

Mac grimaced. "No thanks." He took a closer look and noticed that the plastic milk crates did contain body parts. He spotted an assortment of arms, legs, and even a head. Trying to sound nonchalant and give the impression he was not as squeamish as he felt, he asked, "How long do you keep these?"

Henry looked annoyed. "How long do I keep them? I don't, son. The state keeps them until we find the poor sap that lost them. They turn up in rivers, in the desert, and along the side of the highway. All the fixin's of a person back in there, just no grave or name to put them with."

"Hmm."

"If you ain't missing something, boy, you'd best not be lookin'. Now come on. Dr. Thorpe is waiting."

Within moments they were ready to begin the process. Kristen Thorpe looked directly at Mac. "Have you been in on an autopsy before?"

He avoided looking at Kevin and answered, "No."

"Okay, then. I'll try to explain as we go. First, the sole purpose of this examination is to identify the cause of death. If the cause of death is homicidal, or an unnatural death, then we need to determine if the death is a criminal homicide, which means another person caused the death. It's my job to determine whether or not that's the case.

"First thing we want to do is get her under the x-ray," the doctor went on. "We need to find out if there's any lead in her."

Henry pushed the cart under a large suspended x-ray machine, guided it into place, and then unzipped the body bag, unleashing the terrible odor that had caused Mac to vomit the day before. He started breathing through his mouth.

"Whoa." Henry folded the edge of the outer bag down around the cart. "This is a bad one."

"We can leave the sheet on her for now," Kristen said. "I just needed that metal zipper out of the way for the x-ray."

Mac stared at the sheet, noticing where body fluids had apparently soaked through, creating an outline of the corpse.

Kristen tucked a couple of smelling salts into Mac's hand. "In case you need them. I don't want you to faint on me."

"Thanks." Mac broke one open and took a whiff, thankful for the pungent smell that temporarily overshadowed the odor permeating the room.

Henry gave him an unsympathetic smile as he tied a black rubber apron around his waist and pulled on his elbow-length gloves. "I'll bring the x-rays in to you all. You can wait in the hall if you want."

Feeling sweaty and a little faint, Mac took off his brown sports jacket and stepped outside the room. He placed the jacket on a hook in the hallway near the entrance. Breathing in some fresh air, he loosened his tie and unfastened the top button of his blue oxford cloth shirt. Then stalling for a few more seconds, Mac glanced down at the visitors log near the coatrack. Kevin had already signed them in, listing "investigation" next to their names as the nature of business.

He scanned the names on the list above theirs, noting several area morgues that had listed "deposit" or "withdrawal" next to their names. He was about to go back into the autopsy room when the door opened and a woman stepped inside.

"Allison?" Mac asked as recognition set in. Allison Sprague was one of the agency's top forensic scientists. He knew her by reputation as well as having talked with her when he'd worked in the child abuse unit.

"That's right, the brains of the outfit is here." Allison walked up beside him. "Now we can begin. Just stay out of the way so I can solve another caper and have you macho types take all the credit."

"Sounds good to me." Mac shook her extended hand. "How are things?"

"Good, except for having to work the weekends." She rolled her eyes. "Eric O'Rourke briefed me on the scene and condition of the body. I'm here to take any trace evidence back with me to the lab."

"Hey, Allison." Kevin grinned as she came into the room. "How have you been?"

"Morning, Kevin, great, just great. I hear you're getting ready for retirement."

"I've been ready for a long time. But yeah, only ten months to go."

"Dr. Thorpe will be right in," Kevin announced. "She had to take a phone call. I'm all set up with the camera tripod and evidence bags."

The three of them walked into the exam room together.

Dr. Thorpe and Henry entered the autopsy room a few minutes later, with Henry pushing the body of the victim in front of him. "Negative for traces of lead or metal on the x-rays." Kristen was still examining the black plastic film.

Kevin looked down at his digital pager and, after excusing himself, stepped out of the room.

"I didn't know you were invited to this party too, Allison," Kristen said, noticing the forensic scientist for the first time.

"I crashed it. Didn't want these guys messing up my evidence."

"I heard that." Detective Bledsoe poked his head back into the room.

Allison laughed. "You were supposed to." She grinned at Kevin as he left the room again.

Dr. Thorpe pulled the lace-trimmed apron over her head and tied it around her waist, then placed a surgical cap over her spiked hair. After pulling on the long rubber gloves, she picked up a felt-tip marker and went to a white board.

Henry rolled the body onto the autopsy table and pulled off the sheet. The room quieted as Kristen wrote on the board with the squeaky black pen:

NAME: Doe, Jane
RACE: White
DOB: Unknown

Setting down the pen, she waited until Henry had placed the severed skull with its attached hair mass in the sink area of the table, then she measured the body from the feet to shoulders. "About four feet, six inches. With the head intact, that would make her about five-foot-two." She paused to make the notation on the board.

"What do you say, Henry, one hundred to one-fifteen?" Dr. Thorpe asked.

"I'd put her at, oh, the heavier side of one-fifteen, maybe a little more," Henry replied.

Dr. Thorpe was writing the estimated height and weight on the board when Kevin returned. "We have two missing person hits in the area over the last fourteen days that could fit our victim. One is a Latino out of the Damascus area; the other is Megan Tyson, a woman from Troutdale. Both were in their mid-thirties, with the same general height and weight."

"Any other identifiers?" Kristen asked.

"The Damascus woman should have an appendix removal scar and a scar under the right eye." He glanced at the skull.

"This isn't her." Kristen scanned the victim's abdomen. "No appendix scar."

"The other woman had no remarkable scars, although she would have had a rose tattoo on her left shoulder."

"Bingo." Kristen pointed to a faint discoloration on the shoulder. "Looks like we have a tentative ID. Okay Megan Tyson, if that's who you really are, let's find out what happened to you."

Chapter Nine

I'm going to call Eric back," Kevin told Mac. "We need to get the gang over to the Troutdale P.D. to get a complete rundown on the victim." Kevin punched numbers into his cell as he walked out of the room. "Go ahead and start the procedure, Mac. Get a lot of photos."

"Right." Mac took several photographs of the victim from different angles before Kristen began. Though he struggled to stay objective, his empathy kept getting in the way. He didn't want to see the decomposing corpse as the attractive woman who'd gone missing ten days ago. Anger, disgust, compassion, horror, and a thousand other feelings tangled into a tight mass in the pit of his stomach.

"I'll shoot backup for you, Mac." Allison lifted a camera out of a large bag and began snapping shots. Mac wasn't sure if this was routine procedure or if she didn't trust him to do the job. He kept his comments to himself, deciding that it wouldn't hurt to have a few more photos just in case. He was glad to have her intrude on the job and on his thoughts.

Kristen set out her instruments on the examination table, then depressed the foot activator for the microphone that was suspended above the table. "All quiet, please." She then began her preliminary examination, stepping on the foot pedal while she spoke.

Mac found that focusing on the camera and the smaller images helped him remain emotionally distanced. He used nearly two rolls of film and suspected Allison had as well.

The forensics specialist finally set her camera on the counter behind her and pulled on a pair of rubber gloves. She took a plastic bag from one of the boxes she'd set beside her satchel and approached the body. Allison then removed the paper sack that Kristen had placed on the victim's right hand, placing the bag itself in an evidence envelope.

"Would you hand me some more evidence bags, Mac?"

Mac turned around and picked one off the counter. "Sure, these plastic ones?"

"No, the paper ones, please. Mine can't be plastic; the evidence has to breathe or it will only degrade more. Just hold open those little white envelopes while I take some standards from her, okay?"

Mac didn't ask what standards were. Instead he did what he was told and picked up a handful of plain white envelopes, holding them open one at a time for Allison as she collected the samples. She pulled hair samples from the head and pubic area, placing them in separate envelopes. "Go ahead and mark the envelopes, noting the sample and the part of the body I took them from."

Mac dutifully wrote a description on the front of an evidence standard, sticking his tongue out to seal the envelope. He quickly put the package down, realizing he almost licked the envelope's seal. He glanced at Allison, hoping she hadn't noticed. She had.

"Yeah, you may not want to do that." Allison smiled. "Just stack them up so I can seal them with evidence tape and initial the seal as the collecting agent."

"Good idea." Heat crept up his neck and face.

Allison clipped the fingernails on the right hand, collecting the shavings to examine later. "Hopefully we can get a standard from our bad guy. If she put up a fight, she might have scratched the offender and captured some DNA under her nails."

"I hope she did." Mac pinched his lips together. *Come on, Megan. Give us something to work with so we can catch the scum who did this.*

Allison collected dozens of hairs, fibers, pieces of vegetation, and flesh for eventual lab analysis. "The flesh may be degraded to the point that I can't get a good molecular standard for DNA comparison. Kristen, would you give me a four-inch piece of her femur when you're done, so I can recover some marrow? I'd also like some of the large muscle from her thigh. Hopefully I can extract some DNA from them for comparison later."

"I'll get those now. You want the skull too?" Kristen asked. "If the other two samples fail, I can try to extract a sample from the roots of a tooth. That's a tough one, though. I've only had that work two or three times."

"Save it. I'll get back to you if I need the teeth."

Getting into the scientific aspect of the procedure and listening to the two professionals helped to put Mac's intense feelings aside. The wooziness had left him and he was beginning to feel both confident and competent.

They took standards from the victim's anus and vagina. "I'm going to take some swabs of the genitalia in case there's trace evidence from a sexual assault. Any opinions, Kristen? The area is fairly degraded."

"I checked during the preliminary examination. There are no fissures around the body openings, so no overt signs of forced entry trauma. She's been in the elements too long to say for sure. Go ahead and take a sample, although I'd be surprised if you were able to recover anything of evidentiary value—even if it was there."

Allison went ahead with the attempt to recover any evidence of sexual assault, in the event the perpetrator had left saliva or semen. While she was doing that, Dr. Thorpe packaged the bone and muscle samples for Allison to take back to the lab.

"Thanks," Allison said. "Now if you can extract a urine sample, I'll get this stuff to the lab and get going."

Henry pulled a large syringe from the cabinet behind him. "You want blood too?"

Henry pushed the large syringe into the patient's abdomen, pulling a reddish-brown liquid back into a six-inch long plastic receptacle.

"Looks like her bladder has also degraded," Kristen frowned. "The urine looks contaminated."

"It'll do, Henry," Allison said. "I can still test for illicit or prescription drugs. Just can't do the alcohol."

Henry deposited the samples into temporary glass jars and placed them in prefabricated cardboard containers for transport to the lab. Allison gathered the recovered items Mac had labeled and placed them in a large paper bag.

"I'll give you a call when I get my results. Don't expect anything until the middle of next week."

"That long?" Mac asked then wished he hadn't.

Allison shook her head. "Welcome to the real world of forensics, Mac. Unlike the *CSI* actors, we can't wrap this up in an hour."

"I know," Mac stammered. "I didn't mean . . ."

"It's okay, Detective." Allison tossed him an understanding smile. "Everybody wants results right away."

"All done?" Kevin said as he reentered the room.

"Ha," Allison laughed. "Like you didn't plan this down to the last second. Just like you to leave your partner holding the bag."

Mac chuckled. "Holding the bag. That's a good one."

Detective Bledsoe rolled his eyes. "Here's my card with my pager number on the back. Please call me when you know anything."

"Like I said, I'll take care of you guys. When I have the name and number of the bad guy, you'll get a call."

"Yeah, yeah." Kevin grinned. "Really—thanks, Allison. I for one know we couldn't do our jobs without you."

"We'll do our best to get you something. You two be careful now." She glanced back at Mac. "You did good in there. Thanks."

Mac nodded his appreciation.

"My turn." Dr. Thorpe turned back to the victim.

"You mean we're not finished?" Mac didn't mean to make the comment out loud, but no one seemed to mind.

"Not by a long shot, Mac." Dr. Thorpe washed the maggots and debris from the body with the table's hose. "Okay, Henry, time for some fancy cutting."

Henry produced a shiny new scalpel from a paper package. He made the Y cut from the shoulder blades to the sternum, then a straight line down the patient's stomach to the navel area. The flaps of skin were pulled back to expose the dull yellow fat layer covering the ribs.

Mac's wooziness came back full force. He reached into his pocket and extracted the second whiff stick.

"Her insides aren't too bad," Dr. Thorpe said. "Go ahead and remove the rib cage, Henry." Henry walked past the shiny medical instruments on the table before him, taking an old pair of garden shears from a hook on the wall. "Nothing works as well as this old thing," Henry said.

He cut each rib, one at a time, and removed the rib cage and sternum from the body. Dr. Thorpe examined the organs, removing and dissecting them after Henry weighed them on the overhead scale. He wrote the respective weight on the grease board behind him, as Dr. Thorpe verbally recorded the procedure on her Dictaphone. "No obvious outward sign of trauma to the victim, and all internal organs are in good shape, under the circumstances."

"What about that cut on her right hip?" Mac interrupted.

"You mean this one here?" Dr. Thorpe pointed to a three-inch-long, football-shaped wound.

"Yeah, it looks like a stab wound or something."

"See the stringy layers of flesh connecting the wound? Those are called skin bridges. If a knife or blade cuts flesh, these skin bridges are not present due to the cut. With these present, the wound is an obvious sign of skin tearing. In this case, the wound occurred postmortem, due to the bloating of the body. Bloating puts extreme stress on the skin where it covers bone. As a result, the skin stretches and rips.

"These jagged edges on the flesh also indicate a tear. A slash or stab wound would be much cleaner. There are some curious marks around the base of the throat, see those dark lines? It could be the imprint of some type of ligature, but I can't say for sure with the animals eating on her."

She sighed. "Let's take a look at that skull, Henry."

Henry washed it off with the disinterest of a cook cleaning a head of lettuce. He squeezed the fluid from the mass of hair, placing them both on the examination table. Dr. Thorpe positioned the skull and what was left of the flesh on top of the patient's shoulder area. She examined the lower mandible, peeling the remaining flesh away. "You may want a photograph of this, Mac." Dr. Thorpe pointed to a rough groove, about an inch long, at the base of the jawbone. "She's had some trauma here. I'd guess her throat was cut."

Mac took photographs, once again glad to be watching through the camera lens, while Kristen held a small ruler next to the wound.

"I'm going to rule this one a criminal homicide," she said. "My official report will be that her death was a result of trauma to the head and/or neck area. My unofficial opinion is that someone cut her throat with a heavy blade, which may or may not have been what killed her. The fact that the animals were eating away at the neck first supports this opinion; there must have been a wound there for them to get at.

"There isn't much activity around the genitals or anus, which is just as accessible to the maggots and birds. They were more interested in the neck, so there must have been an easy access wound there. I'll bet on it. You guys should be looking for a stout blade, possibly even a box cutter–type instrument."

"Thanks, Doc," Kevin said. "We'll keep it in mind as we get further into the investigation. Anything else?"

"Just catch the creep who did this to her." She walked past Mac, making eye contact with him as though offering a personal challenge. "You get him." Mac's heart quickened at her words.

"Sew her up, Henry," Kristen pulled off her gloves. "We'll wait until the family confirms her identity before she's released."

"You got it, Doc." Henry pulled a large needle and heavy twine from a floor-level cabinet. He placed all the internal organs in a clear plastic bag then pushed the bag into the chest cavity like he was kneading bread. The rib cage and sternum were then set on top of the bag and the skin stretched over the entire molded heap. Then Henry went to work with his needle, stitching the incision with large loops through the flesh.

"I hem my own pants too." He smiled at the stern-faced detectives. "But I don't do windows." His laugh sounded hollow in the big room. "I don't do windows."

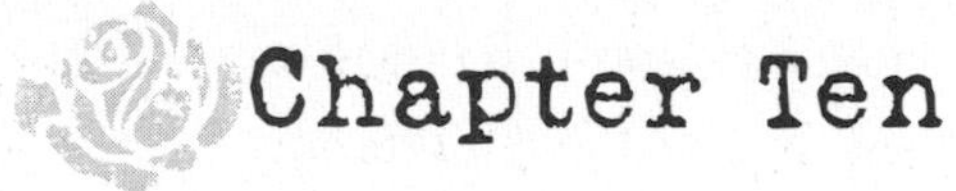

Chapter Ten

Kevin opened the door to his car and backed up as the hot air assaulted him. No problem; he'd just make the call while he waited for the car to cool down. "The medical examiner's office ruled it a criminal homicide," he said to Eric when his friend answered. He and Mac were still parked in front of the medical examiner's offices. "Did you get the victim's identification from Russ and Philly?"

"Yeah. Based on the general description and that rose tattoo, it looks like our victim is Megan Tyson. I checked her criminal history and came back with zip. That means no fingerprints on file, unless she had a concealed weapon permit or was in the military. Nothing so far, though."

Kevin ran a hand through his graying hair. "Allison Sprague took some forensic evidence at the post; hopefully she can give us a DNA printout if we can give her something to compare it to. Do you have Troutdale P.D. in the loop yet?"

"I just got off the phone with them," Eric said. "I'm on the way to their office now. Philly and Russ should already be there. They were trying to contact the victim's sister—Cindy, I think her name is. Apparently they both have the same tattoo, got them a couple of years ago in Florida on a spring break."

Kevin pulled at the neck of his shirt. Man, it was hot. "Mac and I will head down to Troutdale and meet you guys. What time is the briefing?"

"Let's see, it's almost noon now. Why don't you grab some lunch and meet us at the Troutdale P.D. about one-thirty? That should give the rest of the gang a chance to finish up their business."

"One-thirty it is."

"Say, how's your new partner working out?"

"Seems like a good guy. Fast learner." Kevin glanced over at Mac, who tossed his sports jacket and briefcase on the backseat before getting into his vehicle. The engine turned over on the first try. Mac flipped on the air conditioning and got back out.

"That's good," Eric said. "'Cause I was just saying to the Lord this morning, 'Lord, I am so glad I don't have to be Kevin's partner anymore.'"

Kevin chuckled, not believing a word of it. Eric missed him as much as he missed Eric. "You're just jealous."

"Me? No way. You are such a drag to be around, I feel sorry for Mac."

"Obviously you're lost without me. Try not to mess things up before I get there, and quit biting your nails." Kevin could almost see Eric pulling his pinky out of his mouth and squinting at his jagged nail.

"How do you do that?"

"Ve haf our vays." Kevin did a fair Arnold Schwarzenegger imitation.

"I'll bet. In the meantime, mind your own business. I'll see you at one-thirty."

"That was Eric," Kevin said to Mac after hanging up. "If you don't mind driving, I'd like to drop off my car at the Portland Patrol Office and ride with you. We need to be at the Troutdale P.D. in a couple of hours for a briefing, so I thought we'd grab a bite first."

"Sounds good, sir—um, partner."

"That's better." Kevin ducked into his car. "I'll see you at the office."

DRIVING BACK TO THE PORTLAND PATROL OFFICE, which was about fifteen minutes away, Mac thought again about the woman Dr. Thorpe had just dissected. Pictures of the petite blonde who had once been Megan Tyson filled his mind. What horrible things had happened to her? Kristen thought the killer had slit her throat. Tears burned his eyes. During his years as a trooper and months with the child abuse unit, he'd seen some horrible things, but none of them had affected him as much as the brutality of this crime. "How could You let this happen?" Mac pounded the steering wheel and glanced upward. "Why her?" He gripped the steering wheel tighter. He remembered Kristen's challenge at the end of the autopsy.

"Just catch the creep who did this to her." She'd looked right at him as if issuing a challenge. "*You get him.*"

"I will, Kristen. Count on it." Mac sucked in cold air through his clenched teeth. He yanked a tissue from the box on the passenger seat and wiped the moisture from his eyes and blew his nose. "You gotta pull yourself together, McAllister. Can't let your boss see you like this."

Static, then voices came across the police radio. A trooper responded to an injury accident in rural Clackamas County, his siren audible on the radio as he spoke to dispatch. Poor guy. Mac had covered his share of accidents during his stint as a trooper, before making the detective rank. Car wrecks, suicides, and domestic assaults had produced their share of victims.

He had never quite gotten used to death and had tried to distance himself from the personal side of tragedy. His efforts usually didn't work. The victim of a fatal car crash wasn't real to him—until he peered into a wallet for identification and found photographs of children or loved ones. Phone numbers of friends and notes written for future meetings were graphic reminders of their reality—their humanness. Dealing with the devastation and heartbreak of those left behind proved even harder than dealing with the dead.

Mac realized he would much rather collect the remains in a body bag than knock on the door to inform family members that someone they loved had died. That was the most agonizing part of dealing with death. That's what he and Kevin would soon have to do. Megan had family, people who loved her and who were waiting to hear what the police had found.

Mac guided his Grand Prix up to the chain-link fence surrounding the Portland Patrol Office. He entered the four-digit code on the gate's alarm system, activating the automatic opener, then eased his car through the gate, stopping near the employee entrance. Kevin pulled his car in behind him and parked in an open space.

While he cleared the front passenger seat for his boss, Mac changed his FM radio station from a modern rock station to an easy listening channel. Although he rarely listened to mood music, he had it programmed in his car radio so he could quickly switch over when he had older passengers in the car. Not that he was all that sensitive. His grandmothers had always made him change the channel when they rode with him. Eventually, to escape the inevitable lecture about his choice of music, he began switching to the alternative station beforehand.

Detective Bledsoe placed his briefcase in the backseat of the Grand Prix, along with his navy blue blazer. He made some notes in his police notebook and slumped down in the passenger seat. "You name it, partner—my treat."

"What's that?" Mac frowned, still trying to rein in his morbid thoughts.

"You know, grub, chow, eats. I'm hungry."

"Oh, right." Mac wasn't quite ready to think about food. His stomach still hadn't returned to normal, but at least he didn't need the smelling salts anymore. "There's a good Asian place around the corner, if you're into that."

"Perfect. I'm always up for Asian."

Mac backed around, driving over the underground sensor that automatically opened the gate. He passed the point where the sensor was located with no response from the gate. "Jesus Christ, this thing is slow."

Kevin gave Mac a sharp look. "Well, you've got His attention, so go ahead."

"Huh?" Mac glanced around.

"Jesus Christ. You have His attention. Go ahead with whatever profound statement or request you were planning to make." Kevin rubbed his temple and leaned back in the seat.

"I . . . it . . ." Mac stammered. "I was just . . . the gate." He felt like swearing again. Mac didn't like being put on the defensive like that. No one had ever come down on him for swearing—except his grandmothers.

"Uh-huh. If you have nothing to say to Him, then let's go to lunch."

The gate opened without Mac moving his car over the sensor again. He eased his foot onto the gas pedal to go out the gate and the car lurched backward.

Kevin's lips parted in a teasing grin. "Shift her into drive, partner. That works better for going forward."

Saying a few choice words under his breath, Mac shoved the automatic into drive and drove out of the lot. *Great impression you're making, McAllister. First you lie to him, then you offend him, and you top it all off by nearly wrecking your car. The guy's going to think you're a real wacko.*

"WHAT'S GOOD HERE?" Kevin slid into the booth, placing his briefcase beside him.

"I'm having the pork noodles." Mac scanned the menu. "That's grilled pork on top of noodles and lettuce, served with some kind of sauce." Mac's pager vibrated on his hip. He checked the number and sighed. Linda.

Kevin scooted out of the seat. "You can order me what you're having. I need to wash up. By the way, my cell is in my briefcase, so help yourself if you need to make a call."

Mac had left his cell phone in the car, so he decided to use Kevin's phone to call Linda. He poured two cups of tea from the white china pot, then moved over to Kevin's side of the table, where he spotted the scarred, black leather briefcase. *This thing's been around the block a few times.*

He opened the case, moving aside the various notebooks and legal pads. His gaze fell on a worn black book. The pages were bent and the leather cover was frayed and creased. Most of the gold lettering had worn off, but Mac could still read the title. The guy carried a Bible in his briefcase? No wonder he made that comment about Mac's swearing.

Great. He'd been partnered with a Bible-toting religious freak. Mac moved aside the book and found the cell phone.

"Isn't she a beaut?" Kevin nodded toward his case. "My wife gave that to me as a wedding gift."

Mac frowned and scooted out of Kevin's seat. "The cell phone?"

Kevin shook his head. "The Bible."

If you say so. Mac licked his lips, not sure how to respond. "I got one once—a long time ago. My grandmother thought it would make a good graduation present."

"So you're a believer."

"Um . . . no, not exactly." Mac eased back into his own seat, preparing himself for the sermon. This was probably where Kevin would make a pitch for the three- or four- or six-point plan of salvation. He'd been getting some pressure from Linda about going to church—he sure didn't need it at work too.

"Hey, did you make your call?" Kevin asked.

"Not yet." Relieved that the sermon he dreaded wasn't forthcoming, Mac punched Linda's number into the cell. She picked up on the first ring.

"Hi, honey," Mac said.

"Where are you?" Linda demanded.

"Working. Why?"

"Mac, we were going boating with my parents."

Mac groaned and pinched the bridge of his nose. He'd completely forgotten.

"I can't believe you didn't call," she went on before he could answer. "I tried to get you at home and on your cell, and when I couldn't, I got worried and called the state police and had the dispatch operator page you."

Mac glanced at Kevin then at the table. "I'm sorry, honey. I got tied up with that case I went out on last night."

"And you couldn't find two minutes to let me know? Don't I mean anything to you?"

"I said I was sorry."

"Well, that's not good enough." Her voice broke.

"Look, this really isn't a good time." By the time he got the last word out, he was talking to a dial tone.

He clicked off the phone and gave Kevin an embarrassed smile. "My girlfriend," he explained. "I was supposed to go boating with her and her parents today."

Kevin gave him a sympathetic nod. "And you forgot to call her."

He shrugged. "Something like that." He handed the phone across the table. "Thanks."

"Too bad." Rather than return the phone to the briefcase, Kevin slipped it into his pocket.

Wanting to change the subject, Mac took another sip of tea. "I heard you were a boxer at one time."

Kevin raised his eyebrows. "What did you do, look up my rap sheet?"

Mac laughed. "Not exactly. I just asked around, and apparently you have quite a reputation. I thought since we were going to work together, I should know something about you."

"I can't fault you there." The senior detective's beefy hand dwarfed the teacup as he curled his fingers around it and took a drink. "Yeah, I was a boxer. In my day I could hold my own in the middleweights. I was the Junior Golden Gloves champ in Chicago. That's where I'm from. I boxed in the military and was division champ for two years."

"Wow! Did you ever box as a pro?"

"Naw. I thought I had a chance to go professional and make some real money, but after my discharge from the army, things sort of fell apart with the boxing career. All I got were a lot of bumps on my noggin and an empty stomach."

Mac's gaze settled on the champ's crooked nose. "Guess that explains the bump."

"This?" He shook his head. "Surprisingly, no. I got this dandy during my early days as a trooper. I'd been searching a barn for a fugitive with a warrant for a parole violation, just outside of Klamath Falls. A deputy and I had entered a horse stall looking for the bad guy, when *whap!* This guy laces me across the face with the tire iron. I was out for the count. Good thing the deputy was there to take him into custody."

Even the thought made Mac's face hurt. "Man, that must have smarted."

"You bet it did; it rearranged my face too. Jean hardly recognized me when she picked me up at the hospital. She was pregnant with our third kid at that time. It scared her so bad she slapped me right across the face when she saw me."

"She hit you?"

"Yeah, but then she followed it up with a hug and told me never to scare her like that again. She told me that when the lieutenant came to the door that day, she thought he was going to tell her I had been killed."

"I still don't understand why you gave up boxing."

"My wife, who at the time was my girlfriend, told me to get a real job or go it alone."

"She gave you an ultimatum? But boxing was your dream. How fair is that?"

"Maybe not fair, Mac, but wise. Very wise. She had a better idea of what God wanted for me than I did. Besides, she didn't want to see me get hurt. I finally gave in, and after we moved to Oregon, thanks to a little pressure from Jean's father, I applied for a job with the state police. The rest is history."

"Somehow I don't think being an officer is safer than boxing."

"It isn't, but at the time we needed the money. Later I realized this is right where I belong."

The waitress brought their steaming bowls of noodles and they leaned back while she placed them on the table. "Anything else?" she asked.

"That will do it. Thanks." Kevin peeled the paper off his chopsticks.

As the waitress set the check on the table, Kevin slid it over to his side. "No arguments; it's on me."

"You don't have to do that. I have money."

"I'm sure you do. So buy your girl some flowers. From what you told me, you're going to need all the ammunition you can get your hands on to gain her forgiveness."

"All right. But I've got the next one."

"More tea?" Kevin picked up the porcelain pot and poured out the rest of the tea. Mac thought he'd crack up watching the big ex-boxer delicately raise his pinky finger as he took a sip.

THEY WERE JUST LEAVING THE RESTAURANT when Kevin's cell phone rang. He pulled it from his jacket pocket and flipped it open. "Yeah. Bledsoe here."

"Hey, we got a slight problem." Eric got right to the point. "Philly and Russ had to cover a situation down in Salem. They couldn't make contact with the victim's sister and wondered if you and Mac could take care of it."

"Sure. Has she been contacted at all?"

"By phone . . ."

"By phone? What's the deal? Someone should have talked to her in person."

"Don't go getting all hot and bothered about it. She called us. She reads the papers. At any rate, you need to take her down to the morgue to make a positive ID."

Kevin frowned. "Come on, Eric, we can't take her down there. The remains are completely unidentifiable, except maybe that rose tattoo."

"Just following the lady's request. She wants to view the body."

"Sheesh. Okay, give me her address and phone number, and we'll get right on it."

Kevin didn't much like having to contact the family—no one did. Still, he was glad he could be there for them. And truth be told, he was glad it could be him this time and not Russ and Philly. The guys were polite when necessary, but they weren't the most empathetic duo in the department.

After getting the details from Eric, Kevin closed up his phone and pocketed it. Turning to Mac, he said, "The meeting has been delayed until three o'clock to give us time to take the victim's sister down to the morgue."

Mac turned the key in the ignition. "I thought someone else was doing that."

Kevin climbed in and fastened his seat belt. "Yeah, well, you know how it is. Russ and Philly got another call. The sister's name is Cindy Tyson. She lives over by the Lloyd Center—shares a house there with another gal. She's been notified and is waiting for us."

Mac bit down on his toothpick, breaking it in half. "Doesn't seem right."

"What's that?"

"Taking a family member down to the morgue in a case like this. How's she going to make a positive ID?"

"She probably can't, but she'll be able to make out the size and position of the rose." Kevin sucked in a decp breath. "And no, it doesn't seem right. But then having your sister murdered and left for buzzard bait isn't right either."

Chapter Eleven

Mac dropped his splintered toothpick in a plastic bag he kept by his seat for litter. They didn't talk much on the way, except for Kevin giving directions while Mac drove. Ten minutes later, they pulled up in front of an older house—a two-story boxlike place with a square front porch. The porch steps had been given a coat of medium gray paint that matched the gray shutters. The house itself was slate blue. In the corner of the porch, Mac noticed several cans of paint and a few pieces of molding lying on a drop cloth. The front door was new and had an oval stained-glass window depicting a single red rose.

A young woman with red-rimmed eyes and a red nose opened the door. Her hair was tucked under a baseball cap, with a blonde ponytail sticking out the back. She was wearing a pink nylon sweat suit, the jacket pocket bulging with a wad of white tissues. Holding one of the tissues in her hand, she sniffed and wiped her nose. "Are you with the police?"

"Yes, ma'am." Kevin showed her his badge. "I'm Detective Bledsoe and this is my partner, Detective Mac McAllister."

"I'm Cindy Tyson." She gave the badge a cursory look. "The woman who called me said you guys would be picking me up." She touched the tissue to the corners of her eyes. "I look awful. When I heard you might have found my sister's body, I kind of fell apart. I still can't believe it."

"No need to apologize," Mac said. "I'm sorry you have to go through all this."

Cindy reached over to an antique table, grabbing a manila envelope and a small handbag, the latter of which she slung over her shoulder. Stepping outside, she closed the door behind her. "These are Megan's dental records." She handed the envelope to Kevin. "I got them from Megan's dentist when I reported her missing. The police officer who took the report said I should. I thought maybe the medical examiner would need them."

"Good thinking." Kevin tucked the envelope under his arm as he opened the back door for Cindy. "This will save us some time."

Once they were underway, she leaned forward. "Do you really think the woman you found is my sister?"

"The identification is tentative," Kevin answered. "Maybe you'll be able to make a positive ID."

She clasped her hands together and leaned back. "Thank you for picking me up."

"No problem," Mac said. A baseball-size knot formed in his stomach as he thought about what lay ahead for her. He wished he could take away some of the pain she must be feeling.

"Wait here," Kevin ordered when they pulled into the medical examiner's parking lot. This time the door was locked, so he had to ring the buzzer. He waited a few seconds, pushing back his sports jacket sleeve to look at his watch. "C'mon, c'mon," he muttered, feeling unusually restless.

"Yes?" The muffled voice came from the intercom speaker.

"Detective Bledsoe, state police. I'm here with a family member to view the remains of our Jane Doe, possibly Megan Tyson."

"One moment please. I'll be right there."

Kevin gave Mac a wave, telling him to bring Cindy in.

Mac got out of the car and came around the passenger side to open the door for Cindy. "Let's go on inside. This will only take a minute." He offered his arm for support as they walked up to the door. "This isn't going to be easy, Cindy. I just want you to know my partner and I are here if you need us."

"Thank you. Um . . . what should I do?"

"Just come with us. They'll let you know."

Kevin held the door for Mac and Cindy. Kristen stood just inside. "Dr. Thorpe," Kevin said, "this is Cindy Tyson, Megan's sister. She's here to take a look at the body you have in your custody."

"I'm sorry to meet you under these circumstances, Cindy. Please, come in. Can I get you anything—a glass of water, coffee, tea?"

"No, thank you. I just want to get this over with."

"Come on back then." Kristen led the trio down the hall to the examination room. A clean white sheet covered the body.

Mac took a deep breath and prepared himself to view the body again. If he felt this bad, how must the sister feel?

Kristen began to pull down the sheet then stopped. "Cindy, there's no way I can adequately prepare you for this. If this woman is your sister, she won't look at all like you remember her."

That's an understatement, Mac thought.

Cindy nodded and dug a fresh tissue out of her pocket. Tears trickled down her face. Her shoulders tensed.

Kristen slowly pulled back the sheet, revealing the detached head, the leathery brown shoulder, and the rose tattoo.

"My God. Oh my God." Cindy dropped to her knees before Mac and Kevin could get to her. "It's her."

"Are you sure?" Kevin asked.

Without answering, Cindy pulled off her jacket and stretched her knit top to the side to reveal her shoulder. "The rose. We had them done together. Same time. Same colors. She was my best friend and my sister." She looked at the detectives and tears filled her eyes again. "That's Megan. I don't need to see any more."

Kristen pulled the sheet over the victim's head and pushed the cart back into place. Mac hunkered down beside Cindy and helped her to her feet. She leaned into him, sobbing so hard her shoulders shook. He settled an arm across her shoulders, feeling awkward but at the same time wanting to do what he could to ease her suffering.

Kevin handed the manila envelope that Cindy had given him to Kristen. "Dental x-rays."

"That was fast."

"Wish we could take the credit, but Cindy already had them."

"I'll take a look at these later. In the meantime, I'm tentatively ruling this as a positive identification. I'll compare the dental records and give you folks a call one way or the other."

"Sounds good, Doc," Kevin said.

When Kristen stepped toward them, Mac lowered his arm.

Kristen placed a hand on the sobbing girl's shoulder. "Cindy, I am very sorry for your loss. Do you have any family members around?"

"Just Megan. Nobody now, I guess," Cindy pressed a mangled tissue to her face. "Our mother died when we were little. Our father passed away last year. Oh God, I'm so glad Daddy wasn't around for this; it would have broken his heart." She looked stricken. "Oh no—Tim. I've got to call Tim."

"Tim?" Kevin pulled a notepad out of his inside jacket pocket.

"Tim Morris is Megan's fiancé. They were supposed to be married August thirty-first, next Saturday."

Kevin glanced at Mac. "We'll want to talk with Mr. Morris, Cindy. Can you tell us how to get hold of him?"

"He's flying in tomorrow. I'm supposed to pick him up at the airport. Um . . . Tim lives in Florida. He's been worried sick since he got the news. He flew out here as soon as he found out she was missing. He stayed, too, until a few days ago when he had to get back home to take care of some business."

"What kind of business is he in?" Kevin asked.

"He sells exercise equipment. Actually designs the stuff and markets it to the big health clubs. That's how he and Megan met. She works—worked at Fitness First in Troutdale." She released a shuddering sigh. "Can we talk about this at my house? I'd like to leave now."

"No problem." Kevin guided her toward the door. "We'll set up a time that's more appropriate."

"Hold on a minute." Dr. Thorpe left and came back a moment later with a business card. "You'll need to make arrangements to recover Megan for a service of your choice. You can give us a call or have a funeral director make the arrangements."

Cindy stared at the card for a moment then placed it in her jacket pocket with the soggy tissues. Tears came again as she turned to go. Kristen escorted her down the hall to the front entrance. "I'm very sorry. Please don't hesitate to call if I can be of any assistance."

"Thank you. I will. I . . . you've all been so nice to me. God bless you."

Kristen looked up at Mac and Kevin, who were trailing behind. "These gentlemen will see you home now, Cindy."

Kevin opened the heavy door while Mac hurried to unlock the car.

Cindy settled into the backseat, her face turned toward the window. She stayed that way for a long time as they drove down Grand Avenue, past houses that had been a part of Portland's initial growth in the late 1800s.

When they reached the freeway, Mac heard Cindy whimper, "What did you get yourself into, Megan? What happened to you?" She pulled her knees to her chest and cried.

Chapter Twelve

The detectives dropped off Cindy at her house, with a promise that they would be calling in the next day or two to make an appointment. She nodded, but Mac wasn't at all sure she heard or understood.

They waited until she was safe inside before heading toward the Troutdale P.D. for their briefing. They arrived at a quarter of three.

Kevin pounded on the gray metal door to the Troutdale P.D. Mac glanced at the department ring on Kevin's right hand as he cupped his hands around his face to peer into the small window on the door. The gold-colored ring was engraved with the five-point-star badge, with a dull red stone in the center. The words *Honor* and *Fidelity* had been etched into the metal.

"I know they're in there. Eric's and Philly's cars are in the lot." Kevin knocked harder.

Philly Johnson stuck his head out of the second-story window. "Your papers," he shouted in a thick German accent. "Show me your papers or you vill be shot."

Mac shook his head. "You guys and your crazy accents."

Eric opened the door for Mac and Kevin and glanced up at Philly. "You look like Sergeant Schultz from *Hogan's Heroes.*"

"Thanks. I'll take that as a compliment on my acting ability."

"Ha! I said you look like him, not sound like him."

Philly lifted his nose in the air, attempting to look insulted. He laughed and yelled back. "What do you know, you red-headed geek?" He chomped down on the massive hamburger he was holding. A glob of sauce dropped to the ground, and Mac ducked out of the way just in time.

"That's Phil Johnson." Eric directed his comment to Mac. "I think he and Russ were gone by the time you got there last night. Mac saluted Phil, who was still leaning out the window.

Kevin leaned toward Mac and said in a voice Phil couldn't hear, "Don't let the appearance fool you, kid. He's sharp as a tack."

"You guys made good time." Eric motioned them inside then led them up the stairs. Turning back to Kevin and Mac he said, "Troutdale P.D. has two guys here already. They've done some pretty good legwork on the missing person case. They want us to run with the homicide. I brought in the rest of the gang from Salem to run down follow-up with us. I'll make the assignments after our briefing."

When they walked into the conference room, Phil's hamburger was gone. Philly wiped his hand on a napkin, tossed it, then pulled a black plastic comb from his back pocket, shaping his thinning hair over his scalp. He placed his thumbs in his belt to tuck in his sagging shirt, sucking in his hefty stomach.

Eric leaned his narrow hips against a table. "Mac, I'll have to apologize again for making you work with Kevin. I hope he doesn't depress you too much. He's hard of hearing, you know." A slight grin told Mac that Eric was teasing. "You need to speak up when you talk to him. And he falls asleep a lot."

"Just keep talking, pal." Kevin patted Eric on the back.

"Don't worry, I will." Eric indicated for the men to take a seat. There were already nine plain-clothes officers and one uniform from the Troutdale Police in the room. "Gang, you all know Kevin. This is Mac McAllister, from the Portland office child abuse unit. He'll be working with us on this one until further notice. Mac, this is the gang."

Mac stood at the sidelines while the others sized him up. There were detectives from drug enforcement units, pawn details, and auto theft. Most of these guys would do the dirty work—rattling informants, addicts, and dope dealers for leads. Mac could pretty much tell their respective assignments by their dress and issued equipment.

He also knew that the only people cops trusted less than cops they didn't know were the criminals they arrested. Mac hadn't been a detective long enough to gain a reputation, so he needed to make a good first impression. He hadn't done all that well so far—at least not with Detective Bledsoe.

"Welcome, Detective McAllister." Phil stood and reached across the table. "Phil Johnson at your disposal."

"Good to meet you." Mac shook Detective Johnson's hand. His own came away a tad greasy.

"Tell me, Mac. Do you have any naked pictures of your mother?"

"No," Mac said slowly, taken aback by the question and not quite certain he heard correctly.

"Want to buy some?" The room erupted in laughter.

They all looked at Mac as if waiting for his reaction.

"That depends." Mac replied with a straight face as he pulled out his wallet. "Do you have change for a twenty, or did you spend all your money at the antique store on those polyester pants?"

They laughed again and Philly pulled out the chair next to him, offering Mac a seat.

"He's quick on his feet," Eric whispered to Kevin in a tone loud enough for Mac to hear. "If he can stand up to Philly, he should do okay in an interview."

"Yeah, he's a good kid," Kevin replied as the other detectives in the room introduced themselves to Mac. Mac felt like he'd passed the first initiation and wondered how many more there were to go.

Eric held up the clipboard with the respective assignments,

then addressed the rowdy group. "Okay, you clowns, settle down. We've got work to do."

Eric stepped to the front of the room while the others adjusted their chairs and opened their notepads. He turned over the large top sheet of the drawing pad on a metal easel. "I'm Detective Eric O'Rourke. I'll be the lead on this while Sergeant Evans is out of state. I'll be making the assignments during this investigation, so here are my pager and cell phone numbers," he said while pointing to the prewritten numbers on the chart.

"This is the Oregon State Police case number; below it is the missing person case number for the Troutdale Police Department. Please use these numbers on all subsequent reports as connecting reference numbers so I can keep the case jacket together."

Eric flipped to the next page, containing the victim's biographical information. "Here is our victim. Her name is Megan Ann Tyson, thirty-four years of age. Her sister, Cynthia Tyson, last saw Megan on Tuesday, August thirteenth. Cindy filed a missing person report the following day to Troutdale P.D." He glanced at the uniformed Troutdale officer, who nodded in agreement.

"Troutdale Police want us to take the lead on the homicide since they're strapped right now for detective resources due to other cases. They will continue to offer any support we need. Since the victim lived here in Troutdale, we can use their office for our briefings. Right now, we have every reason to believe the crime scene at Bonneville State Park was a body dumpsite only. Therefore, gentlemen, we have a primary crime scene somewhere else. It may be in her home, a car, a parking lot, or whatever. That's what we need to find out.

"Detectives Bledsoe and McAllister are the lead interview team. That means these two will interview all persons of interest." Eric checked the notes on his clipboard. "Philly and Russ, you two have the background gig. I want to know everyone Megan ever knew or was associated with. You can start with her apartment in

Troutdale. The sister has given consent to search the place, and since they roomed together we don't need a warrant. Make sure that consent goes into writing, though; we don't know if she's dirty at this point."

Mac tapped his pen on his notepad. He found it hard to imagine that Cindy Tyson could have had anything to do with her sister's murder, but he knew better than to jump to conclusions.

Glancing at his clipboard again, Eric continued. "The primary information we have from the missing person report was that the victim was due to be married next Saturday. From what her sister said when she filed the missing person report, Megan didn't have a lot of close friends, although she seemed to know a lot of people. Megan worked as a trainer at Fitness First here in Troutdale. I'm told she was in good shape—her DMV printout puts her at five feet, two inches and one hundred thirteen pounds.

"Her fiancé, Tim Morris, has been informed of the death and will be in town tomorrow. Mac and Kevin, I want you on him ASAP. We all know that she was probably murdered by someone she knew. We'll start with the fiancé, then spiral out to other family members. If that doesn't cut it we'll go to friends, coworkers, and associates. If still no leads, then we have the toughest nut to crack. A stranger-to-stranger murder, where she didn't know the perpetrator."

He rubbed the back of his neck. "I want the rest of you guys to roll every junkie and crack dealer in the county, call in all your markers. We need information, folks, the sooner the better. Any comments, questions?"

"Yeah," Kevin spoke up. "Mac and I attended the post. Due to the degraded state of the body the M.E. couldn't come up with a cause of death by a foreign object. All we know for sure is there was no remarkable trauma from the clavicle on down. However, since animals ravaged the head and neck she thinks we have a probable neck or facial wound that may have caused an opening for predators. In other words, we think her throat was cut. Be on the lookout for blades or sharp instruments. But remember, just because we didn't recover any bullets doesn't mean our guy isn't armed."

Eric nodded. "That reminds me. Philly, Russ, find out when the funeral is; we want to be there with a video. I wouldn't put it past this sicko to show up at the funeral to put the last nail in the coffin. Let's get permission to have a camera set up discreetly to film the attendance."

"You got it, boss." Philly made a note on his pad. "Your word is my command."

Eric rolled his eyes. "I think that's 'your *wish* is my command.'"

"Okay. Hey, you all heard him." Philly grinned. "I'm now officially the boss."

Eric folded his arms. "Keep up the smart-mouth remarks and I just might take you up on it." Looking back at the others, he said, "Anything else, gentlemen? I'm passing around this sign-up sheet. Please fill in your name and horsepower—rank, phone numbers, vehicle, and so on. I'll get copies to everyone. I also set up a tip line and had a flyer made up for the public with a phone number to call. Grab a few on the way out.

"There'll be color copies of the victim's photograph for each of you. We've got a planned press release for information on the death, so hopefully that will generate the tips. I'll be reviewing them for assignment when they are received. And Dr. Thorpe just called; she has reviewed the victim's dental records and reaffirmed the sister's positive identification, so we will proceed with a media blitz.

"What else am I missing? Oh yeah. Troutdale P.D. conducted a credit check on the victim and served subpoenas on the respective banks and credit card holders for PIN numbers and account information. We should have that information by Monday or Tuesday, so we can start tracking her credit card use. Her checking and savings have been frozen, although we don't know if there were any transactions after she was reported missing.

"I'd like to turn the briefing over to Troutdale right now, so they can bring us all up to speed on the investigation prior to the discovery of the body."

The uniformed Troutdale police officer walked to the front of the room, looking nervous as he flipped through his leatherbound police notebook. "Here's what we've got so far. Like the detective said earlier, the victim's name was Megan Ann Tyson . . ." The uniform repeated the stats Eric had given them earlier then added, "The victim lived here in Troutdale with her sister, over in some apartments on Bellevue Court. She was boxing up most of her belongings prior to the wedding, leaving most of the furnishings to her sister. I guess she was going to move to Florida, where her fiancé lives. The sister, Cindy, was in the process of moving in with a girlfriend to a place in Portland. The sister said she stayed overnight at her new place the night of the thirteenth. When she came back the next day to the apartment she shared with her sister, she found the residence had been burglarized."

A burglary gone sour? Mac jotted down the new information. *Or maybe the killer wanted it to look like a burglary.*

The officer flipped the page in his notebook, placing a paper clip over the last page. "She, the sister, noticed the television set was gone, along with the stereo and some compact discs. The television was a color, nineteen-inch Sony with a remote. The stereo was a Sanyo compact disc player, with four speakers. The bad guy also took some smaller items—compact discs, silver candleholders, stuff like that. I have a complete list I can copy for you. We couldn't come up with the serial numbers on the audio equipment and TV, but we do have a photograph of some of the items. Apparently, Megan had taken a picture of her sister on the couch that had the TV and stereo in the background. We made a copy of the picture and placed it in these briefing packets with the victim's photograph."

Eric passed around a stack of briefing packets while the officer continued. "The victim had a blue Mustang, one of those sporty convertible jobs. It was in the driveway of the victim's residence—no keys. The sister found the vehicle when she returned home on the fourteenth, the day she called us on the missing person case. Like I said, most of their stuff was packed in boxes for the move, and Cindy told us she had already removed most of their valuables from the residence."

"Did you process the Mustang for trace evidence?" Kevin asked.

"Sure did, the next day. Your forensic lab processed the vehicle, with nothing remarkable located. They took plenty of latent prints. She'd had the vehicle for a couple of years, so it had a lot of use. We released it back to the sister.

"That's about all I have." He perused his notes. "Oh, one more thing. Megan, the victim, reported her purse stolen several days prior to turning up missing. She lost her identification, gas cards, and her checkbook—the whole ball of wax. We don't know if she had a key in the purse or if the theft is related at all. There were no signs of forced entry at the apartment, so we assume the perpetrator had a key. Or, there's always the chance he was invited in and something went wrong. We just don't know."

"When was the credit check done on her cards?" Eric asked.

"The day she turned up missing, the fourteenth. The bank's been a real son of a gun to work with because we don't have Megan here to give consent like in a normal purse snatching. We had to obtain a grand jury subpoena for the records. I'm told we'll have them tomorrow so we can see if the cards have been used."

The officer thumbed through the notebook. "That's all. You'll find her photograph on the last page of the briefing packet. That's the one you've seen on television and the newspaper. Cute gal, what a shame." He nodded to Eric and then sat down.

"Okay, thanks in advance to all of you who are working on this assignment," Eric told everyone. "If there are no more questions, let's hit the streets. Don't forget, all assignments and information go through me. I'll be seated right here, running the tip line, so give me updates every so often."

Mac flipped to the last page of the briefing packet, examining the color photo of Megan Tyson. It had been taken at the coast. Mac thought he recognized the famed Cannon Beach Rock in the distance.

A wide grin stretched across her face as she assumed a model-like pose. Mac could almost hear the waves crashing and the gulls squawking. He could almost hear her laughing. The bright rose tattoo was clearly visible as Megan knelt next to a large piece of driftwood in a sleeveless top and cutoffs.

He thought about the grotesque, decomposed body he'd photographed last night and again this morning. How could this be the same person? Mac looked up from the picture to see Kevin standing at the door, arms crossed and watching him, waiting for him. When he caught Mac's eye, he said, "Ready to get to work, partner?"

"Ready."

Philly stood up and yawned, looking back at Russ. "Let's go, partner. I want to grab one of those teriyaki chicken sticks over at the Bento stand on the way out."

"What are you, a wolf?" Russ asked. "You need a meat fix every hour on the hour?"

"If God didn't want me to eat animals, he wouldn't have made them out of meat," Philly joked as he left the conference room with Russ.

"Hey, you guys be careful," Eric called after the group as they funneled down the stairs. "Let's catch this creep."

Chapter Thirteen

Kevin was punching in Cindy's home number by the time Mac started the car. "Humph. No answer. I'll try her cell." He dialed another number, and Cindy answered.

"Hi, Cindy. This is Detective Bledsoe, Oregon State Police. We'd like to talk to you as soon as possible. I know no time is a good time, but could you give us a few minutes this afternoon?" After a few moments' hesitation, he replied, "Thanks, we'll be right over."

Hanging up, he said, "She's getting the rest of her stuff moved out of their old apartment. Said we could meet her there."

"Okay, you direct. I'll drive."

"According to the briefing packet, she's at the Chinook Run apartments on Bellevue Court, number 315."

"I know where that is."

Less than five minutes later, Mac pulled the car into a visitor parking space. He turned off the engine and reached for the door handle.

"Hang on a sec, partner." Kevin unlatched his seatbelt. "This will be our first interview together, so I want to set some ground rules. I'm sure you know your business, but I'd like to brief you on how I operate. When I'm talking to a potential witness or suspect, you don't interrupt. That goes for me too. It kills a rapport with the person you're interviewing when he is shotgunned with questions. If he's a suspect, it gives him time to think, to come up with an excuse. I may be working an angle, and my point may or may not become clear to you during the interview. Just sit back and relax so you don't jump my line of thinking. We never ask the big questions first; we lead up to them. That way the perp is less likely to ax the interview."

Mac nodded his head. "Got it."

Kevin buttoned his top shirt button and straightened his tie. "These are the rules Eric and I worked under. You'll know when I'm releasing the interview to you for any questions I missed, so be thinking of follow-up questions. It's not critical at this point, but if we get a big fish on the line we don't want to give him any slack. Remember, a provable lie is as good as a confession. So let's be thorough."

"Gotcha, partner. I'm ready."

Kevin removed a mini cassette recorder from his pocket. "I'm going to take some quick notes in the daylight, in case we need them for a warrant affidavit later." He held the microphone to his lips, activating the pause button when he wasn't speaking. "Megan Tyson's apartment—interview with her sister, Cindy Tyson. I'm looking at a two-story wood frame apartment building, constructed for single-family dwelling, standard lap siding. It has a shake shingle roof, brown with tan trim. The single and primary entrance is located on the second-floor residence, with the numbers 315 displayed boldly to the left of the door in white letters. The entrance door is at the top of twelve painted metal stairs, black in color, facing to the south." He pocketed the recorder. "Okay, Mac, that's good. Let's go on up."

"Wow, it's really hot out here." Mac wiped perspiration off his brow with a white handkerchief he kept in his jacket pocket. He started to take off his jacket when Kevin stopped him.

"Sorry, Mac. It's important you interview witnesses with your jacket on."

"Why's that?"

"We don't need to get jammed up on the witness stand when a suspect or witness claims he was coerced to give a statement because your gun is visible. I know it sounds silly, but I speak from experience. The defense lawyer will claim the witness or suspect was intimidated because he could see your gun or handcuffs or whatever, so we don't give him the chance to give an excuse to confuse a jury."

Mac grabbed his briefcase and slipped his coat back on. "Makes sense. Guess I never really thought about it."

Mac and Kevin climbed the stairs. Kevin was reaching for the doorbell when the door opened. Cindy Tyson was standing in the entryway, holding her cell phone to her ear. She covered the mouthpiece and whispered, "Just a sec." To whomever was on the phone, she said, "Right. I'll see you at PDX tomorrow."

Mac could hear a male voice but couldn't make out what he said.

"I know you did. 'Bye, Tim." Cindy set the phone on a box in the entryway and greeted the detectives. "Hi. Thanks for calling ahead. I appreciate that."

She ran a hand through her blonde hair. "I'm sorry, where are my manners? Come on in; you'll have to excuse the mess."

The entire apartment was scattered with personal belongings in various stages of packing for the move. There were sealed cardboard boxes and dismantled decorative items stacked in the family room. A number of paintings and prints were stacked in the corner of the room by the fireplace.

"Can I get you two something, some coffee? If I can remember where I put the pot." Cindy rubbed her temple.

"No thanks," Mac answered.

"Um . . . you can sit on the couch." She moved a stack of photo albums and some newspapers she'd apparently been using as packing material to the coffee table.

Mac and Kevin seated themselves. The love seat, Mac noticed, was covered with chintz fabric with rose designs. Mac pulled out his notepad, as did Kevin. He hoped the routine action hadn't made Cindy nervous. She didn't seem to notice as she pulled a chair from the kitchen table and settled into it.

"Again, we are very sorry for your loss," Kevin said gently. "We'll be investigating your sister's death. To do that we'll need to ask you a lot of questions. Some of them will be difficult for you. But we'd like you to answer to the best of your ability. Remember, you don't have to talk to us if you don't want to. If at any time during the interview you wish to terminate the questions, just say the word and we'll leave."

"I understand. Believe me, I want to cooperate one hundred percent. I want to catch the monster who killed my sister."

"Then we have the same objective. Why don't you start from the beginning?" Kevin said. "I mean the very beginning. Tell us about Megan, everything you can think of. I want to know her past, her friends, her hangouts, what she liked to do—everything."

"Oh." She clasped her hands and settled them in her lap. "I don't know where to start. You mean, like when we were kids and stuff?"

Kevin nodded. "Yes, a brief synopsis of her family background would be fine."

"Well, we were born and raised in Troutdale. Megan is—um . . . was, four years older than me. Our mother died a few days after giving birth to me. Internal bleeding that they couldn't get stopped in time. Our father was the priest at St. Paul's Episcopal Church on the south side. He passed away about a year ago. It was just the two of us." She bit her lip as tears filled her eyes. She caught them with her fingers and sniffed. "Now it's just me, huh?" Cindy forced a weak smile.

Mac looked around for a box of tissues and, spotting them on the kitchen counter, went to retrieve the box. He handed one to Cindy and set them on the coffee table within easy reach.

"You're doing fine, Cindy." Kevin said. "Go on when you can."

"Megan went to Troutdale High School. She was really smart. Graduated with honors. Then . . . let's see. She went on to the U of O. She got a bachelor's of science degree. Megan was a real exercise buff and wanted a career in physical fitness training. She took a lot of classes like sports therapy, nutrition, weight training. Megan wanted to go to work for professional athletic teams, you know, helping athletes who got hurt and setting up training programs. She never got the chance to do that." Cindy looked down at her hands. "She ended up working odd jobs at fitness clubs."

Kevin nodded. "Tell me what she did at Fitness First."

"Mostly she worked at the front counter. They liked having her out front 'cause she was so pretty and bright. She brought in a lot of new people. Megan was a shift manager, which meant she had to open the club at five in the morning and then worked until around one in the afternoon. She also worked as a fitness trainer, giving consultation to new members of the health club, and did personal training when people requested it. She got extra money for that."

"Any interests outside of work?" Kevin asked.

"Lots. Megan was really involved in the church growing up, probably because of Dad. They were real close. She went on some mission trips to Mexico and South America during her teens."

"Missions?" The question popped out before Mac could stop it. The remark got him a stern look from Kevin.

"Yes, missions, with the church. She would go to places where God's Word was not always readily accessible, in an attempt to spread the gospel. Megan knew the Bible front to back. I'm sad to say it, especially now, but I was always jealous of her for that. Dad was so proud of her. She had real talent; her future was so promising before . . ."

"Before what?" Kevin urged her to go on.

"Before Dad died. He suffered so much. He had cancer. Megan got really mad at God. She quit going to church and for a while would hardly talk to me."

"Yet you were living together."

"We made up. About six months ago her roommate left and she asked if I wanted to move in. My lease was up so I did. She wasn't engaged then—in fact, at that point she hadn't even met Tim. Once she did, that's all she talked about: getting married and planning the wedding. It was like a fairy tale. Tim has a lot of money and he told her she could have anything she wanted. She was really excited about marrying him and moving to Florida. She loves warm weather and the ocean."

"Tell me about Tim," Kevin said. "It's Tim Morris, right?"

"Uh-huh. Megan met him at work. Like I said yesterday, he's into exercise equipment. Tim is more than a salesman. I mean, he designs fitness equipment and markets the stuff. Megan met him at Fitness First, when she was working at the front counter. Tim came in one day to meet with the general manager on some equipment deal, met my sister, and the rest is history."

"Can you remember when they met?" Kevin asked.

"Only about three months ago." She sucked in her cheeks. "I guess it was love at first sight."

Mac caught some sarcasm in her voice. Kevin must have as well. "Sounds like maybe you didn't approve."

"I didn't. Don't get me wrong. Tim's a nice guy and all, but she hardly knew him. You don't meet a guy, talk to him on the phone for a few weeks, and then agree to marry him. But she said time wasn't a factor. They were in love."

"Does Tim know you are in contact with the police?" Kevin glanced at Mac then settled his gaze back on Cindy.

"Yeah. He wants to talk to you when he comes in tomorrow. You guys can come with me to the airport if you want."

"That would be good, if you don't mind." Kevin jotted

something down on his notepad. "Can you tell me about her friends—other than Tim?"

"Megan didn't bring friends around much—it was like she really didn't want me to meet them. I wasn't sure if she was ashamed of them or me. She didn't have a lot of girlfriends. Megan was one of those girls who got along better with guys than she did with other women."

"Did she have any other boyfriends? You know, before she was engaged?"

"No, um . . . not that I know of. She would go out sometimes, but . . ." Cindy leaned down to straighten a stack of magazines that was lying on the carpet beside her chair. "Not really."

"Cindy, I apologize if I'm wrong, but I get the feeling you are being less than truthful with me. I want you to understand, at this stage you must be totally honest with us. Time is crucial to us if we are to catch your sister's killer." Kevin's voice took on a stern, no-nonsense tone. "We don't have time for half-truths or intentional omissions."

"You don't understand." She squeezed her eyes closed and grabbed for a tissue. "I need to protect her dignity."

"And we need to catch this killer before he goes after someone else."

Wrapping her arms around herself, Cindy stood up and walked over to the sliding glass door that opened onto a small balcony. "Okay, but this goes no further, right? I mean . . . I don't want her name dragged through the mud." She turned back toward Kevin. "I mean it; you can't let these reporter hounds know what I'm going to tell you. They've already done enough."

Kevin leveled a concerned gaze on her. "I can't make that kind of promise; I'm sorry. What we can do is hold the information for now. Eventually all our reports will be public record. That will be a long time from now, though, and hopefully public interest will have waned by then."

Cindy sat back down in her chair. "If the information I give you isn't important to the investigation, would you keep it out of the files? Could you at least do that?"

"That I can do, although at this stage it will be difficult to tell what's important and what's not." Kevin glanced down at his watch.

"Okay. Guess I don't have much choice. Just remember, Megan was a nice girl. She just got mixed up and started hanging out with the wrong people." She sat there a moment, staring at the floor as though she hoped it would swallow her up.

Kevin rolled his pen through his fingers while he waited.

Cindy blew her nose and bunched up the tissue in her hand. "Awhile back Megan started talking about her biological clock ticking away. She dated a lot of guys and sometimes it seemed like she was almost desperate to find someone to marry. She was going about it all wrong, you know, with the wrong type of guys."

"Are you saying she was sexually active with these partners?" Kevin asked.

"Um . . . I'm not really sure about that. She knew better. She was over thirty and had never had a serious relationship. She wanted a man to love her and to start a family with. Please don't get the impression that Megan would just sleep with anybody. I mean . . . these were guys she dated for a while and, you know, liked, I guess."

"Do you know any of their names?" Kevin started a fresh page in his notebook.

"I only met one guy other than Tim. There were others, but I haven't lived here that long and like I said, she didn't always tell me things. His name was Gordon . . . um, I can't think of his last name. Starts with an R, I think. He works as a roofer. The last I heard he was working at that new strip mall in Gresham. He's sort of scruffy looking, short." She wrinkled her nose as though she disapproved. "Kind of short and skinny with dark hair and a mustache."

"When was the last time you saw him?"

"A few days before Megan disappeared. They were on a date, if that's what you call it. He didn't even have a car—well, he did, but he said it wasn't working. She had to go and pick him up." Cindy shook her head. "I told her not to go and reminded her that she was engaged."

"Do you remember the exact date?"

"It was a weeknight. Maybe the eighth or ninth. They were going out to dinner somewhere. They came back a couple of hours later so she could grab a jacket and headed out again. We argued because they'd both been drinking. I begged her not to go. I didn't think either of them should be driving, but she wouldn't listen."

"Do you have any idea where they planned to go?"

"Well, she had the top down on her car, and she liked going up the gorge and into the hills southeast of here. She came home at four in the morning. She was so drunk she could hardly stand up. Gordon wasn't with her, so I figured she'd dropped him off."

She ran a hand through her hair, but the limp strands fell forward again. "There is one more thing. I don't know if it means anything. Did you guys know about the purse Megan reported stolen from the athletic club?"

"Yes," Kevin said. "It's in the missing person report."

"Well, Megan lied about that to the police. Actually, she lost the purse when she was off drinking with Gordon. I wouldn't be surprised if Gordon stole it. You'll see what I mean when you meet the guy."

"Did she say where or how she lost the purse?"

Fighting tears again, Cindy covered her eyes with both hands. "I can't believe the things my sister got herself into. She just wasn't that kind of person. Um . . . Gordon was driving her car up some logging road out east of here—up around Oxbow Mountain. Megan said they met up with some teenagers who were drinking and sitting around a fire. She and Gordon got out to talk to the kids and have a few beers. She told me they—she and Gordon—left about half an hour later. They went farther up the logging road to some great view he wanted to show her. Megan said when they reached the top of the hill, she noticed her purse was gone. She figured one of the kids must have stolen her purse while they were sitting by the fire."

"Did she have any valuables in the purse, any cash or the like?"

"The usual—her identification, driver's license, credit cards, keys. The worst was the diamond necklace that Dad had given Mom as a birthday present the year before she died. Megan was going to wear it on her wedding day and wanted to get matching earrings made. The necklace was mine and she was only borrowing it. Now it's gone. Megan was just sick over it."

"That's a major loss. Why would she lie to the police?"

"I guess she figured it was only money. She didn't want Tim to find out where she'd been or what she'd been doing. She told me she'd buy something for me to replace it. But how do you replace something that belonged to our mother, you know?"

"Protecting her reputation?"

Cindy ducked her head. "Yeah."

"You said her keys were in the purse."

"Um . . . right. Her spare apartment key and the key to the fitness center. I'm not sure what else. I've been terrified to sleep here since it was stolen. I couldn't stand the thought of someone having a key to our apartment. I would have had the locks changed if we were staying here. We told the landlord and he plans to change the locks when I finish moving out."

"That's a good idea," Kevin agreed. He tapped his pen on his clipboard while he quickly scanned his notes. Then he asked, "When was the last time you heard from Megan?"

"On Tuesday, August thirteenth, sometime around two o' clock. I called her to let her know that I was going to stay overnight at a girlfriend's house. She said she was going shopping that afternoon and . . ." Cindy's voice cracked as she stifled a sob.

"That's the last time I heard her voice. When I came home the next day, she was gone." She dabbed at her eyes with a tissue. "So I called the police and reported her missing."

"I understand you had some items taken from here after Megan disappeared." Kevin glanced around the room.

"The police said it didn't look like a break-in so we figured the burglar must have had a key or that Megan knew the person. I was staying at my new place. I came home—here—about noon on the fourteenth, after my morning classes. That's when I noticed stuff was missing."

Kevin asked her to list the missing items for him, even though he already had a list. Cindy mentioned several of the items then added, "We didn't have much. The necklace was the most expensive thing we had and that was only worth about a thousand dollars."

"Mac, do you have any questions?"

Mac snapped his head up. He'd been so busy making notes and listening, he hadn't had a chance to formulate any questions. "Just one. Did anyone else live here with you and Megan?"

"No, it was just the two of us."

Mac shrugged. "That's all I have."

"What now?" Cindy asked.

Kevin folded his notepad and placed his pen back in his pocket. "Now comes the hard part. Because we don't know who the killer is and have little to go on at this point, we'll start the process of eliminating possible suspects. We do that, in part, by having anyone connected with the case submit to a polygraph."

"You mean a lie detector test?" She frowned. "Are you saying you want me to take one? You think I had something to do with Megan's death?" Her voice rose as she spoke.

"We have no reason to believe you meant your sister any harm, but we can't take anything for granted. The polygraph is a great tool to help us eliminate people as possible suspects so we can narrow down the search and focus on the actual suspects."

"I don't know. Shouldn't I, like, have a lawyer or something for that?"

"You are always welcome to have an attorney present. That would be up to you," Kevin advised. "The polygraph is done by a qualified polygraph examiner from our Salem office. I'll ask her to come up here sometime later next week after we've had a chance to talk to some of these people."

"How does it work?" Cindy asked.

"I'll let the expert explain it to you. Her name is Detective Melissa Thomas, the best we have in the business. She'll explain everything to you before you make the final decision to take the examination."

"Well, I guess, but I had nothing to do with Megan's death." Cindy closed her eyes and turned toward the balcony again. She slammed her fist against the molding along the sliding glass door. "That's not exactly true," she sobbed. "In a way I did kill my sister."

Mac and Kevin exchanged glances while they waited for Cindy Tyson to continue.

Chapter Fourteen

"I'm afraid I don't understand," Mac said.

"I should have done something to stop her." Cindy sobbed. "I should have made her stop drinking and going out with those losers. Oh, Megan, I am so sorry. I'm so sorry."

She looked far too fragile to be carrying such a heavy burden. Mac fought back the urge to go to her and hold her in his arms and tell her everything would be all right. He wouldn't, of course. Mac didn't want her to get the wrong idea. *He* didn't want to get the wrong idea.

Cindy took a deep, shuddering breath and turned around to face them. "I'm sorry. I know you guys are doing your job. It's just so hard. Are we done?"

"Can you think of anything else?" Kevin asked.

"No, I think that's it." Cindy grabbed a fresh tissue and dabbed at her eyes.

Mac looked around the room. "We would like permission to search the apartment for evidence relating to her death."

"Sure. I already told someone that was okay."

"It's a visible search as well as a forensic one. A team of scientists from our crime lab will look over the apartment for microscopic clues."

"Whatever you have to do, just do it. You have my permission."

Mac pulled a white form from his binder. "Good. We'll need to get your permission in writing. Before any search is made, we want to be sure you understand your rights."

Cindy nodded and Mac read the passages aloud.

"You may refuse to consent to a search and may demand that a search warrant be obtained prior to any search of your residence. If you consent to a search, anything of value as evidence seized in the course of the search may be used in court against you."

Cindy winced at the comment but didn't object.

Mac went on. "I have been read this statement and understand my rights." He set the form on the coffee table and offered her a pen. "Sign here if you agree with the statements I've read."

A smile cracked her somber face. "It all sounds so formal."

"We have to cover all the bases."

Cindy took Mac's pen and signed the form.

"There's one more line I need to read to you." Mac picked up the form again. "I hereby authorize the Oregon State Police to seize, open, examine, and analyze any article which they consider to be of value as evidence. This statement is signed of my own free will, without any threats or promises having been made to me."

Cindy signed the bottom of the form, dated it, and handed the pen back to Mac. "Is that it?"

"That's it," Kevin told her. "We'll have the forensics team come over right away if that's okay with you."

"Fine with me. I'm going over to my new place anyway. I don't want to stick around here today." Cindy swung her purse over her shoulder.

"Just out of curiosity," Mac said. "You mentioned taking classes."

"Oh, right. I decided to go back to school and get a teaching degree."

He nodded. "Any particular area?"

"Art." Cindy smiled back at them as she headed toward the door. "I want to be an art teacher."

"Thanks for your cooperation, Cindy." Kevin opened the door for her. "We'll swing by and take you to the airport in the morning if that works for you."

"Sure, come by around nine. I'll be at my new place. Tim will probably want to get dropped off at the Sheraton after you've talked with him. That's where he usually stays."

Kevin handed Cindy his business card after writing down his cell phone and pager numbers on the back. "Call me if you think of anything important or if tomorrow doesn't work for you on the polygraph."

"I will. Thanks. I really hope you catch whoever did this to Megan."

Mac started to say, *We'll try,* but before he could respond, Kevin jumped in with, "You can count on it."

"For some reason I believe you, Detective." She glanced at his business card. "Don't forget to lock up."

Mac watched her climb into a blue convertible Mustang—Megan's car. Cindy was sweet, cute, and seemed genuinely grief-stricken over her sister's death. But she had lied to them. Maybe she had only wanted to protect her sister's reputation. Maybe she was protecting herself . . . or someone else. Mac closed off his errant thoughts.

"Man, what a bunch of ugly leads," Kevin muttered after he closed the door. "Is the bad guy the jealous fiancé, the construction guy, one of the teenagers who stole her purse, or maybe even the sister?"

"Or none of the above." Mac stared out the glass patio door and beyond to the park, where children played on the modern equipment and ran across the lush green lawn. Mothers watched and talked to other mothers. Latent grief pricked at his heart.

Mac knew all too well what it was like growing up without a mother. His had died of pancreatic cancer two months after his eighth birthday. He also knew how easy it was to get on the wrong track in life—to make the wrong choices. Was that what Megan had done? Had someone killed her here in her own apartment—someone she knew? Or had she been the victim of a burglary gone bad? They'd find out soon enough. They had to.

Chapter Fifteen

"Hey, Mac." Kevin drew Mac away from his thoughts.

"Yeah?"

"Got your cell phone? Eric paged me during the interview and I left mine in the car."

"Sure." He fumbled through his briefcase for the phone and handed it to Kevin.

"Eric. Yeah, it's me." Kevin frowned as he listened to what Eric had to say. "Okay, we're on our way. Also, while I've got you on the line, I need a crime lab team at the victim's residence right away. We have a consent to search so I want to get right on it." Kevin hesitated again. "That's good. Thanks."

Handing the cell phone back, Kevin looked pleased. "The tip line is already paying off. Some teenage girl said she has information on the victim, said she saw her with some guy out on Oxbow Mountain, up in the hills near Corbett. Hopefully she was with the kids who stole the purse. Eric's sending a uniform over here right away to stand by for the forensic scientists' arrival."

"Where does the girl live?" Mac couldn't believe how quickly things were moving.

"Springdale—east of Troutdale. That new housing development on the hill. The girl won't be home till after five, so we should get there right on time."

Moments later, a trooper pulled into the parking lot of the

apartment complex. Kevin and Mac were just coming down the stairs. "Look who's here!" Mac smiled and waved as the trooper exited the car. Up until yesterday, he hadn't seen Dana in two, maybe three years; now all of a sudden she was showing up everywhere.

"Hi again, guys." Dana grinned and walked toward them. "My sergeant said you guys needed some help."

Kevin reached out a hand. "Right, thanks. Dana Bennett, isn't it?"

"It is. I can't believe you remembered."

"Hard to forget."

Mac would have added *someone as attractive as you.* He frowned at his lack of professionalism. It's a good thing he'd kept his mouth shut. He doubted Kevin would have appreciated a remark like that. Dana probably wouldn't have either. He wasn't even sure where it had come from. After all, he was supposed to be engaged. He and Linda hadn't made an official announcement yet, and after his blunder today, maybe they wouldn't. While Mac took in Dana's blonde hair and aquamarine eyes, he managed to sound businesslike. "We'd like you to stand by until our crime lab arrives to process the victim's residence for trace evidence."

Dana nodded. "Is this regarding the body we found yesterday?"

"Yeah." Mac set his briefcase on the hood of her patrol car, rummaged through it for the right form, then handed her the blank crime scene log. "Make sure everyone who enters the residence signs the log. We'll be back later to pick it up."

"You got it." She seemed almost excited to be assisting. "I saw on the news that you've already identified the body. Fast work. I'm impressed."

"Don't thank us." Kevin added, "That's the M.E.'s department. We're heading to Springdale, Dana." He walked past the trooper. "Be back in about an hour."

Even though he'd had little to do with the efficient team that made the ID, Mac felt proud to be part of the process—pleased at Dana's compliment. He wondered if Linda would even notice what he'd been working on. He thought seriously about asking Dana out, but he knew he couldn't.

Despite the rabbit trails his brain kept taking, he cared about Linda. Still, maybe he and Dana could meet for coffee. He wanted to know what she'd been doing since they'd stopped going out. They'd parted on good terms, and seeing her brought back happy memories of dates consisting of hikes, studying, coffee shops, battling it out at the shooting range, and talking shop.

Less than fifteen minutes later, Kevin and Mac were driving along Bell Road in Springdale, looking for an address.

"It's an even number, Mac, so it should be on your side of the street." Kevin pointed to a large brick house that hugged the hillside and undoubtedly offered its occupants a beautiful view of the Columbia River gorge. "There it is, 928 Bell Road. Over by the white mailbox."

Mac eased his car over to the curb.

"I'll do the report on the interview with Cindy," Kevin said. "You can run the interview on this one and do the paperwork. By alternating, neither of us will get too bogged down with reports. We need to stay on top of them with a case like this or they'll snowball on us."

Mac's heart hammered a little harder than he thought it should. Kevin was giving him a long leash and that was good. Very good. His mouth went dry. "Sure." Mac nodded. "Anything in particular I should ask?"

"With any interview you want to let the other person do most of the talking. Try not to finish thoughts for her, and never, never give her information we have—especially the cause of death or evidence we may have gathered. You know the drill."

"What was her name again?"

"Rachel Winslow. Eric said she was sixteen."

Mac concentrated on breathing slow and steady as they approached the new two-story home. He rang the doorbell. Moments later, a tall slender woman in a lavender pantsuit opened the door. "Can I help you?"

Mac double-checked the address then introduced himself and Kevin, showing her his badge. "We're here to talk to Rachel Winslow. She called our office saying she might have some information relating to a case we're working on."

"Oh, right. Rachel told me. I'm her mother, Sherry Winslow. I'd like to sit in while you talk to her. She's underage and—well, she hasn't done anything wrong, unless you count lying and going out behind our backs with a boy we don't approve of as wrong." She frowned. "It's wrong, of course, but not in a legal sense."

"We'll see how the interview goes," Kevin said. "If she feels she needs to speak with us in private, we may ask you to leave the room."

"Sounds fair." She opened the door and stepped back, ushering them inside.

As Mac suspected, the house was fantastic. Windows and sliding glass doors made up most of the back part of the house. The foyer had marble floors that extended into a great room. He suspected that no matter where you were in the house, you had a view. It was a house to dream about, though he doubted his salary would ever allow anything like this.

"Rachel," she called toward the balcony on the second floor. "The police officers are here."

Within seconds, Rachel came down the wide carpeted stairs. "Hi." She grinned, revealing a full set of braces. "I saw on television what happened to that lady." She grimaced and rolled her eyes. "I totally flipped out when I saw her picture and found out who she was. I told my mom about seeing her, and she and Dad said I should tell you just in case. I got the number off the screen."

"It's good that you called," Mac said. "We'd like to ask you a few questions, if you don't mind."

"Sure."

"Rachel, take them into the family room." Turning to Mac and Kevin, she asked, "Can I get you something? I just made some iced tea."

"That sounds great." Mac's mouth felt bone dry.

"Make yourselves comfortable." Sherry Winslow moved into the kitchen area and picked up the tall pastel glasses already waiting, then filled them with ice chips from the refrigerator door and poured in the tea. She carried four of them in on a matching tray with sugar and long-handled spoons for stirring.

Mac drank nearly half of his tea, then set his glass down. It had a slightly fruity taste. "Good tea. Thanks." He cleared his throat. "First, Rachel, we'd like you to tell us about yourself—name, age, that sort of thing. I'd like to see some ID, too, if you have it."

Rachel provided her full name and date of birth and handed him her high school student identification card. "This is all I have for ID. I haven't gotten my license yet."

"This will be fine." Mac cleared his throat. "Now tell me exactly why you called us."

"Well, like I said before, I was watching television when this news thingy came on. They showed a picture of Megan Tyson and said she was dead—that somebody had killed her. I freaked. I thought, *No way.* I saw her up on Oxbow Mountain a couple of weeks ago. She was with this creepy guy. I remembered thinking she was really pretty and wondered why she was hanging out with a guy like that. Man, I can't believe she's really dead." Rachel ran a hand through her fine straight hair, pushing it out of her face. As soon as her hand dropped to her lap, her light brown hair cascaded forward again.

"Let's take this from the beginning, Rachel." Mac said. "Tell us about what led up to your seeing her. Where were you and who were you with?"

She licked her lips and glanced at her mother.

"I, like, got into a lot of trouble for being there." She glanced over at her mother again and her shoulders rose and fell in an exaggerated sigh.

"I'm sure this is difficult for you, Rachel," Kevin said. "Especially since you got into trouble, but we are looking into a murder, not a curfew violation or possession of alcohol. Besides, it looks like your parents are already dealing with whatever you did wrong."

"Go ahead, Rachel," her mother urged.

"Okay. I was supposed to be staying with Becky. She's my best friend."

"Can you give me an exact date?"

"Thursday, August the eighth." Her mother supplied the information.

"Right, the eighth. Anyway, my mom dropped me over at Becky's around six. We ate dinner and watched television. I left around ten." Rachel ran her hands over her denim-clad legs. "My boyfriend picked me up in his truck and we went dancing."

"What's your boyfriend's name?"

"Jay Nichols. Becky wanted to come, but she chickened out."

"She was smart," Mrs. Winslow interjected.

Rachel rolled her eyes. "I know, Mom. Anyway, we went downtown, to the Dakota Dance Club. We partied until around one. Jay and I were leaving when he saw one of his buds in the parking lot. I guess you want his name too."

Mac nodded.

"It's Brandon King. They both go to Troutdale High, him and Jay.

"Jay said Brandon and some other kids were going up to the lookout on Oxbow Mountain. I was getting tired, so I didn't want to go. Jay broke me down, promised we wouldn't be out there very long." She sneered. "He, like, totally lied to me. I broke up with him after that night. I still kind of like him, but my parents don't want me to see him anymore."

"It's for your own good, Rachel." Sherry took a sip of her tea, wiping down the sweating sides of the glass with her napkin.

"Tell me about your trip to Oxbow Mountain," Mac urged, steering Rachel back to the subject.

"Oh, yeah. Well, we drove up there in Jay's Toyota pickup. It's got these big wheels that Mom says looks like a toy truck on steroids."

Kevin sent the mother a knowing grin.

"I'm, like, smashed in the middle between him and Brandon. They are these hunks, you know. Both of them play football. They take up the whole front seat by themselves. I wanted to climb in the back, but Jay wanted me next to him. When we got there, I was disappointed 'cause I didn't know any of the kids. They had this bonfire going. That part was cool."

"Was this on Oxbow Mountain, in the National Forest?"

"I guess. I don't know for sure. There were about eight kids, only two other girls. They looked like real losers, if you know what I mean. They were hanging all over these guys, all drunk and stuff. I mean, I'm not exactly being judgmental. I had a couple of brews too. But I wasn't making a fool out of myself."

"Right. Now let's get to the part where you thought you saw Megan Tyson," Mac said, trying to get her back on target again.

"Okay." Rachel picked up her glass and took a drink. "I was sitting on the tailgate of the truck, you know, when this totally cool convertible comes up the road. I thought they must be crazy to bring a nice car like that up into the woods. I don't think it had four-wheel drive or anything. Anyway, this guy gets out and he's totally bombed. He can hardly stand up. Then his girlfriend gets out and she's not in any better shape. I'm thinking these people need a designated driver or something. They walk over and start talking to us like we're long-lost friends or something."

"What did they look like?"

She shrugged. "They were a lot older than us—maybe in their thirties."

Mac tossed Kevin a smile when he frowned at her definition of *older*.

"The woman looked like Megan Tyson," Rachel chewed on her bottom lip. "She had long blonde hair and had on a white jacket and a pink tank. Khaki pants, I think. Um, they were both white—Caucasian. The guy was short, probably weighed around one-fifty. He was my height. I'm five six. The woman was small too. She was pretty and had her hair fixed like mine, kind of straight and long."

"Did they say anything to you while they were there?" Mac asked.

"Not to me personally. The guy asked where the lookout was and if the road was in good shape. Jay told him it was. They stayed for maybe ten minutes and took off toward the lookout."

"Are you sure this woman was Megan Tyson?" Mac opened his briefcase and pulled a photo of Megan out to show her.

She stared at the picture. "It's her. I know." She looked like she wanted to say more.

"Do you need to talk to us in private?"

Rachel glanced at her mother and sighed. "No. She can stay."

"What makes you so certain the woman you saw was Megan Tyson?" Mac asked.

"I know it's her and not just because I recognize her. Something else. After they left, I saw Brandon standing by the fire with her purse. He was bragging about how he snatched it while the guy and Megan were talking to us."

"Oh, Rachel." Rachel's mother covered her mouth. Looking at Mac then Kevin, she said, "I didn't know about this."

Rachel gripped the sides of her chair. "I was in enough trouble already. Besides, I didn't have anything to do with stealing her purse."

"Go on with your story," Mac said.

"Brandon took out a bunch of credit cards and some cash and

threw the purse in the fire. It was one of those small bags that looks like a backpack."

"Do you remember seeing any jewelry in it?"

She shook her head. "No. Just the cards and some cash."

"Did you or the others use the cards?"

She hung her head. "Not me. I mean, I didn't want anything to do with it. Jay stopped to get gas, and Brandon handed the attendant the card and said it was mine. They made me sign it. The attendant didn't ask any questions. He just handed the card back. When we got into Troutdale, he tried the debit card at an ATM machine, but it wouldn't work 'cause he didn't have her PIN number. Jay told him it was stupid to try to use it. I said he should give the cards back to the woman and apologize, but he just laughed and threw them out the window. I would have called you guys earlier if I'd known she was dead, really. Jay was mad at Brandon about the whole thing."

Mac tapped his pen on his notepad. "Did you have any questions, Kevin?"

"Yes." Kevin leaned forward, resting his elbows on his knees. "Are you sure Brandon didn't keep any other items from the purse, maybe a set of keys?"

"I don't think so. All I saw were the credit cards and some cash." She frowned. "You don't think Brandon killed her, do you? I mean, he wouldn't hurt her."

"Do you think Brandon or Jay would use her keys to gain entry to her home—maybe to burglarize it?"

"Not Jay. I don't think Brandon would either. I mean, he's a friend of Jay's. They had been drinking and . . . They're not bad guys, just not too bright sometimes."

"What's the difference between stealing a purse and using a woman's credit card, and burglarizing her home?"

"I . . ." Rachel sat motionless. "I don't know."

"Is Rachel going to be arrested as an accessory?" her mother asked. "If she is, we should get a lawyer."

"It's too soon to tell at this point," Kevin answered. "If she's been honest with us, possibly not. Rachel, can you tell us how to contact Brandon and Jay?"

"Brandon works down at the video store in town, by the grocery store off Tenth Street. I don't know his home address." She stood. "I can get you Jay's address, though."

"That would be very helpful."

Coming back a few minutes later, she handed Mac a pink Post-it. "I'm really sorry I didn't call you sooner. I thought she would just get her cards canceled like people do when they lose a purse or a wallet. I didn't want to be a snitch."

Kevin gave her his business card. "The important thing is that you came forward. It takes a lot of grit. Thanks for all your help. I'm going to ask that you don't try to contact Jay or Brandon, or anyone else for that matter while we are making inquiries. Understand?"

"You don't have to worry about that, Detective Bledsoe." Sherry put an arm around her daughter's shoulder and pulled her close. "Rachel is grounded from everything except school. I don't think she'll be seeing those boys anytime soon."

"I wouldn't anyway." Rachel tipped her head against her mother's shoulder. "I sure hope Brandon didn't do anything stupid."

"So do we, Rachel," Kevin replied as the two men walked out the front door.

"Let's go, Mac," Kevin said as soon as the door closed behind them. "She'll be on the phone in about thirty seconds to her friends. We need to get down to that video store and take a statement from Brandon."

Kevin's comment surprised Mac. "You really think Rachel will warn those guys? She seemed so sincere."

Kevin chuckled. "She's sincere to a point, Mac. With her mother and us right there, what was she supposed to say? She's good—leaning against her mother like that. She might not call Brandon, but you can bet she's calling her boyfriend. He'll warn his friend."

Mac shook his head. "You read people better than I do; that's for sure."

"Don't feel too bad. Remember, I've got a few years on you. Besides, I've raised three kids."

"You don't think Rachel was involved in Megan's death, do you?"

"I'd hate to think so, Mac. But at this point we can't rule anyone out. Not even Rachel."

Chapter Sixteen

Kevin had his ear pressed to his cell phone and was talking to Eric before Mac even had the car started.

"This thing's starting to rock and roll. We've got a lead on the kid who stole the victim's purse. We're heading to his workplace now for an interview. Do we have anything on the victim's residence? Right, we'll head back to the apartment as soon as we can."

Kevin signed off. "Eric said the lab is still at the residence, and they'll be there for a while. Pick it up, Mac. Let's get to this kid fast. Hang a left at the next intersection and it will take us right by the place." He dialed the phone again. "Yeah, babe, it's me. I'll be home when you see the whites of my eyes. I will. Love you too." He tipped the phone toward Mac. "Want to call your girlfriend, let her know you'll be working late?"

"Naw, it's okay. She's probably still boating with her parents. Besides, I doubt she cares."

"Don't be too sure of that. Worry comes in all sort of packages and one of them is anger."

"We're coming up on the video store." Mac nodded toward the red storefront.

"Pull into the parking lot. We'll go into the store like customers."

Mac pulled into a parking place. "I hope he hasn't already split."

"If so, we'll see if the manager's available. He should be able to provide us with the kid's address."

Kevin and Mac approached the front entrance. They stopped as a young man walked out the front door wearing a polo shirt and a nametag that read Brandon. He wore headphones and carried a backpack.

"Excuse me." Mac stepped in front of him, barring his exit. "Do you work here?"

The kid stepped back, almost colliding with the door. "Yeah, what of it?"

"Are you Brandon King?"

"Who's asking?" The kid looked scared. Good.

"State police." Mac and Kevin displayed their badges. "We'd like to talk with you," Mac said.

Brandon looked from one man to the other as though seeking a path of escape.

Mac was more than a head taller than the teenager and probably outweighed him by about thirty pounds. He leveled a steady and what he hoped was an intimidating gaze on the kid.

The boy's shoulders sagged. "I'm Brandon. What's this all about? I haven't done anything wrong. Do I need a lawyer or something?"

Kevin stepped in front of Mac so that he was practically in Brandon's face. "Listen, pal, we are engaged in the homicide investigation of Megan Tyson. If you killed her, yeah, you need a lawyer—big time. If you didn't, and your only crime is ripping off her purse, then maybe you won't. You need to tell us everything you know about Megan. This is your first and last chance to be honest before I tack you to the wall with criminal charges. Understand?"

Brandon's Adam's apple shifted up and down as he pressed himself against the door. He managed a faint, "Yes, sir."

"Good. You're smarter than you look." Kevin backed off a bit. "Let's go out to our car and talk."

After their discussion, Mac wasn't about to trust the guy not to run. He took hold of Brandon's arm and led him to his car. Kevin opened the door and instructed Brandon to sit in the backseat. He followed the kid in, settling himself behind the driver's seat. Mac stood outside the car at the ready in case the kid decided to bolt.

"I'm not kidding, Brandon," Kevin said. "I don't have time for any nonsense. You lie to me once, just once, and you'll be spending the night in jail."

"I got it." Brandon leaned back, looking as though he wanted to fade into the upholstery.

"Okay. We already know you took a purse on the night of August eighth, when you and some friends were partying up on Oxbow Mountain, right?"

"Look, we were just having some fun," Brandon protested.

"Help me out here, Mac. I told him not to lie to us, right? Didn't I say that?"

"Yep. You sure did." Mac leaned into the car. In a way he felt sorry for the kid. Kevin could be pretty fierce looking.

"Just one time I said," Kevin warned the boy.

"All right. Yeah, I took her purse. So what?"

"That purse belonged to a woman who is now dead. Were you aware of that?"

The boy's eyes widened. "No way, man. I didn't do nothin' but take the purse and use a credit card. You got the wrong guy, man."

"No, we have the right guy. We have the jerk who stole her purse. Tell me what happened."

"Um . . . this drunk couple came up to Oxbow Mountain where my friends and me were partying. I'd had a few drinks but nothing like those two. They were driving this sweet convertible with mag wheels. While they were yakking it up with the others, I was checking out the car. I took the purse. I mean, hey, she left it lying in plain sight on the front seat, man. Easy pickings." He lifted his lips in a sneer. "Turned out it wasn't worth taking. Nothing in it but a few bucks and some cards."

"Any jewelry?"

"Just a cheap rhinestone necklace." He tipped his head and gave them a lopsided grin. "Not my style."

"That wasn't a fake, mastermind." Kevin's jaw stiffened. "What did you do with it?"

"No joke? I thought it was too big to be real so I left it in the purse and chucked it in the fire. All I kept was a gas card and a debit card. That and a few bucks."

"Anything else? Like maybe a set of keys?"

"Yeah, there were some keys. They went in the fire too."

Mac shook his head. The kid was lying.

Kevin must not have believed him either. "Are you sure you didn't pocket the keys and go back to her house later?"

"No way. I didn't even know where she lived."

"The truth, Brandon."

"That is the truth. Why won't you believe me?" he whined.

"Because, bonehead," Kevin said, "when you steal someone's purse, there's usually some identification—like a driver's license—that would tell you where she lived."

"I swear to you guys, I didn't even look at her ID. I just took the two pieces of plastic and a few bucks."

"Now, why don't I believe you?" Kevin muttered. "Have you ever been arrested before, Brandon?"

"Once or twice."

"For what?"

"Theft, curfew violations, and um . . . once for possession. I had less than an ounce of marijuana on me. How bad is that?"

"How old are you?"

"Eighteen, man, I'm out there now."

"You're out there, all right. It means you get to go to prison instead of Juvenile Hall. It means I'm going to make you a personal project if I find out you lied to me."

"I didn't lie, dude. Chill out. All I did was lift a purse. I didn't kill the broad and I didn't break into her place."

Kevin grabbed the front of the kid's shirt and pulled him to within two inches of his face. "That broad was a human being. Her name was Megan Tyson. She lived and breathed and had friends and feelings. And maybe, just maybe, she would still be alive today if some punk hadn't stolen her purse for a tank of gas. You think about that, mister. You think about that for the rest of your life."

Kevin sat back in his seat, the veins in his neck protruding. "Get his stats, Mac, and cut him loose. If he gives you half a reason, book him." Kevin climbed out of the car. "I'm going for a walk. Be back in a few minutes."

Stunned by Kevin's anger, Mac wrote down Brandon's name, date of birth, address, friends, and phone number, then told him they would be in contact.

"Are we done? Can I go now?"

"Almost," Mac said. "We'll want you to come in for a polygraph test in a day or two. Are you agreeable to that?"

"Sure. I guess." Brandon glanced at Kevin's receding back. "What's with him?"

"Like he said. A woman is dead. Now get out of here before I change my mind and arrest you for theft."

Brandon didn't need to be told twice. He scooted out, leaving the car door open, and jogged to the back part of the parking lot where he climbed on a motorcycle. He spent half a second revving up the engine before laying a patch of rubber as he peeled out of the parking lot.

Mac rubbed his temples. What had gotten into Kevin? Mac hadn't known him long, but the display of temper was far from professional, and if the kid ended up with a lawyer, Kevin could face charges of harassment. Mac closed the car door the kid had left open, then climbed into the driver's side, starting up the car and turning on the air conditioner.

Kevin rounded the corner of the video store moments later, his hands in his pockets. Climbing into the car, he said, "Sorry about that, Mac."

"For what, partner?" Mac replied as if nothing had happened.

"First of all, I apologize for losing my cool. Second, I'm sorry I walked away. Truth is I needed to cool down and have words with someone."

"Who?" Mac glanced back at the store. "You mean the kid's boss?"

Kevin smiled and fastened his seat belt. "God."

"Oh." Mac wished he'd kept his mouth shut.

"I needed some perspective, and prayer gives me that. God helped me to remember who I am and why I'm here."

"Okay." Mac shoved the car into drive and backed out of the parking space, hoping this line of conversation would end.

"Do you ever pray, Mac?"

"Used to." Mac didn't have much use for prayer. For some reason, he heard himself blurting out a memory from the past. "When I was a kid, and my mom was dying, I spent a lot of time praying. She died."

"And you felt as though God hadn't heard?"

"Something like that."

"You blamed God for taking her away?"

"Yeah. Why wouldn't I? God is supposed to be this all-powerful being who answers prayers. Well, why didn't He answer mine?"

"He did."

"How? By taking my mother and letting my father kill himself with alcohol?"

Kevin licked his lips. "First of all, God didn't give your mother cancer. Cancer is part of our imperfect world. Was your mother a believer?"

"Yeah."

"Then how do you know she didn't pray for God to take her? Maybe she was in a lot of pain at the end." Kevin glanced down at his hands. "As for your dad, God gives everyone free will—we make our own choices. He didn't force your father to drink. In fact, I imagine God worked very hard to get him to stop."

"Humph." Mac shook his head.

Kevin loosened his tie and tossed a knowing smile in Mac's direction. "I can see you're not buying it. That's okay." He opened his briefcase and lifted out the Bible. "Your answers are all right here, buddy, if you'll just take the time to read it."

Kevin opened the Bible. "Now, to get back to my problem. I got really ticked with that kid—more so than I should have. There's a verse in this book that tells me I messed up and need to ask forgiveness." Kevin found the page he wanted and began to read. 'My dear brothers . . . be quick to listen, slow to speak and slow to become angry.' Anger isn't the answer, Mac. While I was walking, God reminded me of this passage."

"Like your conscience." Mac knew a lot about that. His was constantly on him about what he should or shouldn't do.

"That's part of it." Kevin closed the book and set it back in his briefcase. "What do you say we pick this up later? We should head back over to Megan's apartment and see how the crime lab's doing."

"Fine with me." Mac didn't much like getting into this religious stuff. He'd had his fill of it as a kid. "Oh, hey, Brandon agreed to take the polygraph. I think we scared him out of his wits."

"The kid deserves a lot more than a good scare."

"Are you going to arrest him?"

"We'll leave that to the locals—unless he turns out to be our killer."

Chapter Seventeen

Mac and Kevin drove back over to Megan's apartment to see what kind of progress the CSI technicians were making. Allison Sprague stood in the parking lot next to a blue Ford pickup, stripping off her latex gloves.

"Look what the cat dragged in." Allison grinned as the two detectives stepped out of Mac's car.

"What do you have for us?" Kevin pulled his notebook from his pocket.

"Oh, gee, thank you for asking, Kevin. I'm just fine. And how are you gentlemen?"

"Sorry about that." Kevin pinched his lips together. "Been a rough couple of days."

"I know, I know." She removed her glasses and placed them on the tailgate. On the pickup bed Mac noticed a bunch of white plastic bins with blue covers. Allison removed her once-white lab coat, rolled it up, and tossed it into an open container.

"Nice set of wheels." Mac admired the sturdy four-wheel drive vehicle with the large lug tires. The truck was equipped with a heavy-duty winch, mounted to the front, and four spotlights mounted alongside. There were two more spotlights mounted to the rear of the cargo bed, providing work light for outdoor crime scenes.

"She's a real beauty, isn't she?" Allison slid the open tray back into the cargo bed and closed the lid. "I've had this rig out in all hours in every weather condition. She takes a lickin' and keeps on tickin'. I have to keep the trays and bins all locked up or you detective types will rob me blind of all our crime scene supplies. Right, Kev?"

He chuckled. "I plead the Fifth."

"Why don't you two follow me inside and I'll show you what we've done."

Mac followed Allison and Kevin up the stairs. As they entered, Allison pointed to the boxes in the entryway. "I'll let you boys look through the packed goods. We did a cursory search of the contents, nothing in-depth. Then we screened the entire apartment for possible directional blood spatter and/or cleanup residue with high intensity lights."

"Blood splatter?" Mac wrote the phrase down in his notebook.

"Actually," Allison replied, "it was directional blood *spatter*, which is the fancy forensic name for blood spray. I'll show you what I mean."

Allison ran a small amount of tap water from the kitchen sink onto her hand and flicked her fingers across an empty packing box. 'See how the droplets of water have little points off their main body? That tells us the direction the fluid was moving when it struck the surface. The more oblique the image of impact, the greater the angle the fluid struck the solid surface."

"What's the value in that?" Mac asked.

"The size of the directional blood spatter combined with the angle can tell us where the victim was standing or the velocity of impact. If the blood spatter was large and heavy on a ceiling, for example, that would give me a clue the evidence was transferred via a knife or a blunt instrument that lifted the fluid to the ceiling from the victim. Now if the spatter is in mist form over a large surface, I'd know we had a high velocity transfer from a gunshot. It's really quite amazing what you can read from directional blood spatter evidence."

"Wow, I had no idea." Mac was embarrassed by his lack of knowledge. As a trooper he'd had some courses in preserving evidence, but he hadn't worked this closely with the forensics specialists.

"We found no evidence of obvious blood spatter on the walls in here," Allison went on, "but we did find a few spots we thought might turn out to be cleanup samples."

Mac wanted to ask what those were but didn't want to look foolish. To his relief, she went on to explain. "Sometimes the bad guys try to clean up their handiwork with detergents or bleach products. They may remove the topical appearance of blood but they actually do us the favor of locking the trace evidence into the paint or dry wall. The high intensity lights gave us a few hopefuls, but none of them panned out."

Allison turned on one of the high intensity lights, and Mac squinted his eyes as she illuminated the hallway between the bathroom and the two bedrooms. She pointed to a circular swirl on the wall. "See the rust-colored stain on this obvious cleanup spot?"

Mac nodded.

"Now you see it." Allison turned the light off. "Now you don't."

She placed the high intensity light on a black metal tripod. "This stain looked promising, but I'll show you how we eliminated it." Allison pulled a cotton swab and a clear bottle of liquid from an open tool kit in the entryway. "This handy little solution is called phenolphthalein. Now I take a swab of the area of the stain." She rubbed the cotton end of the swab over the wall. "Then we add some of the fluid to the swab. If this were blood, the end of the swab would have turned bright pink. The phenolphthalein reacts positively to the iron present in blood, which results in the brilliant color change." She examined the tip of the cotton swab. "In this case, we are dealing with a regular old stain. Maybe a kid colored on the wall with a marker or something years ago and someone cleaned it off, but it's not blood."

Allison turned off the light in the entryway. The heat from the lamp and the humidity inside the apartment had turned the place into a steam room. Sweat trickled down the small of Mac's back.

"Let's see, what else?" Allison tapped her chin with her index finger. "We photographed the entire residence, of course, along with drafting a working sketch, and pulled all the drain traps from the sinks and shower. Came up with zip."

"You may want to see this," Allison said as she led them into Megan's bedroom. "Looks like most of her stuff had been packed for the move. We didn't find much in the room, although these may be of interest." She pointed to the open bedside drawer.

Mac and Kevin peered into the drawer at a large opened box of latex condoms.

"It's not too earth shattering," Allison said, "but we did find an open wrapper under the bed. I seized it—maybe we can get prints or something. Too bad we didn't have the condom; that would be a great DNA sample to take back to the lab. I'll send the wrapper down to the identification bureau in Salem, since I didn't dust it for latent prints here. Figured it would be too fragile."

"Good work, Allison," Kevin said. "Let us know what you find out."

"You got it. I think that's about it. I'll write up a supplemental report and get it over to you in the morning."

"Perfect. Mac and I are heading back to Troutdale P.D."

"Good. You can walk me out. I'll turn the keys over to you so you can release the apartment."

Mac and Kevin helped her pack up her equipment and carry it out to the truck.

"Is she the smartest person alive or what?" Mac watched Allison get into her pickup.

"Yes, she is," Kevin replied without so much as a hint of sarcasm. "If Allison said there was no blood in that apartment or sign of a crime scene, you can bet your last dollar there's nothing to be found. She's the best."

"You said you wanted to go back over to the P.D.?"

"Yeah." Kevin glanced at his watch. "But it's late. How about we head back to the office so I can get my car? We'll call in our report and head home. Tomorrow's going to be another long day." He tipped back his head and yawned.

On the drive into Portland, Kevin talked with Eric, giving him the latest updates on the investigation and getting reports that had come in from other team members.

When he hung up, Kevin filled Mac in on the call. The canvass that had been done around Megan's neighborhood by a couple of uniforms from the Troutdale P.D. hadn't turned up much. Apparently, Megan hadn't struck up friendships with any of the neighbors, and as luck would have it, the apartment next-door and the one below the victim's were currently vacant. If there had been some type of struggle at the apartment, it was unlikely anyone would have been around to hear it. The detectives working the pawnshop details and the narcotics informants hadn't turned up any new leads. Eric wanted all the detectives back at Troutdale P.D. at 6:00 A.M. for the next day's assignments, but they were all to keep their pagers on in case something came up.

By the time the detectives caught up on their notes and left the Portland office, it was after nine o'clock. "We did good today, partner." Kevin slapped Mac on the back as they exited the building and headed for their cars. Mac agreed.

Kevin climbed into his car. "Good night, and good luck with that girlfriend of yours. You put on your best smile for her, you hear me? And maybe bring her some flowers."

"I hear you." Mac turned on his headlights. Once out of the parking lot, he headed west toward I-205.

While Kevin looked forward to going home, Mac didn't. He'd be walking into an empty apartment, with a near-empty refrigerator and no sweet woman to cuddle up to. No one to kiss him good night. It was too late to call Linda. He doubted she'd want to talk to him anyway.

Chapter Eighteen

Mac eased the car into his driveway. The light he usually left on in the living room gave the false impression that someone was there, waiting. He loosened his tie as he walked up the exposed aggregate path to the front door. Lucy, his golden retriever, peered at him through the front window then jumped down, most likely to take her usual place by the door. Mac could barely squeeze inside as the dog barked and whimpered her greeting. "Hey girl, did you miss me?" Mac rubbed the dog's head, received a series of doggie kisses, then opened the closet door and hung his jacket inside.

"Mac?"

Mac stopped cold. The feminine voice had come from his living room. Was his imagination working overtime? Linda stepped into the hallway. "It's about time you showed up. I've been waiting for hours." She walked up to him and wrapped her arms around his waist.

He held her close, hesitant at first. Linda looked rumpled and sleepy. She wore a soft powder blue sweater and jeans and smelled like gardenias. She felt perfect in his arms. "What are you doing here?" He kissed the top of her head.

"Waiting for you."

He leaned back. "Were we supposed to do something tonight? Did I forget to call you again?"

"No. I felt bad about what I said to you earlier. I wasn't being fair." She moved away and took his hand, pulling him into the living room. "You look tired. Want something to eat?"

"Is there something?"

"I made spaghetti and meat sauce. It won't take me long to heat it up."

"That's nice." Mac grinned. "I'm glad you're here."

"Me too." She stretched up on her toes and kissed him, reminding him why he'd asked her to marry him. Moving away again she said, "Why don't you sit down and relax? I'll get your dinner."

"Do I have time to take a shower? I feel grungy."

"Sure." She kissed his cheek and padded barefoot into the kitchen. He watched her graceful moves, wishing they were already married. Wishing they could forget about food and head straight to bed.

In the bedroom, Mac removed his brown leather shoulder holster and set it on his bedside table. He tossed his badge and pager next to it, yawning as he slipped out of his shoes and peeled off his sweaty socks. Seconds later he stood under a steaming shower, relishing the water laced with soap as it cleaned away the day's grime.

The tantalizing scent of dinner prodded him to dry off and get dressed in record time.

He put on cargo shorts and an Oregon State T-shirt, ran a comb through his short dark hair, and headed down the hall. Linda had set up a tray in the living room and turned on the gas fireplace. He thought it was a little too warm for a fire but wasn't about to break the mood.

While he ate, she sat next to him, feet curled up under her in a delectable pose. He enjoyed his main course but was anxious to finish the meal and sample dessert—kisses from the woman seated beside him. Linda was acting every bit as wonderful as she'd been when they first met. After he'd eaten, they snuggled together for what seemed to Mac a terribly short time before Linda announced that she needed to leave.

"It's too late for you to go home." He nuzzled the back of her neck as she leaned forward. "Why don't you just stay here?"

"Mac, you know I can't do that. It isn't right."

He leaned back, stretching his arms toward the ceiling. "No, I suppose not." Mac wasn't the kind of guy who slept around. In fact, with school and work he hadn't had a lot of time to pursue a serious relationship—until Linda. His luck he'd fallen for a virgin who intended to stay that way until she was married.

She kissed his cheek. "Besides, we'll see each other tomorrow, right?"

Mac frowned. "Tomorrow?"

"You promised to come to church with me, remember?"

Mac groaned. "I have to work. The case is really heating up."

"But you said . . ."

"I know, and I would like to go with you." That wasn't quite true, but Mac wasn't about to antagonize her again. "I can't very well tell my sergeant to put the murder investigation on hold. It's not like I'm delivering newspapers, honey. This is serious stuff."

"And they really need you? Don't they have someone else?"

"No. My partner is counting on me to be there." Mac wrapped a stand of her silken hair around his forefinger. "Maybe I can make it next Sunday."

"PLEASE TRY." Linda pinched her lips together, afraid she'd reveal too much. She was disappointed but didn't want to tear apart the fence she'd worked so hard to mend. Mac was a cop. She'd known that when she met him. As much as she hated his being gone so much, she decided today that she loved him and needed to be more understanding about his job. She had been selfish in her demands. Linda still felt he should have called but wouldn't push it. She didn't want to lose Mac. Men like him didn't come along very often. She debated whether to tell him about the appointment she'd made with the pastor to set up premarital counseling.

Though Mac didn't come right out and say so, Linda doubted he shared her faith. She wanted him to and thought maybe if he would spend a few sessions with her pastor, he'd come around. At least she hoped that was the case. She wouldn't tell him about the appointment she'd made—at least not tonight. She wanted to leave on a positive note.

Linda reluctantly stood up and turned around, clasping both of Mac's hands in hers, pulling him up. "I love you."

Mac drew her back into his arms and kissed her long and hard. She took his passion as a sign that he loved her as well. He'd never actually said he did. But why else would he propose?

Chapter Nineteen

Sunday, August 25
5:50 A.M.

Mac ascended the stairs to the briefing room at Troutdale Police Department. Philly and Russ were already seated in the back row of the small room, which was now equipped with three rows of tables and chairs.

"Good morning, sunshine," Philly waved at Mac with one hand and stuffed half a maple bar into his mouth with the other. "We didn't ruin your beauty sleep, I hope," he added with a muffled laugh through the mouthful of pastry.

"Morning, guys. Yeah, I'm a little tired. Late night."

Kevin and Eric came into the room moments later, cups of coffee in hand.

"Morning, Mac." Eric settled into a chair toward the front of the room. "We have some coffee and doughnuts in the break room."

"Sounds good." Mac started for the break room.

"Hey, Mac, bring me back one of those apple fritters, would you?" Philly asked.

"You got it."

"I like that kid more every minute," Philly chuckled.

Shortly after six o'clock, Eric had the weary group of detectives assembled in the briefing room. "Let's recap yesterday's events for the group. Kevin, why don't you start with your interviews?"

Kevin stood up and walked to the front of the room, taking a sip of his coffee. "Mac and I met with the victim's younger sister, Cindy Tyson, over at their shared residence. We found her credible," he said to the group. Mac nodded in agreement. "She verified that Megan had gone missing on August fourteenth. Cindy reported that the last time she'd heard from Megan was on the thirteenth when they'd spoken on the phone—apparently the victim was going shopping. The sister, Cindy, spent the night with a girlfriend and came home on the fourteenth to find their apartment had been burglarized. There was no sign of forced entry to the apartment and the crime lab could find no evidence of a crime scene."

Kevin took another sip of coffee as he looked through his notes. "We also talked to the guy who admitted to stealing Megan's purse on August eighth—a kid named Brandon King. He claims he took her gas card, debit card, and a few bills and then threw everything else into the fire, keys and all. He's not too bright—didn't even recognize the thousand-dollar diamond necklace inside the purse, so he chucked it in the fire too." He looked at Eric. "By the way, we need to send someone out to Oxbow Mountain to see if anyone turned in a diamond necklace. I can give you a pretty good description of the area the kids were in that night. Diamonds won't burn in a small bonfire, so let's hope it's either still in the ashes or that someone was honest enough to turn it in."

"Got it," said Eric, jotting down the info in his notebook.

Kevin flipped the pages in his police notebook. "Megan was engaged to be married this month on . . ." He paused and glanced at Mac.

"August thirty-first," Mac said.

"Thanks, on August thirty-first to a guy named Tim Morris, who designs and sells athletic equipment to health clubs. The couple was to reside back in Florida after the wedding. From what Cindy says he's well off financially."

Kevin took another sip of coffee. "We learned from the sister that Megan had dated several men prior to and during her engagement to Morris, one as recently as a week prior to her death."

"My kind of girl," Philly chimed in from the back of the room.

"What, two legs and a pulse?" Russ commented. The detectives burst into laughter.

Kevin glared at them, obviously not amused. "Cindy didn't think much of the guy. Name's Gordon, and he's reported to be roofing the new strip mall here in town. Mac and I will be heading over there in a few minutes to see if we can track him down.

"This guy's a good lead for us." Kevin went on to tell them about the stolen purse and the interviews they'd had with Rachel and Brandon, placing Megan at Oxbow Mountain a week prior to her disappearance. "Both Cindy and Brandon have agreed to take polygraphs, so we'll want to get them lined up with the polygraph detective tomorrow."

Kevin slapped his notebook against his hand. "Things are moving pretty fast. Lots of leads. After we talk to this Gordon fellow this morning, Mac and I will be picking up the sister and taking her to the airport to meet the fiancé, who's flying in from Florida. We'll try to get them lined up to take polygraphs too."

"Sounds good." Eric moved up front. "I'll call the polygraph detective right away. Not much else to report. The rest of the crew will get to work on the tips coming in. We've got about a hundred already, with a lot of the usual Elvis sightings and helpful citizens calling in. Kevin, there is one tip you and Mac might want to check out. A guy called saying Megan had commissioned him to design and make a set of earrings to go with a necklace she'd planned on wearing to the wedding. He reported seeing her two days before she'd disappeared. He'd been trying to get hold of the sister to let her know he had the earrings done but hadn't had any luck."

Eric covered his mouth and turned aside to cough. "Also, the credit report finally came in along with the bank's authorization to access Megan's account records. It appears she received a temporary ATM and debit card combination after her purse was stolen. They'll be sending a transaction printout. Hopefully we'll get that by tomorrow. If someone used her card at an ATM we may get lucky and get our killer on tape. I'll put Russ and Philly on that detail as soon as I get the info."

"You got it, boss," Philly replied.

"We're going to take off, Eric," Kevin started toward the door. "We need to see if we can track down this Gordon character."

"Keep me advised, Kev. Let me know when you guys get done with this morning's interviews."

Mac and Kevin jogged down the stairs. "Do you know where that new mall is going in off the freeway, Mac?"

"Sure do. I'll drive."

Minutes later, the detectives pulled up in front of the construction project and were stopped by a security guard holding a clipboard. Kevin rolled down his window.

"Morning." The guard bent down, exaggerating a stomach that would have given Philly some serious competition.

Kevin showed his identification. "Morning. I'm Detective Kevin Bledsoe with the state police."

The guard brought the clipboard to his side. "What can I do for you?"

"We're looking for a guy who might be working on the roof."

"Shouldn't be a problem. The roofer is J. B. Collins—Collins Roofing. His crew is already up top." He pointed to the ladder.

"Thanks. Do you know who's in charge?"

"Nope, but I'd lay odds the owner isn't here—foreman either—

seeing as it's a Sunday. None of them would be working if the project wasn't so far behind. Why are you asking?"

"Just looking to talk to a fellow," Kevin assured him. "Nothing big."

The guard stepped back into the small building. "You can park in that lot over there. Just be careful."

"Will do," Kevin said.

Mac parked beside a flatbed truck and had barely come to a stop when Kevin climbed out of the car. "I'm heading up the ladder to see if this guy is up top. Wait here in case he bolts. Stay far enough back so you can see me on the roof."

"You got it, partner." Mac's adrenaline had been running along normally until Kevin indicated there might be trouble. Now his heart hammered in his chest, keeping rhythm with the sound of the jackhammer *rat-tat-tatting* somewhere in the construction zone. This guy could well be their killer.

Kevin leaned back into the car. "Um . . . just a word of caution, Mac. We don't have anything to hold this guy on at this point. We just want to get a statement from him. I don't want to scare him off by Mirandizing him. We want to make sure he doesn't feel like he's in custody. He needs to know he's free to leave so we don't run into any static if he gives us good statements. If he looks like our guy, we'll go ahead and read him his rights."

Kevin started up the ladder, hoping the guy they were looking for was working. He climbed to the top of the one-story complex. As his head cleared the roof, he spotted a five-man tar crew spreading the sticky black substance in the far corner of the building. The pungent smell of the hot tar made his eyes water.

A kid covered in black soot came toward him. "Hey, this place is off-limits." He didn't look to be much older than eighteen, but the guy was clearly in charge.

"Not to me." Kevin reached into his pocket for his badge. "I'm Detective Bledsoe with the Oregon State Police."

He shrugged. "Can I help you?"

"Maybe. I'm looking for a guy named Gordon. I was told he might be working out here?"

"He might be. What do you want with him? Is he in trouble?"

"No. I was hoping he'd have some information that will help me with a case I'm working on."

"Yeah, I bet." He turned around and yelled. "Hey, Gordy, you got company."

A man with a slight build who was working in the corner about twenty feet from where Kevin stood turned and looked at the detective. He put down his tar brush and removed his rubber gloves, set them on an air-conditioning unit, and headed toward the ladder. He had a heavy beard, and Kevin had a hard time telling where his facial hair stopped and the soot ended. He was only about five-six and about 150 pounds. He had on jeans and a wide leather belt with a western-style silver buckle.

"Gordon, this guy says he's a detective."

Kevin produced his badge and introduced himself. "I'm working on a case, and I was hoping you could answer a few questions for me and my partner down in the car. You're not in trouble or anything, but I think you might be able to help us out."

"I'm kinda busy right now. Can't it wait?" His gaze darted to the kid beside him.

"This is pretty important."

"Go ahead and take five, Gordo," the kid told him.

"Thanks."

Kevin frowned. The kid looked too young to be a supervisor. Heck, everyone looked too young these days. The price one paid for growing older.

Gordon used his arm to wipe his face, leaving a streak of dirty flesh. When the guy lifted his arm, Kevin got a look at his belt and the knife secured in a leather sheath.

Chapter Twenty

"We'll be more comfortable on the ground," Kevin told Gordon. *And if you try to pull anything with that knife,* he thought, *we'll be on even footing.* Ordinarily he'd have secured the knife, but it looked to be the type of large box cutter or utility knife a roofer might carry to cut tar paper or shingles. *Which,* he reminded himself, *is more than ample for cutting a throat.* He'd let it go for the moment, as he didn't want to scare the guy too much. The guy might be a big catch, and Kevin hoped to keep him cooperative.

"Sure." Gordon didn't sound any too pleased, but at least he was cooperating. For now.

"Hey, I appreciate you taking the time to talk with me and my partner, Gordon." Kevin began descending the ladder with Gordon following his lead.

"No problem. You gonna tell me what this is all about?"

"Yeah, let me introduce you to my partner first." Mac was standing next to the car when the two walked up. "Gordon, this is my partner, Detective Mac McAllister."

Mac nodded, keeping his arms folded. "I'm sorry, I didn't catch your last name."

"Reed. Gordon Reed."

Kevin, who was standing behind Gordon, gave Mac a thumbs-up sign. "Let's sit in the car so we can hear over the generator. Hop in the backseat with me."

Mac winced. No way did he want that smelly dirt bag in his car. Not that he had much choice.

"Sounds good to me." Gordon rubbed the back of his neck. "Hard work."

"Looks like it." Kevin climbed into the backseat with Gordon while Mac eased himself into the driver's seat.

Kevin took the lead. "Gordon, I just want to make a few things clear. Once again, we are both detectives with the state police. You are not under arrest and are free to leave anytime you want."

He frowned. "Yeah, but . . . I don't understand what this is all about."

"We'll get to that. Detective McAllister and I are currently working a homicide investigation. The victim's name is Megan Tyson. Ring a bell with you?"

Gordon flinched then seemed to recover. "Why didn't you say so in the first place? I figured you guys would show up eventually."

Kevin shot Mac a look, warning him to be ready in case the guy pulled anything.

"I didn't have anything to do with her getting killed. I mean, if someone's trying to frame me or something. We were just friends, you know?"

"Why would you think someone wanted to frame you, Gordon?"

He shrugged. "Her sister didn't like me. She's the one who told you I went out with Megan, right?"

"Why don't you tell us what you know about Megan?"

"Do you think I should get a lawyer before I say anything?"

"You tell me, Gordon." Kevin leaned nonchalantly into the corner and picked a piece of lint off his trousers. "If you murdered Megan, then I think you should probably get one. If not, you might want to save your money and my time." Kevin studied Gordon's face for any sign of emotion. Something about the anxious look in the guy's eyes and the way he didn't make eye contact put him right up there in the suspect category. *It's too soon,* he reminded himself. *Way too soon.*

"Hey, I got nothin' to hide. What do you want to know?"

"Tell me about your relationship with Megan Tyson and the last time you had contact with her."

"Where do you want me to start?"

"Tell us when and where you met Megan."

He smoothed his mustache. "I met her about two months ago when I went up to Murphy's Tavern after work to hang out. She was in there by herself and looking pretty hot so I started talking to her. She was kinda standoffish at first, but after I bought her a few drinks, she loosened up and gave me her phone number."

"She was alone that night?"

"Yep, all by her lonesome."

"And where was this pub?" Kevin asked.

"Right there. Murphy's." Gordon pointed to the building directly across the street. "Some of the guys started drinking there after work when we started this project a few months ago."

"Did you consider her your girlfriend?"

"I wish. I met her at the pub a few times. We danced and made out some. Then one weekend she shows up at the pub wearing this big diamond engagement ring. She never mentioned this guy to me, and all of a sudden she's getting married and moving to Florida." Gordon shrugged, but his expression seemed pained.

"Did she say much about her boyfriend?"

"Just that he was some rich dude and had a cool house. She really threw it in my face, you know. It was like, 'Buy me some drinks and dance with me 'cause I'm getting married and I want to celebrate.' I told her where she could take her celebrating. 'Buy your own drinks,' I said. Then I took off."

"Where did you go?"

"I don't remember. It wasn't that big a deal. I probably went home and got drunk."

"How old are you, Gordon?"

"Thirty-three. Why?"

"We just need your stats for our report." Kevin thought the guy looked closer to fifty.

"Do you do drugs, Gordon?" Drugs had a way of hardening people. And guys on drugs could do some bizarre things.

"No way. My shrink has me on Zoloft for depression, but I'm clean."

Kevin jotted that down on his notepad. An antidepressant and alcohol—not a nice mix. "How about Megan? Did she do drugs?"

Gordon glanced toward the door. "I don't know. When she was with me, she just drank beer."

He was lying, but Kevin decided not to call him on it. At least not yet. "Okay, you went home mad. Was that the last time you saw her?"

"No. She called me about two weeks later saying she wanted to go out."

"Do you remember the date?"

"I have no clue. Just that it was a workday. I know because I called in sick the next morning."

"Could we check with your boss and verify the date you called in sick? It would be helpful if we could establish a timeline."

"Sure, be my guest. Just don't say anything that might get me fired."

Kevin nodded. "Okay. Go on with your story. She called you and wanted to go out."

"Right. I called Megan back at her apartment, but her sister answered. I asked for Megan and then I heard them arguing. I know the sister doesn't like me, doesn't think I'm good enough for Megan." Gordon's eyes narrowed in defiance.

"Why would you think that?"

"According to her I'm a psycho doper who slaps tar for a living."

From what he'd seen so far, Kevin would have to agree. "So you called and asked to talk to Megan. Then what?"

"Megan comes on the line and acts like she's my best friend. She starts telling me she's having second thoughts about getting married. She wants to go have some drinks and I figure, why not? I told her my car was acting up, so she would have to drive."

"And did she pick you up?"

"Yeah. I couldn't believe it. Here, the chick doesn't pay me the time of day for weeks, and now she wants to hang out with me. I say, heck, maybe she wants to sow some wild oats or something. Who am I to say no to a lady, right?" Gordon chuckled.

You're a real prince, aren't you? Kevin let the remark pass. "Was Megan alone when she came to pick you up?"

"Yeah, she came alone. She drove her convertible, had the top down. She was lookin' pretty fine. I wasn't looking too bad myself. I had on my new boots and Wrangler jeans." He glanced at Mac, then at Kevin. "I don't always look like this, you know."

"I'm sure you don't," Kevin said. "Was Megan wearing any jewelry?"

"Just this cross necklace she always wore. She said her dad gave it to her. Oh yeah, and she was wearing that big engagement ring too, except she had it on her right hand. I didn't bring it up because I didn't want to upset her."

"Did you leave your place right away?"

"Yeah. Went to a joint just outside of town—I don't remember the name. I already had a pretty good beer buzz and didn't want to lose it. We went down to the pub and had a couple of beers each."

"Did you talk with anyone else that night?"

"No, man." He grinned. "That's what I'm trying to tell you. She acted like I was the only guy on the earth. She was totally into me. We line-danced to some country music, danced the slow songs. It was great, man." Gordon smiled at the memory.

Kevin shuddered at the thought of Megan dancing with this lowlife. But maintaining his professionalism, he asked, "What happened then?"

"At about nine or ten, we went down to the Country Inn Restaurant in town. I left because the bartender wouldn't serve me. Said I was drunk. Megan had a Long Island iced tea before we cruised."

"Where did you go from there?"

"Over to the Safeway store in Troutdale. I bought a six-pack of ale—she likes that fancy expensive stuff. We sat in the parking lot of the store and drank the six-pack. I rubbed her feet and we talked."

"What did you talk about?" Kevin almost wished they'd taken the guy downtown. The car was getting hot and smelly. The guy's attitude made his stomach churn.

"Shoot, man, you want my life story?"

"Just tell us what you remember."

Gordon sighed and his right hand drifted dangerously close to the knife.

Kevin tensed and held his breath, releasing it when Gordon just wiped his hands on his pants. A quick look at Mac told him his partner had noticed it too.

"I told her I wanted to be with her and I thought she shouldn't get married because this dude didn't sound like he was satisfying her."

"What do you mean?"

"Do I have to spell it out, man? The dude didn't exactly rock. He was older than her. He told her he didn't want kids and she was ticked about that."

"She told you that?" What was Megan Tyson thinking, hanging out with this guy? Her sister had said she was confused, but was she blind too? What did she see in this guy?

"Well, mostly. Megan said she didn't know him that well. I told her she should just take it slow."

"Did you ever have sexual relations with Megan?" Only age and experience allowed Kevin to keep probing. That and the fact he wanted to nail Megan's killer no matter how far into the gutter he had to dig.

"No way, man. It's not like I didn't try." He gave them a knowing look—as though being men put them on the same sleazy level.

"How hard did you try, Gordon?" Kevin leaned forward.

"I didn't rape her, if that's what you mean. We fooled around and stuff, but never home base. She kept telling me she wasn't that kind of girl."

"How much had you had to drink?" Kevin didn't like the guy, but again, he had to be careful in the way he handled him. He couldn't afford another scene like the one he'd had with Brandon.

"A lot. I was sailing."

"Was Megan still driving at this point?"

"Oh yeah, man, I was in no condition." Gordon laughed. "She wasn't either."

"What happened after that?"

"We went by her place so she could get a jacket. A couple of minutes later she jumped in the car, pulls this condom out of her pocket, and sticks it in her purse. Megan had this big grin and I was like, all righty then—whatever you say. I thought that pretty much set the stage for the rest of the night."

"Where did you go from there?"

"First we stopped and got gas in town, then we drove up the road toward Oxbow Mountain. We'd been driving for about half an hour when we came across this bunch of kids, partying and drinking. We got out to get directions and find out if the road to the lookout was okay." He shifted in his seat. "It's hard to remember all the details. We were so wasted. I think we stopped at a place on the way there to have a couple of drinks too. By the time we got to where the kids were, Megan was slurring her words and laughing at dumb stuff. I remember she had to lean against a tree a couple of times so she wouldn't fall down. I helped her back to the car after a few minutes and we motored up the road. We came to this area with a bunch of radio towers. She got out and pretended she was a stripper, spinning around this radio tower and unbuttoning her shirt when she came around each time.

"She tells me to go get the rubber in her purse. I was like Flash Gordon, man. I booked over to the car but couldn't find the purse. I told her and she starts cussing at me like it was my fault. We figured the kids must have stolen it. She got dressed, and we headed back down the road to find the kids."

"Did you find them?"

"No. They were either gone or we took a wrong turn. We drove around a lot and got lost. Ended up coming out on the highway nowhere near where we went in."

"What happened next?"

"Well, I was still pretty horny and wanted to mess around. I reached over while she was driving and touched her leg. She went ballistic on me, started screaming at me not to touch her. I told her to chill out, but she kept saying everything was in her purse and I wouldn't understand. I guess her spare apartment key and her credit cards were in there too. She said something about losing the necklace she was going to wear at her wedding." Gordon slowly wagged his head from side to side. "The woman was crazy. She took me home and barely stopped the car to let me out. I don't know what time it was for sure, but it was starting to get light."

"Did you have any more contact with her?"

"The next day, I was so hung over, I had to call in sick. I called Megan around noon to see how she was doing. She was in a bad way too. She talked about all the banks she had to call and hoped those kids didn't try to use her key to break into her pad before she moved or had the locks changed.

"I asked if she wanted to go out again and she told me she didn't. Said I was a bad influence. I was cool with that."

"You were cool with that?" Kevin rubbed the back of his neck. "She rejects you and you are cool with it?"

"Yeah. Hey, it wasn't like I was in love with her. I just told her to call me if she wanted to." Gordon shrugged as if he didn't care, but his tone conveyed a touch of bitterness.

Kevin didn't press the issue. "Any more contact with Megan after that?" he asked.

"No, that was it. She never called, never stopped by, nothing. I figure she'd decided to go ahead with her wedding until I saw the news reports about her being missing. Now I find out she's dead." He rubbed a hand across his mouth. "I started wondering if maybe her boyfriend found out that she'd been with me. Wouldn't put it past her snoopy sister to tell him. Are you going to talk to him?"

"That's the plan." Kevin grabbed the back of the car seat and leaned forward. "Are you sure you have been completely honest with us, Mr. Reed?"

"I swear." He glanced over at the work site. "Look, I got to get back to work."

"That's fine." Kevin thanked him. "Like I said, you're not under arrest and you are free to go."

Gordon opened the car door.

"Just one more thing." Kevin stopped him. "Do you think you could talk to us again later, maybe tomorrow?"

"Why? I told you everything I know."

"You've been very helpful, but there are a few more things we'd like to discuss with you. We'd also like you to take a polygraph test."

"I don't know, man. Can't you just talk to me now?"

"Actually we have another appointment right now, so we'll let you get back to work. Can you meet us tomorrow at the Troutdale Police Department—say around eleven-thirty?"

"Um . . . I guess I could go over on my lunch break."

"We'd appreciate that. Like I said before, you're not a suspect. We're just gathering information."

"Yeah." He patted his shirt pocket and pulled out a pack of Camels. "I'll be there."

"Good. We ask that you don't take drugs or drink alcohol for twenty-four hours prior to the test."

"Yeah, okay."

"Could you give your address and phone number to Detective McAllister so we can get hold of you in case our schedule changes?"

"Can't you get it out of your computer?" The guy could hardly wait to get away.

"If it's no problem, Mr. Reed, we'd just as soon you tell us." Mac took out a pen and poised it over his notepad.

"Whatever."

Mac took down the information and thanked him for his cooperation. As Gordon walked away from the detectives, he stopped to light up a cigarette, then took several drags before dropping it to the ground and stepping on it. He looked back at them and started up the ladder.

"What do you think, Mac?" Kevin got into the front seat and fastened his seat belt.

"He's an odd duck. Somehow I don't think he was being completely honest with us."

"I know he wasn't."

"He looked pretty scared to me."

Kevin laughed. "That's an understatement. We'll let him simmer until tomorrow and see if he shows up for the appointment. Hopefully we'll have our polygraph examiner in town so we can run a few of these guys over the box."

"Did you notice that box cutter on his belt?" Mac started the car and put it in drive. "It could have been the murder weapon."

"You're wondering why I didn't secure it?" Kevin asked.

"Crossed my mind."

Kevin rubbed the back of his neck where a good-sized knot had developed. "Mine too, but I decided to take the chance. Didn't want to spook him too much. Too bad the victim's arms weren't intact; I'd like to know if she had any resistance wounds."

"I have to tell you, Kevin. Mr. Reed just moved up a notch on my suspect list. I'd put him slightly ahead of our purse snatcher."

"I know what you're saying, but let's not get too focused on one suspect yet. It may cause us to miss subsequent clues. When you write your report on this interview, make sure you leave these guys as 'mentioned persons' in the data entry section so we don't get hurt later in court."

"What do you mean?"

"I don't want some defense attorney throwing barbs at us if we make an arrest on a totally different suspect down the road. We need to be careful about who we call 'suspects' in our reports until we narrow in on someone. We don't want any avenue for doubt if and when we make an arrest and go to trial. What we write in our reports now may be subject to questions a year from now when the defense is trying to sway the jury."

Mac nodded. "There's a lot to think about, and I definitely don't want to mess things up. What time are we picking up Cindy?"

"We said nine o'clock." Kevin looked at his watch. "I have ten after eight. What do you say we head over to Starbucks and grab a cup of coffee?"

"You read my mind. I could use a little caffeine in my blood before we meet up with Megan's fiancé." Mac grimaced. "Besides, we need to air out this buggy."

Chapter Twenty-One

After stirring his coffee, Mac stuffed his wallet into his back pocket, picked up his cinnamon roll, and took the armchair across from Kevin.

Kevin took a tentative sip. "Ah, this hits the spot. Thanks."

"No problem. Thanks for the training sessions. You're good. A lot of the questions you asked probably wouldn't have occurred to me." Mac licked the cream cheese frosting from his finger and bit into the treat. He needed to stop eating this kind of stuff, but passing up that cream cheese frosting was like saying no to coffee.

Kevin nodded. "When you're old and gray like me, you're bound to remember a few tricks."

"What's this 'old and gray' stuff?" Mac asked. "You look like you're in better shape than I am. And definitely younger looking than old Gordon." He meant it too. Kevin still had the physique of a well-toned athlete.

Kevin sneezed and apologized.

"Bless you." Mac offered the obligatory remark.

"Thanks." He reached into his pocket for a tissue. "I wish these allergies would go away. That tar and soot must have set me off."

"Yeah—I meant to say something about that. I doubt the smell or the soot will ever come out of my car. I'll have to have the upholstery professionally cleaned."

"Sorry about that." Kevin put away his tissue and took another sip of coffee. "Send the cleaning bill to the department. I'll okay it."

"Really?"

"Really." Kevin grinned. "Say, did you take my advice with your girl last night?"

Mac shook his head. "I didn't have to. Linda was at my place when I got home. *She* apologized to *me* and made me dinner. She didn't even seem upset that I got home so late."

"Sounds like a nice gal. It takes a special kind of woman to put up with jobs like ours. My Jean hated the long hours at first, but she got used to it. If you want, maybe we could get the two of them together. Jean could give her some tips."

"Sounds good." Mac tucked the thought away, wondering how Linda would react. Maybe he wouldn't tell her. It seemed easier to schedule a dinner out and let Jean just talk.

Kevin leaned back in the chair and settled his right foot over his left knee. "Jean wasn't always so understanding. In my early days as a detective, my partner was a woman. I spent more time with Gail than I did with Jean." He shook his head. "My wife was one jealous woman. She tried not to be, but there was a lot of tension for a while. It didn't help that Gail was one of the first woman detectives in the department at that time. Luckily the partnership didn't last. Gail transferred to San Francisco, where there was a more liberal view of women detectives."

They drank coffee and talked shop and watched people until ten till nine when Kevin checked his watch. "We better get going."

The detectives pulled up in front of Cindy's place at two minutes after nine. Cindy appeared at the door before they could get out of the car and jogged toward them.

Kevin got out and opened the back door for her, directing her to the cleaner side of the backseat. "Sorry about the obnoxious smell," Mac said. "My partner here insisted we put a human tar pit in here while he talked to him."

"It's okay. I'm glad you're taking me. I hate to drive around the airport."

"How are you doing today?" Kevin asked.

"Better. I'm sad, but on the other hand it's good to finally know what happened. The medical examiner released Megan's body, so we're having the funeral on Tuesday."

"Is anyone helping with the service?"

Mac wondered why Kevin had asked.

"I called the church where my father was priest. The priest there agreed to do the service and the women's guild is putting together some food for a reception after the interment. Tim is going to help financially since Megan didn't have insurance or anything."

"That's nice of him." Kevin twisted around in his seat so he could see her without straining his neck.

"Like I said, he's a nice guy. He called this morning and said his flight was going to be about twenty minutes late. I hope I didn't mess things up, but I told him you guys would be coming along with me."

"That's fine," Kevin assured her. "We're not trying to surprise or trick anyone here. Did he seem concerned?"

Cindy removed her hair band and shook out her blonde hair. "No, not really. He's not a very excitable guy, really mellow and soft-spoken." She gathered her hair up again and secured it with the beaded hair band. She wore makeup this morning, Mac noticed, and looked much more put together. Mac couldn't help but wonder if her improved appearance might be for Tim Morris's benefit.

Mac drove north on I-205, taking the Airport Way exit just prior to crossing the Columbia River into Washington State. He drove west to Portland International Airport's lower terminal and parked in the Police Only Tow Away Zone spot right in front of the entrance to the baggage area. Mac draped his blue raid jacket over the steering wheel of the car, displaying the large yellow State Police lettering.

"I need to get me one of those." Cindy smiled. "That would come in handy at the mall when I'm looking for a parking spot."

Mac chuckled and followed Cindy and Kevin as they passed through the automatic door of the terminal. Cindy seemed more animated today, using comical expressions and waving her arms as she talked. *I bet her sister was like that—bubbly and cute.* Cindy's image faded as the autopsy photographs came to mind. He cleared his throat and set his jaw. *I'll catch the guy who did this to you, Megan. I promise.* Mac hurried to catch up.

"Can I get you a cup of coffee or anything while we wait?" Kevin asked Cindy.

"No thanks. I'm good. I'll just end up having to use the bathroom all morning if I do."

Kevin studied the arrival times on the video display in the terminal. "There it is. Looks like Tim is coming in at gate C-16, so let's head down there."

At the passengers-only checkpoint, the detectives showed their badges and got clearance to go all the way to the gate. Once there they sat in the gray plastic seats to wait.

"I'm going to grab a paper," Cindy told Mac and Kevin after a few minutes. "Be right back." They watched her hurry down the concourse and disappear into the store.

"She seems kind of restless." Kevin turned back around.

"Maybe she's nervous about our being here." Mac stayed focused on the storefront. "Do you think I should keep an eye on her?"

"That's not necessary. I'm thinking she's more nervous about meeting Mr. Moneybags. Notice how she's had nothing but good things to say about him today."

"Yeah. Looks like she spent a lot of time in front of the mirror this morning too. You don't suppose she's got a thing for this guy, do you?"

Kevin leaned back in his chair. "You thinking motive? Like with Megan out of the way she has a straight shot at this guy?"

Mac shrugged. "Somehow I don't see her as the type of person who would commit a brutal crime like that."

"I don't either, but that doesn't mean she couldn't have hired the job out."

Cindy came out of the store with a paper tucked under her arm. "I don't see it," Mac said, watching the pretty blonde walk toward them. "She's not the type."

"I hope you're right, Mac. I do hope you're right."

Cindy settled into the chair she'd occupied earlier and flipped through the pages of the *Oregonian,* pausing at the metro section. "The story is in the paper again." She held it open for them to see.

Mac leaned over and read the headline: "Troutdale Woman's Death Still a Mystery." He glanced at the article, which detailed Megan's disappearance and the recovery of her body.

"Nothing new, just asking for information on leads," Kevin said. "Of course, I wouldn't trust anything in that publication anyway. You might as well grab a tabloid off the grocery store stands; it's probably more accurate with less exaggeration."

Mac was surprised by the comment. He'd never really thought about it. The paper seemed to cover things adequately, even though it did tend to be on the liberal side. He and Cindy had read most of the paper by the time Tim's plane touched down on the tarmac. The Northwest Airlines jet taxied up to the arrival gate, and several minutes later they were standing beside the door waiting for passengers to disembark.

"I take it you know what he looks like." Kevin leaned against a pillar.

"Yes. He's about six foot and maybe 180 pounds. He's got a nice build and blondish hair. Looks like he spends a lot of time in the sun. He's got a tan to die for."

Passengers spilled out of the tunnel and headed toward the baggage claim area. Before the tightened security, family members and friends could come right up to the gate to wait. Now the greeters had to stay outside of the security gates. About two dozen people had come out when Cindy touched Mac's arm and pointed. "That's him." She waved at a bronze-skinned man wearing a tropical print shirt and khaki pants and moved forward to meet him.

Cindy was right. The guy had a perfect tan and the kind of hair women spent big bucks on. Even dressed as casually as he was, the man exuded wealth.

Kevin leaned toward Mac and said softly, "Family money."

"You think?"

"I'd bet on it."

Tim set his briefcase on a chair and released the handle of his carry-on. When he saw Cindy, he stretched out his arms in welcome and she went into them. "Hey, kid. I won't ask how you are, 'cause I don't imagine you're doing any better than I am."

"That's the truth." Cindy stepped away from him. "Thanks for coming."

He nodded. His gaze shifted from Cindy to Kevin and Mac. "You must be the detectives Cindy told me about."

"Tim." Cindy looped her arm through his in an almost protective manner as she drew him forward. "Um . . . Detectives McAllister and Bledsoe with the Oregon State Police. They're working on Megan's case."

"I'm pleased to meet you." He extended his hand, displaying an expensive-looking watch.

"Welcome to Oregon, Mr. Morris." Kevin shook his hand. "I'm sorry for your loss."

"Thank you." Tim's response was a hoarse whisper. Tears shone in his eyes.

"You can call me Kevin. And this is my partner, Mac."

Mac shook the man's hand as well. Tim seemed sincere in his grief and Mac revised his earlier thoughts about him. "How was your flight?"

"Okay." He picked up his briefcase and settled it on the top of his wheeled carry-on. The four of them headed for the main entrance. "Can you tell me how the investigation is going?"

Not certain as to how to answer, Mac left the question to the senior detective.

"We've identified some strong leads but haven't made an arrest yet."

Tim shook his head. "I just don't understand how someone could murder Megan. She was one of the most likable people I've ever met. She liked and trusted everyone. Maybe that was the problem. She trusted the wrong person."

"I can't say a great deal at this stage. I hope you understand."

"I do. It's just that I really want answers. You know how it is."

Kevin nodded.

"Cindy said you wanted to talk to me." He looked up at the signs indicating the direction of the baggage claim and rental cars.

"Yes," Kevin answered. "We're interviewing everyone who might have known Megan."

"That's fine. I'd have been surprised if you hadn't wanted to talk to me. Do you want to talk here?" He glanced at the restaurant area as they passed.

"We were hoping you would come back to the police department with us so we could talk in private."

Tim nodded. "Is that all right with you, Cindy? Do you need my help with the funeral arrangements or anything?"

"Yes, but it can wait."

"If you guys don't mind, I'll pick up my rental car and meet you. I'll need directions."

"That's fine." Kevin ripped a page out of his notepad and wrote out the directions for the Troutdale P.D. "We'll drop off Cindy and see you in an hour or so."

"Um . . . if you don't mind, I'd like to go with Tim," Cindy said, tipping her head toward Tim. "Is that okay with you?"

"Of course," Tim replied.

"We can meet you at the police department," Cindy said to the detectives. "I know the way."

Kevin frowned. "Are you sure?"

"Positive. I'd like to talk to Tim about some things."

"Seems like a nice enough guy," Mac commented as they stepped onto the escalator that would take them down to the baggage claim area. "You worried about him being with Cindy?"

"Not especially. Mr. Morris seems stable and down to earth. Let's get his story before we write him off, though. Ted Bundy was a nice guy too—at least he seemed that way to the people who worked with him. I want Tim to take a polygraph." Kevin looked at his watch. "If you don't have any other bright ideas, we should head over to the Troutdale P.D. and see what the rest of the gang is up to."

Chapter Twenty-Two

When Mac and Kevin entered the briefing room at the Troutdale Police Department, they found Eric with his back to the door, reading a stack of computer printouts. "Wake up, Eric," Kevin teased. "The hard workers have arrived."

"Hardly working is more like it." Eric replied without turning around.

Mac took off his sports jacket and hung it on the back of an empty chair.

"We've got the fiancé coming in for an interview in about an hour." Kevin removed his jacket as well. Loosening his tie, he hitched his hip onto the front table where Eric had been working.

"Good." Eric stood up and put his hands on his almost non-existent hips. "I've been looking over these tip sheets all day long. People are still reporting eyewitness accounts all over the state, some as recent as last night. Don't they understand she's not missing, she's dead?"

"Easy, Big Red, maybe you ought to take a time-out from those for a while."

"You may be right." Eric turned around and smiled at Mac. "You know, I think that's the first time I've ever said that."

"Yeah, I know you have a problem, Eric, but admitting you have a problem is the first step toward recovery."

Mac shook his head. Didn't those two ever quit?

"I hope you haven't corrupted Mac too much." Eric thumped Mac on the shoulder.

"Naw, my new partner is quite a bit smarter than my old one," came Kevin's quick response to the dig. "He can read and write—the whole nine yards."

"You are such a pleasure to be around, you know that, Kevin?"

Mac stood back as he watched the two ex-partners interact. Eric seemed less a threat than he had at first. Not once had he made a remark about Mac's family history and the fact that Mac's grandfather had been a gangster or that his father had been a dirty cop. In fact, he acted like they weren't even related—like Mac was just another detective. Which was fine with him.

"You guys might want to take a look at these updated faxes from Megan's bank relating to the temporary debit card they issued after she reported her purse stolen." Eric handed both detectives a copy of the list. "As you can see, we've got seven transactions on her card on the fourteenth and fifteenth of August. The fourteenth was the day her sister reported her missing. Her account was exhausted after that."

Kevin glanced over the list. "Is there a pattern?"

"I haven't drawn it out. The first three were at a Plaid Pantry on Halsey. They were all on the fourteenth during the early morning hours. The first for fifty dollars at 2:11 A.M. There was a second attempt for two hundred dollars at 2:12 A.M., but it was unsuccessful because the card only allows an ATM withdrawal of two hundred dollars a day. The third attempt at 2:14 A.M. worked and the bad guy received one hundred dollars. The guy actually returned to the same machine inside the Plaid Pantry at exactly 10:00 A.M. for another try at two hundred dollars without success, again because he was already over the daily limit."

"Any more that day?" Kevin scanned the printout again.

"Nope, doesn't appear to be. The next day, the fifteenth, there was a transaction at the Gresham Fred Meyer store at 11:37 A.M., a debit for fifty dollars. It looks like it was used at the store itself, not an ATM machine. The perp then used an ATM machine inside the Clackamas Mall at 3:41 P.M., attempting to withdraw two hundred dollars. There weren't enough funds in the account at that time, so he tried again at 3:44 P.M. for an even hundred and received the money."

"Couldn't he read the transaction slip to see the balance?" Mac asked.

"Yeah, we thought that was odd, too, until I talked to a bank rep. She said this particular account didn't show a balance with the receipt because the primary account was attached to the stolen card. She said it's for security on the account to discourage thieves, like the two-hundred-a-day maximum."

"Who do we have on this?" Kevin asked.

"I pulled Philly and Russ off the neighborhood canvass and her place of employment to track these down. If we get lucky, these ATMs or maybe the stores will have video cameras. Keep your fingers crossed and say a prayer."

"Good." Kevin cracked his knuckles. "Are we still on for the polygraphs tomorrow?"

Eric nodded. "I've got Detective Thomas coming up from Salem. She'll bring her gear with her and perform the examinations here."

"Sounds good. We've got three or four folks to put on the box tomorrow."

"Oh yeah, Kev, I almost forgot." Eric grabbed a second stack of paper. "I ran up some criminal histories on the folks you have been talking to. The sister, Cindy, is as clean as they come. Not even a parking ticket. Same goes for the fiancé. He had one ticket for speeding from the Florida Highway Patrol in 1997."

"Did you check them in the law enforcement data system and the national crime index computer?"

"Yep, according to state and federal records, they're both clean. Now, the other guy—Gordon Reed—is another story. He's been arrested twice for driving under the influence, both in the last three years. His license is currently suspended."

"Humph. He said his car wasn't working." Mac gave Kevin a sidelong look. "We'll remind him of that tomorrow when he drives in."

Eric laughed. "Once a trooper, always a trooper. We have a search warrant in process for his residence and car; as soon as that clears I'll get someone over there. He had a concealed weapon permit revoked three years ago, after a noncriminal arrest for possession of a controlled substance."

"What about our favorite teenager, Brandon King?" Mac asked.

Eric shuffled the papers in his hand. "Ah yes, the purse thief. His juvenile criminal history is sealed, of course, so I had to access his contacts through the data system in Multnomah County, where he lives. Looks as though he's had several contacts for truancy and mischief, nothing major. Another contact on this guy too, for less than an ounce of marijuana. I don't see anything big on him. What's your read so far, Kevin?"

Mac leaned against the wall, trying to take in all the information. So Gordon had a record. That didn't surprise him. He'd be interested to see what a search of the guy's residence turned up.

"Hard to say," Kevin answered. "We have a number of possibilities. We'll keep plugging along."

"When's the fiancé coming in?"

"Anytime now."

"I'm going to get a bite to eat then," Eric said, turning around to grab his jacket. "Don't leave until you talk with me. Hopefully we'll hear something on the bank records and the video. I've got to get someone down to Megan's workplace for a two-o'clock interview I set up with the girl she shared a shift with. A gal by the name of Meredith Hoyt."

"If we get done in time, we'll take care of that one, too, before we call it a day." Kevin yawned and leaned back in the chair, settling his legs on the table.

"Can I bring something back for you guys?"

"Not me. If it's okay with Mac, we'll grab a bite after we interview Tim."

"Sure," Mac agreed, but his stomach didn't.

Eric jogged down the stairs and returned seconds later. "Tim is here, Kevin. He's down in the lobby. I told him you would be right with him. Oh, and you can use the captain's office for privacy. He won't be in today, so feel free."

"Thanks, pal; we'll take it from here." Kevin lowered his legs and let his chair drop back into position. "Hey, Mac, would you mind bringing him up? I'll get us set up in the captain's office. We don't have to advise Tim of his rights because he's not in custody, but since we're here at the station, we'll have to be careful. Give him the seat by the door, and don't close it. We want to make it clear he's free to leave and not in our custody."

"You got it." Mac slipped his sports jacket back on and hurried down the stairs to greet Megan's wealthy former fiancé. "Hello again, Mr. Morris. You're right on time." He glanced toward the door. "I thought Cindy was coming with you."

"She did." He offered a wan smile. "I dropped her off at the outlet mall so she could do some shopping while I talked with you."

Mac nodded. He had to admit to being disappointed in not seeing her. Cindy had a way of brightening the mood and making things seem normal.

Tim glanced at the stairs. "Okay, I'm all yours, Detective."

"Right this way." Mac had Tim take the lead up the stairs—a habit he'd gotten from working the streets and knowing you should never turn your back on a possible suspect. When they reached the top of the stairs, Kevin was waiting in the hallway outside the captain's office.

"Right in here, guys. Have a seat, Tim." Kevin pointed to the chair near the door. He and Mac took seats facing Tim's.

"Thanks again for coming down," Kevin said. "Before we get started, I just want to again say how sorry I am that we have to meet under these conditions."

Tim nodded and folded his hands in his lap, looking down at the floor. "This has been very difficult for me. I loved Megan. I still can't believe she's gone. We were engaged, you know."

"Cindy told us." Kevin leaned back in his chair, a notepad in one hand and a pen in the other.

Mac took the silent partner role again and began taking notes.

"Tim," Kevin said, "we need your help to find out who's responsible for this tragedy."

Tim brushed his manicured hands over his thighs. "I'll help in any way I can."

"Great. Before we start, can I get you something to drink—coffee, tea, or water?"

"No thanks."

"Okay, let's get on with it then. Mac, why don't you start the process?"

Mac's heart nearly stopped at the request. "Sure," he said, glancing down at his notes to give himself time to regain his composure. He began by asking Tim background questions about his home in Florida and jotting down biographical information.

When Mac had sufficiently collected his thoughts, he went on to more pertinent questions. "First, I'd like you to know that you are not a suspect in this investigation, and you don't have to talk to us if you don't want to. There's the door right there and you can go anytime you want."

"I'm fine. I want to cooperate in any way I can. Let me tell you something. I know you guys have to take a hard look at me. Believe me, my lawyer wanted to be present and warned me not to talk to you alone, but since I've done nothing wrong I don't see any point spending a fortune to fly him out here. So ask me your questions; I have nothing to hide." Tim bent his head and covered his face. When he raised his head, tears glistened in his eyes. "I'm sorry. It just hits me sometimes, you know?"

Kevin grabbed a box of tissues from the table at the front of the room and set the box within Tim's reach.

"Thanks." He pulled out a tissue and dabbed at his eyes.

"Could you tell us about how you met Megan?"

"I was looking to sell a new line of treadmills to the chain. The president of Fitness First Health Clubs had asked me to meet him at the Troutdale club." He closed his eyes for a moment then went on. "Megan was working the front counter. She was the most beautiful creature I've ever seen. It was truly love at first sight—at least on my part." Tim hesitated as his eyes welled up again. "I'm sorry. I thought I was done with this."

"That's fine," Mac said. "Take your time. We're in no hurry."

Tim took a deep breath and after a moment or two regained his composure. "After that, I made it a point to visit Oregon as often as I could just so I could see her. The phone bill alone was running me around three hundred dollars a month. I finally bought her a calling card so she wouldn't have to call collect anymore. We would talk for hours. When I came for a visit last month, I told her this long-distance stuff was crazy. I asked her to marry me and move to Florida so we could be together every day."

"And she agreed?" Mac asked.

"Oh, yeah. She threw her arms around me and must have said yes a dozen times. We went shopping for a ring and started making plans."

"Did you ever buy a ring?"

"Sure did. It was a beauty. Bought it at Damon's Diamond Imports in Portland. Megan designed the setting herself."

"Could you describe the ring for us and the value?"

"Sure. The diamond was a one-and-a-half carat oval cut—a D color with VS-1 clarity. It had an—"

"I'm sorry," Kevin tapped his pen on his notepad. "Could you repeat that—a little slower and in English?"

"Right. Sorry. I'm kind of a jewelry buff. It was basically a near-perfect diamond—virtually clear with only a slight imperfection. I paid sixty-five hundred for the stone alone. The setting was an additional two thousand, which made the total purchase price a little over nine thousand dollars."

Mac whistled. "Wow. Must have been some ring." He and Linda hadn't gone shopping for a diamond yet. He'd be lucky to afford a quarter carat.

"Yes. A lovely stone for a lovely lady."

Mac's imagination conjured up a headstone instead of a diamond. Shoving the thought aside, he focused back on what Tim was saying.

"Like I said, Megan designed the setting. There were two hearts overlapping and the stone was set in where they joined. The diamond was bordered by sapphires, our birthstones. Megan said the hearts represented our two hearts meeting and becoming one with each other." His voice broke and Mac waited until he could go on.

"Did she actually have the ring?" Mac knew she had from Gordon's testimony, but he wanted to get the whole story from Tim.

"I gave it to her just before I left last time. We went out to dinner to celebrate." He shook his head. "My last picture of her was her holding the ring up to the light. I swear her eyes were brighter than the diamond. I was wondering . . . did you recover the ring?"

Mac wasn't certain he should give him that kind of information, so he looked to Kevin for the answer.

"I'm afraid not," Kevin said in a gentler than usual tone. "We haven't found it. In fact, we haven't had a very good description of the ring until now. There were no personal effects found with her."

Tim nodded. "I shouldn't be surprised."

Mac frowned. He couldn't blame the guy for wanting it back, but the question raised a red flag. His girlfriend had been brutally murdered and he wanted to know about the ring?

Tim stared at the tissue still in his hand. "I suppose you're wondering why I'd be concerned about the ring. I . . . um . . . I was thinking about having her buried with it."

"Why's that?" Mac asked.

Tim met his gaze. "Do you believe in life after death?"

Mac didn't answer. "Do you?"

"Yeah. I know the ring is a tangible thing, but I was thinking the act of leaving it on her finger would somehow let her know that even though we were never able to get married officially that she'd know I really meant to. You know, like we'd be married in eternity."

Mac didn't know how to respond. He let the silence build, thinking that this was a good time to wait for Tim to offer more information. And for him to collect his thoughts.

"Would you guys mind filling in the blanks for me?" Tim finally asked. "The newspaper accounts I read and the report I got from Cindy didn't tell me much."

"What exactly are you asking?" Mac studied the man's face, looking for inconsistencies. The guy seemed a little too perfect. A little too cooperative.

"I'm not sure. I guess I want the details, like where she was found and what the body looked like. Had she been raped?" He bit into his lower lip. "She told me she'd never slept with a man before me. I don't want her to have been raped."

"I'm sorry, Tim," Kevin replied. "We can't divulge that kind of information at this point. The more information we keep confidential, the less chance investigative information can be leaked to the media.

Sometimes we get lucky and the bad guy tells us something he couldn't have read in the papers or seen on television."

"I suppose that makes sense in a way."

Mac kept his gaze on his paper. "Tim, you indicated you and Megan were . . . intimate?"

"Yes, but not until that last night we were together."

"Were you both exclusive at the point of your engagement?"

"Heavens, yes. Megan was a virgin until we . . ."

Mac noticed a slight defensiveness in his voice. Did he know about Megan's relationship with Reed?

"I don't mean to be intrusive," Mac went on. "We're just trying to identify patterns of conduct for Megan."

"I just don't see the relevance, and I'd rather not talk about our sex life."

Kevin gave Mac a slight shake of his head, indicating he shouldn't push Tim on the matter. He covered the action by turning his head from side to side, while he rubbed his neck.

"Could you tell me one more thing? Did you use a condom?"

"Of course. The last thing I wanted was to get Megan pregnant."

"I understand." Mac leaned back.

"Um . . . do you mind if we take a break?" Tim asked. "I'd like to use the bathroom. And I could use that coffee now."

"Sure. The bathroom is right down the hall." Mac pointed toward the briefing room. "Right next to that is the break room. You'll find the coffee in there. Help yourself. The cups are right next to the carafe."

"Thanks." Tim got up and made his way to the restroom.

As soon as he was out of earshot, Mac asked, "What was the deal, turning the questioning over to me?"

Kevin grinned, not seeming the least bit apologetic. "Just testing you. Wanted to see how you reacted under pressure."

Mac frowned. "How did I do?"

"Great. You barely flinched. So, what do you make of this guy?"

"I'm not sure. On one hand, he doesn't strike me as the killer type, but I don't know about that business with the ring."

"Uh-huh. That was rather odd." Kevin folded his arms. "But all in all, I'm getting good vibes. Though I've been fooled before."

"He's got motive," Mac ventured. "Did you see how defensive he got when I asked about Megan being with other men?"

"The jealous boyfriend. A real possibility there. You never know how a man will act when he discovers the woman he loves has betrayed him. Why don't you let me take over the interview when he comes back in? I'm going to let him in on some of the information we learned from Gordon and Cindy's interviews in regard to Megan's purported indiscretions."

"Do you think that's a good idea?"

"I'm not sure, but I'd like to see his reaction to the information regarding Megan's recent encounter with Gordon. We may not have another chance to talk to Tim again, so we better put all our cards on the table now. Oh, and Mac, let's not ask him to take a polygraph until the end of the interview."

Chapter Twenty-Three

Tim walked back into the interview room a few minutes later, holding a cup of coffee. He sighed heavily and sat back down in the chair, staring intently at the dark brew.

"Find everything okay?" Kevin asked.

"Yes, thanks. The coffee is good—I half-expected mud. But then I understand you Pacific Northwest types pride yourself on good coffee."

"Yep." Mac smiled. "An espresso joint on every corner."

Kevin nodded. "We need something to compensate for the rainy days."

"It might rain a lot, but it's beautiful here—the mountains, the trees. It's August and things are still green."

"We like it." Kevin's smile faded and he leaned forward. "We still have a few more questions for you if you don't mind."

"Sure. Um . . . I was thinking about something in the break room. You're probably wondering about my whereabouts from the time Megan disappeared until the time she was killed."

Kevin rubbed his chin. "Well, that is something we'll probably check out."

He gave the detectives a sheepish grin. "I watch a lot of detective shows and they're always talking about means, motive, and opportunity. I just wanted you to know that I might have had the means, but certainly not motive or opportunity. I took the liberty of typing up my schedule from August twelfth through the sixteenth." Tim picked up his briefcase and set it on his lap. Opening it, he took out a two-page, neatly typed itinerary. "Thought I'd save you some time."

Kevin took the proffered pages and glanced over them. "Thank you."

"As you can see, I wasn't in Oregon during that time period. I can send you actual records, if that's any help."

"I appreciate your help, Tim. Looks like you have all your bases covered."

Bases covered? That's putting it mildly, Mac thought. The guy was being a little too efficient. He made a quick note to himself.

"There is one more thing, though." Kevin studied Tim's face as he spoke.

"What's that?" Tim asked.

"Could you send a record of the actual businesses you visited in these cities along with addresses and phone numbers?"

"Sure. I'll call my secretary and have her get on it right away."

Kevin set the itinerary on the table and moved it in Mac's direction. "Right now we are in the process of proving who didn't kill Megan, rather than working on any particular suspect. Those records will be made part of our case jacket, but I'm willing to take your word for it at this time."

"Thank you." Tim took a sip of coffee.

"Just a few more things and we'll get you on your way."

"Okay."

"I want you to understand that we have talked to a number of people already. One of those people claims he, too, had a relationship with Megan, at least a short-term one. Were you aware of that?"

He shook his head. "No. I'm sure Megan dated a lot of men before we met."

"This person claims to have had a relationship with Megan

before the two of you met and that they were intimately involved as recently as two weeks ago."

Tim rubbed his temples. "I don't believe you. This is some sort of trick to get me flustered, isn't it? Well, guys, it's working, but I find your tactics in very poor taste."

"I'm sorry, Tim, but this is the story we were given."

Tim leaned forward, setting his cup on the desk. "I can't believe this. I won't believe this. Megan was in love with me and I was in love with her. We were to be married and spend the rest of our lives together. I was going to take care of her, provide for her. Now I ask you, why? Why would she run around with another man? Answer me that!"

Tim's gaze fled from Kevin to Mac and back again. "Do you have any more profound bits of information you would like to pass along to me about my fiancée? Because if not, I would like to go."

"No, nothing more today. I'm sorry I upset you; this was just a question that needed to be asked."

"Right, for patterns of conduct. I remember." Tim placed both hands on his thighs and stood up. "Let me tell you something, gentlemen. Megan was the kindest, most beautiful woman I ever met. I didn't really care about Megan's past. I'm sure if she saw this guy recently there's a perfectly good explanation. Unfortunately, she isn't here to defend herself. I loved her. When she died, a part of me died with her. I hope you don't plan on dragging her name through the mud. I refuse to."

Kevin nodded. "We never had the pleasure of meeting Megan. I'm sure everything you say about her is true. You just need to understand that we're trying to catch a killer before he kills again—before he takes some other man's fiancée or wife or daughter. We take this grim responsibility very seriously and we ask the hard questions because someone has to."

Tears watered Tim's eyes again as he ran his fingers through his thick blond hair. "I'm sorry. I just wasn't prepared to hear that from you. If it happened, if Megan was involved with someone else, I'll just have to come to grips with that. Do you think he might have been the one who killed her?"

"We don't know at this time. Mac and I are still working on him. We'll be meeting with him tomorrow, in fact."

"For an interview like this?"

"Not exactly. We've spoken to him in-depth already. Tomorrow he'll be coming in for a polygraph examination."

"A lie detector test?"

"Exactly."

"Do you guys want me to take one of those, too, just so you can be sure I'm not involved so we can work together and catch this . . ." His jaw clenched. "This maniac."

Kevin walked him to the door. "It would be great if you did. The polygraph coupled with your business records would certainly be of help."

"Do want me to take it now?"

"Tomorrow. I know it's a hassle having to come back, but we aren't set up for the examination today. We have to bring up a specialist from Salem."

"Tomorrow's good. I'm staying at the Riverside Inn—it's not that far away." He reached into his still-open briefcase and pulled out a business card. "I'll give you my phone number at the hotel." He jotted the number on the back and said, "I'll call my secretary right away and have her send those records you wanted." He hesitated a moment and added, "If you give me the number here, I can have her fax them over—you could have them later this afternoon."

"We can do that," Kevin replied. "One of us will call you in the morning to set up the polygraph. I'd ask that you don't consume any alcohol tonight and try to get as much rest as possible. The polygraph detective prefers that the subject of the exam use no drugs or alcohol twenty-four hours prior to the examination."

"Drinking myself under the table was definitely on my agenda tonight, but I'll abstain. Thanks for the warning."

"Do you have any questions for us?" Kevin asked.

"Yeah." His eyes went hard as blue ice. "Could you tell me a little about this other guy she was seeing?"

"I don't think that would be a good idea right now," Kevin said. "If it's any consolation, I doubt Megan would have chosen him over you."

"Thanks for that, at least. Have a good afternoon. I guess you'll be in touch."

Mac and Kevin thanked him for coming. After he'd gone, Kevin picked up Tim's card and itinerary. "I don't think he's our guy, but we'll take a look at these business records and see how he does on the box tomorrow."

Mac chewed on the end of his pen. "Kevin, you know this stuff better than I do, but it wouldn't be hard for him to find out about Gordon Reed. I mean, all he has to do is ask Cindy. If she gives him as much info as she gave us . . ."

Kevin agreed. "Good point. We don't want another homicide on our hands, do we? We'll need to be careful about staggering the times of the polys tomorrow so Tim and Gordon aren't in the same place at the same time."

Mac hoped that precaution would be enough. He'd caught the hateful look in Tim's eyes. A look that could translate to murder.

Kevin led the way back to the briefing room.

Eric was already there, seated at the front row table with his cell phone pressed to his right ear and the office phone in his left hand. "Right, great. Thanks, Allison," Eric said into the cell phone as he flipped it shut and put the office phone to his ear. "Sorry, go ahead, Philly. Uh-huh. Shoot. Okay, let me know what you find out at the Fred Meyer store. Great, looks like the Wonder Twins are out of their interview, so I'll get them over to the club." Eric hung up and turned to face them.

"What was that all about?" Kevin asked.

"Philly and Russ went by the Plaid Pantry store on Halsey to check out the ATM where Megan's card was used on the morning of the fourteenth. The machine doesn't have a built-in camera. However, the store has a video camera that monitors the door and cashier area. The bad news is they recycle their tapes after a week so if we had the bad guy on tape, it's already been recorded over twice. Philly and Russ are heading over to the Fred Meyer store now to see if they can come up with anything there."

"Was that Allison Sprague on the other line?"

"Oh yeah, got some good news there. She was able to extract DNA from the victim's thigh bone marrow for a baseline sample. Now it's up to us to find something to compare it to."

"Humph." Kevin slipped off his jacket. "A murder weapon dripping with blood would be nice."

"You wouldn't be getting the big bucks if it were that easy, old buddy," Eric laughed.

"If I had half your money, I'd burn mine." Kevin replied with a grin.

"Speaking of money, how did Tim shake out in the interview? Looked like he was wearing my year's pay on his wrist."

"Hey, his Rolex might be nice, but it's not as fancy as my Wal-Mart special." Mac lifted his arm to display his black plastic digital watch.

Eric laughed. "Very chic. I picked up a similar one in the south of France over the summer." He showed them an inexpensive watch similar to Mac's.

"If you two ladies are through showing off your jewelry," Kevin said, "I have a couple of items I'd like to discuss."

"By all means." Eric gave Mac a wink.

"Actually, Tim did okay in the interview. I don't think he was aware of Megan's indiscretions, which shoots the jealous boyfriend theory. I don't think he killed her. The polygraph tomorrow should tell us if he's being honest with us." Kevin went on to tell him about the itinerary Tim had provided.

Mac rubbed his chin, not certain if he should express his opinion. He was, after all, the new kid on the block and he'd already made a fool of himself a time or two. He didn't share Kevin's feelings about Tim. To him the boyfriend had done all the right things, including the printout of his itinerary. Wanting to look over it himself later, he decided to ask for a copy.

"Oh by the way, Kev," Eric said after Kevin had finished briefing him on Tim. "While you were in the interview, there was another homicide in Salem so we lost part of the crew."

"Perfect. What now?"

"State Penitentiary in Salem, an inmate was set on fire in the vocational rehab center. Looks like someone threw some combustible fluid on him and lit a match. The victim was a convicted child rapist, so even in prison he wasn't the most popular person."

"Any suspects?" Kevin asked.

"Yeah, about forty-five of them. Of course none of the inmates saw or heard anything. They are all in lockdown while our guys respond. The lieutenant pulled four guys off this case to deal with all the interviews on the new call, so you two, Russ, and Philly are the only guys from homicide left working this caper right now."

"Why am I not surprised?" Kevin rubbed his deeply lined forehead. "Tim gave us a good description of Megan's engagement ring, so I'll get that information to you right away. In the meantime, did we get anything from the narcotic detectives or pawnshop guys?"

"Negative. No victim property turning up and no dopers are coming up with any information from the street. We'll just have to keep going through the motions until we get a break."

"We have a long list of characters associated with this murder, Eric. Unfortunately, none of them meets the three criteria as yet."

"Ah yes—the old motive, means, and intent," Eric recited.

Kevin winked at Mac. "Exactly. I suppose I should add not yet—at least not with the information we have so far. Personally, I don't think we've met our guy. And don't say it, Eric; I know what you're thinking."

"Don't form an opinion; stay objective," Eric and Kevin said at the same time.

"Yeah, a wise old coot taught me that." Eric looked at Mac and cocked his head at Kevin.

"I think he's trying to teach me the same thing." Mac grinned.

"I just hope you're quicker than your cousin," Kevin joked.

Cousin? So Eric had told them they were related. He felt himself tighten up again. What, if anything, had Eric said to Kevin? Had he talked about him to the other men as well? *You're being paranoid,* Mac told himself. *Just because your dad was a dirty cop doesn't mean they'll expect it of you. Besides, maybe they don't know.* It had been years ago, in another state. Maybe Eric didn't even remember. He was only a teenager at the time and the families weren't all that close.

While his thoughts had taken him on another foolish rabbit trail, Eric and Kevin were still clowning around. Kevin had Eric in a headlock, messing up his hair.

"All right, all right." Eric shook his head. "I give up. Get out of here so I can get some work done." Eric finger-combed his hair back into a semblance of order.

"Hey, buddy." Kevin chuckled. "I noticed your hair is feeling a little thin on top. Could be pattern baldness setting in. I'd make an appointment with the wig salesman if I were you—though I doubt they'd ever be able to match the color."

"I said get outta here." Eric spoke in a stern voice but couldn't quite hide his grin. "Don't forget you have a two o'clock at Fitness First to interview Megan's coworker."

"What's the name again?"

"Meredith Hoyt. Better write that down, old-timer, so you won't forget."

"Don't worry, baldy, my new partner's mind is like a steel trap. He's also better looking."

"No argument there. You two be careful; I don't want to cut a one percent check this month."

Mac hadn't heard that phrase used in a while. It reminded him that even though he was no longer a uniformed trooper, the job still held its dangers. It was a morbid joke among state troopers in Oregon. If you were killed on duty, all members of the force paid the next of kin one percent of their monthly income. The money went toward the burial of the trooper. From what Mac had heard, it was a long-held tradition to show their honor and appreciation to the fellow officer and the family.

Kevin started for the door. "Hey, Mac, are you ready for lunch?"

"More than." As if on cue, Mac's stomach growled loudly in agreement.

"Let me know what you find out at the health club this afternoon," Eric called after them.

"Yes, Mother," Kevin yelled as he and Mac jogged down the stairs to the exit.

Chapter Twenty-Four

Mac settled into his car and secured the seat belt.

"What did you think of that ring Tim described?" Kevin asked. "It sounds like a real dandy."

Mac laughed. "I'm not going to tell my girlfriend about it, that's for sure. I don't want her getting any ideas."

"If she's like my Jean, she won't care whether it's a diamond chip or the Hope diamond. It's what the ring stands for, not the physical appearance or price tag."

"Do you think the killer took Megan's ring?"

"I'd put money on it. Either he thought he could make a quick buck or wanted to keep it as a souvenir. A ring like that would probably bring him over five hundred from a fencer, or a dishonest pawnbroker. We'll get the description of the ring to local pawnshops, in case he sold it. Or the killer may want it for a keepsake, a token to remember the victim by when he relives the murder."

"Sounds sadistic."

"Hopefully we aren't dealing with someone who actually enjoys killing. That would fit the profile of a serial killer."

"You don't think that's what this is, do you?" Mac thought about the Green River murders and how long it took to finally find the killer.

"You never know," Kevin said.

Mac suddenly had an idea. "Would the cleanup guys out at the body dumpsite have used a metal detector to check for the ring or any other jewelry?"

"Good question, my friend. They should have." Kevin got on the phone to Eric, who told him that no metal detector had been used.

"Make a little detour, Mac. Head back to the P.D. Our fish and game troopers have a detector stored inside that little office they share with the patrol troops. I'm sure it's still there. They use it during big game season to scan illegal deer and elk kills for bullets. I understand it's a pretty sensitive machine."

Mac made a U-turn and less than a minute later was back at the Troutdale P.D. He left the engine running and jogged inside. The receptionist led him to the small office, where he found the detector propped in a corner. He jotted off a hurried note and left.

"Got it," he told Kevin as he popped the trunk, moved his equipment aside, and set it in.

"We'll grab a bite on the way down to Bonneville State Park. We should have time to scan the area and make our two o' clock back in Troutdale."

They stopped at the Burger Barn, a local restaurant known for its one-pounders with the works, and ate their hamburgers and fries on the run. Mac was finished with his before Kevin had taken two bites. "You guys right out of patrol always amaze me," Kevin said.

"How's that?" Mac stuffed his garbage into the fast food bag.

"You eat like there's no tomorrow. You really ought to take your time and chew your food. And I don't want to hear the excuse that you get used to eating fast because you might get a call and have to run out on your lunch."

"I get used to eating fast because I never know when I'll get a call and have to run out on my lunch." Mac grinned.

"Smart guy." Kevin smiled back. "Well, unless you want to look like Philly in a couple of years, you better reprogram yourself."

"Good advice." Mac took a sip of his twenty-ounce Coke. "Are you going to eat those fries?" He reached for Kevin's bag.

Kevin grabbed the bag and set it out of Mac's reach. "I'd throw them away before I gave them to you. Now get your meat hooks out of there." By the time they reached the park, Kevin had finished his burger and fries.

"Eric said we had the Explorer Scouts from the sheriff's office walk through the entire park. They turned up a lot of junk, old clothes, and mail. Nothing of obvious evidentiary value, though. We have it in an evidence locker. Might not hurt to go through it."

Mac drove past the main entrance and took the dirt utility road he'd taken the day they recovered Megan's body.

"Mac, remind me when we get back to check my box at the main office. I asked the state park folks for a list of campers for the first two weeks of August. The info should have been faxed or mailed by now."

Mac whistled. "You're talking hundreds, even thousands of names. You aren't going to check all those, are you?"

"Not me, you." He grinned. "Actually, we may not need to—at least not for a while. If and when we run out of leads or are unable to make an arrest, we'll go to the roster and start checking names. The important thing in a case like this is that you secure any possible item of relevance while it still exists. We don't want to lose it like we did the tape at the Plaid Pantry store Philly and Russ went after. That videotape would have been great evidence, but we couldn't get on it immediately so we lost it. Consequently, we don't want to find out six months or six years from now that things like the park registry records are gone."

Mac nodded, amazed at how many details detectives had to keep track of. Pulling onto the dirt shoulder just past a big maple tree, he cut the engine, popped open the trunk, and got out. As his gaze settled on the body dumpsite, he remembered the smell and condition of the body. The hamburger and fries he'd eaten rolled over in his stomach. *Don't think about it,* he told himself. *Think about why you're here.*

Mac hauled the detector out of the trunk and turned the power button on to its maximum sensitivity setting. With Kevin walking beside him, Mac worked his way over to the ditch along the debris-strewn ground. The metal detector sounded as it revealed every bottle lid and scrap of litter along the roadside. He worked his way over to the ditch where the body had been recovered and was surprised that it still smelled. He asked Kevin why.

"There was quite a bit of sloughing because of the heat. Parts of her body virtually melted into the earth. We recovered what we could, but unfortunately some fragments were left behind because the body was so degraded."

"Wonderful." Mac began breathing through his mouth as he waved the Frisbee-shaped detector over the ground. The hair rose on the back of his neck as he walked the ground where Megan's body had been. As before, the stench in the stale air was almost unbearable. He was starting up the slight incline of the ditch, about to abandon their search, when the metal detector sounded.

"I've got a hit." Mac stopped and waved the disk over the area, holding it still above the strongest signal.

Kevin pulled a latex glove out of his pocket and stretched it onto his right hand. He hunkered down to examine the fern under the detector.

Kevin searched through the big leafy fern with his right hand, holding his mini mag flashlight in his left. As he pulled back the base of the fern, the flashlight beam revealed a metallic object.

Kevin brushed the debris and lifted up a broken silver chain, but no diamond ring.

"Looks like I led us on a wild-goose chase." Mac turned off the machine, disgusted with himself.

"Not at all, Mac." Kevin examined the chain more closely. "It hasn't been here too long. Since it's so close to the dumpsite, we'll bag it as evidence. Remember, Megan supposedly wore a cross around her neck. This chain is broken, so it could have come off when the body was brought here."

"Do you really think it could be hers?"

"It's a long shot, but we'll ask Cindy if she recognizes it. I'm glad you suggested the search, though. We may not have found the ring, but it does tell us that the killer probably has it."

Kevin and Mac returned to the car, where Mac removed his evidence kit. "This should do." Mac held out a small manila envelope.

"Perfect," Kevin replied as he dropped the silver chain inside.

Mac pulled off a section of blue evidence tape to secure the package, signing the seal. Kevin removed his latex glove and brushed the powder off his hands. Mac placed the metal detector in the trunk alongside his crime scene gear. "I could use a little more trunk space."

"Just be happy it doesn't leak," Kevin replied. "Those squareback Chevy Caprices they used to issue us leaked like a sieve. The rubber molding would freeze to the trunk lid in the winter, tearing out a hunk every time you opened it. Then in the spring, they would start leaking. Nothing better than finding out your gear has fuzzy mold growing on it when you arrive at a crime scene."

"Humph." Mac grinned. "Sounds suspiciously like one of those tall tales parents tell their kids about how they used to have to walk to school in a blizzard, uphill, both ways."

"No, seriously, if you doubt me, take a look at Sergeant Evans's car—if you can call it that."

Mac closed the trunk and within minutes they were back on the freeway heading back into town.

"Set a course for the fitness center." Kevin placed the evidence in the glove box. "Let's see what Megan's coworker has to say."

"Right." Mac slipped on his sunglasses as they headed into the bright early afternoon sun.

"The old pager is going off." Kevin checked the numerical display then pulled his cell out of his pocket and punched in some numbers. "Detective Bledsoe here." Kevin glanced over at Mac. "Yeah, Gordon. What can I do for you?"

"Um, I was talkin' to some guys on my crew and they told me I shouldn't take that lie detector test tomorrow. They said maybe I ought to get a lawyer."

"Well, that's certainly your right, Mr. Reed. But like I said, if you didn't have anything to do with Megan's death you don't have anything to worry about."

"I still feel like this is a setup or something."

"Why do you say that?" Kevin was losing patience with the man.

"That's what you dudes are all about. You make things fit your little case and tack a guy with a trumped-up charge."

"Tell you what, why don't you meet with us as planned and see what the polygraph is all about? If you don't want to take it then, that's fine. But it would help put to rest any doubt that you may be involved."

"I don't know. Let me think about it."

"You do that, Gordon—it's entirely up to you."

"Um . . . okay, maybe I will, but I need to come earlier because of some things I got to do."

"That's fine. We could make you our first appointment at, say, eight or eight-fifteen."

"What do you mean your first? You have other people taking the test?"

"Yes. Several other individuals who want to cooperate."

"Okay then. This better not be some trick, man, or I'm outta there."

"No tricks, Gordon; you have my word." Kevin turned off the phone and tipped his head back against the seat. "Lord, give me strength—and patience."

"Our roofer getting cold feet?" Mac asked.

"Like icicles. He's afraid we're setting a trap for him." He tucked the phone away and rubbed his eyes as weariness set in. Maybe he was getting too old for this business. He certainly was losing patience with people like Gordon Reed. "We need to pin this guy down; he's going sideways on us. If he doesn't show up in the morning for the polygraph, he moves to the top of the list."

Mac adjusted the visor. "I'd be very surprised if he comes. I think we should take him into custody before he has a chance to run."

"I think you're less patient than I am. Remember, slow and steady wins the race." Kevin pointed to the strip mall on their left. "There's the fitness center."

Mac turned into the left lane, pulling into the mall parking lot. "Well, if the guy cuts and runs, don't say I didn't warn you."

Kevin just smiled.

Chapter Twenty-Five

Kevin and Mac walked in the front door of the modern-looking health club. The entrance opened to an enormous room with multiple rows of exercise machines. In the far back corner, mirrored walls reflected several free weight stations along one side and two rows of treadmills on the other.

"Welcome to Fitness First! You must be my afternoon date," an attractive brunette in her early twenties said as they approached the front counter. She grinned at them and winked. Her hot pink two-piece spandex exercise suit pushed Mac's temperature up a notch, and judging from the rosy blotches creeping up Kevin's neck, he wasn't immune either. Mac read the name Meredith on her nametag.

"Hello, I'm Detective McAllister," Mac said when Kevin didn't say anything. "This is my partner, Detective Bledsoe. Are you Meredith Hoyt?"

"Live and in person." She flashed them an even wider smile. "I thought you two were the cops; most people don't come to work out in suits. Although you both look like you're no strangers to the gym."

"We try to stay in shape." Kevin straightened his tie.

"I'll be with you in a minute. You can wait for me in the client-orientation office right behind you." Meredith picked up the phone and paged another employee on the intercom.

Mac and Kevin walked in the small room that barely held the desk and three chairs. "You're no stranger to the gym," Mac mimicked when they sat down in the chairs. "She had you hook, line, and sinker. I bet you're ready to sign up for a two-year health club membership."

"Oh, hush. What do you know about muscles? The poor girl couldn't help herself. She's only human, you know." Kevin fluffed his hair and gave his eyebrows a double raise.

Mac laughed so hard his gum flew out of his mouth and landed on the floor under the desk. As he reached for the gum, Meredith entered the room. He sat back up in the chair, intentionally avoiding eye contact with Kevin so he wouldn't break up again.

"I've got my trainee running the counter, so I apologize in advance if she has to interrupt us. Since Megan . . . um . . . left us, we've had to hire someone else to fill her shift."

"We appreciate you taking the time to talk to us." Kevin cleared his throat and started the interview. "Could you tell us a little about your relationship with Megan Tyson and anything you think is relevant to this investigation?"

"Do you want me to, like, talk about what we did here at work?"

"That would be a great start. Tell us about work."

"Megan and I were, like, the most radical team. We had more new signs than any other shift at the club."

I'll bet. Mac couldn't imagine himself turning down the pert brunette.

"New signs?" Kevin interrupted.

"Yeah, you know, new clients for the club. People would come in for trial visits and our job was to sell the club membership to them. We ask about their fitness goals and show them how to use the equipment and stuff."

"Did she have any problems with the customers, or anyone else that you know of? Let me put it this way: Do you know of anyone who would want to cause Megan any harm?"

"No way." Meredith shook her head. "All the women at the club loved her. Well, some of them hated her because she had such a rad body. I mean, not an ounce of fat. But it was nice hate; everybody liked her here."

"How about the men who came to the club? Any of them take a fancy to Megan and get upset because she turned him down?"

She frowned and picked up a pen. "A lot of guys requested her as their personal fitness trainer. Megan was an awesome trainer, but, to be blunt, I think most of them were, you know, trying to get in her pants."

Kevin leaned back in his chair. "Did any of them succeed?"

"Megan had a few male friends she liked to hang out with. I don't think she was sleeping with any of them, but she definitely made it known that she was available."

"How did she do that?"

"You know, she would always mention she was single. It's easy for guys to get the wrong impression around here. Megan was really personable and she would tell them things like, 'Hey, your bod is looking rad. Keep it up.' Part of our job is to play to our clients' egos and keep them happy."

Mac gave Kevin a churlish grin.

"Yes, well, can you think of any members from the club she dated recently?"

"There were a couple of guys she met with on and off, for drinks and stuff. I don't think there was any major love connection or anything. Just Tim."

"That would be Tim Morris?"

"Right."

"What can you tell me about him?"

"He's okay, likes to hit on the girls when he comes into town to make his pitch. See those four rows of stationary cable resistance machines? Those are Tim's product line. They isolate target muscle groups—pretty cool really."

"Sounds as though you don't think much of Tim."

"He's okay, I guess. He asked me out once, but I was like, no thanks, Grandpa. Just because he has bucks, he thinks a gal is going to go for him." She licked her glossy hot pink lips. "Megan didn't pay much attention to him at first. She thought he was just a salesman until I told her Tim owned a company and was a multi-millionaire. Then she decided to fall in love." Meredith shrugged. "I suppose I shouldn't be so cynical. Maybe she really loved the guy. Whatever, you know, they seemed happy."

"Did she mention her engagement or wedding plans to you?"

"Are you kidding? That's all she talked about. She was always showing off this massive ring he gave her. She had it all planned out, the wedding, the move to Florida, and the kids she planned to have."

"How did Megan act toward the other men in the club after her engagement?"

"The same, as far as I could tell. She didn't miss a beat."

"How about contacts outside of the club? Did she continue to date anyone that you were aware of?"

"No. Well, I'm not sure. There was this one guy she was interested in, said he had asked her out and she didn't know what to do because of Tim. I can't remember if they were engaged by then. He was kind of cute, but I've only seen him a couple of times."

"Do you remember the name?"

"No, I'm not very good at names. He was already bulked up—about six feet, maybe two hundred pounds. Looked like he had been lifting for a while."

"Can you tell me more about him?"

"He had dark skin—looked like he spent a lot of time in the sun 'cause I think he was white—or he might have been Native American. He had long black hair down to his shoulders and wore it tied up in the back when he was in the gym. I'd say he was in his late thirties."

"So he was a member here."

"I think so."

"Is there any way we could get this guy's name?"

"I'd have to ask the manager. We can't really give out client information."

"It would be a big help to us," Kevin replied. "We're up against the wall for time here. We'd like to find the guy responsible for Megan's death so we're checking out any lead, no matter how small it may seem."

"Tell you what: Leave me your number and I'll see what I can do. I know he had a photo taken for the membership orientation, so I bet I have him on the computer. I'll scroll down the pictures entered in the last couple of months and see if I can recognize him."

"That would be great, and let us know if you recognize anyone else who took a special interest in Megan. Here's my card." Kevin wrote down a phone number on the back. "This is my pager number. Please give me a call if you turn up anything."

Meredith took the card and cupped it in her hand. "I'll do my best."

"Before we go, can you think of anything else that might be of interest to us?"

"Not really. I mean, we were, like, good friends at work and stuff but we didn't really hang out when our shift ended. I went to school and she took off to do her thing."

"Okay. We appreciate your cooperation." Turning to Mac he said, "Do you have anything?"

"Not right now. Thanks for your help."

"I'll call you tomorrow. My shift ended for the day. I just have to wrap up a few things with my trainee and get down to Mount Hood Community College for an afternoon class. Could you tell me, I mean, maybe I don't want to know . . . Did Megan suffer much? I mean, was she abused or raped?"

Mac deferred the question to Kevin.

His partner pursed his lips and looked out at the gym. "Let's just say we believe it was very unpleasant and we want to catch the person or persons responsible."

"I still can't believe it. Stuff like this doesn't happen to people you know." Her deep brown eyes caught Mac's. "Is there a possibility I could be in danger too? I mean, if the guy is from here and is taking the stuff we say the wrong way . . ."

Wanting to reassure her, Mac said, "There's no reason to think that."

She nodded and put Kevin's card in the bag she pulled out of her desk drawer. "Well, I hope you catch the creep."

"So do we, more than you can imagine," Kevin reached across the desk to shake Meredith's hand. "Thank you for your time."

When Meredith left, Mac took the opportunity to pick up his gum off the floor, throwing it in the garbage can beside her desk.

"Sounds like Megan was popular with the guys," Mac said as he and Kevin walked to the car.

"That makes this caper all the more difficult. Hopefully we can eliminate some folks tomorrow on the polygraph and start to narrow our focus. We still have a few high school kids to track down from the Oxbow Mountain purse-stealing incident. I'll ask Eric to get Philly and Russ to bring Brandon King in for the poly tomorrow."

"It'll be interesting to see whether or not Reed shows up."

"Yeah. Let's head back to the P.D. We may call it a day after we meet up with Eric and the gang."

"What about the tip we got from the jeweler who called about Megan's earrings?"

"Oh, right. Sorry. Guess I'm just anxious to get home. How about we set that up for tomorrow or the next day?"

They drove in silence for several minutes. Mac couldn't stop thinking about Meredith's comment about her being in danger too. He sipped his watered-down soda from a straw and finally spoke. "You know, Kevin, Meredith might be right. She could be in danger and our killer could be a psycho who works out at the center or even one of the guys who work there."

"I was thinking the same thing, partner." Kevin folded his arms and fixed his gaze on the traffic ahead of them. "Which means we better come up with a solid lead—and soon."

Chapter Twenty-Six

The sun was especially hot when Mac and Kevin pulled into the Troutdale P.D. parking lot. Late August to the first part of September were Oregon's warmest weeks. Even so, the temperatures had soared well above average.

"Man, it's hot." Mac tossed his jacket in the backseat of the car and tugged on the back of his dress shirt, where moisture dripped down his back. "Feels more like the Midwest than the Northwest."

Kevin agreed as they entered the building. "What I'd give to be sitting on the sand in Cannon Beach right now, watching the surf roll in."

"Oh, yeah." Images of running on the beach with cool westerly breezes blowing in his face filled Mac's head. They grudgingly climbed the stairs to the briefing room, where Philly was seated at the table with Eric.

"Well, if it isn't the Hardy Boys." Philly fanned his face with a folded newspaper. "Have you and junior solved this caper, Kev, so I can get out of here?"

"Not even close. We're hooking up one red herring after another. Everybody looks good at this point."

"No kidding." Philly leaned back in the chair, lessening the bulge over his belt but widening his berth. "You might as well stick a fork in me, 'cause this old boy is done." Philly placed his hands behind his head, displaying stained underarms with today's sweat ring extending an inch lower than the previous one.

"Where's Russ?" Kevin asked as he and Mac sat down on the opposite side of the table.

"He ran some evidence to the lab. I think we're going to call it for today." He picked up a half-full bottle of water and glugged it down.

"Speaking of evidence, Mac and I took a metal detector out to the body dumpsite today and found a broken chain. We were hoping her engagement ring would be there, but no such luck. As I already told Eric, we do have a description of her ring, though. The fiancé gave it to us. We'll send that around to the pawnshops and hope the killer tries to sell it."

Kevin made an entry in his notebook, indicating he had transferred the evidence to Eric.

Philly sat up in his chair and tugged the front of his shirt away from his distended belly. "Why are you just taking the metal detector out today? If you guys had done the crime scene right the first time, you wouldn't have had to go back." The smirk on his face told Mac the guy was in his joking mode. "I knew I shouldn't let you bumblers work without my supervision."

"Supervision?" Kevin mocked a deep frown. "Oh, you mean like that crime scene out in Silverton?"

"All right. King's X."

Mac winced at the use of the familiar phrase used in police circles. When someone was about to tell a story on you, saying "King's X" reminded him of a story you could tell on him. Police loved having *dirt* on each other. Eric had a lot of dirt on Mac. He hoped he wouldn't feel compelled to use it.

Philly tossed the rolled-up newspaper at Kevin. Kevin caught it and tossed it back. It bounced off Philly's stomach and landed on the floor.

Mac tapped his pen on the table. "What crime scene is that?"

"Never mind," Philly said. "I make one mistake and these guys haunt me with it for the rest of my life."

"You should have been there, Mac." Kevin chuckled. "We had a great shoe imprint outside the bedroom window of a stabbing victim and Philly walked right through the middle of it drinking his milk shake."

"If you guys had marked your evidence better, that might not have happened." Philly grunted as he stretched over to pick up the newspaper.

"Luckily we still made that one," Eric told Mac. "A sixteen-year-old kid stabbed a ninety-year-old guy to death for about twenty dollars in cash. Philly redeemed himself by tracking down the kid and getting a confession."

"I rest my case," Philly said. "Another dirt bag behind bars because the master was on the case."

"All right, you guys, let's get back to this case." Eric handed them several sheets of paper. Tim's itinerary was on the top. "Thought I'd better give you copies of this stuff to carry with you in case something breaks. The fiancé's itinerary, the ATM stuff—also, I pulled out several viable tips I thought were worth checking out. There's a jeweler who has Megan's earrings. Who knows? Maybe he saw the ring and got greedy."

"We've got that penciled in for tomorrow," Kevin reported.

"Good. You can read over the rest and let me know what you think tomorrow." He leaned back against the table and folded his thin freckled arms. "Philly, what did you and Russ come up with on the ATM use?"

"Nada. Zilch." Philly licked his index finger and flipped over a page in his notebook. "As you know, the videotape at Plaid Pantry had been taped over. At Fred Meyer's in Gresham, the dirt bag used Megan's card on the fifteenth just before noon. There's no ATM inside the store, and according to the bank the card was used at the actual checkout counter. The store received the credit for the charge. I guess he bought groceries or something, I'm not sure why it came to exactly fifty dollars."

"Maybe he bought something and got some cash back," Mac suggested.

"That's what we figured. The store has those debit machines on the counter that you just swipe your card through. The teller doesn't ask for identification as long as the personal identification number is good. The store recycles its videotapes every week so we struck out on that one too."

"How about the charges later in the day at the ATM inside Clackamas Mall?" Kevin asked.

"I was getting to that, if you'd keep your shorts on." Philly referred to his notes again. "The card was used after three in the afternoon at a machine near the top of the escalator close to the ice rink. The perp tried to take out two hundred bucks, although the account was down by then. He tried a second attempt a few minutes later for a hundred bucks and got the cash. That's the last use on the card. Once again, no camera in the machine, no videotape from the mall."

Eric examined the bank records on the printout. "Okay, a video of the guy would have been nice, but we can't use what we don't have. So here's what we do have: The withdrawals were made after the sister reported her missing. That means either Megan was being forced to use her debit card by the bad guy, which is unlikely due to the public places it was used, or—and I'd have to go with this one—the perp somehow got her PIN number and she was already dead or at least in captivity."

They all agreed. Kevin added, "I think it's safe to assume Megan Tyson was dead by two in the morning on August fourteenth. That's consistent with the use of her card and the opinion of the medical examiner on the state of her remains."

"What next?" Philly asked no one in particular.

Kevin deferred to Eric. "It's your call, buddy, but I'd like Mac and me to stay on Gordon Reed and Tim Morris. We'll also follow up on some of the other leads we've gotten. There are several people we need to talk to."

"Yeah," Mac muttered, "like a whole health club full."

"What about the high school kids from Oxbow Mountain—the purse thieves?" Eric asked.

"Russ and I could work that end," Philly offered.

"Sounds okay to me." Eric rubbed his chin as he stood up. "Are Gordon and Tim still taking the box in the morning?"

"Gordon is coming in at eight, at least we hope so," Kevin answered. "We need to make sure the examiner is here by then."

"Detective Thomas is still a go," Eric replied.

"Good. We should schedule Brandon King after Gordon and then Tim so there's no chance the two men come into contact."

"Humph." Philly sneered. "You ought to get the two of them in here to butt heads. Maybe they'll take each other out and save us the trouble."

"You are a real beaut, you know, Philly?" Kevin shook his head. "He hasn't changed a bit since we worked the road together, Mac. Except that his belt is bigger than it was fifteen years ago."

Philly patted his stomach. "I have big bones."

Mac laughed and shook his head. "You guys are something else. Don't you ever quit?"

"Yeah." Eric glanced at his watch. "Right about now. Let's call it a day." Turning to Philly, he said, "I'd like you and Russ to get Brandon King in here tomorrow morning."

"You got it. Just pull the Hardy Boys' report on their interview so I can track down the little delinquent and give him a talkin' to. I'm heading for Murphy's. I could use a drink. I'd ask you to join me, but I already know the answer." He winked at Mac. "These two are a couple of teetotalers."

"I think I'll have a cool one when I get home," Kevin said. "A nice tall glass of Jean's sun tea."

"That's what I thought, Mary Poppins. How 'bout you, Mac, want to tip a few drinks?" Philly asked.

The invitation surprised Mac. "No, thanks, I'm going home too." That wasn't exactly true. He could have stopped by, but Mac didn't drink. His father had taught him well on that score. Even if he did, he wouldn't relish the thought of hanging out with Philly for the next couple of hours.

"Ah, Kevin." Philly sadly shook his head. "You've already converted the kid? That's a record, isn't it?" He sighed and shuffled out of the room. "Okay, suit yourself. I'll call Russ; he's always good to go."

Eric stacked the tip forms on the desk then reached for his jacket. "Let's go, then. My lovely bride is waiting at home and she's a heck of a lot more pleasant to be around than you two. Hopefully our team will wrap up the murder in Salem, so we get some bodies back. Oh, that reminds me—Sarge called from Hawaii today to check on the case. He said he's having a heck of a good time, wanted to thank us for taking this off his plate so he could go."

"That's great," Kevin said. "Is he still coming back next weekend?"

"Looks like it. I hope we have this thing on the way to an arrest by the time he gets home so he can ease back into the routine."

"That would be nice." Kevin collected his briefcase. "Say, did we get the warrant to search Reed's place?"

"Yep. I'll get someone out there tomorrow—maybe while he's here. Thought it might be best to wait on the search until we got him in here."

"Good thinking," Kevin said.

"I'll see you two bright and early," Eric said. "Seven-thirty okay with you, Mac?"

"I'll be here." Mac picked up his briefcase as well and joined the men as they headed for the door. Unlike the others, Mac was in no hurry to go home. He'd have preferred to keep working, following up on tips that would eventually lead to Megan Tyson's killer. While he wouldn't interview anyone personally without Kevin, he could maybe make a few phone contacts.

The three men stampeded down the stairs, sounding like a herd of cattle on the old wooden steps.

Mac eased into his oven-hot car, turned on the air, and started for home. On the police radio, voices went on nonstop as metro area troopers made traffic stops and responded to fender benders. As he drove, Mac thought about Philly's comment about Kevin converting him. Since when did not drinking mean he'd converted to Christianity? Something about Philly's assumption annoyed him.

On the other hand, he didn't mind being compared to Kevin. The senior detective had a sense of normalcy about him. While he joked around with the others, he seemed more mature, sensible, steady. Traits Mac wouldn't mine having. He thought about Kevin's reaction to the teenager who'd stolen Megan's purse. The anger had surprised Mac, but Kevin's response surprised him more. He'd openly asked for forgiveness and talked about his reasoning. *The answers are in the Bible,* he'd said. Kevin really believed that. Maybe that was it. Kevin seemed to live out his faith.

Mac had seen a lot of hypocrites, professing to believe in God and living immoral lives. His father had been a Catholic—insisting they go to mass at designated times throughout the week when he'd go to confession then go home and get drunk. Instead of coming home to his family, like Kevin and Eric were doing, he'd stop off at a tavern; and by the time he got home, he'd be staggering drunk and mean. At some time or other he'd crossed over the line from enforcing the law to taking bribes and looking the other way.

His maternal grandfather had been much the same, outwardly

a pillar of the church. Instead of drinking, he used his wealth and position to get anything he wanted. Now he was serving a life sentence for his connection to the murder of a federal agent who'd infiltrated the ranks of his organization. His grandfather's ill-gotten wealth had allowed Mac to go to the best schools.

"Be a lawyer," his grandfather had said.

A lawyer. Humph. Someone who could keep DiAngelis and his *family* out of jail. It didn't happen. By the time Mac reached college he'd decided to walk away from the family money and corruption. He went to college, paying his own way, and earned a degree in criminal justice. Ironically, he did end up in law enforcement, not as a lawyer, but as a cop—a clean one. He'd insisted people call him Mac instead of Tony. He lived modestly, and everything he owned had been paid for with his own moderate salary.

Mac's heart leapt to his throat as he thought about Eric and how much he might have revealed to his coworkers. *Calm down,* Mac told himself. *So far they haven't held it against you. Whatever Eric said can't have been that bad.*

Mac liked to think he'd put his past behind him. But there were always reminders. Once a week, usually on Sundays, Mac would head over to the Mountain View Retirement Inn about three miles west of where he lived to visit to his maternal grandmother, Dottie DiAngelis. His paternal grandmother, Kathryn McAllister, suffered a major stroke last year doing what she loved best—baking pies. She died three days later without ever regaining consciousness.

Since it was Sunday and he was already ruminating about his history, Mac headed for the retirement inn. Even though she brought to mind painful memories, Mac loved his grandmother. Dottie and Kathryn had raised him after his mother died and his father walked out. Though he had lived with Kathryn, he saw Dottie several times a week. He realized now that Dottie had wanted him to live with her, but she didn't want him growing up too close to her husband and his people. Mac had been brought up in the church and for a short time considered going into the priesthood. Private school had been a good experience for him and he'd excelled in all of his subjects. Mac smiled as he thought about those years. Even with the negative influence of the men in his life, he'd emerged with a strong sense of justice, of right and wrong. Perhaps that had come from the positive influence of his grandmothers or perhaps from the training he'd received as a kid, or maybe he wanted, in his own way, to undo the damage his relatives had done. All he knew was that he'd decided early on to be a cop, and nothing could turn him away from his goal. He had gotten a position with the Oregon State Police right out of college as a trooper and had worked his way up to detective. Now he was working his first murder investigation.

Traffic slowed ahead, bringing his attention back to the honking cars and the scores of people heading home from their weekend of fun. I-205 northbound slowed to about five miles an hour as he crossed the Glen Jackson Bridge into Vancouver. He admired the view of the mountain and the colorful sails dotting the river as sailboaters and windsurfers took advantage of the sun and the wind and the vast Columbia River.

The traffic slowdown had been caused by a traffic stop on the Washington side of the bridge. Watching a sheriff's deputy step out of his car sent his mind skittering in another direction. *If a deputy or one of our troopers could have stopped Megan and Gordon that night when she'd been driving drunk, maybe she'd be alive today.*

Then again, maybe not. It did little good to speculate.

The traffic moved freely as he exited I-205 and headed east on Highway 14. Ten minutes later he pulled into the upscale retirement community and parked.

You should have stopped for flowers. You should visit more often. Guilt broadsided him as it often did when he came to visit. Dottie never complained about his infrequent visits, but he could tell in her dark eyes and her wistful smile that she wished he'd come more often. Maybe he would—soon.

The residents were just finishing their dinner when Mac came in. Dottie, who must have been watching for him, waved. "Antonio, Antonio, come give your nana a kiss." She was the only one who used his given name. He'd tried to get her to change it, but she never would. His grandmother may have been old in years, but she had the booming voice of a high school cheerleader. Mac wove around the tables until he reached hers, which sat in front of a window overlooking the courtyard. Linen tablecloths covered the tables and flowers from the garden had been placed in small vases. The place smelled of roast beef and mashed potatoes, reminding Mac of his own hunger. He'd stop on the way home and pick up something. In the courtyard, late summer flowers, roses and dahlias, bloomed profusely in the gardens, made even more brilliant by the emerald lawn.

Mac leaned down and planted a kiss on his grandmother's cheek, inhaling the familiar scent of her floral perfume. Dottie had been a beautiful woman in her time. In a way she still was. Her dark eyes shone as bright as ever and her hair, though peppered with gray, showed no signs of thinning. She had the figure of a model, and though she had never worked outside the home, still dressed as though she were heading for the office. Mac had never seen her without makeup or perfectly manicured nails. The facility had a beauty shop, and Mac suspected Dottie visited at least three times a week.

Kathryn, on the other hand, had never worn makeup. She was beautiful in her own way. Grandmother McAllister cleaned other people's houses as well as her own. Her perfume was often freshly baked breads and cookies. She'd had a sturdy shape and a soft bosom, perfect for holding and comforting a child.

Dottie gripped his hand and Mac raised it to his lips. "Sorry I'm so late, Nana. I'm working on an important case."

"On the Sabbath?" She clucked her tongue. "What could be so important you have to work on Sunday?"

"It's a murder case."

"Oh." Her eyes clouded. "You're trying to find out who killed Megan?" She glanced over at her tablemate. "Did you hear that, Estelle? My Antonio's going to find out who killed our Megan."

Estelle, a woman in her mid-eighties with Alzheimer's, stared at the wall.

Several residents murmured their support. One elderly man at the next table nodded. "It's about time."

"Your Megan?" Mac sat down in the empty chair. "What do you mean? Did you know her?"

"Of course I did. She used to come here once a week and teach our tai chi class." Dottie pursed her lips. "Lovely girl. We prayed for her every day when we heard she was missing." She squeezed his hand even harder. "I'm glad you are working on this. It feels good to know you'll have that horrible man behind bars soon."

"I hope so. There are a lot of suspects."

"Maybe, but as far as I'm concerned Matthew did it."

Mac frowned. "Matthew?"

"You're a detective and you don't know about Matthew?"

"I-I don't think so." Mac couldn't remember Eric saying anything about a Matthew, nor could he remember seeing the name on the tip list.

She rolled her eyes and threw up her hands in a dramatic gesture. "Matthew is an aide who works here. None of us likes him very much. He doesn't like us either. God only knows why these places hire people who don't like being around old people." She shrugged and leaned closer. "But he liked Megan. He watched her all during the classes while he was supposed to be working."

Mac pulled out his notebook and jotted down this new information. "What's Matthew's last name?"

"Um . . . DeLong. Yes, that's it. Matthew DeLong."

"What makes you think he had something to do with her death?"

"He was lusting after her and she didn't want to have anything to do with him."

Mac looked skeptically at his grandmother. "Nana, did Megan actually tell you that?"

"She didn't have to. A woman can sense these things. At any rate, the last time she was here, he followed her out to her car and talked to her. I couldn't tell what they were saying, of course, but it looked like an argument to me."

"Where's Matthew now?" Mac glanced around, spotting a balding man pouring coffee into one of the resident's cups. A mix of adrenaline and fear surged through him as he realized Megan's killer could be here in this facility—in this room.

"Don't you see?" Dottie released his hand. "That's why I think he did it. I haven't seen him since Megan disappeared."

The high alert settled into high interest. Mac could hardly wait to call Kevin.

Chapter Twenty-Seven

Mac went back to Dottie's one-bedroom apartment with her. The unit was attractive and full of antiques, books, and treasures she couldn't quite part with when she moved out of her home and to the retirement community three years ago. As far as Mac was concerned, she didn't need to be in a place like this, but Dottie herself had made the decision. The house was too big—too full of bad memories. Here she had a social life, meals served three times a day, and elegant surroundings. The community not only had the retirement inn, but an assisted care facility and a nursing home. She seemed to be thriving.

While Dottie used the bathroom, Mac paged Kevin and got a call back seconds later.

"Hey Mac—what's going on? You miss me?"

Mac chuckled. "No way." Mac relayed the conversation he'd had with his grandmother.

"Hey, I'm impressed."

"Anyway, since I'm here, I thought I'd check with the supervisor and see if I can get his personnel records."

"You can try, bud. With your looks you might be able to charm your way around, but I doubt they'll release anything. Tomorrow we can get a grand jury subpoena for the employee records and start tracking the guy down."

"Sounds good. I'll let you know if I turn up anything."

Dottie came back out to the sitting room just as Mac hung up. They visited for about half an hour before Mac told her he had to go see what he could find out about Matthew. She seemed pleased about that and for the first time in a long while didn't urge him to stay.

He tracked down the evening shift supervisor, Annie Jenkins, and talked to her about Megan. Annie, a redhead in her forties, claimed she didn't know Megan personally but said the residents thought highly of her. "I'm sorry we had to lose her."

"My grandmother tells me I should check out a guy named Matthew DeLong."

Annie rolled her eyes and shook her head. "I've heard the rumor about Matthew possibly being responsible. I wouldn't put too much stock in that. Old people don't have a lot to do, so they make up stories."

"Just the same, if he showed interest in Megan we should at least talk to him. Could you give me his address and phone number?"

"Not a chance." Annie slipped her glasses down on her nose and peered over them. "Our personnel records are confidential and I'm really not in a position to give them out."

Mac didn't argue. He could get the information from other sources.

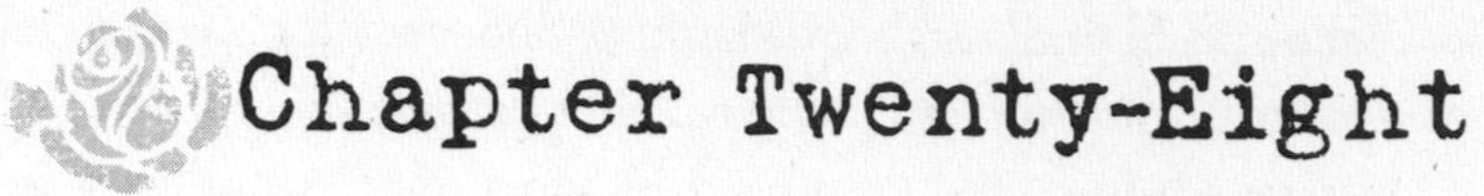

Chapter Twenty-Eight

Monday, August 26
7:20 A.M.

When Mac arrived at the Troutdale Police Department, Kevin and Eric were already in the briefing room, talking to a tall brunette in a suit jacket, soft pink blouse, and slacks. She slipped off her jacket, revealing a weapon in a leather holster on her belt at the small of her back. She had an exotic, multiethnic look about her—maybe Asian, Polynesian, and African American.

"Morning, Mac," Eric lifted his coffee cup in a salute. "Have you met Detective Thomas?"

"No." Mac stretched out his hand. "Nice to meet you, Detective."

"Melissa." She tossed him a crooked smile. "I'm a polygraph examiner from the Salem office."

"Oh, right."

"Eric and Kevin were just going over the details with me. I think we're set for the first one anyway." She glanced at Kevin, who nodded in the affirmative. "I'll get set up." Melissa gestured to the empty office adjoining the briefing room. "Is this office okay?"

"Yeah," Eric replied. "We reserved it for you all day."

Melissa picked up a large black plastic case and left the room.

"Have a good night's sleep, Mac?" Kevin asked.

"Not really."

"I hear you. Five o'clock came early this morning. I was searching for an excuse not to put on the old running shoes today, but . . ."

"You went running?" Mac asked.

"Don't look so surprised. Been doing six miles, four times a week for nearly thirty years."

"Wow. I'm impressed." Mac hadn't been keeping up with his exercise regimen and felt a stab of guilt.

"You mean, goody two shoes for you." Eric chuckled at his own joke.

Kevin shook his head. "Use it or lose it." He turned to Mac. "Why don't you tell Eric what you uncovered last night?"

Mac cleared his throat, eager to share his information. "I went to visit my grandmother after work and ended up getting some potentially valuable information on our case."

"What's that?" Eric asked."

"You're not going to believe this." Mac went on to tell them about Matthew DeLong and how he'd gotten nowhere with the evening supervisor. After talking to Annie, Mac had gone back to get a description from Dottie and had ended up with a photo taken at a resident's birthday party showing Matthew serving cake to the birthday girl. Mac set his briefcase on the table and, after opening it, took out a new folder he'd labeled DeLong.

Kevin looked pleased.

Eric shook his head and in a sarcastic tone said, "Good work, Mac—all we need is another lead. You sure you can trust the residents?"

Mac bit back a sharp retort. Was Eric implying that Dottie couldn't be trusted? "Yeah. Even if it's a rumor, like the supervisor seemed to think, we can't afford to pass this one up."

"And you are so right." Kevin headed for the break room. "I could go for a cup of joe."

Mac and Eric followed, each filling their disposable cups with coffee.

"Kevin," Mac said, "when we spoke last night, you mentioned getting a subpoena for DeLong's employee records . . ."

"I'll take care of that, Mac," Eric said. "Nice work. Tell Dottie I said hello next time you see her."

Mac nodded. "Is Gordon coming in this morning?"

Kevin shrugged. "He didn't call to say he wasn't."

Moments later, a code enforcement officer from the P.D. stuck his head in the break room. "Any of you guys with the state police?"

"We all are." Eric took a sip of coffee. "Can I help you with something?"

"There's a guy named Gordon Reed out front. Says he's here to see the detectives he talked to yesterday."

"He showed up. How about that?" Kevin looked at his watch. "He made the appointment with time to spare." To the officer he said, "Thanks, we'll go down and meet him."

Kevin walked around the corner to the office where Melissa had set up the polygraph machine. "Mr. Reed is here a little early. Are you ready to proceed with the exam?"

"Ready to go." She plugged a cord into the back of her laptop computer. "Bring him on in."

"It might be a few minutes. The last time we talked to him, he was dragging his heels. I think we can convince him, though."

Kevin gave a thumbs-up sign. Mac jogged down the stairs to the ground floor then opened the door leading to the parking lot. Gordon Reed was standing by the door, smoking a cigarette. He had cleaned up pretty well and was wearing a pair of jeans and a polo shirt. Without the soot, he actually looked pretty normal. The knife was gone. Mac wondered if the guy had talked to a lawyer and gotten some advice.

"Hello, Mr. Reed." Mac shook his hand. "I'm glad you could make it."

"I tried to get in through the front door, but it was locked." Gordon blew out puffs of smoke as he talked, then took another drag before dropping the butt on the asphalt and grinding it in with his tennis shoe. "Hope you're not planning to write me a ticket for that."

"I'll let it slide this time. Sorry you had to wait. The office here doesn't open up until eight o'clock. You're a little early but that's fine."

"I just wanted to get this over with."

"The polygraph?"

"That's what you wanted me to come for, right?"

"Right." Mac led him up the stairs. "Come on up, Gordon; she's all set up for you."

"She?" Gordon glanced back at Mac as they ascended the stairs. "You mean a broad is going to do this thing?"

"Detective Thomas will administer the test. She's a licensed polygraph examiner. Not just anyone can run those things. It takes quite a bit of advanced training."

"Cool."

Mac introduced Gordon to Eric, and within a few minutes they had introduced him to Melissa and seated him in the small office where Melissa had set up her equipment. Although Mac had arranged numerous polygraph tests during his tenure in the child abuse unit, he had never actually sat in during an exam. He was especially curious about Gordon, however, so he asked if he could observe. Neither Gordon nor Melissa had an objection, so after Kevin excused himself, Mac picked a spot in the back and leaned against the wall.

"Have you ever taken a polygraph examination, Gordon?"

"No." His gaze drifted over the unit. "I remember seeing it on television, though. Some dude was hooked up to a machine with wires and another machine that looked like the kind they use to measure earthquakes."

"They used to be like that. We don't use as many electrodes. I just place a few on your arms and put this strap around your chest." Melissa held up three wires. "These lead from my laptop to some very sensitive devices. When I ask you questions, these devices measure physical responses like your heart rate, breathing, and other biorhythms."

"Whatever." Gordon glanced at Mac then back to Melissa.

"Before we start, I need to clarify something with you. I understand you have not been charged with any crime and you are here today on your own free will."

"Yeah, I guess so. I don't think these guys will leave me alone until I take the thing, so I decided to get it over with."

"You realize that you don't have to go through with the exam."

Gordon held his hands up in mock surrender. "I got it. I'm here on my own free will. Let's get on with this. I have to get to work."

Melissa scratched some notes on her legal pad. "All right then. I know you are not in custody, but I always advise test subjects of their Miranda warning before I administer the test."

Gordon nodded.

"It is my duty as a police officer to inform you of the following," Melissa read from a prepared form. "You have the right to remain silent. Anything you say can and will be used against you in a court of law. You have the right to talk to an attorney before any questioning if you wish. If you cannot afford to hire an attorney, one will be appointed to you without any cost, if you wish. Do you understand these rights I have explained to you?" Melissa looked up at Gordon, who nodded his head in the affirmative.

"I need a verbal response for my record, Gordon."

He sighed. "Yes, I understand my rights."

"Having these rights in mind, do you still wish to proceed with the polygraph examination?"

"Yes," Gordon answered.

Melissa wrote his verbatim response on the form. "Please sign the form to acknowledge you understood your rights and waive them at this time." She turned the form around and handed a pen to Gordon, who signed and dated it.

"Before I hook you up, I want to ask a few more questions. Have you taken any unlawful narcotics or alcohol in the past twenty-four hours?"

"No."

"How about any prescription medication?"

"I take Paxil twice a day."

"What's the Paxil for and what is the dose?"

"My shrink has me on ten milligrams a day."

"And the reason for the medication?" Melissa asked again.

"Doc says I have recurrent major depression with schizoid traits." Gordon grimaced. "I think it's bull, if you ask me. I'm not supposed to drink alcohol, which is just plain stupid."

You're the one who's stupid. Mac bit his lower lip to keep from showing his disgust. And what was this Paxil business? Gordon had told them he was on Zoloft. Mac wondered if Eric had sent a crew out to Gordon's place and what they'd find.

"Have you been taking your medication on a regular basis?" Melissa asked.

Gordon shifted uncomfortably. "Why is this so important?"

"Because certain medications and drugs could affect the examination. I have to document the use of substances before the test is administered."

Gordon picked something off his jeans. "I've been pretty good about it the last few days."

Melissa wrote some additional notes on her tablet then removed a loose sheet from the back of a binder. "These are the three relevant questions the detectives would like me to ask you, Gordon. They are the questions I will be scoring you on, or actually the computer will. I'll ask you baseline questions, which I assume will get truthful answers, before asking you these relevant questions for scoring."

She handed Gordon the questions.

"You mean I get to see them first?"

"It isn't a pop quiz." She smiled. "Look them over and tell me if you object to any of them."

Melissa studied Gordon for an initial reaction while he looked them over. "I'm okay with them." He handed the paper back to Melissa.

She then attached the sensitive equipment to Gordon's right wrist and index finger with one wire. She attached a second wire to a Velcro harness around his left bicep. A third measuring instrument was wrapped around his chest to measure his breaths. "These aren't made for comfort," Melissa said with a slight grin as she secured the wires.

"No kidding. I feel like I'm in the electric chair already."

"Okay, we'll begin with the baseline questions first. What is your name?" She posed her fingers above her laptop and typed as he answered.

"Gordon Dean Reed."

"In what month were you born?"

"June." Gordon straightened, looking more uncomfortable.

"Good. Here's a relevant question. Do you know the whereabouts of Megan Tyson's engagement ring?"

"No, I don't." He licked his lips and glanced furtively at Mac.

"Do you know how Megan Tyson died?"

"No."

Mac watched the screen while the machine measured Gordon's bodily functions on a colored chart. "Now, the last relevant: Did you kill Megan Tyson?"

"No way, lady. I didn't hurt her." Gordon's Adam's apple shifted up and down as he looked at the machine then at Melissa.

"All right. Here are a couple more baseline questions. What is your mother's first name?"

"Margaret."

She asked a couple more family questions, then said, "You did fine, Gordon. I'm going to repeat those questions twice more before scoring your responses. Are you okay with that?"

"Yeah, go ahead." Gordon examined the fingernails on his left hand.

Melissa asked the same questions twice more in the same order. Once she was finished, she removed the polygraph equipment from Gordon's body. "How do you think you'll score on the test?"

"Okay, I hope. Unless you guys are trying to frame me or something."

"I can assure you, that's not the case. We don't operate that way. It will take awhile for the machine to score your responses. Do you want to use the restroom while I'm completing the test?"

"I could use a smoke." Gordon pulled his cigarettes from his shirt pocket.

"That would be fine." Melissa opened the door.

Kevin was standing in the hall as Gordon, Melissa, and Mac walked out. "All done?"

"I am," Melissa answered. "Mr. Reed is going to take a smoke break if you and Mac don't mind."

"Sure, Gordon, help yourself." Kevin stepped aside to let Gordon by.

He walked straight ahead without making eye contact, placing a cigarette in his mouth as he passed.

"We'll come and get you in a few minutes, Gordon. You can wait in the lobby after your smoke break," Kevin called after him.

When he'd gone, Kevin asked Melissa how it went. "Did you crack him?"

"The poly is still scoring the examination. It takes a few minutes, but it's better than the old days when I had to do it by hand."

"Do you have a gut feeling?" Kevin pushed the wires aside and seated himself in the chair Gordon had just vacated.

"I've got some concerns about the medication he's taking. Gordon is on Paxil, which is an antidepressant medication. His doctor reportedly diagnosed him with major depression and schizoid behavior. You may want to contact his therapist. He was hard to read. Even though he answered the questions in a matter-of-fact way, he never made direct eye contact. Seemed almost paranoid that we were out to get him."

"He told us he was on Zoloft," Mac said.

"He may be on others as well." Kevin acknowledged the comment. "Some of these guys have several different doctors prescribing different drugs. Then you add their recreational drugs and alcohol." Kevin shook his head. "You gotta wonder how they live through it. Of course, some of them don't. By the way, Mac, we have a unit out at Gordon's place as we speak."

Melissa studied the computer screen, which showed a lot of up-and-down lines Mac couldn't decipher. Mac folded his arms, willing himself to breathe normally. Gordon was hiding something. He didn't trust the guy and had a feeling the polygraph would indicate that he'd been lying about Megan.

"Shoot." Melissa frowned and typed something in.

"What?" Kevin stood and bent down to look at the screen.

"The test is inconclusive. That's what I was afraid of. It's probably skewed because of the meds."

"Or the alcohol," Mac muttered. "I'll bet he ignored our advice to lay off."

"What were his scores on the relevant questions?" Kevin squinted at the computer screen.

"As you know, an answer doesn't score a deceptive response unless it's beyond a negative three from the baseline scale on nonrelevant questions. On the flip side, an answer doesn't score a truthful response unless it's beyond a positive three from the baseline. Gordon's answers to the relevant questions are all positive ones or twos. No, wait. He actually had a dip below the baseline on one of the relevant questions, but nowhere near the area where I would rule it a deceptive response."

"Should we run the test again?" Mac asked.

"No, that would be a waste of time. A personality disorder coupled with high-powered medication would probably give us the same result time after time. His responses are leaning toward truthful, if I had to make a professional guess on his chart in addition to his demeanor when asked the questions. I'm still going to reflect the test as an inconclusive examination for reporting purposes."

Kevin straightened. "Well, thanks for trying."

"Sure. I wish we could be more precise sometimes."

"Can I get you some coffee or tea?"

Melissa rubbed the back of her neck. "No thanks. I'll get my own—I need to stretch a bit before the next victim comes in."

Kevin and Eric headed back into the briefing room. Eric glanced up at them. "How did it go?"

"Inconclusive," Kevin answered.

"What now?" Mac asked. "We can't just let the guy go."

"We won't, believe me." To Eric he said, "Mac and I are going to have a talk with Mr. Reed while we still have him—if we still have him." He frowned. "Did we turn up anything on the search of Reed's premises?"

"No surprises so far," Eric said. "The place is pretty seedy and there's a stash of marijuana. We'll have the narcotics unit deal with him on that. I'm told he has an interesting array of prescription medications as well."

"I'll bet." Kevin nodded. "Do me a favor, would you, Eric? See if you can contact Megan's sister, Cindy. I'd like to have her take the box."

"Sure, pal."

"Have Philly and Russ checked in yet?"

"They called. They're on their way out to pick up Brandon King."

"Good."

Melissa walked in with a cup of coffee in one hand and a folder in the other. "Here's a printout of the test. I'll get the complete report to you tomorrow."

Eric took it from her. "Thanks."

"Now, brief me about the other subjects we have coming in." She settled into a chair and crossed one slender leg over the other.

Kevin went through the list and added, "We can keep the questions basically the same with the rest of the folks we parade in here today." Turning to Mac, he said, "Let's get Reed; he's probably making the front desk receptionist a little nervous by now."

Chapter Twenty-Nine

Gordon Reed was waiting in the lobby, reading the sports section of the paper.

"You want to come up and have a chat, Gordon?" Kevin asked.

"Do I have a choice?" Gordon folded the newspaper over in his hands.

"Of course," Kevin said.

"Well then, I'd just love to." He dropped the newspaper on the seat beside him and slowly got to his feet.

The detectives led him back upstairs and into an unused office. Kevin flipped on the lights and offered Gordon a seat near the door. Mac sat down behind the desk while Kevin slid a third chair up within inches of the guy's knees.

Obviously disturbed by Kevin's closeness, Gordon leaned back in his chair and placed his hands on his thighs.

"So, what did you think of the test, Gordon?" Kevin moved even closer.

"I don't know. Okay I guess." His gaze darted to the door, then over to Mac, then to his hands.

"Gordon, you've been telling us that you had nothing to do Megan's death. What if I said I didn't believe you?"

Gordon made a squeaky sound. "Why don't you guys believe me? I talked to you. I came in and took the test." He looked at the door, panic rising in his eyes. "What did that test say?"

"What do you think the test said?"

"I don't know, but I told the truth. Why don't you believe me?" Gordon slumped in the chair.

Kevin moved even closer. "I didn't exactly say I didn't believe you. I was just wondering what you would say if I said that I didn't believe you. I'll say it straight out this time, Gordon."

Kevin placed both of his big hands on Gordon's shoulders. When Gordon finally raised his gaze to meet his, Kevin asked, "Did you kill Megan?"

"No!" Gordon pushed Kevin's hands away and looked toward the door again, tears welling up in his eyes. "I knew this was going to be a setup. You guys can't keep me here."

"You were jealous because Megan had a new boyfriend and was getting married. Isn't that right?" Kevin placed his hands on the guy's narrow shoulders again.

"No. You got it all wrong. We were just . . ." He batted at a tear rolling down his cheek.

"You can tell me how it was, Gordon." Kevin persisted. "I know what it's like to have a gal come on to you and then drop you just like that. She was a flirt, wasn't she? And she led you on, right?"

He sniffed. "Well, yeah, but . . . a guy doesn't kill a girl for something like that."

"What would cause a guy to kill a girl, then?"

"I don't know." Gordon's tears had evaporated, and anger replaced the fearful look in his eyes. "Look, I liked the broad a lot. She screwed around with my heart, but I didn't kill her." Gordon shrugged off Kevin's hands. "Now back off and don't ask me that stuff again. I didn't kill her."

Kevin slid back on the wheels of his chair. "Okay, Mr. Reed, settle down."

Gordon leaned back in his chair, glaring at Kevin.

Unfazed by Gordon's response, Kevin leveled a steady gaze on him. "Where were you the night of Tuesday, August thirteenth?"

Gordon groaned. "Man, I can't remember that far back. Probably at Murphy's Tavern with the guys from work. Like I told you, several of us go there after our shift."

Kevin made a mental note to have Russ and Philly check Gordon's alibi. Hopefully one of the construction workers would remember whether Gordon was at the bar that night—or not.

"Are you going to tell me how that stupid test went or what?" Gordon said. "If it said I was a liar, then it's more screwed up than the two of you."

"The test was actually inconclusive, Gordon, probably because of the medication you're taking."

"Well, I told the truth. I don't know what else I can say." Gordon sat up straighter in the chair. "I knew you were trying to frame me. Do I need to call a lawyer?"

"Maybe you need a lawyer; I don't know, Gordon. As to framing you, we wouldn't do that. We're just asking the questions that need to be asked. You had intimate contact with the victim within a day or two of her death. You had your emotions rejected because she chose another man over you. Now, if you were in our shoes, wouldn't you take a hard look at someone like yourself?"

"Yeah, whatever. I . . . I guess so," he stammered. "I just need a break right now. You guys can call me later if you need to. I'll cooperate. I just need a break."

"The door's right there, pal. You are free to go." Kevin moved his sports jacket back and checked his pager, then turned back to Gordon. "We appreciate your coming."

Gordon reached for his cigarettes as he walked out of the room.

"See him out, will you, Mac? I need to make a call."

After making sure Gordon had left the building, Mac made his way back to the room where they'd questioned him.

"Wow. That was quite an interview," Mac said. "I thought the two of you were going to be sharing the same chair."

Kevin nodded. "I intentionally pushed him. He's wound up

pretty tight, so I hoped he'd give in if I pushed hard enough. He actually held up pretty well."

"He did? Didn't you see how he reacted?" Mac couldn't believe Kevin's response.

"You have to remember his mental state, Mac. The guy is on medication and who knows what all. He isn't the most stable person in the world. Not the smartest either. Don't get me wrong. I'm not saying he's innocent. In fact, the personality disorder shot him way up to the top of my list."

Mac reined in his indignation. "I'm glad to hear that. For a minute there, I thought you were losing it."

Kevin smiled. "Uh-huh. Your impatience is showing, Mac . . . and your lack of experience. We'll pay him a visit tomorrow, after the funeral. We still have to make sure we don't get too focused, though. I don't like being in the fourth day of this gig and not having a defined suspect yet. The longer this goes on, the less our chances are of making this case."

"No kidding. And thanks to my grandmother, we've got another person of interest."

"We'll just have to work extra hours." Kevin tipped his head from side to side, rubbing his neck muscles as he headed for the door.

"Kev, just one thing. Do you think we should set up surveillance on Gordon? See where he goes, who he talks to?"

"That sounds like a good plan if we can find the manpower. That reminds me—the page I got during the interview was from Meredith Hoyt. She found a photograph of a guy Megan dated a couple of times. She's working at the health club right now. My inclination is to get that info and hold off on Tim and Matthew DeLong for a bit."

After briefing Eric, Kevin and Mac hurried out to Mac's car and arrived at the athletic club at ten. Meredith greeted them as they came in and motioned for them to go into the same office they'd used the day before. She grabbed a sheet of paper from underneath the counter and stepped into the room.

"If my boss finds out about this it could mean my job, so don't mention it to anybody, please." Meredith brushed her hair back. "I'm only doing this because I really want you to catch whoever killed Megan."

"We understand," Mac said. "What do you have for us?"

"Um . . . like I told you, Detective Bledsoe, I found a picture of a guy Megan seemed chummy with, in the club directory." Meredith handed the computer printout to Mac. "We take a picture of all our clients so they can't loan their membership identification to others. His name is Joe Higgins. He's been a member for about four months. He and Megan joked around a lot, and I think she might have dated him."

Mac held the picture between them so Kevin could see it. He was a decent-looking guy with a square chin and thick neck muscles. Long black hair curled around his face. He had a friendly smile.

"Looks like a football player," Mac commented.

"Actually," Meredith said, "I think I heard him tell one of the other guys that he'd been a wrestler."

"I can see why Megan might be attracted to him," Kevin leaned back in his chair.

"He's an average-looking guy, really. He looks better in the picture than up close. He has some pockmarks on his face from acne or something."

"Do you remember when you last saw him?" Mac asked.

"I ran up his club history, which lists every time he comes in to work out. He came in four or five times a week for the first three months, but he's slacked off in the last month. Joe's last visit was on the eleventh. That's not unusual. People always decline on their club use after the initial membership weeks. Heck, some folks don't come back at all. The last time he came in, he also used a visitor pass."

"Visitor pass?" Kevin glanced at the photo again.

"Yeah, you can bring in visitors if you're a club member. We encourage it to get new club members."

"Any idea who the visitor was?" Kevin asked.

She smiled. "I'm way ahead of you. I found the signature of the guest." She handed them another sheet of paper. "This was the guest list for the eleventh. There are only seven names on it, and five of them were tanning appointments from nonmembers. I crossed those off. Joe usually came in around seven in the evening for his workout, and he had made an appointment with Megan as his personal trainer that night. I'm assuming that the second-to-last name on the list was his guest because of the time of day and because the only other name that wasn't a tanning appointment is the first name on the list, which would have been before eight in the morning." She paused for a breath.

"How do you know that?" Kevin looked over the list.

"Am I good or what?" Meredith grinned. "The tanning appointments helped me zero in on the guest names. So number six here must be Joe's friend. I can't make out the first name, starts with an M, though. Last name is Wallace."

"I agree, looks like M. Wallace." Kevin handed the paper to Mac. "Can we keep these? They may come in handy later."

"Sure, I made copies. Just don't tell anyone."

Kevin nodded. "Thanks for your help. We'll let you know if we turn anything up on this information. We're talking to quite a few folks right now."

"I hope you guys catch Megan's killer. I'm afraid of my own shadow lately." Meredith folded her arms. "The other gals and myself walk each other out to the parking lot after work, even in the middle of the day. We're all pretty freaked out."

"That's understandable," Mac said. "We'll do our best. Thanks again, and please call if you think of anything else." The two men showed themselves out.

"Great, another guy to track down." Mac turned the air on full blast and grabbed his sunglasses from the visor. "We can put him on the list with the other hundred or so guys Megan liked to flirt with."

"No kidding," Kevin said, looking at the papers Meredith gave him. "Joe Higgins's address isn't far from here. We may as well drive by on our way back to the P.D. Do you have your Thomas Guide in here somewhere?"

"Under your seat."

Kevin retrieved the map book. "Hmm. I was right. It's not too far. Just go east to 242nd in Gresham and go north a couple of blocks at the most. You know, down by where the old greyhound racetrack was before they turned it into a Home Depot. That'll take us right into Parkview."

Mac shifted the car into gear. "I'm going to need to get some gas sometime this morning. I don't suppose you'd want to take your car."

"Out of the question." Kevin tossed him a smile. "Besides, you need the experience."

"Experience!" Mac shook his head. "I drove over two hundred miles a day as a road troop."

"That's different. This is detective driving," Kevin said with a serious look on his face. "It takes much greater skill."

"Oh, brother." Mac rolled his eyes. Truth was, he didn't mind driving at all.

"Turn here, 242nd. Okay, Parkview should be right up here. There it is—1300."

Mac pulled into the parking lot of the two-story apartment complex, located across the street from a city park. The plain-looking apartments were constructed in an L shape, with open-air parking structures along one of the buildings.

"Looks pretty run-down." Mac's gaze traveled over the faded yellow paint.

"There's apartment fourteen right there, on the ground floor."

Kevin pointed it out and Mac parked in an empty spot under one of the covered parking structures. They walked toward the apartment, noticing the curtains were drawn on the single front window. The door was metal, with brown paint flaking off the bottom half.

Kevin knocked on the door as he removed his identification from his jacket. Both detectives took posts on opposite sides of the door out of habit. Years of training and horror stories had taught them never to stand directly in front of the door when knocking, as that was the usual path a bullet would travel if a suspect opted to answer the knock with gunfire.

Kevin knocked again as Mac kept his gaze trained on the window, looking for a glimpse of movement. "Looks like nobody's home," Mac said.

"Yeah. Let's go hit up the manager and see if he has any information on the tenant."

They walked around the first apartment building to the second, finding the lower-level apartment with a manager sign on the door. Kevin and Mac stepped up to the sliding glass door. "Is this the back door or what?" Kevin asked.

"It's the front," a little girl told them as she came up beside them on her tricycle.

"Thank you." Mac hunkered down beside her. "What's your name?"

"Mary Ross. I'm five."

"Well, hello, Mary Ross. Do you live around here?"

"No, but I stay here with Theresa when my mommy is at work." Mary got off her three-wheeler and ran into the apartment. Moments later a woman in her late forties came to the door carrying a dishtowel in her hands.

"Are you looking to rent an apartment?" She looked them up and down.

"Are you Theresa?" Kevin asked.

"Yes, my husband and I manage the complex. I run a day care too." She nodded her head at two toddlers in a playpen and another child sitting at the table coloring. "These aren't all mine."

Kevin displayed his identification. "I'm Detective Bledsoe and this is Detective McAllister. We're with the Oregon State Police. Do you mind if we ask you a few questions about a tenant?"

"Which one?"

"Could you tell us who lives in apartment number fourteen?"

"No one now. It's been empty for about a week. A guy named Joe Higgins lived there for about two years. He said he needed a bigger place."

"Do you know where he moved to?"

"No, I don't. My husband usually deals with the tenants, so I didn't know him that well. I can get you a copy of the rental agreement if you think it might help. Um . . . not today, though. Would tomorrow be okay?"

"That would be great." Kevin handed her his card. "Give me a call when you have it and we'll swing back by. Do you know if Mr. Higgins had any roommates or if he was married?"

"I don't think so. I'll have to ask Bernie. Fourteen is just a one bedroom, so there's not much space. Like I said, he told us he was moving to a bigger place. Is he in some kind of trouble or something?"

"No," Kevin replied. "We're just looking to talk to him to see if he could help us out with a case we're working."

"Oh, that's good. He seemed like a nice enough guy. I'll get that file when Bernie comes home and I can shed some kids."

"That would be fine, ma'am. You have a good day," Kevin said.

He and Mac walked back toward their car. "Let's give Tim Morris a call at the hotel. Maybe we can swing by and pick him up on the way to the P.D."

Mac was beginning to feel like a ricocheting bullet the way they were popping from one place to another. "Mind if we stop for gas and a coffee first? I could really use a latte."

"Lead on, partner. A cup of coffee sounds mighty fine." Kevin made the call to Tim as they drove. A moment later, he folded the phone and settled it into his pocket.

"What's wrong?"

"Maybe nothing. Maybe a lot. Tim checked out of his hotel room this morning."

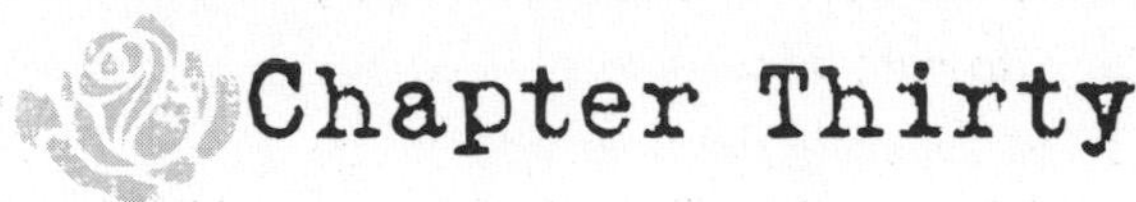

Chapter Thirty

"Do you think the fiancé skipped?" Mac turned onto the main road and pulled into a gas station. He rolled the window down and told the attendant to fill it up.

"I don't know what to think. I doubt he'd leave before the funeral unless he killed her and thought we were on to him."

"The guy could be on his way to Mexico by now."

"True, but let's not jump to conclusions. I better give Eric a call." Kevin picked up his phone again and dialed the number to the P.D.

Eric answered the phone almost immediately.

"Hi, it's Kevin."

"Hey, fatty, what's shaking? You guys heading in?"

"Shortly. I just called the fiancé and found out he's checked out of the hotel. That raises a red flag."

"Not to worry, pal. Tim called just after you left. Said he'd be in around noon if that was okay. I told him it was."

"Hmm." Kevin frowned. "Wonder what he's up to? Well, if he's coming in, I won't worry just yet."

"Did you find out anything at the health club?"

Kevin reported their visit with Meredith and the subsequent visit to the vacant apartment. "So far, just another guy to talk to, nothing hair raising. Say, did Philly and Russ get hold of Brandon King for the polygraph?"

"He's in the hot seat as we speak. Philly went by his apartment and got him out of bed."

"Ouch." Kevin grimaced. "How'd you like to wake up and see old fabulous Philly's face staring down at you?"

"Yeah. Waking up to Philly would give anyone a scare. Probably will give the kid nightmares for years to come."

Philly spewed a verbal response in the background that made Kevin's hair curl.

"Philly says good morning to you and Mac," Eric translated.

"I heard."

"Mac and I are going to grab a cup of coffee on the way back; you want to join us for a break?" Kevin glanced at Mac and pointed to the Starbucks on the opposite corner.

Mac gave a thumbs-up. After taking his gas receipt, he twisted the key, revved up the engine, and took off.

"No thanks, I'll meet you another time," Eric answered. "I'm already on my second pot here so I'm off the java for the rest of the day. Besides, I want to hang out here until the poly exams are done."

"Sounds like a winner." Kevin glanced at his watch. "Give me a call if the kid flunks the test. I want to conduct the postexam interview."

"Will do," Eric said.

Kevin tossed the phone back into his briefcase. "This one is on me. I feel like a frou-frou drink this morning."

"A frou what?" Mac laughed.

"You know, one of those espresso things—like a latte or a mocha. A frou-frou, touchy-feely drink. The ones that run about three or four bucks a pop."

"Oh, *those* fooh-fooh drinks." Mac pulled into the parking lot and grabbed his briefcase out of the back, thinking he might take a look at the notes. They had too many leads they hadn't even made contact with.

Kevin opened his case and grabbed something out of it before joining Mac in the coffee shop. At the counter he read through the offerings and reached for his wallet. "What are you having?"

"I'll have a latte with a bagel." Mac reached for his wallet as well. "But let me get it."

Kevin elbowed him out of the way. "Would you relax for the first time in your life and go sit down? I said I'm buying. Here, take this and go grab the comfy chairs."

"Okay, suit yourself, moneybags." Mac took the book Kevin handed him. "In that case, I'll have a grande mocha and don't hold back on the whipped cream."

"Yeah, yeah."

Mac sat down in one of the cushioned chairs and set Kevin's book on the table. When he realized what it was, he slid it down beside him, as if he was somehow breaking a rule by merely possessing a Bible in public. After a few seconds, he lifted the top cover and started reading the names of various chapters. He was surprised at how many he remembered. As a kid he'd memorized all the books and a lot of passages.

"You ought to get one this size."

Startled, Mac shut the Bible and glanced around. His gaze landed on a man dressed in a flannel shirt and jeans at the next table.

"What was that?" Mac asked. "Were you talking to me?"

The burly man held up a navy blue book no bigger than his palm. "I said you ought to get one this size. These pocket Bibles are a lot easier to pack around. I only carry my big one like that when I go to church."

"Oh, yeah. That's a handy size."

The guy stood up, tucked his hard hat under his arm, and gave Mac a wave as he left. Mac picked up the Bible again and turned it. He liked the feel of the soft leather against his skin. And strangely enough, he liked the way holding it made him feel. Mac set the book on the table. The sensation had been nothing more than a visit to his boyhood when reading the Bible had been his comfort just before he turned off the light and went to sleep.

"A mocha and a bagel for his highness." Kevin set the items down on the table that separated the two easy chairs and eased into his chair with coffee in hand.

"Thanks." Mac took a sip of his mocha then set it on the table so he could scarf down a few bites of bagel and cream cheese. Until this moment, he hadn't realized how hungry he was.

"Don't mention it. So tell me, how are you and Linda doing?"

Mac shrugged, mentally kicking himself. He'd been so focused on the case, he hadn't even thought about calling her last night. "Um . . . okay I guess."

"Are you sure you really love this girl?"

"Sure. She's beautiful and kind. And I think it's about time I settle down and start raising a family. I'm not getting any younger."

Kevin looked like he was about to say something but instead took a drink.

Mac had the distinct feeling that Kevin didn't think too much of his answer. Not surprising—Mac hadn't liked it either. He took advantage of the uncomfortable silence to change the subject. "So how's your family?"

"Good. I'll be marrying off my oldest later this year."

"Great, congratulations." Mac raised his coffee as if to toast the occasion.

"Thanks. Jean and I are really excited. She's marrying a good man who loves her and shares her faith. And most important, he loves and fears her dad." Kevin grinned. "Yes sir, it's really rewarding to raise your children with the best intentions and have them turn out all right. I just can't believe my baby is getting married. It seems like yesterday we were picking out baby things and trying to decide on a name."

Kevin teared up and Mac, not knowing how to respond, changed the subject again. "Good mocha. Mine's just right."

"Yeah, not a bad cup of joe." Kevin cleared his throat. "Mac, I know it's none of my business, but I'm not hearing the kinds of things I'd expect from a man in love and soon to be married. I'm not saying you should or shouldn't marry this girl, but I am suggesting you ask God about it. Ask Him to clarify things in your own mind. God will let you know if she's the right girl for you."

Mac frowned. "How can I know what the right answer is? When I'm with her I feel like I'm on the right track, but then I get involved in stuff at work and forget she's even around."

"Only you can answer that, Mac. For starters, I'd suggest you start going to church. You could come with Jean and me out to Good Shepherd Church in east county. We have a couple of great pastors and—"

Mac held up his hand. "Not a good idea. Linda has been bugging me to go to church with her since we started dating. If I go at all, it would have to be with her."

"That's fine. It really doesn't matter where you go so long as you go. But even more important than going to church is developing your relationship with God."

"I'll think about it." Mac wasn't about to argue with his boss. He'd play his noncommittal role—neither agreeing nor disagreeing.

"Well, I get the feeling God is chasing your sorry behind. Why He would want you, I have no idea." Kevin chuckled as he gathered his empty cup and paper plate. "Let's get back to work, partner. I'm anxious to see how our purse snatcher did on the poly."

They arrived at the Troutdale P.D. just after eleven o'clock. Mac pulled into the crowded parking lot.

"Over there, Mac." Kevin pointed to a shady spot under a tree.

"Great, must be my lucky day." Mac backed into the parking spot. After a short walk across the parking lot, they jogged up the stairs and entered the briefing room, where Eric and Melissa were eating lunch from a nearby takeout.

"She just got done with Brandon King." Eric tore open a packet of ranch dressing and drizzled it over his salad.

"How did Mr. King do?" Kevin slipped into one of the empty chairs.

"Passed with flying colors." Melissa set down her sandwich and reached for her drink. "Positive sixes and sevens on all the questions."

"Philly and Russ just cleared out about a half-hour ago," Eric said. "They're taking him to the campsite on Oxbow Mountain—hopefully the diamonds are still in the ashes somewhere. Our check with the main office turned up nothing, so let's hope another camper hasn't pocketed it. After they check out the bonfire site, they're going to take Brandon back to work and chat with a few more of the kids. Looks like their stories are checking out, though. Brandon used the gas card once after he lifted the purse, then tried to use the original ATM card with no success."

"What was your feeling on him, Melissa?" Kevin asked.

"I got good vibes. I'm going to write this one up as a truthful exam. I don't think he's your man."

"Well, let's keep running them through. I'd like to get the other guys we've learned about in here too. Not sure that's going to happen today, though. We have Tim Morris and hopefully Cindy Tyson." Kevin glanced over at Eric. "By the way, did you get hold of her?"

Eric shook his head. "She has classes all day today."

"Okay then. Tim Morris will be here soon. He's a long shot, but let's run him through the box and see how he shakes out."

"The same base questions?" Melissa stood up and dusted a few crumbs off her lap.

"Yeah, the same ones. Let's see if he has any knowledge regarding Megan's stolen property or her death."

"I need a few moments to boot up the laptop. I'll be ready by the time he gets here."

Mac checked his watch. "Hey, Kev, if you don't mind, I think I'll run over to the deli and pick up something. That bagel didn't quite do it for me."

"Sure. Bring me a roast beef on rye—everything on it."

"Right." Mac took off and several minutes later, with a bag of sandwiches and some drinks, headed back through the main entrance. Tim held the door open for him.

"Thanks."

"No problem." Tim was dressed more formally this morning, wearing a dress shirt, open at the neck, and dark suit pants. "I'm a little early."

"Glad you could make it. Why don't you have a seat while I go upstairs and make sure the polygraph examiner is ready for you."

"Sure. Are there any new developments?"

"Just a couple more leads to follow up on. Nothing substantial."

"So you still want me to submit to the polygraph?"

"If you're still willing."

"I spoke with my attorney this morning. He still recommends I refuse to take it. But I told him I had nothing to hide and wanted to get on with the investigation so there was absolutely no doubt."

"That's great, Mr. Morris. Now, if you'll excuse me, I'll run upstairs and let the examiner know you're here."

Mac wanted to ask Tim why he had checked out of his hotel but thought it better to wait until Kevin was there. The last thing Mac wanted to do was to bungle things with this guy.

Mac hurried into the briefing room and deposited the lunches. "Tim is downstairs. I ran into him on my way in. He wanted to impress on me how cooperative he's being. Brought up the fact that his lawyer didn't want him to take the test. I thought that was a bit weird."

Melissa popped in to say she was ready.

Kevin went downstairs to usher Tim up to the polygraph exam

room. In the hallway, Mac heard Kevin asking Tim if he wanted coffee.

"Thank you, but no," Tim replied. "My stomach is a bit upset this morning. I've been up most of the night."

"I'm sorry to hear that," Kevin said. "Are you sick?"

"Just upset, I think. Stressed."

"I can certainly understand that." Kevin showed Tim to the small room and asked him to take a seat, then he introduced Tim to Detective Thomas.

"Thanks, Kevin, I'll take it from here." Melissa began the paperwork while Kevin closed the door and stepped into the hall, nearly bumping into Mac. "Did you want to observe this one?"

"Um . . . no, that's okay. I don't imagine it'll be much different than the one she did with Gordon. It would be interesting to watch his face during the responses, though."

"Melissa is good. She'll give it to us straight. Besides, we've got tons to do before we can call it a day, and we should eat that lunch you just bought."

"Oh, yeah." They returned to the briefing room where Eric was finishing up his lunch. Mac pulled his corned beef sandwich out of the bag. He loved those things—probably because once a month Grandma Kathryn would cook up a brisket of corned beef and make sandwiches piled high with the spicy meat and sauerkraut.

"How goes the battle, boys?" Eric leaned back and patted his flat stomach. "Are we making any headway on this caper?"

"Nothing new since we last talked to you." Kevin removed his suit jacket and unwrapped his sandwich. "So far there's only one guy who gets my hackles up and that's our old buddy, Gordon Reed. And he doesn't really get me too excited."

Mac stood back up to take his jacket off as well, checking to make sure his badge wallet was still inside the left pocket before laying it on the table. "Gordon's on top of my list too, but I really want to get to the other guys."

For several minutes, the detectives focused on food. When he'd taken his last bite, Kevin crumpled his napkin.

"I'll make some phone calls and see if we can't set up some interviews," he offered. "Eric, do we have that subpoena yet?"

"Yep. It's all ready for you to pick up."

"Good. We'll try to get to the retirement inn this afternoon."

"While you're doing that, I can plug these names into the computer and see if they have any criminal history," Mac said.

"Good idea." Kevin opened his briefcase and handed Mac the information they'd gotten from Meredith at the health club.

Mac sat down to enter the name into the law enforcement data system terminal in the briefing room.

"Who are you doing first?" Eric asked.

"Joe Higgins."

Kevin picked at his teeth with a toothpick. "Meredith seems to think Megan dated this Higgins guy," he explained to Eric. "He's the one who moved out of his apartment about a week ago. The manager said she'd page us when she got a copy of the rental agreement—hopefully there'll be a forwarding address. I think after Tim is done—"

"Hey, Kevin, Eric," Mac interrupted. "Take a look at this guy's criminal history."

Kevin and Eric walked over to the computer terminal's screen, where Mac was seated. Mac was still typing on the keyboard when they crowded around. "Joe Thomas Higgins was born in Phoenix, Arizona. He's listed as five feet, eleven inches and one hundred ninety pounds, brown eyes. His DMV printout still has him at the Parkview apartment."

"His first name is actually Joe, not Joseph?" Kevin asked.

"According to this, it's just Joe." Mac scrolled back a page. "Here's the big news. Our Mr. Higgins has done some pretty hard time in the federal lockup for manslaughter."

"Really." Kevin placed a hand on Mac's shoulder and leaned closer to the screen. "I wonder why he did federal time for manslaughter? That's usually a state charge. Does it say where the crime was committed?"

"I can't tell." Mac typed additional inquiries. "This thing says 'DOS—Convicted Felony (Manslaughter).' FCI Houston is written in the disposition column. I don't know what all this means."

"I'm on the phone right now," Eric said, reading the 800 number on the face of the computer terminal.

"Well, isn't this interesting." Kevin folded his arms. "FCI means Federal Correctional Institute. There must be one in Houston. This guy must have killed someone during the course of a federal law violation or something."

Eric had reached someone at the 800 number and appeared to be having an interesting conversation with the person on the other end.

"Close, but no cigar," Eric said as he settled the phone into its cradle. "Military. This guy committed manslaughter while in the active military. 'DOS' stands for active duty overseas. That's why Higgins served time in a federal prison. The manslaughter is probably similar to our state charge, recklessly causing a death through some form of negligence."

"If the federal system is anything like ours, then he probably plea-bargained his way down to that charge," Kevin said. "Who knows what he was charged with initially?"

"You're one of those glass-half-empty guys, aren't you?" Eric slapped Kevin on the back.

Mac grinned at the clowns he'd inherited with the department. Turning back to the computer, he clicked on the "print" button. Adrenaline trickled into his bloodstream. Mac wanted to move now. He didn't want to wait for the managers to call. He didn't want to wait, period.

Chapter Thirty-One

Eric rubbed a hand over his carrot-top. "I've got a military contact down in Salem who owes me a favor. I'll see what he can tell me."

"You think everyone owes you a favor, ya big goober." Kevin tossed a crumpled napkin in Eric's direction.

"That's because most everybody does, my old friend, and I stress the word *old.*" Eric was grinning as he left the room to use the phone.

"You see what I have to put up with, Mac?" Kevin frowned, but the corners of his mouth had stretched up into a smile.

"While Eric is checking out Joe Higgins, I'll see if I can get something on the guy from the retirement inn." Mac shifted screens and typed in the name Matthew DeLong. It didn't take long to find a photo match. When DeLong's rap sheet came up Mac released a long low whistle. "I don't believe this. Megan sure knew how to pick 'em. Of course, from what I've heard, she turned this one down." He read through the arrests and conviction list: "Ouch. There's a rape charge in here." Mac read the record aloud:

ARREST#1: 1993—RAPE THIRD DEGREE, P.D.—SALEM DISPO—CONVICTED WITH THREE YEARS PROBATION.

ARREST #2: 1995—CONTRIBUTING TO THE SEXUAL DELINQUENCY OF A MINOR—P.D. SPRINGFIELD—CONVICTED.

ARREST #3: 1996—PUBLIC INDECENCY—SO. MARION COUNTY—CASE DISMISSED.

"Whoa." Kevin shook his head. "What is that retirement inn thinking, hiring a guy like that?"

"Maybe he lied and they were so hard up for help, they didn't bother with references." Mac spoke from experience. He'd seen several questionable employees at Dottie's place.

"Maybe. He's a hot one, for sure."

"You were right, old-timer," Eric said as he returned to the briefing room.

"Of course. What was I right about?" Kevin asked.

"I just got off the phone with my source on that Joe Higgins character. The arrest was made while he was serving in the military. He was a marine, assigned to the First Division as a recon grunt. Apparently Mr. Higgins got into a fight with a fellow crewman over a prostitute about eleven years ago, while they were on shore leave in Japan. They'd both been drinking heavily. Joe stabbed the sailor during the fight and then cut the guy's throat. Higgins was arrested for murder and took a reduced sentence in a plea-bargain that resulted in the nine-year federal prison term in Texas."

"Huh." Kevin rubbed his jaw. "So he was arrested for murder."

"That's the unofficial version. I got a number for the Naval Criminal Investigative Service out of San Diego from my friend. I'll order a copy of all the reports surrounding the arrest and conviction for the case. Higgins was paroled a little over a year ago and tagged with a dishonorable discharge."

"Moved up to the Northwest to start over." Kevin nodded at Mac. "Did you find any arrests on his recent criminal history?"

"Nothing, not even a parking ticket." Mac scanned the pages he'd printed. "Maybe he cleaned up his act."

"Maybe he didn't." Kevin tapped his pen on the report he was working on. "Eric, could you get his social security number off his rap sheet and see if we can track this guy's work activity over the last year?" Kevin got to his feet and began pacing. "I also want his past addresses, credit history, and whatever else you can come up with."

Eric jotted down some notes to himself. "You got it, pal. I'll have it by tomorrow morning."

"Oh, and, look up the number for those apartments we visited this morning. Tell the manager we need a current address now, not later."

Melissa walked into the room. "Do you have a minute? I'd like to go over the results of number three."

"Let me guess: He confessed and all you need is a transport to the jail." Eric looked up from his notepad.

"Sorry. I'm afraid you guys will have to go back to work. Tim passed with flying colors. He scored in excess of a positive ten on all the relevant questions. I'm confident he was truthful on all his answers."

"Is he still in the room?" Mac asked.

"Yes, I already told him the results. He's still sitting in there looking like he has nowhere to go. Looks pretty bummed out."

"He's had a rough go of it." Kevin slipped on his jacket and started for the door. "Let's go and talk to him, Mac—that is, if Melissa is finished."

"He's all yours. I'll gather my gear when you're done with him, unless you have more tests scheduled for today."

"We may, but I don't want to keep you around all day," Eric said. "Philly and Russ are still rounding up some juveniles, and there's still the sister, although she's a low priority and I probably won't be able to reach her for several hours yet."

"I'll be on pager if you need me. I'm only about forty minutes away at my office in Salem."

Kevin and Mac left Melissa and Eric in the briefing room while they walked in the interview room where Tim was still seated.

"Well, I guess I'm not a liar." Tim forced a smile. "But then I knew that all along." He looked up at Kevin, then Mac. "What now?"

"I'm curious about something, Tim. I tried to call you earlier and learned you'd checked out of your hotel room. I have to admit you gave us a few tense moments."

"Thought I'd left town?" He shook his head. "I wouldn't do that. There's no way I'd miss Megan's funeral. I checked out because an opening came up at the Sheraton—that's where I usually stay when I'm here. It's closer to the airport and just all around more convenient. Besides, my other hotel didn't have a pool or weight room." He grabbed a pen and notepad from the desk and jotted down a phone number. "Here's my new hotel number if you need to reach me."

Kevin took the slip of paper and nodded. "Well, Tim, unless you have any questions you're free to go."

"I do have one question. I know you guys said Megan was seeing other men. I just want you to know she was a nice girl. I imagine a lot of guys hit on her—she was so attractive. No matter what you learn or hear from these guys, I want you to remember that." Tears gathered in his eyes and for the first time, Mac saw him as more of a victim than a suspect.

Kevin placed a hand on Tim's shoulder. "No one is claiming the contrary, Tim. I want to reassure you that we're doing everything we can to catch Megan's killer. We won't stop until we do—that's a promise."

"I believe you. It's just that I miss her so much."

"Mac and I are making more contacts today. Why don't you go back to the hotel and get some rest? You look like you could use it."

"Thanks. I'd like to, but I need to meet up with Cindy to make the final arrangements for tomorrow's service."

"Is there anything we could do for you, Tim?"

"No, just remember what I said. Please just remember that."

"We will." Kevin stepped away so Tim could leave. "Just one more thing before you take off. We'll have some officers at Megan's funeral tomorrow. They'll be at a distance with a camera. It's not uncommon for a killer to attend the victim's funeral, and if he shows up we'll have him on film."

Tim stopped in the doorway. "You think he'd dare to show his face . . . ?"

"Stranger things have happened. I just wanted you to be aware of it. We already mentioned it to Cindy."

"Okay, well, maybe I'll see you two there tomorrow. Thanks for all your hard work. I can show myself out." Tim shook their hands and with his shoulders hunched made his way down the stairs.

Kevin and Mac walked back into the briefing room. Kevin snapped his briefcase shut while Mac gathered the papers he'd printed off and handed them to Eric.

"Any luck on that forwarding address on Higgins?" Kevin asked.

"How about 4621 Southwest Macadam Court?" Eric looked pleased with himself. "When I entered his social security number to check his financial history, the system automatically checked the Department of Fish and Wildlife's database and found a good address for Joe Higgins. He purchased a salmon tag less than a week ago and used this address." Eric handed Kevin a Post-it note.

"We're on our way." Kevin grabbed the note from Eric.

"That's his phone number below the address if you want to call first."

"Thanks, but I want to cold tap this guy." Kevin and Mac grabbed their briefcases and turned to leave.

"Hey, Kev," Eric called after them, "I'm going to run all the evidence out of temporary holding here at the P.D. down to our office in Portland. You want anything taken over there?"

"No, the only thing we've tagged recently is the silver chain."

"Yeah, I've got that. Give me a call later and let me know what's going on."

"You've got it, buddy." Kevin and Mac started peeling off their jackets as they crossed the scorching asphalt.

"Hey, Mac." Kevin turned toward him, as if about to ask a serious question. "Do you know where you're going?"

Mac was caught off-guard. "Is this one of those trick questions you Christians ask? I'm supposed to say heaven and if I don't you go into a long spiel about salvation and grace and all that stuff?"

Kevin gave him a perplexed look and said, "No, I just wanted to know if you knew how to get to Macadam Court."

"Oh." Mac imagined red blotches creeping up his neck. "Um . . . yeah. I do. So sit back and enjoy the ride. Make sure your seat belt's fastened; please don't hang your hands outside the window."

"Can't you Gen Xers just answer a simple question?" Kevin laughed, but Mac couldn't tell if it was at his blunder or his smart-mouth comeback.

"We should be there in about twenty minutes." Mac paused. "Do you think we'll catch him at home this time of day?"

"Depends what time he gets home from work, or if he works at all." Kevin popped a cinnamon Altoid into his mouth and offered one to Mac.

They left Troutdale, heading west toward Portland. The greater Portland-Metro area changed from suburb to city with little notice due to the dense population. A sign along the road was usually the only way people had of knowing they'd entered a different town. The sign read Portland, City of Roses. They continued west on I-84, merged onto I-5 south, and at Barbour Boulevard turned onto Southwest Macadam Court.

Kevin checked the number against the houses and apartment buildings and finally told Mac to pull over. "That's got to be it." He pointed to a duplex that looked like it had been built in the early sixties. It had a brick front with white trim and had been well maintained—at least on the outside. "The guy is moving up in the world," Mac said as they pulled into the wide driveway in front of the garage door.

"Hold on a second, partner," Kevin pulled on Mac's jacket sleeve before he could exit the car. "I'd like you take the lead on this interview. Don't forget about that Wallace fellow on the health club roster. Don't let on that we got the information from Meredith; just keep in mind that we might be dealing with two or more guys."

"Got it." They walked up to the door and Mac rang the bell. He stepped back and off to the side, taking his badge wallet from his coat pocket.

Kevin reached over and covered the peephole view with his police notebook. No answer. Mac rang again. His heart thudded in his chest at the thought of conducting the interview himself.

"What do you want?" someone from inside yelled.

"State police, Mr. Higgins," Mac yelled back. "Could we have a word with you?"

"Hold on just a second." Deadbolts turned, and both detectives posed themselves to react swiftly if need be. The door swung in. Joe Higgins was wearing black sweatpants and a plain white T-shirt. His long black hair met his collar, although the top and sides were trimmed short. "What can I do for you?" he asked, still holding onto the doorknob.

"Are you Joe Higgins?" Mac asked.

"Yeah. What's up?"

"I'm Detective Mac McAllister, Oregon State Police." Mac displayed his photo identification. "This is my partner, Detective Kevin Bledsoe. Mind if we come in and talk to you for a few minutes?"

"What's this about?" The smell of onions and spices permeated the room.

"My partner and I are working a murder case and we were hoping you might have some information," Mac said.

"Oh, does this have anything to do with the call I made to your office?"

"What call is that?" The question took Mac by surprise.

"I saw this program on TV—about you guys wanting information on Megan Tyson, so I called. I'm the jeweler she hired to make earrings to match her necklace."

Mac glanced at Kevin, trying not to look too surprised.

"Come on in." He stepped back. "I'm not sure how much help I can be, but you're sure welcome to ask. Excuse the mess. I just moved in a short time ago. But you guys probably already know that."

"No problem," Mac said. "This shouldn't take long. Where'd you move from?"

"Troutdale." Joe moved into the kitchen area. "I was fixing an omelet. That's why it took me so long to get to the door. Can I get you guys something?" he asked while picking up a plate off the counter. "I just made some coffee."

"No thanks," Kevin answered. "Omelet for lunch, huh? Do you work nights or something?"

"Nope," Joe replied with a smile. "I just love eggs." Joe picked up his plate and fork and walked back into the family room, taking a seat in a brown vinyl recliner.

Mac scanned the duplex, which appeared to have two bedrooms. A breakfast bar separated the small kitchen from the family room. The place was strewn about with litter and boxes, partially from the move, but Mac guessed that even in the best circumstances Joe's housekeeping left something to be desired.

"Have a seat, gentlemen." Joe took a bite of his omelet and gestured to the couch. He set his plate on the stained oak coffee table.

As Mac and Kevin seated themselves, Mac noted a stack of *Hustler* magazines under the coffee table. "Hey, thanks for taking the time to talk with us, Joe."

Joe nodded, his mouth full of food. He swallowed and said, "I hope you don't mind if I hurry up and eat this. There's nothing worse than cold eggs."

"Not at all." Mac pulled out his notebook and pen. "Now Joe, we're going to ask you some questions. I want to make it clear you aren't in any trouble and that if you don't want to talk to us, at any time, just say the word and we'll leave."

Joe nodded and kept chewing. "Sounds cool. I got nothing to hide. Ask away."

"As you've already guessed, we're here to talk to you about Megan Tyson. You indicated you knew her?"

"Yes, I did." Joe set the near-empty plate down again. "Not that well, though. Boy, it's terrible what happened to her."

"What did happen to her?" Mac asked.

"Come on guys, you know better than I do." He shrugged. "All I know is what I heard on television. She turned up missing and a little while later someone found her body; that's all I know."

"Can you tell me what you knew about Megan? Anything that might help us with this case?"

He folded his hands and brought them to his chin. "Let's see. I first met Megan when I joined Fitness First. She was a personal trainer there. Mostly she worked mornings, but every once in a while she'd be there in the evening and work out with me. She was a big flirt, but after a while I realized it was all for show."

"And did that bother you?"

"Not at all."

"Did you ever see her outside of the club or date her?"

"No. Not that I wouldn't have taken her out, but it wasn't like that with us. She had a boyfriend."

Mac glanced at Kevin and could almost hear his partner's caution not to push too hard or too fast.

"What kind of work do you do?"

"I'm collecting unemployment right now. The contractor I

worked for went under a few weeks ago—couldn't make the payroll, so I quit. I've got a claim in at the Bureau of Labor and Industries for a retro-check, but I doubt I'll ever see it."

"Construction, huh? Anything else?"

"Yeah, I make jewelry. I do a lot with silver and turquoise stuff—some beads and stones. That's what I was saying earlier. Megan knew about the jewelry business I had going on the side and commissioned me to make a pair of earrings for her to wear at her wedding." Joe pointed to one of the bedrooms. "That's why I moved in here. So I'd have more room to work. In my old place I had to set up in my bedroom and there wasn't much room."

Through the open bedroom door, Mac caught a glimpse of a small desk and chair with a light mounted on the side. There were boxes of beads and tools and wire sitting on the top of the desk and underneath. "Make any money with the jewelry?"

"I don't do too bad. I run a booth down at Portland's Saturday Market. I make enough to pay for the booth and buy a few groceries." He grinned. "Last Saturday I had a woman who runs a gallery in Ashland come by. Wanted to carry some of my stuff. I'm hoping that business will pick up to the point where I can do it full time."

"Anyone live here with you, Joe?" Mac had no idea what direction to take the interview. He seemed nice enough—like a guy trying to get back on track.

He shook his head. "I'm a bachelor. 'Course you can probably tell that. If I had a wife the place would be cleaned up already."

"Have you had any visitors in the last few weeks?"

"None to speak of. I mean, a few friends but no family or anything."

"Got a girlfriend?" Mac asked.

He raised an eyebrow. "There are a few on the line."

"Right. Say, does the name M. Wallace ring a bell?"

Joe's friendly expression faded. He picked up his plate and fork and took them into the kitchen.

Mac's adrenaline kicked in. What was this guy up to? "You brought a fellow named M. Wallace to the health club as a guest," Mac reminded him.

"Oh, Mitch. Yeah, I know him. It took me a minute." Joe grabbed a Pepsi out of the refrigerator and popped the top. "Did you guys talk to him too?"

"We've been talking to a lot of people. This Mitch guy, how old is he?"

"Early forties maybe."

"Where does he live?"

Joe came back in and sat down. "Right now he's in the State Pen. Got picked up on a warrant a couple weeks ago."

"What kind of warrant? How come he's in prison and not at County?"

"I don't know for sure. I thought he was free and clear from the joint, but I guess he still owed some time or something. The cop said he had an abscond warrant out of Washington. I guess he wasn't supposed to be out of state."

"How'd you get to know Mitch, and what was he doing in Oregon with you at the gym?"

Joe shook his head and crossed his arms. "That, my friends, is a long story, but I'm sure you ran me up in your little computer and could put it together."

"You met in prison?" Mac asked.

"Bingo." Joe pointed his index finger at Mac. "I got into some trouble when I was in the marines, a drunken bar fight while I was on leave in Tokyo. It was self-defense; I cut a guy during a fight. My defense lawyer said I could get life, so I took a deal. I went to military lockup for two years, although I got tagged with a rat jacket so they shipped me out to FCI Houston."

"Rat jacket?" Mac asked.

"Yeah. I testified against an army sergeant who ran a shank through the neck of a punk. I cooperated for a reduced sentence."

"I'm not up on my prison lingo, Joe. I know a shank is a makeshift dagger, but what's a 'punk'?"

"Punk," Joe said with a smile as he looked at the ceiling, displaying an unusually large Adam's apple that looked like it was going to tear the skin on his neck. "'Punk' is the term for an inmate who takes on the role of receiver, for lack of a better term. They do it for protection usually, or favors. Punks can be traded or sold, whatever turns you on."

"So a punk is basically a gay sexual partner for the inmates."

"They weren't necessarily gay. Most were straight—at least in the beginning. Let's just say, they weren't always the most willing partners. Anyway, I testified against this sergeant and word got back to the general population in, oh, about two seconds. A jacket is prison slang for, like, your title or something. Since I cooperated with the cops, I wore a rat jacket."

"I see," Mac replied. "So they rolled you up and shipped you off to Texas."

Joe snorted. "Shipped off. That's a good one. When I got to Houston, they put me in with Mitch. We bunked together for several years, until I was paroled a little over a year ago. I thought Mitch had around four years to go when I got out of the joint, but he called me a few weeks ago and told me he's on his way down."

"From Washington?"

"Yeah, man. He said he got an early work release and was coming to visit. He showed up at my place and crashed for a couple of weeks, then *wham!* He gets busted by the cops out in Gladstone. I got pulled over for a burned-out taillight. The guy questioned Mitch because he didn't have his seat belt on. Mitch isn't too bright. He tried to give them a fake name and birthday, but the idiot couldn't figure out how old he was. They took him in. I found out later that he shouldn't have left the state. Like I said, Mitch isn't too bright."

"Were you guys pretty close?"

"I guess. He watched my back and I watched his." Joe shook

his head. "He's not the kind of person I'd hook up with on the outside. I've been trying real hard to stay clean. Regardless of what my records show, I'm not a bad guy."

That's what they all say. "What kinds of things did the two of you do when he was in town?" Mac asked.

"The usual stuff. We partied some, drank, and met a few girls. Most of the time we hung out at the old apartment reading, watching television and movies, and playing video games."

"When was Mitch arrested?"

Joe frowned. "I think it was like the fourteenth or fifteenth. Something like that."

"What was he in for, prior to the escape charge?"

"Bank robbery. That's why he was in the federal joint. The nut tried to take down a federally insured bank. Pretty hard time for the amount of money you get."

Mac looked over at Kevin, signaling for him to take over the interview.

"What kind of rig do you drive?" Kevin asked.

"A real babe magnet." He laughed. "It's a 1990 Ford Escort, that white junker parked out front. She's not pretty, but she gets me from here to there."

"How long have you owned it?" Kevin asked.

"I bought it off my folks when I got out of prison."

"Joe, you said you never associated with Megan outside of the health club, right?"

"That's right." He took a drink from the Pepsi can he'd taken out of the fridge.

"So, there would be no reason your prints would be inside her apartment then?" Kevin rolled his pen between his fingers.

He frowned. "Shouldn't be."

Mac caught the hesitation, and apparently Kevin did as well.

"Let's get one thing straight, Joe." Kevin's voice took on a hard tone. "You don't want to get jammed up on this if you don't have to.

Like I said earlier, we've talked to a lot of folks. Now we have information that says you dated Megan, independent of the gym. If you want to stick with your story, that's fine. But if I find your prints on her belongings, that's not going to look good for you."

Joe stared at the coffee table for several minutes, taking another sip of his drink and swallowing hard. "Okay, you want the truth, I'll give you the truth."

"That would be refreshing," Kevin replied.

Chapter Thirty-Two

I haven't done anything wrong." Joe Higgins's Adam's apple bounced up and down as he swallowed. "But I know how things can be misconstrued. I went down for one incident that wasn't even my fault. I was afraid if you knew I'd gone out with Megan you might try to pin her murder on me." He pinched his lips together. "It was stupid. But it's scary, you know—being involved with somebody who gets killed like that. Megan and I went out once—to a movie and had some drinks. When we got back to her place she asked me in."

"What else happened, and why would you be afraid to tell us about that?"

Joe slumped back in his seat and folded his hands. "It was weird, you know. We started making out a little. I got her blouse off and everything was cool until I sat up to take off my belt. She freaked. Jumped off the couch and covered up, telling me she wasn't that kind of girl. I tried to apologize, but she just asked me to leave. I grabbed my coat and took off. It was a nonevent." He splayed his hands. "That's why I didn't tell you guys the truth in the first place. I figured you'd look at my prison record and I'd go right to the top of the bad guy list. I don't need that right now. I'm clean and making a life for myself. It isn't easy being an ex-con. People aren't real quick to hire you. But I got a chance to make it in the jewelry business."

"Did you force yourself on her?" Kevin asked.

"Like rape? No way. I'm not that hard up. I was mad, sure. Here I spend fifty bucks and she blows me off after she's half-naked. But hey, a woman's got a right to say no and I respect that."

"Did you ever see Megan after that night?"

"Yeah. I saw her at the club and we talked. She acted like the whole thing never happened. I didn't ask her out again, but she still wanted to be friends. A week or so before she disappeared she called me and asked if I'd make the earrings for her. She offered to pay me three hundred bucks and supply the materials and the design. That was more than I would have charged her, but I figured, what the heck. She can afford it. She brought in the stones and I put it all together. Like I told the person I talked to at the police station—I tried to get hold of her sister, but I guess she moved out of their apartment. I was thinking I might go to the funeral tomorrow and give the earrings to Cindy. I don't care about the money. I mean, I do, but it doesn't seem right getting money for them now." He laced his fingers together. "Anyway, I'm sorry I wasn't totally clean with you, but you can understand my dilemma."

"Sure, we understand." Kevin jotted something down in his notebook. "Mac, do you have anything more to add?"

"Just a few things. Can you tell us where you were the night of Tuesday, August thirteenth?"

Joe rubbed his temples. "The thirteenth . . . that's been a while. I can't remember for sure, but Mitch was here then. Like I told you, we mostly hung out at the apartment, so we were probably watching a movie or something."

Mac winced at the thought of Mitch and Joe watching what was surely a pornographic video. He quickly turned his attention to the matter at hand. "Have you ever taken a polygraph examination, Joe?"

"No, and I don't plan on taking one either. I've heard about how unreliable they are."

"Well, I hope you'll reconsider. We'd like to offer you the examination. You may or may not be aware that in Oregon, the polygraph can't be offered as proof of guilt in a criminal trial. It's only a tool we use during the investigation. We've already administered several tests during this investigation. And you might be interested to know you're not the only man to have dated Megan. I'd really like you to consider it."

"I'll think about it." Joe checked his watch. "Um . . . could we hurry this along? I have a couple of job interviews today. Maybe I could get back to you on the polygraph thing."

"Sure, that would be great. Here's my card and my pager number." Mac wrote the number on the back of the card. "Give me a call when you make up your mind."

"I'll do that." Joe walked the detectives to the door.

"It was nice to meet you." Mac reached out to shake Joe's hand when they reached the door. "Thanks again for your cooperation."

On the way to Mac's car, Kevin scribbled down the license plate number of the white Ford Escort parked at the curb.

"What do you make of Mr. Higgins?" Mac asked as he started his car.

"He just claimed the prize as my number one suspect, partner. I've got a feeling about this one. Don't let his friendly attitude fool you; he's not as slick as he thinks."

"He didn't seem very interested in the polygraph either," Mac said.

"I'd be surprised if he came in to take the examination. I'm going to give Eric a quick call. I want to verify that Joe's buddy, Mitch Wallace, is really in the State Pen. If so, I'd like us to start recording his phone calls."

"Good idea. Are we going to talk to Wallace as well?"

"You bet. If he's as dense as his friend claims, he may be the weak link here—providing Joe is guilty. I'd like to hear old Mitch's take on Megan."

"Me too. I'm not sure what to think about Joe. I almost hate to say it, but I'm not with you as far as him being the killer. I don't trust him, but I don't think I'd go with him over Gordon. It's funny how similar his experience with Megan was to Gordon's. Megan led both of them on and then rejected them when they tried to go too far. I guess I'm not ready to give Joe higher billing than Gordon at this point, at least not until we talk to the guy from the retirement inn. He's got a record too."

"Yes, he does, Mac. Thanks for the reminder. We're nowhere near ready to single out anyone. But we do need to put the guys we have under the microscope and see what turns up."

ERIC'S PAGER VIBRATED on his hip as he pulled out of the parking lot of the state police office after having dropped off several evidence items with the property custodian. "Hello there, Kevin," he said out loud as he looked at the number on the pager then hit a speed dial button on his cell phone.

"Ed's Road Kill Café." Kevin answered his cell phone on the first ring.

"Sounds like someplace *you* would eat," Eric replied.

"Look who's talking. Hey, Eric, I got a name I need you to work on."

"Shoot." Eric attempted the awkward task of driving, talking on the phone, and writing at the same time.

"Mitch Wallace." Kevin spelled it out. "Should be a white male adult about forty years old. I need you to check to see if he's a new arrival at the State Penitentiary in Salem. If he's not there, check the Snake River Facility and Pendleton."

"You got it, pal. Had a good interview with this Higgins guy, I take it?"

"I don't want to get too excited, but he's a good one to start learning more about. If you locate this Wallace character, can you run us up a background on him with a complete criminal history? According to Higgins, he was arrested in Gladstone after a traffic stop. I need you to see if it was by one of our troops or one of the other agencies."

"Ten-four. Any thing else I could do for you, like wash your car or chew your food?" Eric tossed the pad and pen on the seat.

"Just page me when you get the info." Kevin ignored the smart remark. "I'd suggest placing a tap on Wallace's inmate identification number and recording his calls if you find him in the system."

"Got it, Kevin. Are you and Mac heading back to Troutdale P.D.?"

"No, we're going back over to Joe's old apartment in Troutdale. I want to get into that place and take a look around. Hopefully the landlord can let us in. Now that Joe has moved out, we don't need his permission to search."

"Sounds good, Kev." Eric checked his rearview mirror and switched into the far left lane on the freeway. "We've got that subpoena for DeLong's records."

"I'm not sure we'll need it, but it's good to have access just in case. Mac was able to get an address, so we'll head over there after we visit Joe's old apartment and try to make contact today."

"Do you ever get tied in knots with all these loose ends?" Mac asked when Kevin finished his call.

"All the time. That's why I write everything down. Then, whenever I can get to them, I write up the reports. I also keep a journal of notes just for myself. I look through them in the morning and pray for guidance." Kevin ran a hand down his face. "This is a tough one, Mac. There were a lot of guys in Megan's life, and any one of them could have killed her. It may have started as a rape and ended up a murder. None of the characters we've talked to admit to actually having sex with Megan—except for her fiancé."

Kevin sighed. "Did you hear what I told Eric about Joe's old apartment?"

"Yeah. I'm heading there now."

"Good," Kevin said. "We'll get written consent to examine the place. I want to see why Joe moved so close to the time Megan disappeared. I'm not falling for the 'needing extra space' line."

Less than twenty minutes later, Mac and Kevin pulled into the parking lot of the apartment complex that Joe Higgins had called home. They swung around back, parking near the manager's apartment.

Theresa came out of the apartment, holding a toddler on her hip. "Hi. I was just going to call you. Bernie's home now; he's over at unit number twelve fixing a problem with the stove. You can go right over."

"Thanks." Mac slid back into the car.

"I'll walk over." Kevin placed his hands on his lower back and stretched. "I can use the exercise."

Mac pulled the car back over to the carport directly across from apartment number fourteen. As he set the brake and put the car in park, he noticed a heavyset man in blue coveralls approaching him from the rear. The man was smoking a cigar and carrying a yellow portable radio.

Mac climbed out and walked back to greet him, reaching him at the same time Kevin did.

"You the cops?" He spoke around the cigar.

"Yes, sir." Mac shook his hand. "Detective Mac McAllister, and this is my partner, Detective Bledsoe. You must be Bernie."

"In the flesh." A wide smile lit up his bearded face. "Theresa called me on the walkie-talkie and said you were here."

"Appreciate you taking the time to talk to us," Kevin said. "We'd like to ask you some questions about the former tenant in apartment fourteen."

"You mean Joe Higgins." Bernie took the cigar out of his mouth and dropped his hand to his side. "To tell the truth, I had to look up the rental agreement to see who the guy was. I couldn't remember much about him. He kept to himself. Theresa said she gave him his deposit back. He left the place spotless when he moved out."

"We'd like to take a look in the apartment if it's okay with you—unless you have it rented to someone else," Kevin said.

"Fine with me. No one is in it right now. I was fixing to change the locks. What are you expecting to find, dope or something?"

"We're not sure," Kevin replied. "Let's just say it's a hunch."

"Suit yourself." Bernie placed the cigar back in his mouth. Mac hadn't noticed until now that the cigar wasn't even lit, just a saliva-soaked pacifier. Maybe the guy was trying to quit.

Mac went back to the car and pulled a consent form out of his briefcase, along with a clipboard. "Bernie," Mac said, moving alongside him, "we'll need to have you sign this search-by-consent form if you don't mind. Since you are the agent of the property owner, your signature will do fine."

"Sure, but I don't have my glasses."

"I could read it to you. It basically saves us from having to obtain a warrant and says we will seize any evidence for the case we are working on."

"I'll take your word for it. I trust you guys." Bernie signed on the line Mac pointed to. "My cousin is a cop down in the bay area. Name's Todd Anderson—ever run into him?"

Neither Mac nor Kevin had. Mac slipped the consent form back into his briefcase then opened his trunk to grab his tool kit, a fishing tackle–type box used for collecting evidence.

"Good guy. I think he's in charge of the SWAT team." Bernie dug a large ring of keys out of his pocket as they walked up to the door. Taking the key he wanted, he let the detectives inside. "It's all yours, gents." Bernie stepped aside, peering inside the apartment as if he expected something to emerge from the shadows.

"Bernie, you there?" Mac recognized Theresa's voice coming out of Bernie's coveralls.

He pulled out his walkie-talkie and answered, "Yeah, what is it?"

"Twenty-two has a problem with the toilet again."

"Tell her to jiggle the handle. I just replaced the float bulb."

"She said she already did that. You better get over there before it floods again."

Bernie rolled his eyes. "It never ends. You guys help yourselves. I'll be over at apartment twenty-two; it appears the sky is falling. Just lock up if you leave before I get back."

After Bernie brushed by them, Mac and Kevin stepped through the doorway. To their immediate left was the small family room with the kitchen directly ahead. Kevin stepped into the family room and pulled open the curtains to allow light to enter the room. A moldy smell permeated the apartment. It had beige-shag carpet and cream-colored linoleum in the kitchen that matched the countertops. A small hallway separated the kitchen and the family room. The single bedroom was to the right of the hall and the bathroom at the end. The same shag carpet covered the bedroom floor.

"He had a king-size bed by the looks of those memory lines on the carpet." Kevin turned on the light in the bedroom. "Maybe even a waterbed." Kevin stood in the middle of the bedroom, staring motionless at the closet area. "Have you got any clues for me?" Kevin asked of the place as he walked from the bedroom into the bathroom.

Kevin looked over the small cramped bathroom. It came equipped with a bathtub-shower combination. He noted the shower curtain was missing, probably an item owned by the tenant due to hygiene issues. Mac followed along behind him. Kevin seemed to be concentrating intensely, so Mac kept quiet and tried to read the place himself.

While Kevin examined the bathroom, Mac went back to the kitchen area and unlocked the sliding glass door that led to a small concrete patio and a shared courtyard. Several cigarette butts littered the bark dust next to the patio. Mac conducted a cursory search of the patio then stepped back into the apartment. He opened what appeared to be a pantry in the kitchen and was surprised to see it opened up into a large closet approximately six feet deep and three feet wide. Mac pulled the string on the single hanging light bulb. No light. "Must be burned out," he muttered to himself. Even without the light Mac could see the bare studs and insulation. He pulled his small flashlight from his jacket pocket to illuminate the room. The wood studs and insulation were covered with a thin layer of dust. Putting on his latex gloves, he knelt on the floor and ran a finger over the smooth concrete as Kevin leaned in.

"Find something?"

"Not really. The floor is so clean you could practically eat off it." Mac lifted his light so Kevin could see the walls. "But the walls look like they belong in a haunted house. Look at those cobwebs."

"The whole place is like that, Mac. Floors are spotless, but not much attention was paid to the walls."

Mac got to his feet. "Judging from the appearance of his new place, I'd say he left this apartment too clean."

"Maybe. On the other hand, he might have just wanted his deposit back." Kevin stepped back into the kitchen. "Hey, let me see your flashlight, Mac. I want to go over the closet in the bedroom—there's a shelf I couldn't quite see."

They walked into the bedroom, with Kevin sliding open the closet door. He stood on his tiptoes to shine the light on the closet shelf. The veins in his neck strained as he peered up on the shelf. "Nothing, clean as a whistle."

Kevin twisted the flashlight beam adjuster. "How do you turn this darn light off?"

Mac took it from him. "There's a button here on the end of the . . . Wait. Hold on." Mac shined the light back on something he thought he'd seen in the corner.

"What are you looking at?"

"I'm not sure. Something caught my eye while I was waving this thing around." Mac illuminated the far right corner of the room, focusing in on a spot just inches from the bed's imprint on the carpet.

They both hunkered down, examining what looked like a dime-sized rust stain. "I didn't see that the first time." Kevin slipped his own gloves out of the pocket of his jacket and put them on. "Good eyes, Mac."

The adrenaline rushed in again. "It's pretty small. I wouldn't have seen it if the light hadn't hit it just right. What do you think it is?"

"Hard to say, but I know who can tell us." Kevin removed his pen from his shirt pocket and probed the small orange stain. "Grab me an evidence bag, Mac, and make sure it's paper. Those plastic ones would degrade the sample. I've got some in my tool kit—and I should have some tweezers and scissors in my first-aid pack that'll make a nice clean cut." Mac was already out the door by the time Kevin finished his sentence.

"Bring in your camera," Kevin yelled after him. "I want to get some pictures of this little beauty."

Mac could hardly conceal his excitement. The dark stain on the carpet looked like dried blood to him, and it might be just the break they were looking for. He returned to the bedroom and took several photos. With every shot his excitement grew.

"Simmer down, Mac. You look like a kid with a straight-A report card. It's best not to get your hopes up. We might have a crucial piece of evidence. But I've been in this business too many years to jump for joy at this stage. There have been too many blood stains that turned out to be juice and too many fingerprints on murder weapons that ended up belonging to the cop who recovered the gun or the knife.

"Why don't you cut the fibers, Mac?" With a gloved hand, Kevin held half a dozen carpet strands. "Cut it as far down as you can. We want to be sure we have the entire thing."

Mac snipped the sample from the carpet with the razor-sharp scissors then held the bag while Kevin dropped the carpet pieces inside.

Kevin grunted as he got to his feet. "Let's finish up here and get this down to Allison Sprague at the crime lab and find out what we have."

"Sure. I found some cigarette butts out on the patio. Thought it might be a good idea to collect those too."

"Good thinking. If there's saliva on them, Allison could probably extract some DNA samples. I didn't notice if Joe smoked, did you?"

Mac stepped out to collect the cigarette butts on the patio with a pair of tweezers. "I didn't see any ashtrays, but he might be an outside smoker."

The two men scanned the remainder of the apartment for clues relating to Megan's death, searching under sinks and behind the refrigerator. After spending nearly an hour surveying the small residence, and finally satisfied they had searched every nook and cranny for additional evidence, they decided to head out.

"Let's get back over to the Troutdale P.D. and see what Eric found out about this Wallace character." Kevin removed the latex gloves, pulling them inside out and stuffing them back into the plastic package they'd come in. "I'll call the lab on the way over and have Allison send a lab rat to collect our sample. I want some answers on this carpet ASAP."

Chapter Thirty-Three

The detectives gathered their gear and started for the car, locking the door to apartment fourteen behind them.

"You fellas all done in there?" Bernie yelled at them from across the parking lot. He came toward them, mopping his brow with a red rag.

"For now," Kevin answered. "Say, Bernie, could I ask you to keep the apartment locked up for a day or two?"

"Sure. Did you find something in there?" Bernie glanced at the package in Kevin's hand.

"We may have. Bernie, I'll be up-front with you. The guy who used to live here is a person of interest in a homicide case we're working. It may be nothing, but we took a couple of samples from the apartment that we want tested by our crime lab. I'd appreciate it if you would keep that to yourself, but I want to convey the importance of leaving that apartment undisturbed."

"Sure. I'll tell Theresa to hold up on showing it to anyone until I hear from you." Bernie tucked the disgusting cigar into the corner of his mouth.

Kevin shook Bernie's hand. "We appreciate your help."

"Sure, sure. I'm cool with that," Bernie said. "You want me to ask around or anything? Maybe one of the tenants saw something . . ."

"No, no. I'd just like you to lie low. I'll call you if we need anything. Like I said, it will be just a day or two."

Mac handed Bernie a business card. "That's my pager number on the back. Give me a jingle if you need anything or have any questions."

"Will do." Bernie placed the business card in the breast pocket of his coveralls.

Once in the car, Kevin phoned Eric to let him know they were on the way.

"Mother Goose, this is Flapjack," Kevin joked when Eric answered the phone. "The eggs are in the basket, over."

Eric chuckled. "When you get done playing espionage, maybe you can get to work and give me a hand with this murder investigation."

"Oh, that. We solved the crime hours ago." Kevin winked at Mac. "What did you find out on Mr. Wallace?"

"Plenty. I was just going to call you," Eric replied. "You want the scoop or are you ladies coming in?"

"Hold off on the info; we're en route. By the way, could you twelve-four the crime lab and have them send out a lab tech to recover some possible trace evidence we collected?"

"Anything good?" Eric asked.

"Might be. Keep your fingers crossed," Kevin replied. "Tell Allison we want to put a rush on it, run it up through a serology workup. She may want to come get it herself; I don't know."

"Okay, I'll call down to the lab. See you in a bit. Philly and Russ are here, so we can brief."

"Have they turned anything up?" Kevin asked.

"Unfortunately, nothing on the campsite search. Brandon took them to the bonfire site, but it's been so long that the ashes have been well scattered by now. And nothing has been turned in at the main office either. Another camper must have spotted the necklace in the ashes and, unlike Brandon, realized that it wasn't just a cheap fake. I hate to have to break the news to Cindy."

"That's a shame," Kevin agreed. "What about the tip line?"

"They've followed up on almost fifty calls. I think they've found Elvis, Bigfoot, and D. B. Cooper, but nothing that would help our case. You know how those tip calls go."

"Speaking of tips," Kevin said, "we just talked to the jeweler who called in."

"When did you manage to work that in?"

"That jeweler was none other than Joe Higgins."

"No kidding."

"Small world, huh?"

"Very."

"See you in a bit." Kevin snapped the cell phone shut.

"Everything going okay?" Mac asked.

"Right as rain," Kevin replied. "The rest of the gang will be there by the time we get to the P.D. Eric found some information on Mitch Wallace, so that should be interesting."

Kevin tipped his head back against the headrest and closed his eyes.

"Getting a little shuteye?" Mac asked.

"Praying," Kevin answered.

Mac didn't respond. What could he say?

He pulled into the parking lot at the Troutdale Police Department, easing into a parking spot near the back entrance. Mac turned off the engine and stared over the steering wheel. "Kevin—before we go in, I just wanted to thank you."

"For praying? You're welcome. I asked God to bring you closer to Him—and I prayed for you and Linda too."

"Um . . . okay." Mac cleared his throat. All this talk about praying was making him nervous. "But I was talking about showing me the ropes and all in this investigation. I mean, I've never been exposed to a case of this magnitude. I appreciate you involving me as a partner and not a lackey doing menial follow-up work."

"Don't thank me, Mac. You earned your detective badge and now you're earning your slot in major crime work. Everyone has to start somewhere." Kevin gave him a wistful smile. "I was still wondering what I wanted to do with my life when I was your age."

Mac grinned. "I'll bet." He slid out of the car seat, throwing his jacket in the backseat and loosening his tie. He grabbed his briefcase and the evidence bags and the two of them headed inside.

"Look what the cat dragged in," Philly said when Mac and Kevin entered the briefing room. "It's Boy Wonder and Rat Man."

"Hey, nice polyester suit, Philly," Kevin retorted. "I had one just like it about thirty years ago." He walked by Philly and set his briefcase in the chair. "The thick white stitching around the collar is really sharp. I'm glad to see you're spending your clothing allowance wisely and not just pocketing the money the department gives you."

"And you're just a regular Brad Pruitt, or whatever his name is." Philly held a hand over his heart and fluttered his eyelids.

Mac laughed. "I think you mean Brad Pitt. But hey, what's in a name?"

Russ chuckled then feigned a cough when Philly shot a glaring look in his direction. "Don't start with me, junior, or you either, Russ. Unless you would like me to tell the guys how you left your gun in the restroom at Denny's this morning."

Russ looked over at Philly with a look of disgust, making a zip-it motion across his lips.

"Oh, did I say that out loud?" Philly scooted around the table away from Russ.

"What happened?" Eric asked.

"Mr. SWAT team, sharpshooter nerd, went in to use the john at Denny's this morning after breakfast." Philly howled with laughter and could hardly talk. "The doofus leaves his gun hanging by the trigger guard on the coathook in one of the stalls. We're about ten blocks from the restaurant before ace here figures out his .40 caliber is still swinging on the bathroom door."

"Was it there when you got back?" Kevin asked, his hands on his head.

"Yes, it was there," Russ growled, his face red with embarrassment. He pulled open his jacket to display said handgun. "And it wasn't ten blocks away, we were just leaving the parking lot."

"Sorry, partner, you forced my wrath."

"Have you forgotten the old adage, 'What happens in the field, stays in the field?'" Russ thumped Philly's shoulder.

"That doesn't apply in a situation like this." Philly wiped his eyes with a beefy hand. "Sorry, Russ, it had to be told."

"Okay, okay," Eric interrupted the free-for-all. "Let's get back to work, shall we, gentlemen?" He sat down at the briefing table with a stack of paperwork. "Kevin, why don't you bring us all up to speed on recent developments."

The mood in the room turned serious as the detectives flipped to clean pages in their notebooks, preparing to jot down relevant information. Kevin read his own notes, bringing the others up to date on the investigation so far. "I think you all know that Mac and I worked on a lead supplied by one of Megan's coworkers at Fitness First. An ex-con by the name of Joe Higgins worked out at the club and dated Megan at least once. Mac and I interviewed him earlier today at his duplex on Macadam Court. He was polite enough, but the guy failed the honesty test. Joe initially denied he had dated Megan, only giving it up when pressed. He said he figured his rap sheet wouldn't do much in his favor if he told us he had dated the victim."

"What was his definition of 'date'?" Philly asked.

"Dinner, back to her place for a back rub." Kevin gave him an abbreviated version of the date. "We asked if he would take a poly. At first he flat-out said no, then when we explained it to him, he said he would think about it." Kevin told them about the rest of the interview and the connection with Mitch Wallace.

When he mentioned the video games, Philly leaned forward. "Any idea what they were playing?

"Um, no," Mac said. "I didn't think to ask."

"Might be important to know. Russ and I ran into a weirdo scene about five years ago with a kid down in Molalla who killed his girlfriend—remember, Russ?"

"You mean Jason Fulton?"

"Right. The kid and his buddy played that fantasy game—*Dungeons and Dragons.* It has all these make-believe elf characters. Fulton said they talked to demons and crazy stuff like that through their characters. We didn't think too much of it. You know how kids are with these video games. It turns out this Fulton kid goes from playing basketball to playing murderer in less than six months. He gets a local girl pregnant and then decides it would be better to introduce her to a shallow grave rather than own up to his responsibility. During the trial, old Jason claims that his elf character had actually been the one who killed his girlfriend. He was totally psycho. Ended up hanging himself in his cell before the jury could return a verdict."

"Yeah, I remember that one," Kevin said. "I didn't connect the video games with the *D&D* case. We'll have to check that out, Mac."

Mac nodded. He hadn't thought about the video connection either and he should have. Having been in the child abuse unit, he'd seen several cases where kids acted out their fantasies. But Joe Higgins and Mitch Wallace were grown men.

"Anyway, Higgins and Wallace became friends. Joe was paroled and moved to Oregon. He was working construction and makes jewelry."

"Jewelry?" Philly raised an eyebrow.

"He told us Megan commissioned him to make a pair of earrings for her," Mac said. "I'm thinking we need a search warrant on the guy's duplex. Could be he's got Megan's ring and her cross."

"Could be he sold the stones," Kevin said. "Maybe that's where he got the money for the move. Certainly worth checking into. We have a lot to work with here. Eric, did you get the info on Wallace?"

"Sure did." Eric pulled a sheet off his pile of papers. "Mitch Wallace, born in Bremerton, Washington, to a military family. Father was career navy. Mitch is your basic career criminal, robbing and stealing his whole life. By the looks of his criminal history, he's not much of a mastermind. His last arrest was for bank robbery in California—he actually tried robbing a bank and then running away on foot. He was caught in about ten seconds and ended up serving a sixteen-year stretch in the federal lockup in Texas."

"That's where he met Joe," Philly said.

"Right." Eric glanced down at the form. "He was released on parole earlier in the summer, although restricted to a halfway house by a federal parole officer in Seattle. He'd apparently told federal authorities his mother was ill and they transferred Wallace's parole supervision to Washington. That lasted about six weeks until he skipped town and came to Oregon to meet with his old cellmate."

"What does this guy look like?" Russ asked.

"Here's his release mug." Eric went to the second page and handed it to Russ to pass around. "It's a faxed copy, so it's not very good. He's a white guy, five-eight, one hundred and seventy pounds."

Kevin examined the mug shot. "Were you able to confirm the arrest in Gladstone?"

"Yeah. I actually talked to the officer from Gladstone Police Department over the phone—Officer Sid Vaughan. Apparently Vaughan stopped Higgins for a taillight out at around 2:00 A.M. on the morning of August fifteenth." Eric's story of the stop and subsequent arrest was consistent with the report Joe Higgins had given them.

"What did the officer do with Joe?" Philly asked.

"I'm getting there." Eric tossed him a be-patient look. "This is where it gets interesting. Vaughan conducted a consent search on the vehicle and found a duffle bag in the trunk. Inside the bag he found an old stun gun, some black duct tape, a black sock, one of those ski masks that covers the face, and a box of condoms. He said there was an assortment of tools and a hokey-looking plastic handgun."

Mac straightened in his chair. "Who took credit for the bag?"

"No one." Eric sighed. "Joe said it was Wallace's and Wallace denied knowing anything about it. The officer said he had no reason to detain Joe or seize the property so he cut Higgins loose with the bag. Vaughan thought it seemed shady, but he had no crime to connect it to—we hadn't found Megan's body yet and he wasn't aware of the missing person status. Not that any of that information would have alerted him. Nothing in the bag really connects them to the crime."

"So where's Wallace now?" Kevin asked.

"Still at the State Pen in Salem. He went to County lockup then was transferred to Salem on a roll-up. I guess the state agreed to house him in Oregon for the rest of his sentence." Eric consulted his notes. "Looks like two more years. I've got a tap on his inmate ID number so anytime he uses the phone, we'll catch the recording."

"Good work, Eric." Kevin tucked his papers back in his brief-case.

Eric jumped as the phone rang behind him. Picking it up, he answered, "Detective O'Rourke. Oh great; send her up." He hung up and announced to the group that Allison Sprague from the crime lab had arrived.

Moments later, Allison walked in the briefing room. "Pretty tight security you have down there. I guess they didn't recognize me without my lab gear on."

"Hey, Allison." Eric rose to greet her. "Thanks for coming down so late in the day."

"No problem," Allison replied, setting a small plastic tote on the table. "I'm working swing shift today, trading times with a coworker. What do you have for me?"

Kevin nodded at Mac. "You want to brief everyone on what we found at the apartment?"

"Sure." Mac pulled the two evidence sacks from his briefcase and set them on the table. "We got a consent to search Joe Higgins's old apartment in Troutdale from the landlord. The place was pretty clean—a little too clean if you ask me—so we didn't find much. We collected a few cigarette butts off the back patio in case they are needed for DNA workups in the future, and we found a small stain on the carpet."

"That's it?" Philly rolled his eyes.

"The stain looks like blood," Mac said in a defensive tone.

"And you think this might be Megan's blood?" Allison smiled.

"It's a long shot," Kevin said, "but it's worth checking out. I have a bad feeling about this guy."

"I'll take a look and tell you right now." She opened her container, slipped on a pair of gloves, and pulled out the bottle of clear liquid marked phenolphthalein. "Open her up, Mac, and let's take a look."

Mac tore open the bag to reveal the half-dozen strands of carpet. "See what I mean? It looks like dried blood."

Allison used a pair of tweezers to hold one of the carpet strands and rubbed a sterile cotton swab over the stain until some of the substance was transferred to the swab.

"This will tell us if we need to do further testing." Using a dropper she dripped a small amount of solution onto the swab. The white swab instantly turned neon pink, confirming that the substance was blood.

Mac released the breath he'd been holding. Kevin leaned back and clapped his hands together.

"Don't get too excited, boys." Allison packaged the test fiber into a glass vial. "I'm only going to call it a presumptive positive right now. I'll get the remaining samples back to the lab and see what we have." Allison packaged the remaining carpet samples in a new evidence bag and collected the second bag containing the cigarette butts. "I'll get back to you as soon as I have some results." She pulled off her gloves and discarded them in the garbage can near the door.

"Thanks again for coming down," Kevin said.

"You are more than welcome. I'll get back to you as soon as the results come in. I should have some preliminary results late tonight or early tomorrow. I can't tell you if it's Megan's until I run a DNA, but I can tell you for certain if it is blood and what the blood type is."

"Let's get a uniform on that apartment," Kevin said after Allison left. "I'll call the landlord and make sure he continues to restrict any access to the apartment. We don't have enough for a court order yet, although I'm sure Bernie will cooperate with us. I want an officer to keep an eye on that place until Allison gives us some conclusive analytical findings."

"I'll call the patrol sergeant now." Eric reached for the phone. "Anything else?"

"That's it for now." Kevin leaned back in his chair. "Hey, Philly, are you and Russ still going to video the funeral tomorrow?"

"You betcha. I hope they have a good buffet after the service."

Kevin ignored Philly's food comment. "Good. We don't want to put all our eggs in one basket with this Joe character. I'd feel better if he were locked up, but we don't have anything except the fact that he irritates me." He studied Mitch Wallace's mug shot. "At least we know this guy isn't going anywhere soon."

"We still need to check out DeLong," Mac reminded him.

"Right. No reason we can't do that this afternoon. Let's pay him a cold call too. Did you get his address?"

Mac held up his notebook. "Right here."

Eric hung up. "The sergeant will take the watch until ten o'clock tonight then turn it over to a graveyard troop. I told him to plan on sticking a day-shifter on the apartment tomorrow as well."

"What did he say to that?" Kevin asked.

"He grumbled a little; I guess he's pretty thin on patrols." He frowned. "Aren't we all? Speaking of which—this case has us all spread pretty thin. I think I'll make a quick run down to the Pen tomorrow and see if Wallace has made any phone calls." He glanced over at Kevin. "Are you and Mac going to the funeral?"

"I'm not sure. Philly and Russ can handle things there. If we don't hear from Joe on that polygraph by tomorrow morning, we'll need to pay him another visit." His cheeks puffed out as he exhaled long and hard. "I'm almost afraid to start looking into what this DeLong guy has been up to. Gives me the creeps just thinking about what he's been doing. So far every rock we've turned over has been covered with scum."

Mac and the others agreed.

"Who knows?" Kevin snapped his briefcase shut. "Maybe the blood in Joe's old apartment will be Megan's. It wouldn't hurt my feelings at all to put that guy back in lockup."

Mac picked up his briefcase and headed for the door. "Come on, slowpoke," he said to Kevin. "It's time to rumble."

"Say, Mac. Hold on a second." Eric slipped a small square envelope out of his jacket pocket and, leaning across the table, handed it to Mac. "Lynn wanted me to give this to you. I told her I could just ask, but she doesn't trust me to remember."

"What?"

"It's just an invite to dinner on Sunday after church." He grinned. "Hope you can make it."

"Hey, not fair." Philly pouted. "I've worked with you a lot longer than Mac, and you never invited me for dinner."

"That's because I'd go broke buying enough food to feed you." He chuckled. "Besides, Mac's family."

"Oh, right," Philly said. "I'd forgotten about that. Mac, if you do end up going, just don't let Eric do any of the cooking. At our picnic last month he dropped one of the steaks on the ground, picked it up, brushed off the dirt with his oven mitt, and tossed it back on the grill."

Kevin laughed. "What Philly doesn't know is, that was the steak he got."

Philly tossed his pen across the room. Kevin ducked and it hit the wall. "Time to go, Mac. The natives are getting restless."

MAC AND KEVIN found DeLong's address without any problem. They rang the bell and a woman in her thirties answered. They introduced themselves. "We'd like to talk with Matthew DeLong. Is he in?"

"Um . . . he has to work tonight and he's just stepped out of the shower."

"Who is it?" a guy yelled from the back of the house.

"Detectives, from the Oregon State Police."

There was a pause before he shouted, "Just a minute."

The woman left them at the door and went back into the kitchen, where she was apparently cooking something for dinner. The delicious scent wafted out to them, making Mac's stomach growl.

Several long minutes went by while the detectives listened to a lawn mower, birds singing, someone starting a vehicle and revving it up. A horn honked.

"Um, ma'am," Kevin finally leaned in and knocked on the open door. "Could you see what's keeping your husband?"

"He isn't my husband. He's my brother." She came out of the kitchen looking none too pleased by the interruption. Wiping her hands on a dishtowel, she walked down the hallway to the last room on the left and knocked. "Matthew, get your sorry butt out here; the cops are still waiting."

There was no answer. She pushed open the door and came back toward the two detectives. Holding her hands out, she shrugged. "I'm sorry. He's gone."

Chapter Thirty-Four

Mac charged into the bedroom, with Kevin close behind. The bedroom window was wide open. Mac started to climb through it, but Kevin stopped him. "No point in chasing after him. He's got too much of a head start. Besides, he's not under arrest and it's not illegal to run from us. I'll put a call into Eric for some manpower. In the meantime let's talk to the sister—find out if he took his car, where he might go, what he's been doing, and why he felt he had to run."

"You think this is our guy?" Mac scanned the backyard and moved back inside.

"I don't know, but we sure as heck are going to find out. He's got something to hide; that's for sure."

"Is Matthew in some sort of trouble again?" The sister was standing in the doorway.

Tears had gathered in her eyes, but they didn't match the annoyance on her features. "What has that fool brother of mine done this time?"

"We don't know that he's done anything," Kevin said. "What was your name?"

"Sandra. Sandra Keeley."

Kevin nodded. "We just wanted to talk to him about a case we're working on."

"What case is that?"

“Did he ever mention a woman named Megan Tyson?”

Sandra paled. “Oh, my gosh. You don’t think he . . .”

“No, ma’am. We’re interviewing people who knew her. Your brother met her at the Mountain View Retirement Inn.”

“He never mentioned her.” Sandra’s fists tightened around the towel she still held.

“Do you have any idea why he might take off like that?”

“He’s been in trouble before. I suppose he just got scared. He promised me he’d get his life back in order. Um . . . Matthew has had a really tough time of it. He’s undergone counseling as a condition of his last release from jail. We—my husband and I—told him he could stay as long as he didn’t get into any more trouble.”

While Kevin questioned her, Mac scanned the bedroom. A television sat atop a modern-looking chest of drawers. The furniture was a mismatch—some looking like Goodwill rejects. A fairly new computer sat on one of those single units about the size of a bookcase that held the desktop and all the peripheral items, a printer, scanner, fax machine, CDs, and disks. Though crowded, the room looked neat and orderly. His gaze settled back on the TV, a Sony—hadn’t Cindy listed one as a stolen item? He made a mental note to check it out.

“Do you know why your brother stopped working at the retirement inn?” Kevin asked.

“They fired him. Had some complaints from some of the residents. He didn’t seem too upset about that. Didn’t like working there anyway.”

“You mentioned he was going to work. Where does he work now?”

“He’s a waiter out at Donovan’s Bar & Grill—near Vancouver Mall. Actually they changed the name to Westfield, but I never call it that. It’s a temporary job—so was the one at the retirement inn. He’s into computers and hopes to get a job with Hewlett Packard.”

"Do you have any idea where he might have gone just now?"

She shook her head. "Probably not to work."

Kevin agreed. "Probably not. Since we didn't see a vehicle back out of your driveway, can I assume he left on foot?"

"We can check." They followed her back down the hall and into the main part of the house, veering off to the right. "He parks his motorcycle out back beside the garage." She went to the patio door just off the dining room and peered out. "His bike's gone."

"Great." Mac grunted, angry with himself for being outwitted by the ex-con. The vehicle he'd heard above the lawn mower must have been DeLong's.

Sandra glanced at the clock on the stove. "I'm sorry. I wish I could help you more, but I have to finish dinner before my son comes back from the pool."

"We won't keep you. If Matthew contacts you, could you let us know?" Kevin handed her a card with his number on it. "As of now, we only want to talk to him. Mac, did you have anything?"

"Just one question. I notice your brother had a Sony television set in his room. Do you know where he got it?"

"Um . . . from a friend, I think. He brought it home a couple of weeks ago." Sandra set the card on the counter near a wall phone. "I'm sorry he took off."

"It's not your fault. We may need to come back and talk with you later—maybe have a look through his things."

"You know, he has been worried about the child support situation. His ex-wife is really vindictive. Maybe he was afraid you were going to get him for back child support."

Kevin nodded. "Well, you can tell him that's not what we're here about."

"I will—if I see him. I have a few other things to tell him too." She walked them to the door.

On his way back to the car, Mac was lost in thought, wondering what DeLong was up to. He had a bad feeling about this guy.

"Top of the list is getting crowded." Kevin adjusted the vents so the air was blowing full force into his face. He lowered the window and rested his arm on the sill.

"You can say that again. Want to drive around and see if we can spot him?"

"No. Like I said, we'll turn it over to the uniforms and let them find him. Or we can wait awhile. I have a hunch he'll talk to the sister before long. Good call on the television set. I can't wait to find out what he has to say about that. I'll get a search warrant going, and with or without DeLong's presence, we'll check that room and maybe even the house thoroughly." He yawned. "In the meantime, we should call it a day. I could use some sleep and I'd like some time to go over our findings and pray about our next step."

"Seems like you do a lot of praying."

"I do, Mac. You might try it. Gives me peace of mind, knowing the Lord is working right alongside us."

Gives me the creeps. Mac kept the thought to himself. He liked Kevin, respected him more every day. If the guy felt praying helped, he wasn't going to argue.

Mac didn't want to go home. He didn't want to talk to Linda about getting married. He wanted to put Megan's killer behind bars. After dropping Kevin off at his car in the P.D. parking lot, Mac began his trek west, then north over the bridge into Vancouver. He hardly noticed the mountains or the clear blue sky. All he could think about was Megan. Had one of the guys they'd uncovered been her killer? He wanted things to move faster—much faster.

On the way home he stopped for takeout at a Thai place and ordered salad, rolls, and some kind of chicken dish he couldn't pronounce—pieces of chicken yellowed and spiced by curry and served with vegetables and rice.

At home he checked the answering machine. There were six

messages from Linda. In all of them she needed to talk to him right away. Something about an appointment she'd made for them on Thursday night for premarital counseling. *Premarital counseling?* What was that all about? He had a feeling it had to do with his less-than-perfect attitude toward church and God.

Annoyed and curious, he dialed her number but hung up when he got her answering machine. He'd try later, but chances were, she'd call him back before he got a chance.

Mac took the information they had gathered so far on Megan's case out of his briefcase and set it on the table. While he ate, he went back through all of the suspects: Gordon Reed, Joe Higgins, Mitch Wallace, Matthew DeLong, Brandon King and his pals. The fiancé had slipped through the polygraph exam, but Mac wasn't totally ready to dismiss him either.

Mac rubbed his forehead. What had Megan seen in these guys? Why would she date them? Tim Morris he could understand, but the others? *Megan, where was your common sense?*

Maybe more important, what reason would any of them have to kill her? Jealousy was a strong motive. Gordon and Tim fell into that category. Maybe Matthew DeLong did as well, but Mac suspected his motive, along with Joe's, would be rejection. Dottie had mentioned an argument between Matthew and Megan. With Joe Higgins, the motive may have been the jewelry. It fit—the fact that he made jewelry; he had probably seen the necklace and the ring. But Megan's death had been so brutal, denoting passion and anger—the kind of anger that rose out of jealousy and rejection, not theft. If it were up to him, with the evidence and information he had now, he'd finger Matthew DeLong. Unfortunately, they didn't have enough evidence for a conviction.

The closest thing they had to solid evidence in the case was that bloodstain. It would sure help if they could find the cross and the ring—and those missing items from her apartment. Had the television set he'd seen in Matthew's room been Megan's? Every day brought new trails to follow and more to think about. His head swam with possibilities. Somehow they had to narrow this thing down.

You could pray about it. The thought came out of nowhere, blindsiding him.

Leaning back in his chair, Mac thought about Kevin and what he'd said about prayer. His grandmothers had often told him that God answered prayers. He wondered if Megan had prayed during her ordeal. She'd been a minister's daughter. *I bet you did.*

Humph. Cynicism invaded his thoughts. *God didn't answer those prayers, did He?*

Despite his feelings about God, Mac did pray. "I don't know what to believe anymore. But if You are there and You are listening, please help us narrow our search and find Megan's killer. She didn't deserve to die like that."

He thought about Linda and his uncertainty in that relationship. "And while You're at it, maybe You could help me figure out if Linda is the girl I should be marrying."

The phone both startled and embarrassed him. "Hey, Mac." The woman's voice sounded familiar, but he couldn't place it.

"Yeah. What can I do for you?"

"It's Dana Bennett."

"Dana." He grinned, imagining Dana's dimpled smile. "How are you doing?"

"Good. Um . . . I was wondering—if it's a bad time I can call later . . ."

"No. It's fine. I was just eating some takeout."

"Okay, well, I'd like to talk to you about something. About your work actually. Would you mind if I came over?"

"Please do. I could use some company."

"Okay. I'll be there in about fifteen, twenty minutes."

Dana lived in Gresham, not far off I-84. He doubted it would take her that long. Mac finished eating and cleared the table, putting away his notes and paperwork. His place wasn't all that messy—

mainly because he had hardly lived there lately and because he kept a clean house. He attributed his housekeeping to his grandmothers, especially Kathryn, who had made certain he knew that being male didn't exclude him from housecleaning chores.

When the doorbell rang, a jolt of excitement tore though him. He felt like a kid with a new toy. *Not a good analogy.*

"Come on in."

"Thanks." Dana grinned up at him shyly and he wondered if the visit was just to ask questions.

"Have a seat." Mac gestured toward the living room. "Can I get you anything?"

"No thanks, I'm fine." She chewed on her lower lip. "I feel kind of awkward coming here."

"Hey, no reason to. We're old buds right?" There was that grin again, and blue eyes you could drown in. *You're engaged,* he reminded himself. *Remember Linda?*

"Right. Which is why I called you. Might as well get to the point here. Mac, I want to be a detective."

Mac's gaze drifted over her face and her trim figure, nicely covered with a pale blue blouse and tight jeans. His gaze jerked back to her face. "You what?"

"I want to be a detective. I know I'm new on the job, but I really want to be a homicide detective. I need you to tell me what all to do and maybe put in a good word with your bosses."

Mac paused, collecting his thoughts. "It's no secret. Basically, you need to show them you can do a good job on the road, you know, digging beyond the ticket. You have to make the cases, and that involves looking past license plates to get to the real dirt. Make the arrests and bring the bad guys in. And keep doing what you're doing—show up at the crime scenes, offer to help. Put in free hours. That's what I did—worked a lot of gratis shifts because I wanted the experience."

"That I can do." Dana leaned back and crossed her arms. "I

need someone to sponsor me or I'll never make it. Who's that gonna be if not you? Philly?"

Mac grinned. "I don't think Philly is your guy. Kevin might be, though. Just keep doing what you're doing. The most important thing is being able to back up your arrests with good reports. That keeps you out of court and keeps the sergeant happy."

"Can I show you some of my reports before I turn them in for review? You know, have you look them over and give me some pointers?"

Mac shrugged, thinking he'd do just about anything for the cute trooper sitting across the coffee table from him. "Sure. Just throw them in my box or drop by. You could also help yourself by signing up for as much training as you can get. Even if they turn you down, and they might for a while, be persistent and make sure you spell this out on your annual employee development form during your evaluation. Always put your goals on paper in case your sergeant is reassigned so the new guy knows what ground you've covered."

"I'm way ahead of you there, Mac. The sarge is very aware of my goals." Dana grinned.

"Sounds like you've already done a lot of the groundwork. Let Sergeant Evans know you want to transfer in and wait for an opening."

"Do you think I can do it?"

"I don't know why not. The unit I'm in doesn't have any women—at least none that I've met. There's Melissa Thomas out of the Salem office who's the polygraph examiner. She might be a good one to talk to. I think it's great. Maybe we'll be able to work together."

"Now, that would be a plus. I'm not sure how my boyfriend would feel about me having a guy as good-looking as you for a partner, though."

"Boyfriend?" Mac felt the flush creeping up his neck. She thought he was handsome.

"Jason Smith." She grinned. "That isn't jealousy I'm seeing in your eyes, is it? I mean, you and I broke up a long time ago and I heard you were engaged . . ."

Mac heard a key in the door, but before he could get to it, the door opened and Linda stepped inside. "Mac? I've been trying . . ." She caught sight of Dana and stood there with her mouth open for what had to be five seconds—a long five seconds. To say it was an awkward moment was like saying mountains were big. "Oh . . . I'm sorry. I didn't know you had company."

"Um . . . Linda, this is Dana."

Linda's gaze jerked from Dana to Mac. Still holding the door, she gave Mac a we'll-deal-with-this-later look. "Call me when you're free." Her voice was cold and hard.

Mac nodded, thinking he should go after her and tell her that Dana wasn't a date and that things weren't as they seemed. He did neither. Instead, he watched through the still-open door as she climbed into her car and drove off.

"Mac, I'm so sorry. I hope I didn't mess things up for you."

"What?" He snapped his attention back to Dana. "No, not at all." Linda hadn't bothered to stick around long enough for an explanation. She obviously didn't trust him. What kind of deal was that?

"I should go." Dana picked up her bag and settled the strap onto her shoulder.

"Do you have to?" Mac liked her company. Liked being with her.

"No. I guess not." She offered a pixielike grin and set her bag back down beside the chair.

"Good." Mac went over and closed the door Linda had left open in her hurry to escape. "To tell you the truth, I've missed our times together."

She sighed and leaned back in the chair. "We did have our moments, didn't we?"

"And some good talks."

For the next two hours, Mac and Dana talked shop, swapping horror stories and jokes. She left around eleven and, before going out to her car, wrapped her arms around Mac and kissed his cheek. "I've missed you."

"I've missed you too."

"Hey, I have a great idea." A smile lit her entire face. "Why don't we have a standing date—like for coffee? We can meet for coffee before work once a week to debrief. You can coach me on this detective thing and tell me about your life in the big leagues."

Mac nodded. "Sounds good." *Sounds perfect.*

When she'd gone, Mac flopped on the sofa and lay there, hands behind his head, thinking about the evening's events. He felt no guilt regarding Linda—well, almost no guilt. After all, he'd done nothing wrong. Linda had jumped to conclusions. Whose fault was that? *You don't need a jealous, pushy woman in your life,* he told himself. *If she really loved you, she'd have waited for an explanation. Forget her. You have an investigation that needs more than 100 percent.*

Right now, Linda was a complication he didn't need.

Chapter Thirty-Five

Tuesday, August 27
7:45 A.M.

Kevin was already in the briefing room at Troutdale Police Department when Mac walked in.

"What are you working on?" Mac peered over Kevin's shoulder at a map, marked up with different colored highlighters.

Kevin motioned to a map in front of him. "I've mapped the locations of the ATM usage from Megan's card after she disappeared. These red marks up here on Halsey Street at the Plaid Pantry indicate the usage on August fourteenth in the early morning hours."

"Right." Mac squinted, hoping to see a correlation.

"Now, the green highlighter is the debit card usage at the Gresham Fred Meyer store on August fifteenth. And finally, the pink highlighter shows the Clackamas Mall transaction later that same day."

"Okay." Mac still couldn't see his point.

"Take a look at the red dots for the Plaid Pantry usage." Kevin pointed to the map. "What street do you see within close proximity to both locations?"

Mac squinted to read the small print. "Let's see, Cornelius, Alder, Morrison . . . Hmm, I don't believe it. Parkview—Joe

Higgins's old apartment building. I had no idea the Parkview Apartments were so close to the activity on the victim's ATM card."

"Neither did I." Kevin rubbed the back of his neck. "Not until I plotted it out on the map this morning. I'd asked for guidance the night before and woke up with the idea. Now, I have to admit it's a long shot. Any one of our suspects could have driven to these places—and Clackamas Mall doesn't seem like a place Joe Higgins would spend a lot of time at, but again, it's only about twenty minutes away."

"But you think it's worth following up on. Are you thinking about talking to him again?"

"Yes, but first we go back over to Vancouver to talk with our runaway."

"His sister called?"

"Actually he paged me last night. I told him we just wanted to talk to him about Megan, and he seemed fine with that. The sister was right. He got spooked about the child support payments. Said he'd been paying regularly but missed last month."

"Right. What do you bet he's one of those deadbeat dads?"

"I wouldn't. Whether he is or isn't doesn't concern me at the moment. We'll talk to him while he's feeling relatively safe. I told him the child support issue wasn't on our agenda." Kevin smiled. "However, that doesn't stop us from putting a bug in the sheriff's ear after we're finished with him."

MATTHEW DELONG turned out to be a heavyset guy with the personality of a snake—slithering around their questions and rarely making eye contact. His dark hair was shorter than it had been in the photo. He was clean cut, but there was something dirty about him. Mac wondered if he would have felt the same way if he hadn't known about his criminal record.

Mac shot a glance at Kevin. This guy was scared, which meant they didn't have to tiptoe around him. They could get right to the point.

Kevin took a seat on the couch. "You're in a little bit of trouble, but my partner and I are willing to work out your problems with you, Matt."

"You don't mind if we call you Matt, do you?" Mac added, playing off his partner.

"No, I go by Matt. That's fine. What do you mean, *my* problems?" Matthew's face had grown considerably flushed.

"Your little problem on the child support," Kevin replied sternly, making eye contact for several awkward seconds. "Why don't you have a seat, and we can discuss it."

Mac enjoyed watching the power play and wondered how Matthew would react. It didn't take long. The guy sat down and leaned forward.

"We might be willing to forget the call to the civil unit at the sheriff's office if you cooperate with us fully."

Matt nodded. "You have my attention."

"First of all, some formal introductions. I'm Detective Bledsoe and this is my partner, Detective McAllister." The two men produced their badges for identification. "We're state police detectives working the Megan Tyson case."

"I figured that much," Matthew replied with a touch of sarcasm in his voice. "Like I told my sister . . ."

Kevin interrupted. "I'm not done yet, so hold your horses. I need to explain something to you. You're not under arrest and you don't even need to talk to us if you don't want to. Just say the word and we're gone, although quite frankly I'll leave here with more questions than I arrived with."

Matthew bit into his lower lip. "Look, guys, I got nothing to hide. My life's an open book. Just tell me what I can do to get you guys out of my life."

"Are you willing to submit to a polygraph test?"

"No way. I don't do those things."

"May I ask why not?" Mac enjoyed watching him squirm.

"Just don't trust them. I spent some time in jail—but you know that. Some guys said the lie detector test wasn't accurate and said they'd lied when they hadn't."

"Do you know that these guys were telling the truth?"

"No, but . . ."

Mac explained that the test was not used in the courtroom and was simply a tool. "If you haven't done anything wrong and have been truthful with us, you don't have anything to worry about."

"I don't know." He licked his lips. "I feel like maybe you guys have already made up your mind about me—seeing as I had that rape arrest on my record. But I never raped anybody. The charges were dropped."

"And what about the porn?"

He lowered his head and stared at the floor. "That was a mistake. It was stupid. I got involved with a guy on the Internet who told me I could make a lot of money selling these videos. I didn't know how old those kids were."

Now, why don't I believe that? Mac let the comment slide. He nodded. "Sometimes life just isn't fair, Matt. So what do you say to the polygraph?"

"Okay—I guess I could take it."

"Good choice. Would tomorrow be okay?"

"Yeah. I don't go in to work until four."

"I'll set it up and give you a call to let you know what time to come in."

"One more thing, Matt," Kevin said. "Yesterday when you took off, my partner here got a little overzealous and ran into your room. He tells me he noticed a Sony television set. Can you tell me how long you've had it?"

Matthew looked stricken. "A couple of weeks." He shook his head. "You guys are something else. I guess I could lie—tell you if you want to look at my stuff you'll need a search warrant. Truth is, Megan gave it to me."

Mac could hardly swallow. His heart felt as though it had dropped to his feet. At that moment he'd have bet a year's salary that they had Megan's killer.

Chapter Thirty-Six

"Would you care to elaborate?" Kevin leaned forward slightly, catching Mac's eye.

"She was talking about moving to Florida and having to get rid of stuff. She said she had a television set and some other stuff and asked me if I wanted it. I said I could use it. I like to be alone sometimes you know—watch television in my room."

Kevin pressed his hands against his thighs. "I'd like you to give me a list of all the items she gave you, Matt. Can you do that?"

How could his partner sound so calm? Mac wondered.

"Sure. Let me get a pen and paper."

When DeLong went into the kitchen, Kevin shot a look at Mac that warned him not to get too excited.

Mac couldn't help it. Matthew DeLong had the items Cindy had reported as stolen. Did he also have the ring and the cross?

Matthew wrote down several items and handed the list to Kevin. "Do you mind if we take a look around your room, Matt?"

"No, I suppose not. I've got nothing to hide."

Matthew pointed out the items he claimed Megan had given him and stood at the door to watch Mac and Kevin do a complete search. Mac figured the guy was being too cooperative and doubted they'd find anything other than the items he'd written down.

"Did anyone see you remove these items from Megan's home?" Kevin asked.

"I didn't see anyone. There were a few kids hanging around." He shrugged. "Look, all I know is she gave them to me, and I packed them up, locked up behind me like she said, and left."

"What do you mean, you locked up?" Kevin settled both hands on his hips, legs slightly apart. "Wasn't Megan there?"

"At first. She was in a hurry—guess she had an appointment or something. She didn't say where she was going."

Mac looked down at his shoes, wishing he were a little better at reading people. The guy seemed to be telling the truth, but some people were such practiced liars, you couldn't tell.

Kevin completed the questioning and thanked Matthew for his cooperation, saying he'd call him about coming in for the polygraph as soon as they could schedule it.

Back in the police car, Mac said, "I couldn't get a reading on him. Either he's a good liar or he's telling the truth."

"I agree, Mac. We'll ask Eric to send a couple of uniforms over to Megan's old apartment to talk to neighbors—see if we can find these kids Matt mentioned. Right now I think we should follow up on the blood evidence we found at Higgins's place. I'd like to pay Joe another visit."

"Shouldn't we wait to see if it's Megan's blood?" Mac glanced in the rearview mirror and noticed Matthew coming out of his driveway and heading the opposite direction on his bike. "There goes Matthew. He seems to be in a hurry. Want to follow him?"

Kevin shook his head and grinned. "Yeah, but let's not. We have too much to do to chase around after the kid. He doesn't seem too worried at this point, so let's not spook him."

"You're the boss." Mac pulled into the street and headed for Joe Higgins's duplex.

Kevin got on the phone with Eric, telling him about the items Matt had and asking for someone to canvass Megan's neighborhood again.

Mac pulled up to the curb in front of Joe Higgins's place at 10:00 A.M.

"Let's hit him up on the polygraph again, keep the pressure on," Kevin said as they approached the front door. Kevin rapped on the door with his leather notebook case.

The door opened almost immediately and Mac wondered if Joe had seen them coming.

"Greetings, gents." He had his dark hair pulled back in a ponytail and was wearing the same black sweats he'd had on the last time they'd talked to him. "And to what do I owe the pleasure of your company this morning?"

"Just wondering if you had a few minutes to answer some more questions." Mac slipped his right foot in the door over the threshold.

Higgins peered down at Mac's foot and grinned. "What's this? Did you sell door to door before this job?" His smile faded. "Sorry, that was rude. You don't have to worry. I wasn't going to slam the door in your face and take off. I really can't talk this morning, though. I was about to jump in the shower. I'm planning to go to Megan's funeral today and I have a job interview after that."

"You're going to the funeral?" Mac asked.

"Yeah. I told you that before. I wanted to give Megan's sister those earrings."

"Right." Kevin nodded. "Well, since we're here, I'd like to ask you one thing."

"Just one?" Joe acted surprised.

"Right. We were checking out your old apartment and found a bloodstain on the carpet."

He shook his head and smiled. "Sorry to disappoint you fellas, but that was my blood. I cut my hand while I was moving." He held up his hand to show them the small mark on his palm. "I thought I'd cleaned it up pretty good."

A defensive wound? Mac wondered.

"That's all we need for now, Mr. Higgins. Maybe we could come by later today—say after the funeral and that interview."

"Fine by me," Higgins replied.

"Have you given any more thought to taking that polygraph?" Kevin asked as Higgins started to close the door.

"Some. I'm leaning that way, but I'd like to talk to my attorney about it, you know."

"Sure. We'll talk to you later, Mr. Higgins." Kevin barely got in his response before the door closed.

"He seems pretty confident." Mac opened the car door.

"Yes, very." Kevin glanced back at the duplex. "Let's go over to the old apartment. I want to make sure things are running smoothly."

"On our way."

"My pager." Kevin glanced down. "It's Eric." Kevin reached for his phone. "Darn, I left mine at the P.D."

"Mine's inside the center console." Mac shifted his arm over so Kevin could access the phone.

"Thanks, pal. I was just testing to see if you were prepared."

Mac rolled his eyes. "I'll bet."

"Kevin." Eric answered the phone on the first ring.

"Yeah, buddy. Good morning."

After bantering, Kevin turned serious, finally ending the conversation with, "We're on our way."

"Eric wants us to meet him at the P.D. He's got taped phone calls from Mitch Wallace. I'll bet they're to Higgins."

"What about the Parkview apartment?"

"Eric says Dana Bennett is covering for him until he can get there." Kevin raised an eyebrow at Mac. "Is it my imagination, or is that girl shadowing you?"

"Not me." Mac grinned, glad for the opening. "She's hoping to make detective."

Kevin nodded. "I guess that's why she told Eric she didn't mind staying for as long as he needed her."

"Sounds like her. From what she told me last night, she's working really hard. You might want to talk to her. Maybe you could put in a good word for her."

"Be glad to." Kevin tapped on the dash, then said, "Last night, huh? You two have something going? What happened to Linda?"

"Dana and I are friends. We took some classes together at the University of Portland. I was a senior and she was a freshman—we were both working toward a criminal justice degree. She came over to my place last night to talk to me about what she needed to do to make detective." He sighed. "I don't know what to do about Linda. She dropped by while Dana was there." Mac told him about the incident.

"Whew. Boy, am I glad I don't have those girl troubles any more. There are real pluses to having been married for thirty years."

"Humph. Somehow after last night I don't think wedding bells are going to be ringing in the near future for me."

"From what you just told me, it sounds like you might not be ready to settle down."

"You may be right." Mac didn't want to talk any more about the women in his life. "Did Eric have anything else to say?"

"Just that Philly and Russ are over at the church, getting ready for the funeral service. I guess there's already a big crowd gathering, lots of media. The press is playing this one to the hilt, making a big deal about the girl who is to be buried rather than married." Kevin grimaced in disgust. "Anything for a buck."

Kevin and Mac arrived at the Troutdale Police Department at about the same time Eric did. As they walked across the parking lot together, Kevin said, "I can't believe you can drive from Salem quicker than we can cross town."

"Yeah, this metro traffic is getting worse and worse." Eric opened the door and the three of them filed in.

After checking with the clerk, Eric led the way to the police chief's office and plucked a tape player off the overstuffed bookcase. Once they were seated, he slipped the first tape into the small player. "The tapes were made yesterday afternoon at seven in the evening. The inmates can call collect from the pay phones in the yard between ten in the morning and eight in the evening. There may have been more calls made, but these are the ones we captured after we set the tap in place."

Mac folded his arms and leaned back, stretching out his long legs. "Since we had to ask, I take it not all calls are recorded. If it's a public phone, how do they know when to record?"

"The inmate types his identification number into the phone before the call," Eric replied. "All calls are subject to being recorded for random checks, although they aren't singled out for law enforcement unless requested."

"Got it."

"Here we go with the first one." Eric depressed the "play" button.

"Will you accept a collect call from the Oregon State Penitentiary from . . ." a male voice saying, "Mitch," interrupted the computerized voice.

"Please press one to accept. Your call may be monitored."

"Hey, Mitch, how goes it?" Mac recognized the speaker as Joe Higgins.

"Not bad. What's up?" Wallace's voice was scratchy—probably from too many years of tar and nicotine.

"Not much. Had a visit from a couple of detectives this morning."

"Oh yeah?" Wallace's pitch went up a couple of notches.

"Yeah. They were asking questions about Megan Tyson—you remember, the gal I made those earrings for. I told them I didn't know anything." Higgins tone stayed even and steady.

"Why did you even talk to them, man? You don't have to, you know."

"Mitch, it's no wonder you're back in the tank. Don't you know anything? When cops say jump, you ask how high. I don't want to wind up in the slammer again. No way. Besides, I got nothing to hide."

"Is there anything else I should know?" Wallace coughed.

"They asked about you."

"You told them about me?"

"No, pinhead. They asked."

"How did they know about me?"

"How should I know? No need to get riled up. Just remember, they could be recording this."

"I don't give a rip. Answer my question, Higgins. What have you been telling them?"

"Nothing, I swear. Besides, what's to tell? They're talking to everybody who had some connection to the Tyson woman. I imagine they'll be visiting you too."

"I don't like it."

"Look," Joe sounded patronizing. *"I didn't tell them anything except that you were in town to visit and drink a little."*

"You'd better be telling me the truth, buddy, 'cause a few words to the cops and we'll be cellmates again."

"Simmer down, Mitch. I haven't done anything to go to prison for. I'm clean, remember?"

Wallace grunted and Higgins ended the call.

"It's a bit vague," Kevin said, "but reading between the lines I'd say Higgins is making a promise not to rat and wanting the same reassurance from Wallace."

"No arguments here." Eric took out the tape and put in the second one.

They listened through the same operator-assisted jargon and heard Joe's irritated voice.

"Man, you've got to quit calling me. My phone bill's whacked."

"I forgot to ask you about something. I was wondering if you got rid of all that camping gear we had?"

"Yeah. I sold it."

"Cool. Remember you promised to give me half of what you made for helping you move. I need money for smokes."

"I got your half, but I'm taking out enough to pay for these phone calls."

"Just don't go spending it. Look, I gotta go. Stay cool, man, I'll call you tomorrow. It's time for lockdown. You stay cool, you hear!"

"Don't worry. Sounds like you're the one who needs to stay cool."

"That's it so far." Eric pulled the second tape from the machine. "I wonder what the camping gear stuff was all about."

"Who knows?" Kevin stood up and paced across the room, pausing to examine the contents of the police chief's bookcase. "I doubt that it's camping gear, though."

Mac straightened in the chair. "Wallace sounds a little worried about his friend's loyalty."

"You got that right." Kevin turned back around to face them. "They're worried about something, that's for sure. If you want to break an alliance, you start at the weakest link. Wallace sounds nervous." He placed both hands palm down on the desk. "Eric, how long would it take to have Wallace moved from general population to segregation?"

"About thirty seconds." A smile erupted on Eric's face. "You thinking what I'm thinking?"

Mac looked back and forth at the two detectives, feeling left out of the loop.

Kevin nodded. "I wouldn't be a bit surprised. We move Wallace into segregation and cut off his phone calls to Higgins."

Eric agreed. "He'll be climbing the walls in a couple of hours and ready to crack in twelve."

"Make the call to the Pen and work your magic, my friend. With any luck at all, the guy will tell us why he's so worried about our little chats with Higgins."

Eric left the room to make his call.

"Can we do that?" Mac asked.

"Wallace forfeits certain rights when he is in prison." Kevin sat back down. "The prison officials can move him about and restrict his rights without warning or reason. We aren't doing this to be cruel. We're hoping to cause some friction between Wallace and Higgins. If we want straight answers, we've got to cut their support line."

"Do you really think Higgins and Wallace killed Megan?"

"I wish I could say yes and get this caper over with. They had access to her. We found blood in Joe's apartment. Higgins sold some so-called camping equipment. That could translate to Megan's ring. Or it could be stolen goods that have nothing to do with Megan. We'll know more when we talk to Allison."

Mac blew out a long breath. "I think waiting is the hardest part of this job."

"No, Mac. The hardest part is doing all this work and coming up empty, which could still happen. Like I said before, this could have been a random act and the killer is long gone."

"I hope not." Mac thought about the serial killers who preyed on people for years before getting caught—and those who were still out there.

Chapter Thirty-Seven

"Let's grab a quick bite then head over to Megan's funeral," Kevin said.

"I thought we weren't going to the funeral." Mac felt relieved somehow at his partner's decision. He had wanted to go, and not just as a detective. He wanted to say good-bye.

"Changed my mind. Higgins said he was going, and I'd like to keep an eye on him. Besides, I feel like I've gotten to know Megan Tyson fairly well over the past few days. I'd like to pay my respects."

Eric walked in the room as they were putting on their jackets. "Mr. Wallace is enjoying a suite for one at the luxurious segregation ward in the Oregon State Penitentiary. He's allowed no outside contact, phone calls, or mail. The cell block captain said we could administratively hold him there for one week without reason, but any longer and we're going to need something more substantial."

"We should know in a day or two whether he and Higgins killed her." Kevin adjusted his jacket where it hooked up on his holster. "One more favor, Eric. We need to set up a poly this afternoon for Matthew DeLong from the retirement inn. He's agreed, but he's squeamish about it. Need to get him in before he changes his mind."

"I'll make the call now." Minutes later Eric got off the phone and told them it was all set up. Detective Thomas would be there at 2:00 P.M.

"Great." Kevin grabbed his wallet. "Hey, Eric. Mac and I are going across the street to grab a bite. You hungry?"

"I could eat a horse." Eric patted his flat stomach.

"You may just do that in this joint," Mac joked.

"Ah yes, but I'd take quantity over quality any day." Eric laughed and grabbed his jacket to join them.

"HOW'S MY COUSIN HERE DOING on the investigation?" Eric asked when they'd been seated and given menus.

Mac snapped up his head in time to see Eric send him a wink.

"He's a quick learner," Kevin said. "A lot quicker than you were anyway."

"That's not saying much." Eric laughed.

Kevin glanced over at Mac. "Eric was a really tough case. More stubborn than you are."

Mac crinkled his brow, wondering what his new partner was up to. "What do you mean stubborn?"

"Oh, not as far as the detective work. I'm talking about getting right with God. Took Eric a long time to come around to my way of thinking."

"How do you know your way is the right way?" Mac asked.

Kevin pursed his lips. "I stand corrected. Let's say, God's way. As I was saying, it took Eric a long time to see the light."

"Don't rub it in," Eric said. "'Even a fool is thought wise if he keeps silent, and discerning if he holds his tongue.'"

"Yes, but 'the wise in heart accept commands, but a chattering fool comes to ruin.'"

Eric picked up his menu, not seeming the least bit annoyed. "Can't I ever stump you, old-timer?"

"Not when you're venturing into Proverbs, pal. Bring it on." Kevin picked up his water and drank half of it down.

"I know when I've been bested, Master Yoda." Eric grinned

and nodded at Mac. "You may as well give in, Mac. Kevin is relentless."

"I'll take that into consideration." So his cousin had become a believer. Mac wondered if that was why he'd been so nice—why he hadn't given him a hard time.

"Um, Eric, I should have called Lynn yesterday. Tell her I said thanks for the invitation. If I'm not working, I'd like to come."

"Good. I'll pass it along. How long has it been since you've seen my family, Mac?"

"Since Grandma Kathryn's funeral last year, I think."

Eric shook his head. "Too long. After all, we're cousins—we should get together now and then."

"Yeah." Mac nodded, wanting to change the subject before Eric decided to say any more about the family. "We should order."

After lunch, the detectives headed for the funeral service. Eric opted to take his own car so he could head right over to Joe Higgins's old apartment to relieve Dana.

WHEN MAC AND KEVIN ARRIVED at the large church, hundreds of mourners had come to pay their respects.

"I didn't expect quite this many people," Mac said as they ascended the wide stairs leading into the church.

"Like I said, the press went all out on this one. Everybody feels a connection with Megan. We all have a wife, sister, mother, or daughter who could have died in Megan's place. There but for God's grace. A lot of people feel the need to attend the service of murder victims; some feel they have come to know them during the course of the media coverage." Kevin looked over at Mac. "Sometimes police officers feel a need to bury the victims too."

Mac swallowed hard, glad to hear he wasn't the only one who felt that way. As they entered the sanctuary, Mac noticed Russ and Philly in the balcony with a video camera on a tripod. Russ nodded at Mac in recognition. He and Philly were poised to capture the attendance, in the event the killer was brazen enough to attend the funeral.

Mac noticed an older man standing next to a table that displayed a large photograph of Megan. He was dressed in dark slacks that looked a little too long for his short frame. He tugged at his collar, trying to loosen his tie.

"Look at that guy over there, Kevin, by Megan's picture. Seems out of place."

The man's lips moved as though he were talking to her. He bowed his head, then turned away and walked toward Kevin and Mac.

"I think he set something on the table," Mac said, leaning close to Kevin's ear. "I'm going to go see what it is."

"Hold on, Mac." Kevin stepped toward the older man, blocking his path. "Hello, Mr. Collins."

The man squinted. His eyes widened in recognition. "Oh, hello, Detective. You remember me, huh?" His smile revealed tobacco-stained teeth.

"Sure do, sir." Kevin offered his hand. "I also felt a need to attend the service."

"Well, I'm not much for fancy gatherings, so I'm going to head back to the place. I've got a lot of work to do before the fall sets in."

"It was good to see you, sir. God bless."

"God bless you too, Detective." The man shook Kevin's hand a second time, using both hands. He turned and walked out of the church, disappearing into the crowd.

"Who was that guy?" Mac asked.

"Preston Collins—the unfortunate fellow who found Megan's body. It was nice of him to come by." Kevin straightened to his full height and scanned the crowd. "Have you seen Cindy Tyson or Tim Morris?"

"Not yet," Mac said. "I still can't get over the number of people here."

Kevin pulled his pager from his hip, squinting to read the number. "Got your phone, Mac? It's the crime lab in Portland."

"I left it in the car," Mac answered with an embarrassed grin.

"It's your evidence, partner. You go make the call and see what Allison has turned up for us."

"You got it." Mac wove through the crowd and sprinted to his car, which they'd had to park two blocks away. He hurriedly dialed the number to the lab.

He got a secretary and, after what seemed like five minutes rather than five seconds, got Allison on the line.

"Hi, Allison, Detective McAllister here. You just paged Kevin."

"Right."

"What do you have for us?" Mac could barely contain his excitement.

"I've performed a forensic examination on the carpet fibers and verified that the stain was in fact human blood. I then compared the blood sample to the DNA comparison sample I extracted from the victim's thighbone. I used what was called the polymerase chain reaction method, or PCR. These initial markers give us a probability odds factor in the neighborhood of one in five thousand."

"Can I get that in English?"

"Sorry. It's the initial DNA comparison method that only uses six markers, called loci. Anyway, to make a long story short, the bloodstain on the carpet is not consistent with the DNA I extracted from the victim at the time of autopsy."

Mac closed his eyes and pinched the bridge of his nose. "Joe Higgins said he'd cut himself. I guess he was telling the truth."

"Sorry, Mac. I've begun the more comprehensive DNA analysis, but that won't be ready for several days. I'll fax the report over to the Troutdale P.D. I'll also run an analysis on those cigarette butts you brought in. That will tell us for sure if the sample was Joe Higgins's blood."

"Thanks. I'll let the gang know."

"Do you still want a CSI crew over at the Parkview apartment? We're tied up on another case right now, but I can have someone out there later this afternoon."

"I don't know—I'd say yes, but let me ask Kevin and get back to you."

Mac snapped the mouthpiece shut on his cell phone and stared out the window of the car for a moment, his left foot still dangling outside the open car door. He slammed his fist on the steering wheel. "So much for your big find, *Detective.*" He looked into the rearview mirror. Why couldn't it have been Megan's blood? Mac climbed out of the car and locked it up, then took his time getting back to the church.

"I have some good news and some bad news," Mac said when he joined Eric and Kevin inside. "Allison said it was definitely blood, but the initial test indicated that it wasn't Megan's."

Both men expressed their frustration.

"Allison said she'd test the cigarette butts we found on Joe's patio to determine if the blood was Joe's."

"Thanks, Mac." Kevin looked worse than Mac felt. They had all put a little too much hope in that tiny speck of blood. "Okay, so the blood isn't Megan's. Joe may be telling us the truth, but I'm not ready to let him off the hook. Since we've got things set up for the crime lab to check out Joe's apartment, I'd like to go ahead with it. We have to do at least that much."

Eric agreed. "The consent is still good, so go for it."

"Allison can't get to it until later this afternoon," Mac said.

Kevin nodded. "I'll reaffirm with the landlord when we get there. I don't see any need for a warrant yet."

Mac stepped out to call Allison then came back inside where Eric and Kevin were still talking.

"I'll keep Philly and Russ here to follow through with the funeral." Eric looked around at the massive room full of people.

"I'd like to pay my respects, too, then we'll head over to the apartment."

The service was starting. The detectives filed into the main part of the church and stood against the back wall.

The minister opened in prayer then welcomed people. He looked out over the congregation. "We're here today to mourn the death of a beautiful young woman, Megan Tyson."

From his vantage point in the back Mac could see Cindy and Tim. Tim had an arm around Cindy's shoulders. Two seats behind them sat a man in a black ponytail. Joe Higgins.

"I'm sure many of you are wondering how a God we claim is loving can allow such horrific things to happen."

Mac lowered his head, remembering how he had blamed God. Now the minister was saying much the same thing Kevin had. How God gets blamed for a lot of bad things and how God does not choose pain and suffering—they are part of the human condition.

"Megan is no longer suffering. There is no pain, for the Lord has brought her home. There will always be evil. There will always be suffering and death. But in the end, good triumphs over evil. Even now, detectives are working hard to find Megan's killer. For that we can be thankful."

Mac's gaze traveled back to Joe Higgins. He'd come to give Cindy the earrings. On the surface it seemed a magnanimous thing to do. Was it just for show?

He took it all in—the mourners, the curious, the priest with his words of comfort, assuring those present that Megan was indeed in a better place. One older man who said he'd been a friend of the family for twenty years talked about his old friend, Megan's father, and how proud Father Tyson had been of Megan. "I am grieved at Megan's passing but also must consider their reunion in heaven. How joyous they both must be."

Kevin leaned into him and whispered, "Look off to your left. Gordon Reed just came in."

Looking at Gordon, Mac realized they hadn't visited him at his home. Maybe they were wrong about Higgins. He wondered what besides drugs the other detectives had found at Gordon's place. He wondered why the guy wasn't in jail. Maybe he had been and was out on bail.

"I think we should take a closer look at Gordon," Mac told his partner once the service ended and they were on their way to Mac's car.

"You have a valid point, Mac. The trouble is we can only go in so many directions at once. It's easy to get shortsighted. I haven't ruled out old Gordy, but I'm inclined to wait on him until we exhaust Higgins and DeLong. They have the most violent criminal histories. If the trail runs cold on them, we'll turn our attention to Reed."

"I guess that makes sense." Impatience had hit Mac alongside the head again.

Kevin elbowed him. "Let's run by Higgins's old place and make sure Dana is okay with staying until Eric gets there. We still want to make another run at Higgins this afternoon, before he lawyers up."

They arrived at the Parkview Apartments within twenty minutes. After parking the car in the space reserved for apartment fourteen and waving a greeting to Dana, Mac and Kevin walked to the manager's office.

"Back again?" Theresa came to the screen door. "Do you need back in that apartment?"

"Yes, ma'am," Mac said. "We'd like to have your continued permission to have unrestricted access to the apartment, if that's okay."

Theresa opened the screen door and stepped out. "Did you find something in there?" she asked. "Bernie said you were working a murder or something."

"We found some trace evidence in the carpet that interested us," Kevin responded. "We're having our crime lab do a more thorough investigation."

Theresa looked skeptical.

"I assure you we will pay for any damage we cause."

"Sounds fine with me. I'm sure the state is good for it." She smiled. "The place could use new carpet anyway. Let me call Bernie to make sure it's all right, though."

Theresa disappeared into the apartment.

"Lab rats are here," Kevin said as the crime lab's blue F-250 pickup pulled into the parking lot. "They must have finished up earlier than they thought."

Mac watched two figures in white lab coats emerge from the truck. Allison Sprague was one of them. He wondered what she'd think if she knew she was being referred to as a lab rat.

Kevin looked through the screen door. "Let's hope we don't have to take three hours and write a search warrant affidavit."

Theresa came back, this time toting a toddler with jelly-coated cheeks and lips. "Bernie says it's okay, just as long as you pay for anything you break or whatever. He'll be by later to give you a hand, if you need it. Here are the keys." Theresa slid open the door and handed Mac two keys on a stainless-steel ring. "I'd go over with you, but I've got a house full of little ones."

"That's fine, ma'am; thanks for your help." Mac took the keys, caught the grin on the toddler's face, and smiled back.

They let the lab techs in and told Dana she could go.

"Um, would you mind if I hung around? I have a lunch and a break coming." She grinned and tucked a strand of hair behind her ear.

"Okay by me, but I could think of more appetizing places to spend my lunch," Mac said.

Kevin gave her a knowing smile. "Mac told me about your wanting to move into the detective division. Sounds like he gave you some good advice. We can talk later if you want."

Dana's eyes brightened even more. "That would be great, sir. Thanks."

Mac took out his camera equipment, and Kevin offered to take the photos so Mac could watch the process. Allison pulled on her gloves and went inside with Mac, Dana, and Kevin following. "Where did you find that blood sample, Mac? We might as well start there."

Mac showed her where they'd cut the carpet fibers. Allison opened a window and put on a painter's mask and goggles, then pulled a spray bottle out of her kit. "Stay back guys. I'm going to spray some luminol."

"Is it toxic?" Mac asked.

"Not really. Just better to use it in a ventilated area." She sprayed the luminol on the carpet near the place Mac had found the blood spot. Nothing. She continued spraying all around the area where the bed had been, holding a wand-sized blue light in her left hand. On the other side of the bed marks, nearest to the bathroom, she let out a long whistle.

"Well, would you look at that? We have blood, people—a whole lot more than you'd get from cutting a finger."

Chapter Thirty-Eight

Kevin snapped photo after photo of the telltale carpet. Mac could hardly breathe. The illuminated stain covered a three-foot area alongside the indentation where the bed had been. "Wonder how Higgins is going to explain this one?"

Allison's partner leaned into the bedroom. "I found traces of blood on the concrete in the storage room. Looks like they used an industrial cleanser."

"Right, but cleaners can only go so far. With this much blood there had to be some hand-washing and such. Check out the sinks and pull the drain traps." Looking at Kevin, she said, "We'll need to pull up the carpet in this bedroom. I doubt that was done when they cleaned it. There might be some interesting stuff parked under the carpet and pad."

Several minutes later, the same lab tech reported traces of blood in the bathtub, as well as in the sink.

"There's still blood in the drains?" Mac asked. "How is that possible? Wouldn't the water rinse it down?"

"Fortunately, there was a lot of hair and foreign matter in the drain traps, which formed a substantial obstruction in both. I dried a portion of the matter—it tests positive for blood. We'll get these to the lab and let Allison perform her magic on them."

Mac helped the male tech loosen the edges of the carpet from the tack strips. They rolled up the carpet and pad, revealing dark prominent stains on the floor. He and Mac secured the roll with large plastic ties and carried it out to the truck.

On his way back in, the pager on Mac's hip vibrated. He checked the number, pulled out his cell phone, and punched in the unfamiliar number.

Megan's fiancé answered immediately. "Yes, Detective McAllister, thanks for calling back. I wanted to talk to you before I left town, so I got your pager number from the police station. I plan to fly home tomorrow. Do you need to talk to me before I go?"

"I'll have to get back to you on that, Tim—we're tied up right now, but I'll check with the boss and give you a call."

Mac hung up and went into the house, where Kevin was helping Allison measure a large dark spot on the floor. Mac told him about the call from Tim.

"Tell him he's free to go and that we are still following up on several leads. We have a lot of work to do yet, so don't say anything about these recent developments. I don't want him hanging around or getting in our way."

Kevin bent down to help Allison again, then changed his mind and stood to face Mac. "Hey, Mac. Make sure you thank him for the cooperation he gave us and say that he is not subject to any further scrutiny. Let's put the poor guy's mind at ease. Just tell Tim we're sorry for his loss and that we are doing everything in our power to bring the killer to justice. Just tell him that."

"Killer to justice, got it." Mac acted like he was writing the quote down.

"Just tell him something, smarty." Kevin threw a roll of evidence tape at Mac. "See what I have to work with?" Kevin told Allison.

She laughed and shook her head. "You guys."

Mac returned a few minutes later, meeting up with Kevin in the front room of the apartment. "I told him pretty much what you said."

"What did he say?" Kevin asked.

"Not much; he was real choked up." Mac swallowed back the sudden lump at the back of his throat. "Said he wanted to thank us for coming to the funeral today."

"Anything else?" asked Kevin.

"That's it. He wants to be kept up to speed."

"We're done here," Allison said. "You guys can take off. I'll lock up and get our evidence to the lab. I'll be able to tell you tomorrow morning if this is Megan's blood. We're looking at a long shot here. I'll tell you one thing, though. If this isn't Megan's blood, I'd like to find out whose it is. I really think we have us a murder scene, boys."

Kevin chewed on his bottom lip. "For now I'm going to assume the blood is Megan's. I'm also going to assume that Joe Higgins has been playing games with us. Come on, Mac." Kevin handed the camera back to its owner. "Time for us to make the next move."

"Thanks for letting me observe," Dana said.

Mac had almost forgotten she was there. "No problem, Dana. Thank you for preserving the scene."

"Anytime." She glanced from Kevin to Mac. "Call me when you need an extra hand. And I mean that."

When she'd gone, Kevin put in a call to Eric. "Hey, pal, where did you go?" Kevin told him about their find. "I want to hit Higgins up on this right away," Kevin said. "Just because we put Wallace into isolation doesn't mean Higgins can't get word to him via another convict." He paused to listen to Eric's response.

"No." Kevin eyed Mac and headed for the car. "I don't think we need backup at this point. We're not ready for an arrest yet. I want to hear back from Allison first on the new lab results. If we don't get any admissions from Higgins, then maybe he'll cough up some provable lies."

Kevin shut the car door and Mac started the car. "Think he's home yet?" Mac asked.

"Only one way to find out."

KEVIN AND MAC ARRIVED at Higgins's duplex on Macadam Court in less than thirty minutes. Kevin told Mac to park across the street so they could assess the situation. The driveway was empty.

"Doesn't look like he's home, " Mac said.

"He may want us to believe that." Kevin looked up and down the street. "No sign of his car, but it might be in the garage."

"He did say he had a job interview after the funeral."

"Right, but I wouldn't trust anything he says."

Mac's heart pounded like a drum in a rock band as he flattened against the wall outside the door. Kevin stood across from Mac, also standing away from the door in case Higgins tried to pull something. Mac gave a nod of readiness to Kevin, who knocked on the door.

There was no answer. Kevin glanced at Mac and knocked again, this time announcing himself. "Higgins, you in there? It's the state police."

Again, no response. Mac thought he could hear or feel movement from within the duplex. Or maybe it was simply his own blood pulsing through his veins.

"I still think he's in there. I thought I saw a light go off." He pressed his lips together. "Come on. I got a plan."

Mac went back to the car with Kevin, glancing back at the duplex at least twice during the short trek. At Kevin's instructions, Mac drove around the block, came back, and parked again, farther back but still able to see the duplex.

"Why do you think he didn't answer?" Mac asked. "You think someone tipped him off?"

"I'll bet he's worried his friend Wallace hasn't called like he said he would." Kevin took out his cell phone. "Maybe Higgins is a little concerned his buddy might rat on him."

"Are you sure he didn't cut and run?"

"No." Kevin ran a hand down his face. "I'm not."

"We'll wait here for a few minutes and give him a call."

"Call him?" Mac asked, surprised by the suggestion.

"Yeah. He may not answer his door, but he might answer his phone."

About three minutes later, Mac scanned his previous notes for Higgins's phone number and punched in the digits. It rang six times before Higgins answered.

"Yeah," Higgins answered.

"Mr. Higgins?" Mac asked, knowing full well who it was.

"Speaking," Higgins replied.

"This is Detective McAllister with the state police."

"Oh, hey, how's it going?" Higgins said with an overly friendly voice.

"Pretty good. How'd the job interview go?"

"Oh, we'll see. I think it looks pretty good, though."

"Great, that's good news," Mac said. "So are you going to have time to speak with us today?"

"Couldn't you just ask me what you need over the phone?" Higgins asked.

"We have quite a few questions, and it's usually better to interview in person," Mac replied.

"What kind of questions?" Higgins wanted to know. "I mean, if it's that lie detector thing, I talked with a lawyer and he said those things aren't worth the trouble. I'd rather not take the time—you guys are either going to believe me or you're not. All I can say is I've told the truth."

"That's your right, Joe, so we won't push it. But it'll be available if you change your mind."

"I won't."

"We really need to hook up on these follow-up questions," Mac pressed. "We'd like your opinion on a few things." Kevin gave Mac a thumbs-up.

There were several seconds of dead air before Higgins answered,

"I don't see why you can't just ask me over the phone. But come on over if you have to do it in person."

"Is right now a good time?" Mac asked nonchalantly.

"I'm working on my car," Higgins sighed. "But now is as good as any other, I guess."

"Great, we'll be right over," Mac said.

"Who's we?" Higgins sounded nervous.

"My partner, Detective Bledsoe, and I."

"Oh, right."

Mac turned the phone off. "He said to come right over."

"Well done. You never let him off the hook," Kevin said. "Higgins has to play ball now; he's still hoping to deflect the suspicion. This guy is a pretty cool character, Mac, so we have to be careful with this interview. It might be our last. Don't come right out and hammer him with what we recently learned about the bloodstains. We want to keep him talking, so save that until the end of the interview. Oh, and I'd like you to tape this one."

"Okay," Mac answered with a deep exhale through pursed lips, patting his inside jacket pocket to make sure the mini cassette recorder was where he usually kept it.

"Mac, I have the utmost confidence in you. This interview will be a snap. Just give me the high sign when you're ready to turn it over. I don't care if it's one minute or one hour. Just do what feels right."

Mac nodded, wishing he had the same confidence in himself.

"Um, I don't know if you're interested, but Eric and I used to say a quick prayer before we tackled what could turn into a volatile situation. Would you mind?"

What could he say? No? Truth was, Mac wouldn't mind getting some celestial help.

"I can use all the help I can get," he finally said.

Kevin nodded and bowed his head. Mac instinctively did the

same. Kevin's prayer was simple and to the point, asking for guidance and protection and an end to the search for Megan's killer.

"I can see why you pray," Mac admitted. "It's hard to explain, but I feel stronger."

"I know what you mean. Now let's go talk to Higgins."

"What if he confesses?" Mac turned the key.

Kevin grinned. "Then you'll have to take out your handcuffs and place him under arrest for murder, because I'll be too busy trying to catch one of those flying pigs."

"What?"

He drove the half-block to Higgins's duplex and was pulling into the driveway when Kevin's smart remark caught up with him. "When pigs fly—I get it." He rolled his eyes. "Ha, ha."

"I've got a million of 'em."

"Spare me." The brief banter loosened Mac up a bit, but he was still tighter than an overblown balloon.

DANA BENNETT SUPPRESSED A YAWN as she headed home to her apartment in Gresham. Her shift had ended and she was bone tired. She'd been working way too much overtime, but for a good cause. She wanted to make detective and intended to do whatever it took. She smiled at the way she'd been able to keep up with this last murder investigation and put herself in the right place at the right time. Of course, it helped to have a boss who knew what she wanted.

This last assignment had been fascinating, getting to watch the lab techs gather evidence. All that blood in a place that looked virtually spotless. She didn't know much about the various suspects, or people of interest. The detectives didn't like to call them suspects until they had solid evidence. They had a lot of interest in this Joe Higgins guy. He sounded like a real sleazeball.

A scratchy voice came over her radio. "Need the closest unit to respond to Forty-fifth and Beech Street on a twelve-forty-nine Adam."

Every trace of sleepiness left her as adrenaline kicked in. This time Dana didn't have to consult her cheat sheet. Twelve-forty-nine Adam meant a possible homicide.

"Eleven-twenty-five," Dana responded. "Burnside and Division—I'm about five minutes out." Hitting her lights and siren, Dana flipped a U-turn and headed back to Troutdale.

Dispatch came back in with, "Eleven-twenty-five, reporting party is standing by. We have a DOA in his vehicle. Detectives are paged out, request you secure the scene."

"Eleven-twenty-five, copy, en route."

Seconds later, Dana's patrol sergeant called on the radio asking her to go to open, or what they called the gab channel.

She did. "What can I do for you, Sarge?"

"Are you sure you want to do this one, Dana? A few minutes ago you told me you needed some shuteye."

"Not a problem. I'm wide awake and ready for action."

"Okay, have at it."

REACHING THE DOOR to Joe Higgins's duplex, Mac assumed the role as lead detective and knocked. The door opened slowly and there stood Joe Higgins, again wearing the black sweatsuit. His hair was loose this time, with black curls hiding most of his face.

"Hello, Detectives. C'mon in." Higgins's Adam's apple shifted up and down in a nervous gesture.

"Thanks for meeting with us," Mac said. "This shouldn't take too long, just a few more questions."

"Sure, have a seat on the couch. Make yourself at home." Higgins settled into the brown recliner, leaving the large sofa for Mac and Kevin. The coffee table provided an effective barrier.

Mac noted that the pornographic magazines had been

removed from the base of the coffee table. Higgins sat forward in his seat, as though he were ready to run if necessary.

"Joe, I'd like to record this interview if you don't mind." Mac pulled a tape recorder from his coat. "It saves me time, not having to take notes and all."

"Sure, suit yourself." His eyes darted from the device to Kevin, to Mac, and to his feet. The action negated the indifference in his words.

Mac activated the tape recorder, setting the device on the coffee table. "All right, for the record, my name is Detective Mac McAllister, Oregon State Police. Also present is Detective Kevin Bledsoe, also state police. We are in an interview with Mr. Joe Higgins. Last name spelled H-i-g-g-i-n-s. Mr. Higgins, are you aware that we are recording your conversation?"

Higgins nodded and Mac reminded him to reply audibly, which he did.

"Detective Bledsoe, you are also aware?" Mac added.

"Yes I am."

"Mr. Higgins," Mac continued, "before we get started, I just want to make it clear that you're not under arrest and we have no intention of placing you under arrest at this point. If at any time during our conversation you feel that you don't want to answer a question or want to terminate the interview, you're certainly welcome to do that. Do you understand all of that?"

"Yeah, sure. I've got nothing to hide." Joe curled his fingers and examined his nails.

"Good," Mac said. "I don't have a lot of questions, Mr. Higgins. But before I get started, do you have anything you'd like to ask me?"

"No, I just want this to get over with so I can go about my life and not have the cops showing up every few hours." Higgins leveled a sharp glare at them.

"That's what we would like to accomplish also," Mac said.

"For the record, could you briefly go over your relationship with Megan Tyson again? Just give us the *Reader's Digest* version."

"First of all, we didn't have a relationship," Higgins said, leaning over to the tape recorder when he spoke. "I just lifted at the gym where Megan worked. We went out once and there was no love connection, so there's nothing else to say."

"You went to dinner, then ended up at her place during the date?" Mac asked.

"I wouldn't exactly call it a date, just a couple of friends getting together," Higgins corrected. "But yeah, like I told you guys before, I thought I could get some that night, went for center field, and struck out. That doesn't mean I killed her."

"Of course it doesn't, Mr. Higgins, just trying to give a little history here," Mac said.

"Right, well, don't stress that too much for the record or whatever," Higgins warned. "I don't know where we're going with this. Maybe I need a lawyer . . . I don't know."

"If you murdered Megan Tyson, then yeah, you'll need a lawyer," Mac snapped, stealing one of his partner's lines. "But if you had nothing to do with this, then I suggest you cooperate with us."

"You're right, I'm sorry." Joe lifted his hands in mock surrender. "Please go on."

"You're positive there was no sexual contact between you and Ms. Tyson?"

"Positive." Higgins pressed his lips together.

"So there would be no reason we would find any trace evidence on Ms. Tyson's remains that belongs to you?"

"No." Higgins sat back in his chair.

"What kind of bed do you own, Mr. Higgins?"

"It's a king-size," he said. "A real monster, a waterbed actually."

"You had that in your old place in Troutdale?"

"Yep, I've had it for quite a while." Higgins got to his feet. "Say, do you guys want a Pepsi or something?"

"No thanks," Mac answered. Kevin shook his head.

"Well, if you don't mind, I'd like one."

"Sure, go ahead. We just have a few more questions." Mac tensed. Did Joe intend to flee?

"Okay, just let me know if you want anything." Joe disappeared into the kitchen and reappeared with a can of soda. He popped the top, taking several swallows.

"Thanks." Mac picked up the tape recorder to see how much room was left on the tape. "Tell me about Mitch Wallace again. The two of you celled together in FCI Houston, right?"

"You got it. Mitch came up to visit, said he was just out of the joint. He got picked up by you guys—well, not you two, but the cops out in Gladstone."

"Yes, you mentioned that before." Mac watched the guy's face. "And remind me where you two were going when Wallace was arrested."

"Just heading home. We hit the bars and caught a few shows," Higgins replied.

"Have you had any contact with Mr. Wallace lately?" Mac asked.

"Nope, none at all," Higgins answered without hesitation.

"Did Mr. Wallace have a key to your apartment in Troutdale when he was staying with you?"

"No way! You think I would trust that guy? He's a thief." Higgins bit the inside of his cheek. "I kept the keys to my pad. Mitch came and went with me."

"Would you consider Mr. Wallace a good friend?" Mac asked.

"I suppose, but I still wouldn't trust him," Higgins added.

"Would you lie to protect him?" Mac asked bluntly.

"I might. I wouldn't take a murder rap for him, if that's what you're asking." Higgins came back across the room and sat down. "Did Mitch get into more trouble while he was staying at my pad? That stupid son of a—"

"Would you tell us if Mr. Wallace was involved in Megan's death?" Mac interrupted.

"In a New York second, man, without hesitation."

"Good, I may remind you of that."

Higgins leaned back into the chair.

Mac moved closer to the edge of his seat. It was time to confront him with the blood evidence. "Detective Bledsoe and I went over your old apartment with a fine-tooth comb, Mr. Higgins. Not just us, but a team of forensic scientists. You did a good job cleaning up, but not good enough."

Higgins turned an unflattering shade of gray. "What do you mean?"

"We found blood in your bedroom, Mr. Higgins. A lot of blood."

"That's not possible. You guys are messing with my head. You think because I have a prison record, you can dump this thing on me. Well, I'm not falling for your tricks."

With a voice as solid and controlled as he could manage, Mac delivered the final blow. "Megan Tyson died in your apartment, and we intend to prove it. If you had nothing to do with her death, I suggest you tell us who did. If Wallace killed her, you might want to think twice about lying for him."

"This interview is over." Higgins glared at Mac, then Kevin. "Turn that thing off. From here on out you can talk to my attorney."

"If you say so." Mac pressed the "stop" button on the player and, following Kevin's lead, headed for the door.

"You guys are not going to pin this thing on me."

"Remember what the detective said, Mr. Higgins," Kevin delivered a parting shot. "We'll be in touch."

Higgins stood there staring at Kevin with such a hateful look in his eyes, Mac expected him to erupt in flames. Or, at the very least, slam one of his clenched fists into Kevin's face. Sliding his hand under his jacket, Mac gripped the handle of his Glock pistol.

"Are you going to make trouble, son?" Kevin straightened slightly, showing his extra height and stature.

Higgins hesitated for a moment. "You'd like that, wouldn't you?" He backed inside and slammed the door, sliding the deadbolt back into place.

"That went well." Mac blew out a long breath as he and Kevin walked back toward the car.

"Extremely. We almost had him."

"I thought for a minute there I was going to have to pick you off the floor. I tell you, partner, Clint Eastwood's got nothing on you. Man, I thought you were going to tell him to make your day."

Kevin chuckled. "I almost did."

"Let's head south, to the gray-bar motel, Mac," Kevin said when they reached the car. "We need to have a little talk with Mitch Wallace. Maybe he'll tell us where all that blood came from."

"Sounds like a plan to me." Mac started the car and gripped the wheel. They were getting close.

"Eric paged me while we were in session with Mr. Higgins. I'd better get back to him." Kevin dialed the number as he spoke.

"Hey, Red, what happened to you? Thought you were meeting us out at Joe's old apartment." There was a pause, then he said, "No kidding." Kevin shot Mac a look of surprise. "How long ago?"

"What's going on?" Mac mouthed.

Kevin held up a hand. "Okay, we just finished an interview with Higgins and were headed to Salem to talk with his buddy, but we'll hold up on that." Kevin paused again. "You got it."

Kevin put his phone back into his jacket pocket. "Head on back to Troutdale, Mac. We've got another murder."

Mac frowned. "Another female victim?"

"Nope. Gordon Reed."

Chapter Thirty-Nine

Mac leaned against his car, watching the deputy medical examiner and Russ and Philly process the scene. The sight of the bloodied corpse wasn't what made his stomach churn. It was being yanked back to square one. Another murder, another slashed throat—Gordon's death was obviously linked to Megan's. Had they been going after the wrong man? When he'd first seen Gordon's face, he'd immediately thought of Tim Morris, not Joe Higgins.

"What are you thinking, Mac? You look like you're ready to do someone in yourself." Kevin stood beside him, arms crossed, legs slightly apart.

Mac rubbed at the creases on his brow. "Just trying to make sense of it. My first reaction is that Tim figured out who Gordon was—wouldn't have been all that hard. We told him about the poly and all he would have had to do was to stake out the police parking lot. Maybe he saw him at the funeral and went crazy."

"I hear you, partner. As far as I can tell, he and Cindy are the only people involved in the case who knew about Gordon."

"I feel like we ought to be looking at Higgins—you know, with the throat slashing, but if I wanted to get rid of a guy in public, I'd probably use a knife rather than call attention to myself by using a gun."

The M.E. moved away from the body and Gordon's car. "Due to the lack of rigor I'd say he was killed within the last couple of hours."

Mac did a little calculating. "After the funeral, that's for sure. We went over to Higgins's old apartment. And got that call from Tim."

Kevin gave Mac a wry smile. "And we cut him loose."

Eric, who had just joined them, said, "Let me get somebody on the fiancé. Unless you two want to run him down."

"Excuse me," Dana interrupted. "I'm off patrol duty right now. I could track this guy down for you. Just tell me what to do."

Eric grinned at her. "What are you looking for, a promotion?"

"Hey, with the budget crunch, all the departments are short-handed. There's a lot going on and too few people to handle things. I'm not doing anything right now, so use me." Her cheeks dimpled with that irresistible smile of hers. "And, yeah, I'd like to move into homicide."

It didn't take long for the detectives to take Dana up on her offer. Providing her with pertinent information, including a photo, rental car description, and destination, the detectives wished her luck and sent her off, asking her to check in with them often. "And, Dana," Eric added as an afterthought, "be careful. He may have passed the lie detector test with flying colors, but that doesn't mean he's innocent."

"Right."

Mac gave her a thumbs-up sign as she drove away. Turning to his partner, he said, "So what's our next move?"

"What do you think we should do?" Kevin slipped his hands into his pockets and rocked back on his heels.

"Is this a test?" Mac looked back at Gordon and tipped his head back. "Mitch will keep. I think we should have a talk with Cindy—see if she can tell us anything about Tim and make sure she's okay."

"I'm with you." Kevin nodded. "Give her a call."

Mac flipped through his notes for Cindy's number and dialed. A woman answered, but Mac didn't recognize her voice. "Is Cindy there?"

"Who wants to know?" The woman sounded frightened.

Mac introduced himself.

"I'm Cindy's roommate. I've been thinking of calling you guys. Cindy didn't show up at the reception after the funeral and she hasn't come home. I thought I'd check at the cemetery first, then swing by her and Megan's old apartment. Tim came to say goodbye and seemed upset that she wasn't there. Said he might try to find her but had a plane to catch."

"Why didn't you call us sooner?" Mac's heart shifted into overdrive.

Kevin gave him a what's-up look and Mac covered the mouthpiece to explain. "Cindy may be missing. The roomie says she didn't go to the reception."

Kevin groaned. "What next?"

"It hasn't been that long," the woman said. "I was going to call if she wasn't at the cemetery or her old place."

"Okay. I take it you were at the funeral with her."

"Yes. I was with her the entire time until . . ."

"Until?"

"She was talking to people after the interment. I had to go back to the church to help set up, and when she didn't come, I got worried."

"Who did she talk to?"

"Um . . . some guy named Gordon. He said he was really sorry about Megan and that he'd liked her a lot."

"Was Tim with her at that time?"

"Yes, now that you mention it, and he was sort of rude to the guy. I just figured he was, you know, grieving. There was a guy with black hair—he had it in a ponytail. He gave Cindy some earrings that Megan had commissioned him to make. Neat man. He could have insisted she pay, you know? But he just gave them to her and Tim. Said Megan had designed them and he thought they might want them."

"How did Tim react to that?"

"He seemed impressed. They were gorgeous—had to be worth some big bucks. Tim offered to pay for them, but the guy, I think his name was Joe, said he couldn't take the money in a situation like that. Tim and Cindy thanked him and he left. None of them came to the reception." She hesitated. "Um, there was a guy at the reception looking for Cindy, though. He said something about Megan giving him some things—a TV set and stuff—and said if Cindy wanted it she could have it. He was leaving town and didn't plan on taking it with him."

Matthew DeLong. Mac could hardly breathe. His fuses were all lit and he felt as though he'd explode any minute. He thanked the roommate for her help and briefed Kevin and Eric on the conversation.

"Oh, man." Eric rubbed a hand over his short hair. "This thing is getting out of hand. I'm not sure I'm up to it. Whose idea was it to let Frank go to Hawaii? I tell you, when this thing is over—if it ever is—I'm going on a long cruise."

"Take it easy, Eric." Kevin slapped his former partner on the back. "All we have to do is clone ourselves and be at four places at once."

Mac rubbed the back of his neck, trying to regain his composure. "My grandmothers used to tell me that when a problem gets too big, like this case has, you have to step away from it or it sucks you in and you can't accomplish anything. You think of it in terms of pieces—like working a puzzle, you put it together one piece at a time."

"Good advice, Mac," Eric said. "It's easy to forget that."

Mac checked his notebook for phone numbers. "I'm going to call Matthew's sister and see if she knows anything."

"Smart thinking." Kevin nodded his approval. "We can put out an APB on him and let the troops bring him in."

"Okay," Eric said. "Dana is covering the fiancé—let's hope he's clean and she doesn't have a fight on her hands."

"Who knows?" Mac said. "Maybe Cindy decided to go to

Florida with him. They did seem pretty chummy. I know he passed the polygraph test, but maybe he and Cindy killed Megan so they could be together."

Kevin groaned. "Maybe you ought to be writing mystery novels instead of solving crimes."

"That hurt." Mac joked to cover his embarrassment. "It's not all that far off."

"You're right, Mac. I'm sorry. It's just that we have way too many scenarios on this one. I wish it were more straightforward." He sighed. "We definitely need to narrow the playing field."

"If Cindy is with Tim, Dana should be able to tell us soon enough." Eric jotted a few notes on his pad. "And we shouldn't have too much trouble picking up Matthew. He doesn't have that much of a head start on us."

Mac dialed Matthew's sister's phone number. She sounded pretty upset.

"He was afraid you'd pin that girl's murder on him because he had her stuff and couldn't really prove she had given it to him."

"Did he tell you where he was heading?" Mac asked.

"No. He said he was giving everything back to Megan's sister and heading out. I have a hunch it might be Canada. He has friends up on Vancouver Island."

"Thanks for your help, Mrs. Keeley."

"If you find him—he didn't kill that girl. I know it. He's running scared. I tried to tell him it would be okay and that running would make him more suspect, but . . . Well, Matthew has always been kind of high-strung."

After thanking her again, Mac snapped his cell phone shut. "She thinks he might be headed north."

"I'm on it," Eric said. "We'll get the word out. The guy won't get far."

"Okay," Kevin said. "The fog is lifting. Two suspects down—three, counting the body. That leaves Joe Higgins—Mr. Nice

Guy—and his good buddy, Mitch, who's cool until we can get to him. Let's pay another call on Joe and see if he knows anything about these new developments."

"I don't know how he would have found the time to kill Gordon and be involved in Cindy's disappearance," Mac said, thinking aloud. "We went to his house, what, an hour after the funeral? We know he was home at four."

Kevin nodded. "True, but you'd be surprised at how quickly things can be accomplished when you're organized."

"Okay, I admit Joe is a greaseball, but if he abducted Cindy, wouldn't he have taken off instead of going home?" Mac stopped short. "He told us he was working on his car when I called. The car must have been in the garage."

"I'm thinking the same thing, partner. Maybe he was working on something else."

Mac thought he was going to be sick. "You don't think he had Cindy in his garage when we were there?"

"I don't know, Mac. Let's hope not. I'd hate to think the guy was committing another murder right under our noses."

Kevin and Mac knocked on Joe Higgins's door ten minutes later. Joe didn't respond to the knock. An older woman, who'd been pulling weeds in the flower garden of the duplex next-door, eyed the detectives. After seeing the men peer into Joe's windows, she walked across the grass and confronted them. "Can I help you gentlemen?"

Mac introduced himself and Kevin. "We're with the Oregon State Police."

"My goodness! Has Mr. Higgins done something wrong? He seems like such a nice man."

"Not that we know of, ma'am. We just need to ask him some questions regarding a case we're working on."

She glanced at Mac's car. "You were here earlier, weren't you?"

"Yes, ma'am."

"Well, you won't find him here. He left a good half-hour ago."

"Great." Mac left the thank-you to Kevin and they headed for the car. "Should we search the house?"

"We can call in for a warrant—that'll take about twenty minutes."

"That's a long time." Mac looked back at the house. "I seem to remember something about entering a residence forcefully if we have probable cause—like if someone's life was in danger. Cindy could be in there."

"I doubt it, but I'd feel better knowing for sure. I'm right behind you."

Mac didn't need any more encouragement. He made for the door and, using a straight kick he'd learned in defensive tactics training, he aligned his foot and kicked the door right next to the knob. The doorframe splintered and gave them access.

They did a quick run through the duplex. No Cindy and no sign she'd been there. Mac did note that the bedroom had a large cabinet against one wall. There was a big screen TV and video equipment along with several stacks of videos. Kevin picked up a couple and shook his head. "Snuff films."

"What?"

"They're the lowest of the low, Mac. So-called actors pretend to rape and murder their sexual partners. Looks like Higgins was into it big time."

They found stacks of *Penthouse* and *Hustler* along with a couple of bondage magazines.

"Let's go, Mac. I've seen enough."

As they were passing through the living room, past the kitchen, Mac spotted a pair of earrings on the counter. "Whoa. Aren't these the earrings Higgins made for Megan?"

Kevin looked closely at the diamond earrings. "Looks like it. If Joe gave them to Cindy at the funeral, what are they doing here?"

"I'm not sure I want to know."

"Let's put these in an evidence bag, Mac. We'll seize these under the authority the exigent circumstances case law gives us. I think it would be easy to justify the risk. If we leave these puppies behind, they may disappear."

Once the earrings were bagged, the detectives headed back to the car.

Mac buckled himself in and cranked the key. "We should have arrested him when we were here this morning."

"The evidence, Mac. We still don't have any real proof that he killed Megan."

"But we know he killed someone. Like Allison said, all that blood . . ."

"Suggests someone may have been killed. Mitch Wallace had access to the place—so did the manager. And who's to say the blood wasn't there when Joe moved in? We don't want to make an arrest unless we have enough evidence to hold him. This morning we were working on a hunch, and hunches don't hold up well in court. Now we have the earrings, which in themselves don't necessarily implicate him. We don't even know for sure that Cindy is in any harm. But my gut tells me she's in trouble and that Joe is behind it."

"Mine too. Any ideas on where we might find this guy?"

Kevin secured his seat belt and sighed. "A couple. Remember what Joe said he and Mitch did for fun? And where they got stopped by the traffic cop in Clackamas County?"

"Yeah. Out in Gladstone."

"The area where they got pulled over is known for bars and strip joints. I'd say we head over there and see if we can spot his car." Kevin rubbed his chin and glanced skyward. "Lord, keep Cindy safe and help us find her."

Mac made a beeline for Highway 99E.

They cruised the strip and spotted Joe's vehicle on the second pass by. Mac parked behind it, blocking its exit. He actually said a silent prayer as he and Kevin entered the dimly lighted bar. Even at this time of the day, colored lights illuminated a scantily clothed woman. Mac liked women as well as the next guy, but this one repelled him. He wondered what had happened in her life that she would take such a degrading job. The place smelled of booze and stale cigarettes and reminded him of his father. Mac shook his head. What had turned his father into a slobbering drunk and a two-bit crook?

"My sinuses are already beginning to clog." Kevin stood with his hands on his hips while he scanned the place. Several people glanced in their direction then went back to whatever they were doing.

"A lot of people here for a weekday afternoon."

"After quitting time for some."

They approached slowly at first, getting the lay of the land, hoping to spot Joe before he saw them. Kevin elbowed Mac and pointed to a guy at the bar hunched over a drink and watching the stage. Joe saw them coming and turned away, but not soon enough to keep Mac from seeing the surprise and disgust that crossed his features.

Joe turned toward them again, this time all smiles. "Hey fellas, if I'd known you were into this kind of thing, I'd have invited you to join me."

Mac stiffened. *We're not.*

"Easy, partner," Kevin murmured as if he'd read Mac's thoughts. "We're still in the talking stages here. You take one side; I'll take the other."

Mac forced his personal feelings aside, sauntered up to the bar, and hitched himself up on a stool.

"Can I get you boys something?" The bartender approached them.

Kevin flashed his badge. "Some privacy would be nice."

The guy shrugged, held up his palms, and backed away. "Take all you need."

"So . . ." Joe took a drink of what looked like a second glass of dark beer. "What brings you two to the slums? Must be important for you to track me way out here."

"It is, Joe." Kevin settled an elbow on the bar. "We have another murder. Fellow by the name of Gordon Reed. That sound familiar to you?"

"Can't say that it does." The big Adam's apple shifted uneasily.

Kevin took a hanky out of his pocket and blew his nose. "Strange that you'd say that, seeing as someone saw you talking to him at the funeral today."

He shrugged. "I talked to several people."

"Yes, but this one ended up dead. There's also the matter of Megan's sister."

"Cindy?" He smiled. "She's one cute broad, isn't she? You should have seen the sparkle in her eyes when I gave her those earrings. You'd have thought I was giving her the moon." Something between a sneer and a smile curled his lips. "She even hugged me."

"What did you do with her?" Kevin leaned forward.

Joe backed up, connecting with Mac's sturdy shoulder. "Uh . . . I don't know what you're talking about. I gave her the earrings and left. She was with Megan's hotshot boyfriend the last time I saw her."

Taking the bagged earrings they had found on the kitchen counter out of his pocket, Kevin placed them on the bar in front of Joe. "These are the earrings you made for Megan."

Mac watched Joe's face turn a pasty shade of gray. Joe pushed himself away from the bar. His Adam's apple bobbed; his jaw twitched. "What were you doing in my house?"

"I asked my question first, Joe. Why do you have Megan's earrings? You just told us you gave them to Cindy."

"Those are an extra set."

Kevin shook his head. "You expect us to believe that?"

"It's true. I liked them and thought they'd sell. They don't have the real stones like Megan's did, but they're still pretty."

"Okay, I might be willing to believe you. Now suppose you go outside with us. I'd like to have a look in your car."

He frowned. "My car? What for?"

"We'd like to see what you were working on when we stopped by to see you earlier."

"You want to see my fan belt?" He shook his head. "Whatever turns you on." Joe swung around and slipped off the bar stool then ambled toward the entrance with Kevin on one side and Mac on the other.

At the door, Joe sprinted ahead, slamming the heavy door in the detectives' faces.

Kevin grunted as he took the brunt of the blow on his nose. Mac hesitated for a moment, gripping his wrist where it caught the door. "You okay, Kev?"

Holding his nose, Kevin managed to wave Mac on. "Go. I'm right behind you."

Mac opened the heavy wooden door. "Suspect's heading north."

Kevin lifted his head and felt blood streaming from his left nostril. The bartender handed him a towel. "Put some pressure on it. You should be okay."

"Yeah, but will my partner?" Kevin brushed the towel away and barreled out the still-open door—more mad than hurt. Through watery eyes, he called for backup and headed out after Mac, praying his partner would be able to overtake Joe. He had no doubt now that Joe Higgins was their killer. He only hoped Cindy hadn't been another victim.

Chapter Forty

The bright sun blinded Mac momentarily as he stepped outside the strip joint. He headed north in the direction he'd seen Joe take, spotting him just as he disappeared around the back of another building. Mac sprinted after him. His gun drawn, he yelled for Joe to stop. The guy ducked into the back of another bar. Mac easily caught up, but the door was locked. He reholstered his gun and ran around to the front, nearly colliding with Kevin. He tore his gaze from the blood-smeared face and caught a glimpse of Joe going into the front of another bar two doors down.

"He's zigzagging," Mac told his partner. "You take the front, I'll go around to the back. Maybe we can trap him." Mac sprinted back to the alley and waited for Joe to show up. As he neared the back entrance to the bar, he drew his Glock again.

A full minute passed and Mac was beginning to think he'd blown it big time. He was just about to go inside when the door opened. Mac had never moved so fast in his life. The moment Joe stepped outside, Mac was on him. He spun Joe around and shoved him against the side of the brick building. He had Joe handcuffed before his brain synchronized with his actions. "Consider yourself detained for a police investigation." Mac breathed heavily, winded more from the adrenaline than the run.

"Take it easy, man." Joe's face was still pressed against the wall.

Mac released his hold slightly, grabbed for Joe's arm, and led him to the front of the building where he had left Kevin.

They headed back to Mac's car, where two police cars had responded. Philly and Russ pulled in behind them.

"Having a party without us?" Philly jumped out, his dark eyes taking in the scene.

Mac gave a quick rundown while Kevin dabbed at his bleeding nose with his sleeve.

"We're thinking this dirt bag has Cindy in the trunk." Mac patted Joe down and retrieved his keys. "I suppose we need a warrant to get into this thing."

Philly grabbed the keys. "That may not be necessary. Listen, did you hear that? Sounded like a thump coming from inside the trunk."

Mac frowned, "I didn't . . ."

"Yeah." Russ came up behind them. "I heard it, too, partner."

"You guys are crazy," Joe said. "No way did you hear anything."

"Get rid of this creep, would you?" Philly addressed one of the uniformed officers, who led Joe to his black-and-white car and settled him into the backseat.

"I didn't kill anybody. You got nothing!" Joe yelled back at them.

Mac held his breath as Philly slipped the key into the trunk. When he first saw the large black garbage bag, his heart bottomed out. If this was Cindy, they were too late.

When he thought he heard a muffled sound, Mac tore the plastic away. "Oh, God. It's her." Mac pulled the duct tape and took the rag from her mouth. "It's okay, Cindy. You're safe."

Cindy whimpered, tears draining from her eyes. Mac held back his own tears while he and Philly undid the tape that bound her hands and feet.

Mac lifted the small woman into his arms and carried her to his car. He started to set her in the passenger seat but couldn't. She had wrapped her arms around his neck and wouldn't let go, so he sat sideways with her in his lap. Her whimpers had turned to sobs as she tried to tell them about her ordeal.

"It happened so fast," Cindy said between sobs. "I was in the cemetery alone . . . everyone had just left . . . he came up behind me . . ."

"Shh. It's okay." He held her close as one might comfort a damaged child. "You don't need to talk. We'll get your statement later. We caught him, you know. We caught the guy who did this to you."

"He—he killed Megan." She looked up into Mac's eyes. "He was going to kill me too."

Mac reached into his backseat and grabbed some tissues from the box. "Here." He handed her the tissues and grabbed one for himself.

"I've called for an ambulance, Mac." Philly settled a hand on Mac's shoulder. "We'll get her to the hospital."

Several long minutes later the ambulance arrived. The paramedics took Cindy out of Mac's arms and placed her on a stretcher.

Mac went to stand beside his injured partner. "Looks like you might need a visit to the emergency room too." Kevin's already crooked nose looked like it had another break. Bruising had already started to form under his eyes, and blood still drained from his left nostril.

Philly removed the semiclean rag from his pocket and placed it over Kevin's swollen nose. "You need to keep pressure on it, you dope."

Kevin tilted his head back, finally able to close his eyes and tend to his wound.

"I'm getting too old for this, Philly," Kevin mumbled, taking care not to open his mouth too wide so the blood wouldn't trickle in.

Philly rubbed Kevin's neck, a concerned look on his face.

The guy has a heart after all, Mac thought as he watched the interchange.

Kevin opened one eye, still holding the bloodied rag to his nose. "You aren't going to hug me, are you, Philly?"

Philly didn't flinch, but a smile grew on his round face. "You're not going to get to first base with me without buying me a drink first." The two old friends laughed as the ambulance with Cindy eased out of the parking lot.

"And how are you, Prince Charming?" Philly asked Mac.

Mac stared at the departing ambulance, still trying to take it all in. "Huh?" When Philly's question finally penetrated, he turned around.

"How come Kevin looks like he went twelve rounds and your hair isn't even messed up?" Philly went on.

Mac expected a jab of some kind, but Philly actually looked sincere. About the only response Mac could muster was, "I can't believe what just happened."

"Well, believe it, kid. You just caught a murderer and saved that woman's life." Philly took the bloodsoaked cloth from Kevin's nose. "You saved her life, Mac. Good work."

"Thanks."

Philly glanced down at his own bloodied hand. "Now, will someone give me an alcohol rinse? Who knows what kind of crud is floating around in Kevin's blood?"

Mac was relieved to hear the banter start up again. The joking brought back a sense of normalcy.

Philly and Russ offered to secure Joe's car, have it towed back to the office, and write out a warrant while Mac took Kevin to a medical facility. After securing a Polaroid photo of Joe Higgins sitting in the back of the patrol car in handcuffs, Kevin and Mac left.

Kevin rejected Mac's offer to take him to the hospital, choosing instead to stop at a gas station, where he washed off the blood and cleaned up the best he could. Back in the car Kevin pulled down the visor and checked his face. "Jean's going to freak when she sees this."

"Want me to take you home?" Mac eyed the bloodstained dress shirt. "You might want to change."

"Not yet. We need to head down to Salem to talk with Wallace now—before he hears about Higgins. What we've got so far on Joe Higgins is Kidnap One and Assaulting a Public Safety Officer—namely, me. Those are both felony charges and will hold him for a couple of weeks. We need more, Mac. I want to nail this thug six ways to Sunday. I want to see Joe Higgins in prison for life, and it's our job to make sure nothing—absolutely nothing—goes wrong."

"Can't argue with you there, partner. Salem it is."

Chapter Forty-One

Mitch Wallace was being held in a small segregation cell at the Oregon State Penitentiary in Salem. The eight-by-four-foot cell barely allowed him the room to bounce his small blue handball against the wall. The cell could be accessed only by a single steel door with a small slot used to transfer food and shelter the guards during handcuffing.

Figuring the guy would never talk where other prisoners might see him cooperating with the police, Kevin had asked the prison officials to bring Wallace out of solitary and transport him to the Salem Patrol Office, where they'd conduct the interview.

"Don't go far. I got nothing to say to these guys," Wallace told the guard as he was brought into the interview room.

"We'll see about that," Kevin muttered as he took a sip of coffee.

"Come on in, Mr. Wallace. We've been expecting you." Kevin pulled out a chair for their visitor.

"Yeah, I bet." Wallace's gaze darted from Kevin to Mac as he sat down. He had mousy brown hair that reached the small of his back, a full beard, and small piercing blue eyes.

"Just give me a holler when you're done with him," the corrections officer said. As he closed the door, he added, "Let me know if he gives you any problems."

"How are you, Mr. Wallace?" Kevin stepped around to his side.

"You tell me."

"My name is Detective Bledsoe, and this is my partner, Detective McAllister. Mr. Wallace, we'd like to talk to you about a very important matter, but first, let me make you a little more comfortable." Kevin eyed the handcuffs. "Let's put those things in the front."

"Um, thanks." Wallace eyed him warily. "My arms are getting numb."

Kevin removed one handcuff and allowed Wallace to bring his hands to the front, then placed the restraints back on his wrist.

"Is that better?"

He nodded. "What do you guys want?"

Kevin and Mac each took a chair in the small interview room, pulling their chairs directly in front of Wallace. Kevin scooted so close he was practically touching Wallace with his knees.

Wallace pushed back but hit the wall. His gaze dropped from Kevin's bruised face to the dried blood on Kevin's shirt. "What happened to you?"

Kevin glared at him. "This is nothing." He gave Mitch a wry grin. "You should see the other guy."

Wallace pressed back as far as he could go, obviously scared he might get the same treatment.

"We're investigating a murder, Mr. Wallace," Kevin began, "a murder we think you know something about."

Wallace stared at the cuffed hands in his lap. "I don't know nothin' about no murder."

"Before we get started, there are a few things you need to know." Kevin's gaze fastened on Mitch Wallace's face and remained there. "You're not under arrest, but you're obviously not free to leave because of your incarceration status. So with that in mind, I'm going to advise you of your Miranda warnings. Mr. Wallace, you have the right to remain silent. Anything you say can and will be used against you in a court of law. You have the right to consult with an attorney before any questioning if you wish. Do you understand your rights?"

"Yes, and I don't want to talk to you," Wallace replied.

"Suit yourself, Mr. Wallace." In a move meant to intimidate, Kevin moved his chair closer to Wallace. "But I'll be blunt with you. Things don't look very good for you right now. I'd like to tell you what I know, if you have the time."

"Time's all I got," Wallace mumbled.

"How much time have you served so far in the bank robbery conviction?"

"Around nine years, when you add the escape charge to my jacket," Wallace sighed.

Kevin's tone gentled as he asked, "Do you need anything right now, a cup of water or coffee?"

"No, I'm good. Thanks, though," Wallace glanced around, and Mac thought he saw the beginnings of tears in the guy's eyes.

"All right then, let's lay it on the line," Kevin continued in a gentle tone. "Detective McAllister and I are investigating the death of a young woman by the name of Megan Tyson." Kevin paused, sitting back in his chair.

Mac noticed that Kevin didn't seem to be pushing Wallace as hard as they had pushed Higgins. Probably because Wallace already looked like he was going to crack.

"Never heard of her," Wallace brought his shackled hands up and brushed back his hair.

"Maybe you ought to just listen, Mr. Wallace." Kevin's jaw tightened. "Now, I know Megan Tyson was a bit of a flirt, and I know she flirted some with your pal, Joe Higgins."

Wallace swallowed hard, and his head bobbed up and down once.

"We know you were staying with Higgins when you went AWOL from your parole," Kevin continued. "Now, Mr. Wallace, this is important. Detective McAllister and I have been to that apartment several times and we've had forensic scientists all over the place looking for trace evidence."

"So?" Wallace blurted the word out in what Mac felt certain was an instinctive defense mechanism from years of dealing with and denying police questions. "What does that have to do with me?"

"I'm about to get to that." Kevin leaned closer to him. "We found blood in that bedroom, Mr. Wallace—a great deal of blood. That blood belonged to our victim, Megan Tyson."

"Maybe you ought to talk to Joe. I told you I didn't know no Megan Tyson."

"Hmm." Kevin stroked his chin and in a quiet voice said, "That's why we're here. We talked to Higgins—he told us we should be talking to you. He's probably making a deal with the district attorney as we speak."

"What kind of deal?" Wallace stiffened.

"I suspect he'll be turning state's witness to testify under oath about how you escaped from your parole restrictions in Washington and came to Oregon. And how, on August thirteenth, Megan Tyson came by to visit him while he was out." Kevin leaned forward until their faces were only inches apart. "Then, I imagine Higgins is going to testify that he came home late and discovered that you had murdered Megan Tyson after a rape attempt gone bad."

Mac's heart pounded in his chest. He took in a shallow breath.

Wallace gripped his handcuffed hands together in a fist and began rocking back and forth. He sprang to his feet. "That's a bunch of lies. Higgins killed that girl, not me! No way is he going to pin that girl's death on me!"

"If you didn't kill her, then you had better play ball now, or you, my friend, are going down for the count."

"He's lying," Wallace gasped, tears dripping down his cheeks. He sat back down and buried his face in his hands. "I'll tell you what happened."

Kevin asked Mac for the mini cassette recorder, and once it was in place, informed Mitch that the session was being recorded. "Mr.

Wallace, it's extremely important that you be completely honest with us from this point on. If I get the impression you are being less than forthright . . ." Kevin paused. "If I get that feeling, I'm turning the tape off and you're going back to your cell and we'll work with Higgins."

"I got it man, I got it," Wallace sobbed. "Just tell me where to start."

"First, try to relax. Take a few deep breaths and we'll go on tape," Kevin said.

After a couple of minutes, Wallace looked up at Kevin and nodded. "I'm ready."

"Okay." Kevin activated the tape and went through the introductions. "Mr. Wallace, are you aware I'm recording your conversation?"

"Yes, I am," Wallace answered with surprising calm.

"Detective McAllister?" Kevin asked, without looking at Mac.

"Yes, with my permission," Mac answered, glad to finally say something.

"Mr. Wallace, prior to going on tape, were you advised of your Miranda rights?"

"Yes, I was." Mitch fixed his gaze on the tape recorder.

"And do you understand those rights? Do you wish to have them read to you again?" Kevin looked up from the tape recorder.

"No, I fully understand my rights."

"Do you have any questions before we get started?" Kevin again asked.

"No, I'm ready. That creep is going to fry."

"Okay, Mr. Wallace. Did Detective McAllister or I make any threats or promises to you in order to get you to provide us with this much appreciated cooperation?" Kevin asked, covering every possible defense angle on the tape.

"No, you have been very nice. Thank you," Wallace answered.

"Why don't you tell us about how you met Higgins and about your relationship?"

"Well, I was already in FCI Houston when Higgins came in on a military charge. He bragged about cutting a dude's throat when he was in Taiwan or Japan or something. I think he was playing the tough guy, you know, to keep the goons away."

"You and Higgins shared a cell?" Kevin asked.

"Yeah, for quite a while."

"How did you spend your time?"

Wallace shrugged. "Reading porn magazines." He stopped short. "Um . . . I know it's against the rules to have stuff like that, but—they weren't mine. Higgins got them from—"

"I'm not concerned about that right now," Kevin interrupted. "What else did you do?"

"Made up stories. Higgins bragged that he was going to produce movies when he got out. He'd make up these stories where this stud would rape and kill women. He had some weird hang-up over women."

"What kind of hang-up?" Kevin asked.

"Like I said, his scenarios always ended up with women being killed and stuff. I always assumed it was just jailhouse talk, nothing serious. He never talked about dating girls or anything like that. It was just use them—get what you could out of them and kill them." Wallace grimaced. "I figured it was just for show. I didn't think the wacko meant it."

"So Higgins would make up these scenarios and you would play along?" Kevin asked.

"Yeah." He pinched his lips together. "I wasn't about to argue with the man. The stuff he came up with got worse and worse. He started talking about torture chambers where demon guys would conduct human experiments and feed on human flesh and make sacrifices to the devil. He had some pretty freaky ideas."

Mac's stomach rolled. He was glad he hadn't eaten, because if he had, he'd have been running out of the room about now.

"And how long did this go on?" Kevin asked.

"Till he got paroled."

"So Higgins was paroled and you got out later?" Kevin continued.

"Right. He wrote me a few times saying he'd moved to Oregon and was making jewelry. Gave me his address and said I could move in with him if I wanted. I was paroled and the feds stuck me in this rotten halfway house that wasn't fit for a pig."

"So you skipped out," Kevin said.

"Yeah, I skipped out." Wallace shook his head. "I called Higgins and had him pick me up at the bus station. I didn't think I would make it all the way up here. I don't seem to do too good on the outside; my shrink in the joint told me I'd become institutionalized. Said I secretly liked being in prison. Can you believe that smack?"

"Did Joe know you skipped?" Kevin asked.

"Yeah, he knew. I told him I did. We partied pretty hard when I got into town, drank a lot of beer, and met a lot of girls at these strip joints he liked to go to."

"Tell me about Megan Tyson," Kevin prompted.

"I don't know if I can." Wallace began to weep again.

Kevin gave Mac a look of concern. "You've got to, Mr. Wallace. I know it's rough." Kevin sounded like he really cared about the guy. Maybe he did.

"Higgins said he had this babe on the hook. He took me to the health club where he worked out so I could get a look at her."

"Was it Megan Tyson?" Kevin asked.

"Yeah, it was Megan," Wallace murmured. "You should have seen her, man; she was one friendly gal. Higgins bragged about how he took her out once and almost got her in the sack, but she shut him down. That really made him mad, and he said he'd get back at her for using him."

"Using him?" Kevin asked.

"Using him, that's what he said. See, Higgins figures if a girl puts out the signals and he buys them dinner, then he's entitled to whatever he wants. Megan shut him down, so he was going to get back at her."

"How did he do that?"

"He offered to make some earrings for her." Wallace stared at the floor and cleared his throat. "He called her when he was done and told her to come over to his place to get them."

"And did Megan Tyson pick them up?"

He nodded. "She came over."

"Was that the evening of August thirteenth?" Kevin's jaw twitched.

"Yes," Wallace whined. "I didn't know what he was going to do. You gotta believe me."

"Tell me what happened, Mr. Wallace," Kevin said in a hushed tone. "Tell me everything that happened."

Wallace went on to describe every horrific detail of Megan's death. Several times Mac thought he was going to be sick. He had to clamp his lips together to keep from telling Kevin to make Wallace stop.

"You were there and you didn't try to stop him?"

"Higgins kept telling me he would slit my throat. He'd have done it too. He kept hitting her and choking her."

Mac couldn't imagine any human being torturing another the way Joe Higgins had tortured Megan. Hadn't they heard enough?

"What then?" Kevin asked in a barely audible voice.

"Then Higgins grabs the knife and he . . . he cuts her throat. Said he wanted to make sure she was dead. There was blood everywhere. It took all night to clean up. I thought he was going to kill me too. We rolled up Megan's body in the bedspread and then in the shower curtain and carried her into a storage room next to the kitchen. It had a concrete floor and Higgins said it would be easy to clean. We cleaned up most of the mess and each took a shower before we left."

"Where did you go?" Kevin dragged a hand down his face, wincing as he touched his nose.

"We loaded up the body in the trunk of his car and drove out east of town. I didn't know where we were going. We came to this turnout and we dragged the body down into a ditch and took off."

The testimony was taking a toll on both detectives, but Kevin kept hammering away. "What happened to the shower curtain and the bedspread, and Megan's clothes and personal property?"

"Higgins threw everything in a dumpster somewhere back in town. Sorry I can't say where. I was way drunk and confused by this time."

"What about her jewelry?"

"Joe took the stones out of the ring and sold them. I don't know what happened to the cross. He'd yanked it off her at the apartment. I never saw it after that. He said something about wanting a souvenir."

"What was the camping gear you mentioned in your phone calls to Higgins?" Kevin asked.

Wallace glanced up at Kevin. "The rocks from her jewelry. He said he was going to send me my share of the proceeds, but I never got it."

"How do we know you weren't the one who did all these things, Mr. Wallace?" Kevin leaned back in his chair.

Mac didn't know how Kevin could stay so cool.

"I don't know. I'm telling the truth. I'll take a lie detector test, whatever you want. I know I'm jamming myself up, but I didn't kill her. I just got in over my head. There's no hope for Higgins. He lives in that sick fantasy world of his where he dreams up ways of taking out entire groups of people."

"How so?" Kevin straightened and shot a look at Mac.

Wallace dragged his hands down his face. "He talked about hooking up timers in air conditioning ducts that would release gas into an office or school and knock everybody out. Then he said he would come in and kill everyone after taking money from their wallets. Stuff like that. He scared me so bad—I have to tell you, I was almost glad when I got arrested."

"Speaking of that night, what were you and Higgins up to when you were stopped?" Kevin asked.

"I didn't mean to open that door, but I might as well step through it." Wallace sighed. "Higgins really got off on this thing with Megan and wanted to do it again right away. He made me go to a strip joint with him the next night. He tried to put the moves on this one blonde stripper, but she told him to get lost. Higgins told me she would be the next one to pay, except this time I knew what he meant. We waited in the parking lot for this gal to get off work and followed her. Higgins had his kit with him; he said we would follow her home then break in to her place. He'd have done it, too, if that cop hadn't stopped us."

"This kit—can you tell me what was in it?"

"Yeah. Duct tape, a ski mask, an old stun gun, a sock—I don't know what else."

"Why didn't you tell the police what Higgins was up to that night?" Kevin asked. "You were safe once you got here."

He bit his lip. "I was safe, but my mom wasn't."

"What do you mean?"

"Right after I got sent to the Pen, Higgins wrote me a note. He said he hoped I was doing okay and then down at the bottom he wrote the number 2133 BR. I knew what it meant; 2133 Butler Road is my mother's address."

Kevin nodded. "Detective McAllister, do you have anything?"

Mac wanted nothing more than to get the guy out of his sight and back in prison where he belonged. He wanted to go home and take a long hot shower. But he also wanted to know what had happened to Megan's temporary debit card. Wallace admitted that Joe found Megan's temporary PIN number scribbled on a Post-it in her purse, and he and Joe had used the debit card at all the locations noted on the bank record.

"That's all I have," Mac said, handing the interview back over to Kevin.

Kevin stood up and moved behind his chair. "Just one more thing, Mr. Wallace. What do you think should happen to you and Higgins for your participation in this crime?"

"I think we should die," Wallace said without hesitation. "I think we should both die for this, at least Higgins should."

"That's all I have for you now, Mr. Wallace. Do you have anything you want to add?" Kevin picked up the tape recorder.

Wallace sat back in his chair, wiping his eyes with the back of his hands. "Just that I'm really sorry for what we did. I didn't mean for that girl to die and I wish I had never met Joe Higgins. Please tell her family I'm sorry and I'll do anything I can to make sure Higgins never sees the light of day again. I wish I could kill him myself. That's it; that's all I have to say."

"Get on your feet, Mr. Wallace." Kevin opened the door and signaled for the guard who had brought him in.

"Am I going back to segregation now?" Wallace asked.

"Actually," Kevin said, "I'm going to have you transported out to Multnomah County because I'm charging you with the crime of murder for the death of Megan Tyson. You'll be arraigned in the morning."

Wallace nodded as the guard took his arm and led him out the door.

"That was amazing," Mac said.

"We took a chance and it paid off."

Mac rubbed his still-churning stomach. "I don't think I could have gotten all that out of him. I was ready to leave after fifteen minutes."

"It's tough listening to stuff like that, Mac. I don't think it ever gets any easier, but we had to get everything we could. When this case goes to court, we want the D.A. to have more than enough ammunition to nail those two." He stood up and grabbed his notes. "Right now we need to type up a probable cause affidavit, then we'll take the hammer wagon up to Troutdale and pay Mr. Higgins a final visit. The media will be all over this thing soon. We'll give Eric this last bit of information and get a telephonic search warrant for Higgins's new duplex. It's coming together, partner. It's all coming together."

Chapter Forty-Two

Things progressed rapidly from that point on. After processing Joe's vehicle, Kevin and Mac searched the duplex and found the setting for Megan's ring and the cross that had been ripped from her neck. Allison Sprague reported that the blood in Joe's old apartment was indeed Megan's.

What really cinched the case was the confession from Mitch Wallace. The other suspects were cleared.

Dana had found Tim Morris at the airport. He canceled his flight and went straight to the Troutdale P.D. When he found out about Cindy, he canceled his plans so he could be with her. The Washington State Patrol found Matthew DeLong at a convenience store just north of Longview at the Mount St. Helen's turnoff. Now he was back home, paying alimony and still living with his sister.

As it turned out, Joe Higgins had killed Gordon Reed. The murder weapon—Gordon's own knife—was found in Joe's tool kit, along with the duct tape he had used on Cindy. The lab techs had matched the tape Mac had pulled from Cindy's mouth to the roll in Joe's trunk—a roll that had Joe's fingerprints all over it.

A search of Gordon's place revealed that he'd written a note to Joe saying he knew Joe had killed Megan and wanted money for his silence. Megan had told Gordon about the jewelry, so when he saw Joe giving the earrings to Cindy, he put two and two together, then tracked the guy down with the idea of blackmailing him. Joe kept his money and got Gordon's silence anyway.

The detectives spent a good two weeks processing their evidence before closing the books on the case. They turned everything over to the prosecutor, who felt certain the case would stand up to any attorney Joe Higgins might hire.

Mac had gone home that night exhausted and ready to move on. He'd made it through his first murder investigation and in Cindy's eyes, at least, had emerged a hero. The guys joked about his getting the girls and saying how jealous they were. Kevin didn't say a lot, but what he had said was positive. Mac smiled, thinking about Kevin's remark about God's guidance. Mac wasn't certain if God or instinct or both had led them to Joe and Cindy, but he was thankful either way.

Sitting in front of his fireplace, stroking his dog's silky head, he thought about how well Dana had gained Kevin and Eric's respect. They were both rooting for her and had promised to talk to Frank on her behalf. "It won't be long now," Mac had told her the day before.

"I hope so. I can't wait to show those chauvinists what I can do."

"Chauvinists?"

"Not you, Mac. And not Kevin or Eric. I'm talking about the others—especially Russ and Philly. Those two are something else."

Mac had to agree. His thoughts made the obvious transition from Dana to Linda. He hadn't talked to her since she'd walked in on him and Dana. Kevin had advised him to mend the fences regardless of whether or not they still had a relationship.

Mac went to get his cell phone and punched in Linda's number. He'd apologize for not calling sooner. He'd tell her why Dana had been there. And he'd come clean about his past. Neither Eric nor Kevin held his ancestry against him, so maybe Linda wouldn't either. He might even agree to go to premarital counseling—that is, if Linda was still interested in working things out.